THE IRON ROAD

ALSO BY DAVID WRAGG

Articles of Faith
The Black Hawks
The Righteous

Tales of the Plains
The Hunters
The Company of the Wolf

DAVID WRAGG
THE IRON ROAD

HARPER
Voyager

Harper*Voyager*
An imprint of
HarperCollins*Publishers* Ltd
1 London Bridge Street
London SE1 9GF

www.harpercollins.co.uk

HarperCollins*Publishers*
Macken House,
39/40 Mayor Street Upper,
Dublin 1, D01 C9W8
Ireland

First published by HarperCollins*Publishers* Ltd 2025
1

Copyright © David Wragg 2025

David Wragg asserts the moral right to
be identified as the author of this work.

A catalogue record for this book is available from the British Library.

ISBN: 978-0-00-853382-3 (HB)

This novel is entirely a work of fiction.
The names, characters and incidents portrayed in it are
the work of the author's imagination. Any resemblance to
actual persons, living or dead, events or localities is
entirely coincidental.

Set in Sabon by Palimpsest Book Production Limited, Falkirk, Stirlingshire

Printed and bound in the UK using 100% Renewable Electricity by CPI Group (UK) Ltd

All rights reserved. No part of this publication may be
reproduced, stored in a retrieval system, or transmitted,
in any form or by any means, electronic, mechanical,
photocopying, recording or otherwise, without the prior
written permission of the publishers.

Without limiting the exclusive rights of any author, contributor or the publisher of this
publication, any unauthorised use of this publication to train generative artificial
intelligence (AI) technologies is expressly prohibited. HarperCollins also exercise
their rights under Article 4(3) of the Digital Single Market Directive 2019/790 and
expressly reserve this publication from the text and data mining exception.

This book contains FSC™ certified paper and other controlled sources
to ensure responsible forest management.
For more information visit: www.harpercollins.co.uk/green

*For my daughters,
and the rebellions to come*

PREVIOUSLY, ON TALES OF THE PLAINS . . .

The Hunters

REE, a woman in her early forties with a mysterious past, is trying to run a horse farm out in Mining Country, at the very fringes of the known world, while holding the local chapter of the rapacious SERICAN MINERS' GUILD at arm's length. Meanwhile, her twelve-year-old niece JAVANI, bored of living in the middle of nowhere, has cooked up a scheme that will get her (and *maybe* her aunt) over the mountains to the fabled nation of ARESTAN, land of milk and honey and that sort of thing. She's enlisted a local bandit gang, led by ex-miner and current tough guy MOVOS GUVULI, to rob the local Guildhouse through a plan of her own devising, involving a large blue jewel she borrowed from her aunt.

Before the robbery can occur, the long-expected trade caravan arrives in town, bringing with it a bunch of brutal mercenaries led by THE WHITE SPEAR, a massive Horvaun ex-reaver, who have forced caravan leader and self-described master merchant SIAVASH SAROSH to bring them along.

Also arriving: a foreign prince and his entourage, who have travelled across the plains guided by brother and sister team AKI and ANASHE, failed mercenaries and thieves-to-order. Both groups appear to be after Javani, and battle ensues. Chaos and disaster follow, and a lot of death, and in the middle of it all Movos Guvuli and gang try to rob the Guildhouse. Ree steals their getaway wagon, chucks Javani aboard and brings Aki and Anashe along for good measure, and they race out into the desert . . . but not before the White Spear has informed Javani that she is believed to be a lost princess, the heir to a distant throne. The White Spear has come to collect her and keep her safe; the prince has come for her head.

What follows is a prolonged chase, along with some revelations – Ree worked with Aki and Anashe's late mother fifteen years before, and they've been searching for her along the way; and it turns out Ree is in fact not Javani's aunt but her mother, something she kept secret supposedly to keep the girl safe, but in fact may have been more because she couldn't deal with the pressures of motherhood. Javani loses the blue jewel along the way, throwing it at a chasing Guild rider.

The chase runs on. Guvuli (still after his getaway wagon and its contents) is captured – inadvertently – by Javani, then released after a good scolding and an instruction to think more clearly about his future. Javani makes a deal with the White Spear to return with her if she protects Ree too, after the White Spear proclaims that only death will break the contract (her own, or the target's).

Eventually the gang are cornered in an old mine canyon. Ree is hit in the leg with a nasty crossbow bolt, and Aki gives his life to save his sister. The White Spear is buried in a cave-in, but the prince survives, and Ree packs Javani off through a narrow crack in the wall then turns to face him in a final duel. Javani returns in secret to watch, hoping she can help, and sees Ree badly injured before she outwits the prince and fatally wounds him. As he lies dying, Ree reiterates that he's had the wrong kid all along: her own child, the one he and the White Spear have been hunting, was stillborn, and Javani was a foundling. This is news to the watching Javani.

The prince dies, Javani rushes to Ree's injured side, and as she loses consciousness the White Spear erupts from the rubble. They bind Ree's wounds and dig themselves out, then rendezvous with the heartbroken Anashe. Aki is buried, and the White Spear decides to travel back without Javani – she heard Ree's confession inside the mine, the heir she was sent to retrieve died long ago. Anashe, in search of new prospects and purpose, goes with her. Meanwhile, Movos Guvuli returns to the Guildhouse he earlier tried to rob to find ZIBA RAHDAT, a Guild auditor, has arrived, supposedly to root out the local chapter's corruption. She offers him the chance to serve as her assistant in the purges to come.

Javani and Ree have an uncomfortable chat; Javani deduces as she goes that Ree knew the White Spear was listening when she told the prince that Javani was a foundling, and that the whole thing was a gambit, and she really is a secret princess after all. Sorry, says Ree, your dad was a goat-herd, but he was a fine-looking chap with excellent hair.

As the book ends, Ree and Javani are travelling west, into the mountains, with paradise just a few hundred miles away . . .

The Company of the Wolf

Ree (still limping from her injury) and Javani (now very, very nearly thirteen) have got lost crossing the mountains. They stumble across an unmarked village, and find it full of friendly but slightly odd people, who prize peace and tranquillity above all. To that end, they have engaged a mercenary company to protect them, although the terms of the deal have seemingly degraded to outright extortion by the time Ree and Javani arrive.

Ree sticks her oar in, and things get considerably worse for everyone. Notable villagers include VIDA and MARIAM, the village blacksmith and her wife, and ANRI, a thoroughly disagreeable hunter who lives with his catatonic wife just outside the village and pretends to have nothing to do with it. Javani becomes obsessed with getting Anri to teach her how to shoot a bow (properly).

Meanwhile, in the mercenary camp across the valley, CAPTAIN MANATAS — a generally decent man, if a little long-winded — and his few loyal comrades (including TAURAS, a friendly and uncomplicated pillar of muscle) find themselves usurped by newcomers and entryists, who have decided the village is ripe for the taking and no settlement will ever be enough.

Manatas and Ree encounter each other while scouting, and despite various threats to kill, they find an understanding. However, Manatas is sidelined, the mercenaries attack, and things get bloody. The villagers win the day despite some tragic losses, and Ree comes to Manatas's rescue. In the aftermath of the battle, the two of them return to the now-abandoned mercenary camp, and officially make friends.

With the mercenaries defeated, it looks like the village can return to its peaceful ways, and despite having put everyone's backs up, Ree and Javani are invited to stay – should they want to. As they consider, a band of riders from THE GUILD show up at the village periphery, and inform them that they're all on Guild land, and will start paying their tithes shortly.

The book ends with a collective declaration of war against the Guild, and everything it stands for.

ONE

Maral sat in the gleaming anteroom, her head in her hands, assailed by the serving girls' shrieking laughter echoing from the exquisite carved marble of the hallway, and wondered when she had last felt joy.

She half-turned her head towards Kuzari, who lounged against the cool wall beside her, picking seeds from his teeth with a dirty fingernail. His fingernails were always dirty. It was like he simply didn't care.

'Zari.'

'What?' His mouth was still gummed with a dark crescent of nail.

'What makes you laugh like that?'

'Like what?'

Maral cocked her head, letting the coarse scrub of her hair fall to one side, to indicate the irrepressible giggles that pealed from the direction of the palazzo's upper kitchens. 'Like the laughter we are currently hearing, Zari. That laughter.'

'Hm.' He inspected the tip of his nail, and, satisfied, wiped it on the faded embroidery of his coat. His clothes were a shambles as ever, their fine stitching worn and fraying, their colours bleached and half obscured by an overlapping patchwork of murky stains. Yet still he received more. He didn't wear most of them – there wouldn't be time to weather each outfit to such a rancid degree if they were in constant rotation. Maral imagined he pawned the spares, although she had no idea what he did with the proceeds; they had little enough expenditure even when on assignment. And somehow, infuriatingly, to her he remained elegant, despite the grime: long-limbed and sleek, the reflected glow of the fierce sun beyond the colonnade lighting the planes of his cheeks, adding sheen to the glossy tumble of his hair.

Beralas never gave Maral fine clothes; he had daughters already. And what would be the point, anyway? Maral was not to be seen.

A chamberlain came hurrying down the hallway, robes bright, a palimpsest under one arm, and diverted towards them on catching sight of two grubby figures very much doing nothing to aid in the palazzo's grand preparations. It took him a stride and a half before he realised who they were, and, face blanched and sweating despite the hallway's shaded cool, he diverted back away from them, wobbling in his soft slippers, and padded away as fast as his bowed legs would carry him. She saw it though, as he passed. The look. The distaste. The revulsion.

At least she kept herself cleaner than Kuzari, for all the good it did her.

The distant laughter from the kitchens quelled abruptly at the presumed arrival of the unseen chamberlain, leaving only the buoyant melodies of birdsong and rattle of nervous activity drifting from the terraces beyond the fine-wrought columns at the hall's end. A new sound came with them, a harsh braying, a rhythmic jingle, the whinny of skittish horses.

'Hm,' Kuzari said again, pushing himself up from the cool marble with a languid flex and sauntering to the columns. 'He's arrived. Twenty camels at least, quite a show.' He wafted a leisurely hand. 'Can smell them from here.'

'Which one?'

'Behzad. Raad isn't coming. Sent a delegate in his place.'

'You're joking.'

Kuzari tilted his head, seemingly puzzled. 'No,' he replied slowly. 'Is he mad?'

'I imagine one of us will shortly find out.'

Guildmaster Behzad entered in a flourish of fuss, preceded by heralds, flanked by retainers, trailed by functionaries. His robes were silk, ostentatiously tailored and embossed and shining golden in the mellow light, and his great swollen face barked orders to the palazzo's cringing staff from the moment they came into view. Maral noted the humourless chamberlain nestled among those scraping before him.

One of the great polished blackwood doors beside Maral swung open, and the hallway fell quiet in expectation, even Guildmaster Behzad momentarily stilling his demands. One of the private attendants who ran the inner palazzo slipped through the gap before easing the vast door closed on oiled hinges. She padded past Maral and Kuzari to the guildmaster at the end of the hall, head bowed, and exchanged a few inaudible words. The guildmaster folded his arms in a show of impatience as she padded back towards the doors, then paused before Maral and Kuzari.

'You may join now. The Chairman has asked for you,' she said to them, eyes lowered, then slipped back through the doors as noiselessly as she had come.

Maral stood, brushing dust from her stubby robes, resisting the urge to do the same to Kuzari. He sloped over to join her, one finger back working at his teeth.

'Thrice-damned seeds,' he muttered. Then, 'My work, I think.'

'What?'

'I enjoy my work. It gives me a . . .' He glanced up at the fluted ceiling, the swirling, interlocking tiles in rainbow shades, the gilded drapes that hung from each arch. 'A sense of satisfaction. When I do a good job.'

'But does it make you laugh? Do you feel . . . joy?'

He pondered as they shuffled, side by side, over to the magnificent doors, where the burnished guard motioned for them to stop and pressed an ear to the wood, awaiting a signal from beyond.

'I have smiled sometimes,' Kuzari said slowly. 'When I have overcome a challenge. When I have achieved my goal in a way that others couldn't.'

'That's hardly joy, Zari.'

'I did laugh when I took that one agitator's head off by mistake. I'd only meant to slit his throat, but by the gods, he had bones like butter.' Kuzari's face lit at the recollection. 'His head went spinning off into the air, I didn't even see it land, but I was chuckling the whole ride home. The noise it made!'

Maral nodded in acknowledgement, but she was not convinced. She enjoyed a good dismemberment as much as the next person – who in this case was Kuzari – but she wouldn't have described one as joyous. Amusing, at most.

The guard at the door stiffened and turned back to them, one hand on the pearl-inlaid handle, then his eyes narrowed. 'Are you carrying weapons? No weapons beyond the doors.'

Maral gave him a level stare. 'Are you new?'

The guard's eyes went wide. 'You're the ratcatchers.' He swallowed. 'You're still not allowed weapons—'

Kuzari pushed past the man with a seeded smile. 'My friend, if the mood took us, it would make little difference either way.'

They were in the western audience chamber, and it was even fuller than Maral's last visit. Slanted light entered the vaulted ceiling through panels of coloured glass, casting a slow, shifting pattern of dazzling shafts against the far wall. Two new statues of the brothers, yet to be painted, adorned fresh plinths, while low tables in the room's sunken centre groaned with a glistening array of seasonal fruits from the gardens and candied treats, evidently untouched. Attendants lurked in the periphery, several wafting enormous peacock feathers, sending a cooling breeze across the chamber towards the dais at the tables' far end. Music drifted from behind the ornate screens at one flank, a soft dulcimer and sympathetic drum pair.

A clutch of neat but modest-looking figures huddled before the tables, their backs to the door and the new arrivals, one of their number standing forward, mid-supplication. A couple turned at Maral and Kuzari's arrival, and immediately turned back, their gazes frozen.

Beyond them, the Verdanisi brothers were arrayed: Beralas stood proud on the dais, draped in shimmering silk, beard neatly combed, one arm raised in a pose of triumph, while one of his client artists sketched furiously onto parchment at his feet; Gurbun lounged on a longchair beside the tables, a silver pitcher cradled against his gut, glossy beads of liquid in his stubble, his fine-cut robes rumpled but irrepressibly glorious.

Maral felt squat and lumpen. Beside her, Kuzari folded himself into a posture of perfect relaxation against the wall. He always seemed so at ease in their presence, as if he felt he belonged. Not for the first time, Maral envied him. She shrank back into the shadow of the swirling pillar beside them.

The attendant who'd fetched them slid from behind a partition. 'He wanted you here for the dismissal,' she murmured to Maral and Kuzari, her head bowed. She still refused to look at them. 'It will not be long.' With that she faded once more into the architecture.

Beralas noticed their arrival, and nodded acknowledgement before returning his attention to the delegation before him. 'Please, friends,' he called out, sonorous words bouncing from the marble walls. 'Continue. Despite appearances, my attention is yours. As the great General Diin always said: "my eyes are my own, but my ears are for the world."'

Maral's eyebrow twitched. She had not heard that one, and she'd read all of the great general's works the palazzo library contained.

The foremost supplicant cleared his throat. 'As I was saying, gracious Chairmen, all we're asking is something closer to the original spirit of our agreement . . .' He tailed off, the hunch of his shoulders suggesting he already feared he'd overstepped. The shoulders were well-tailored and neatly stitched, Maral noted; clearly the man had some means, if nothing on the scale of his current surroundings. Beralas made no move from his victorious posture, and Gurbun seemed more interested in the jellied tangerine on the end of his finger than in what the man was saying. One of his companions nudged him to continue, which he managed at the second attempt.

'It's just,' the man went on, his voice thin in the capacious chamber, almost swallowed by the gentle music from behind the screen, 'when we made the agreement, at the start, there were lots of outfits we could sell to, and the Guild offered competitive terms.' He tried a smile. 'We were all doing business, making a good living. But then, well, one or two places joined the Guild themselves, or had, uh, difficulties.' He cleared his throat again. 'Until, you know, today, there's only the Guild left, and – and I'm not saying it's happened with your knowledge – the terms we're being offered, it's just not . . . it's not sustainable.'

The man swallowed, his hands knotted before him. The other

members of his delegation were huddled behind him as if using him as a shield. 'We're not asking for the original terms, we understand . . . business realities . . . but, well, with what the Guild are paying now . . . people can't make enough to survive, you see? Never mind good business, there's people going hungry, not even scraping by, and, you know, the work suffers. We all want the work done, don't we? But it has to be . . . it has to be . . . *viable*.' He almost choked on the last word.

Beralas glanced down at the frantic artist at his feet. 'Have we finished for today, Toran?'

'Um, beloved Chairman, concerning our sessions—'

Beralas dropped his arm and stepped over the artist. 'We have finished for today, Toran.'

'—because I still haven't been paid for—'

'Leave.' The little man dodged Beralas's trailing leg and scuttled backwards and away, his unfinished parchment bundled against his chest. An attendant ushered him towards a side door.

'Jallal, Jallal,' Beralas said, stepping down from the dais to the sunken floor. 'Do you think when our father was a humble mine foreman, he was concerned about . . . viability?' He walked slowly along the length of the first table, stooping to inspect a bowl of gleaming plums and ripe, untouched cherries. 'He was one of the first traders of mined goods to make a name for himself in the expanse, but when he approached the great organs of commerce, the wheels of state . . .' Beralas shook his head with a sigh.

'They laughed at him,' barked Gurbun from his longchair.

'Laughed at him,' Beralas echoed. 'Laughed him from the palace, from the city itself. But he would not be dissuaded, Jallal. He had a vision of what could be. A great Guild, an aggregation of the working man, not hidebound in tradition or beholden to weak-chinned nobility.' He swept his arms around the chamber. 'And look at us now! We are our father's vision made flesh, made stone. And it's incumbent upon us to stay true to that vision.'

Jallal, the lead supplicant, had one finger half-raised to his mouth. 'Does that mean . . .'

Beralas placed a heavy hand on the man's shoulder, and he flinched. 'It means we must stay the course, Jallal. In the words of the Immortal

Pislik: "when the gods open a door, we must march through it, and never look back."'

The woman to Jallal's right had more fight than he did. 'You mean you won't change the terms? People are going to starve! The townships will be up in arms!'

'Oh no,' chuckled Gurbun into his pitcher.

Bolstered by his companion's gumption, Jallal spoke up again. 'The townships' support may waver,' he chanced, voice querulous, 'if word spreads that the Guild is not keeping its side of agreements . . .'

Beralas was still smiling, his hand on Jallal's shoulder. 'You think so? And where do you imagine them realigning their support?'

A third supplicant, a thick-shouldered man, younger than the others, burst out, 'Arowan, of course! The Swan will welcome them back with open arms. All it would take is a nod from us and—'

'*Arowan?*' The bellow echoed around the chamber. The gentle music immediately ceased. Gurbun was on his feet, pitcher discarded, fists flexing. The room was silent but for the rattle of the pitcher coming to rest.

'Where was *Arowan* fifteen years ago?' Gurbun brayed, taking slow, heavy steps towards the cringing supplicants. 'Where was Arowan when the bridges fell? Coiled back in on itself like a fucking snail!' One thick-fingered hand came up. His earrings glittered rainbows as he crossed the patch of coloured light. 'You dunces, you clods. Who protected you when they ditched the forts? Who kept raiders and Mawn from butchering every last body on the expanse?'

He came to a halt before the supplicants, face flushed. 'Who brought trade, peace and stability?' he went on, leaning too far forward. 'Who's still providing it? Who keeps the slavers to the wild places? You simpletons! We fund your bureaucrats, we collect your taxes – and let you keep more of them than we should – we keep your farmers and citizens safe. We're the ones keeping the expanse *viable*. By all means, go running to the crone in her empty ruin and her scuttling conclave. See what happens when we withdraw our indulgence.'

Beralas still held his smile, but there was little mirth in it. 'I don't think we need to make threats. Our friends here understand, don't you?' The edges of his beard tweaked upwards. 'Arowan was decadent and deservedly cleansed, and we rose from the ashes. We are the now, we are the future: the Guild is eternal. My brother and I carry our father's legacy; we are remaking the world as it should always have been, with us all at its heart. We can all agree that's a good thing, yes? But we're not unreasonable. We'll take another look at those terms. In the name of friendship.'

Jallal nodded weakly as he and the supplicants were escorted from the room. Kuzari watched them go with a blank-eyed smile. 'Want me to follow them, boss? Make an example of one or two? Or three?'

Beralas waved a hand. 'No, no, that won't be needed for a while yet. Although . . . Magallu!' Beralas's simpering secretary slid from behind the musicians' screen. 'That young lad, talking of Arowan. Who was he?'

'Javad, Chairman. Nephew of Jallal. No doubt owes his position to nepotism.'

Beralas nodded, one hand stroking the curls of his beard. 'I thought as much. Once this hiccup is resolved, see that he suffers an unfortunate accident, ideally involving something . . . very hot. His immediate family, too.' He smoothed the front of his robe. 'To speak to me like that, in my own house, no less . . .'

'Noted, Chairman.'

'Has my wife returned? We were due to—'

'The lady Yzra has sent her apologies, Chairman. She has been unavoidably detained.'

Beralas's mouth became tight and thin. 'My daughters?'

'Not yet back from—'

Beralas threw up a jewelled hand, cutting him short. 'Who *is* here?'

'Guildmaster Behzad has arrived, Chairman, and is waiting in the east wing. Shall I send him in?'

Beralas and Gurbun exchanged a look. 'No,' Beralas replied, his humour returning, 'let's take him for a stroll. Kuzari . . . Ah, Maral, there you are – follow along. Not too close.'

TWO

Guildmaster Behzad was not permitted his entourage in the central gardens. Chastened and isolated, he trailed the brothers as they walked the shaded promenade between the terraces, his formerly spectacular robes looking tawdry and unrefined beside theirs. Explosions of coloured foliage lay to either side, dazzling in the baking sun, countless ranks of luscious orange, apricot and cherry trees gleaming in the haze, interspersed with plums and pistachios, while beyond the artful fountains, legions of white-robed gardeners toiled in studious silence, each mindful enough to move away at the procession's approach. The birdsong and insect hum were near deafening. Maral did not care for it, but it could cover the sound of a great many things, she supposed.

'Guildmaster Raad isn't joining us?' Behzad enquired, the hope in his voice disgusting.

'He sent a delegate,' Beralas replied over his shoulder.

'You'll be meeting him very shortly,' Gurbun added. He diverted a pace to deliver an idle shove to the back of a slow-moving gardener working at a fountain's edge, dunking the man into the pool below. He might have stayed to watch the man flail and gasp had his brother not summoned him back.

They came to a halt in a small courtyard in one of the less ornate hedge mazes, a refuge of cool and spectacular tiling. The brothers arranged themselves on a marble bench, beside a small gurgling wellspring fashioned into the form of one of the household gods. They directed Behzad to the facing bench, which sat in the full glare of the overhead sun.

He sat, and began to sweat.

'Most honoured Chairmen—' he began.

'Guildmaster Behzad,' Beralas said, 'how are things?'

'Things are . . . they are . . . all is well, my lords.'

'All?' Gurbun inclined his head meaningfully.

'Well, the rebellion—'

'Don't call it that,' Gurbun barked.

'The *unrest* has been . . . challenging, but we have the situation completely under control.'

Beralas leaned back on the bench. 'Ziba,' he called towards an archway at the courtyard's far side, 'is the situation in the east completely under control?'

A silver-haired woman walked stiffly out from the archway and into the courtyard, coming to rest in the shade just beyond the perspiring guildmaster. Maral knew her by gait and reputation, the scars on her lip and the milky cast of one eye – Ziba Rahdat, one of the Guild's top intercessors.

If Behzad had been sweating before, now he gushed.

'I would say,' the newcomer pronounced, 'it is not. Far from it.'

'Gods damn it all,' Beralas cried, throwing his hands up in the air. 'It has been two years. Two years, Behzad! More if you include that fuck-up in the mountains that started it all. And still you lie to our faces?'

'The situation is fluid,' the guildmaster protested, 'but we are taking steps to—'

'Shut up, you twerp.' Gurbun didn't raise his voice or move from the bench, but the guildmaster fell immediately silent.

Beralas tipped his head back and sighed. 'The state of matters please, Ziba.'

Rahdat removed a palimpsest from her long coat. Despite being hard-wearing travel fabric, it was formal in its cut and secured with a ladder of fine-worked silver buttons. Maral eyed the thrice-strung silver chain at her neck with admiration that fell just short of envy. 'The raids started in the south-west of the expanse two springs ago, before spreading north and east, but we believe the original incident was the third-phase expansion into the Ashadi the previous winter, which uncovered a number of unregistered settlements, some of which refused to pay their dues in a . . . most aggressive manner. The perpetrators appear to be a motley mix of ex-mercenaries, ex-Guild riders and motivated citizenry, with perhaps a few nomads mixed in as well.'

'Boring!' Gurbun lowed. 'We know all this. Why isn't it finished already? Why haven't you spread these insolent grass-munchers across the plains?'

'You can speak now, Behzad,' Beralas added wearily when the guildmaster said nothing.

'We can't find them,' Behzad offered weakly, his hands spread. 'They keep running away.'

Gurbun's eyes were showing white around the irises. 'Go to their hideouts! Burn them to ash! Why are you so useless?'

'B – but they don't have hideouts! They just . . .' He swallowed. '. . . melt into the plains.'

Beralas was pinching the bridge of his nose. 'Are you telling me our caravans and supply trains are being raided by ghosts, Behzad? This is what puts the renewal at risk? I hope that is not what you're telling me.'

'Get some trackers together, for the sake of the gods,' Gurbun snarled, 'and fucking follow them! Why do I have to do your thinking for you?'

'We've tried!' the guildmaster cried, and the courtyard was suddenly quiet as the echoes bounced around it. Behzad swallowed again, blinking rivers of sweat from his eyes, one hand dragging instinctively at the collar of his robes. 'We've tried,' he repeated softly as the eyes of the brothers bored into him. 'We just . . . we don't have the people, or the resources. We've never had to deal with anything like this before, nothing this . . . organised.'

Gurbun's fists were folded over one another as he leaned forwards, elbows on knees. 'The Guild equips you and your riders with the best horseflesh and steel this side of the gorge. There are *armies* who gaze at our forces in naked envy, and one of them sits in Arowan. What in hells do you mean you' – he adopted a mewling mimic of the guildmaster – '*don't have the resources?*'

'And those delightful little hand-bows,' Beralas added, miming a shot with his finger. 'Such innovation, such precision. No one else on the continent has them. Not to mention our most recent imports from . . . overseas.'

Behzad's palms rubbed up and down the sides of his head, fingers grasping at his scalp. 'They steal,' he whimpered. 'They steal so much. They're so well informed . . .'

'Someone in the Swan's circle is slipping them tips?' Gurbun seemed to tremble with anticipatory outrage.

Rahdat's nose twitched as if scenting something brief and curdled. Maral was no stranger to the expression. 'No evidence of it. Yet. She knows we're watching.'

'We'll put the notion about anyway,' Beralas murmured. 'This close to renewal, it seems more likely than not.' He pursed his lips. 'Do we have a turncoat in our directorate? Ziba?'

She shook her head. 'My investigations have found nothing so far, but I can . . . dig harder.'

'Delegate. We need a fresh approach. We are bare weeks from the eastward opening now, and everything rides upon it. I don't need to tell you how much this matters. It's time to make some changes.'

Behzad looked up, hands still pressed to his head. His robes were darkened with great rings of sweat. 'Will Guildmaster Raad's delegate be joining us?'

Beralas shot back a brilliant smile. 'No. You will be joining him. Kuzari!'

Kuzari sprang forward, a huge grin on his face, and made for the wall behind the guildmaster's bench. He knew, after all, exactly what was behind the discreetly hinged marble panel, and so did Maral. From the look on his face, Behzad did not, but he was beginning to guess.

'Beloved Chairmen, please!' he squealed, 'I want only to—'

Beralas flicked a finger. 'Kuzari.'

The gag went on over the guildmaster's head, Kuzari's arm around his neck, and he was dragged backwards and out of sight. Into darkness he would go, down slick steps into the cool chambers below the terraces, the network of corridors and small rooms buried in the rock where screams echoed from every direction at all hours no matter the season.

'Ziba, we want you leading on this,' Beralas went on as Behzad's silken slipper-clad feet disappeared kicking into the dark of the hatch. 'What arrangements do you need to make?'

Rahdat sucked at her teeth a moment, stretching the long scars across her lip. 'My man in the north will keep things in hand. I am free to move.'

'Guvuli? Good. Competence is in short supply, it seems. The renewal is in sight, and we can't have this rolling shambles putting doubts where they do not belong. It's time to try new things. Maral!'

She didn't jump at his word, but part of her wanted to. She moved carefully across the courtyard, mindful of their gazes on her, their evident distaste. Beralas did his best to cover it – he always did – but that twitch at the corners of his mouth gave him away every time.

'Maral, my star, my sharpest blade,' he said in a low voice, steeling himself to put a hand on her shoulder. She knew Beralas loved beautiful things. His daughters were swathed in lace and gold tissue, his latest wife a vision of multicoloured silks when she deigned to appear at the palazzo. But Maral knew that to even touch her must take a tremendous effort of will.

'Chairman.'

'I have a job for you, my first.' He swallowed, mouth dry. He was so close to disguising his revulsion. 'Let us discuss the details . . .'

A short time later she greeted Kuzari as he emerged from the darkness and pulled the marble panel into place behind him. He was damp.

He grinned, a seed still stuck between his teeth. 'Arrived through the front door with twenty camels, exits through the hole, not a camel in sight, and shitting his robes all the way down.' He chuckled. 'You've got to admit, Maral, that's pretty funny.'

She smiled. It was. But was it joy?

Siavash Sarosh, self-declared greatest merchant ever to travel the length of the north road and return with all his fingers, was on the verge of losing everything, and he could not have been happier. Not since his daring, unprecedented and near-ruinous expedition into mining country nearly three years before had he felt such a frisson of excitement. His stake on the glossy table before him was all but gone, it was true, but ample coin was no longer a source of concern. His investments elsewhere were on the cusp of bearing fruit, and in a few short weeks' time he would be deluged in enough silver to fill the great lake of Astrum. He had allowed himself to gamble a 'modest' sum by way of reward, and gamble he had, with the derisory stack that gleamed before him in the amber light of the chandelier the result. The next sweep of the tiles would be his last, he was in no doubt, but he would not have had it any other way. The price of admission, and the coin played and lost along with it – enough to have run a caravan three stops along the fort-line – had been worth it to be seated at the top tile table of the *Illustrious Den*.

He marvelled once again at the surroundings, as the players gathered themselves for the next hand, slurping at drinks and rolling ossified shoulders. Siavash had already dispatched his clerk to bring him another of the *Den*'s fine brandies, and was content merely to observe the other players as they made stilted conversation and contemplated their futures in the coin stacks that sat neatly at each of the faces of the hexagonal table. Fine, rich men – for women were not permitted at the *Den*'s top table, for reasons Siavash had never clearly understood but felt it not his place to question – in fine, rich clothes, matching the opulence of the wide chamber at the *Den*'s heart.

The top table was aptly named, sitting as it did on a raised dais at the end of the long, vault-ceilinged hall that contained the *Den*'s teeming tile tables; the walls were panelled blackwood, so finely polished it seemed to suck the light from the oil lamps and chandeliers that glimmered at regular intervals. The place had a cosy, intimate feel – shutters barred what windows the chamber possessed along its side walls, and Siavash had long since lost track of the hour. Conversation was muted, muffled by the velvet coverings on the furniture, the silk banners and hangings, only the occasional distant clink of coin carrying over the background murmur. The place fairly reeked of wealth, and Siavash had to sit on his hands to stop himself clapping with delight.

'Your drink, master.' Ulfat had returned with the brandy, served in a vessel both outrageously tiny and exquisitely carved. The man hovered at his elbow as Siavash sniffed and sipped, a fraction too close.

'What is it, Ulfat?'

'Might we think about departure soon, master?'

Siavash gestured at his diminished holdings with a sigh. 'I'd say our departure was imminent.' He leaned back, taking in the older man's evident discomfort. 'Is our situation not to your liking, Ulfat?'

The clerk shuffled and looked at the floor. 'It is a fine place, no doubt, master. Very fine.'

'Very fine,' Siavash confirmed, smiling beatifically at the players on the table's far side, who were beginning to take an interest. He fixed Ulfat with a meaningful stare and communicated with his eyebrows that he was to stop embarrassing them both.

'Very fine,' Ulfat repeated, his attention fixed on the smooth boards between his less-than-perfectly polished boots. 'Perhaps, master, too fine?'

Siavash affected a broad grin and leaned over in his chair. 'Ulfat, in the name of the heavens, what ails you?' he hissed.

'There are rumours, master,' the man mumbled.

'Rumours?' Siavash was trying to keep his voice down, but the player to his right, a jowly fellow in a sweeping robe of yellow silk brocade, seemed to take his exclamation as a conversational invitation.

'You mean the rebels?' He chuckled, his thick moustache, which might have been in fashion a decade before, spreading around a toothy mouth. 'Your man thinks we're in danger of attack, here in the *Den*?'

Siavash's brows lowered. 'Is that your concern, Ulfat?'

'In the kitchens, they were saying,' the hapless clerk muttered. 'Rebels been seen in the region. They think they're camped nearby.'

'Are they, now?'

'And this place, well . . .' Ulfat gestured to their surroundings, his gaze still fixed on the polished floor.

The man beside Siavash's neighbour laughed too loud, slapping a hand on the table and setting the coin stacks jingling. Alphan Qadib's was the largest stack by some measure, and when he laughed, the two liveried guards behind him, Guild breastplates glittering with the light of six dozen lamps, chuckled along. 'The rebels would never come for this place! Can you imagine?' He turned his head towards the guards who flanked him and screened the strongbox that lay on a table behind him, pressed against the chamber's back wall. 'Guards at the perimeter. Guards at the ingress. Guards above, guards below.' He swept a hand around the chamber, encompassing the armed heavies in their bright sashes who stood watching at each doorway. 'They couldn't get within a thousand strides of this place undetected, and they'd certainly never make it inside. Tell your man there is nothing to fear.'

A quiet voice came from Siavash's left, directly opposite the laughing man.

'You don't fear the rebels?'

The man who'd spoken was young, almost comically so – he played with a wide-brimmed hat pulled down over his face, and Siavash had been tickled to note that the stubble shading the young man's cheeks and jaw appeared to be carefully applied charcoal. He was certainly deepening his voice when he spoke, which Siavash put down to nerves. He could hardly blame the young fellow, given the opulence of the surroundings and the magnitude of the occasion – was a little dressing in borrowed finery and acting up that much different from Siavash's own pretensions at the table?

His eyes slipped to the neat stacks that sat before the boy, second only to the bullish Qadib with his strongbox and Guild minders. The young man could play, that was in no doubt, and unlike every other player at the table, he had not been allowing Qadib to win. Siavash did not know the Guild man's particulars beyond his name, recognising only the air of deference paid to him by not just the *Den*'s staff but the other players too, the armoured men at his elbows and the intriguing-looking strongbox pressed into the chamber's corner.

Now the man placed both hands onto the table's smooth wood, fingers luminous with rings, and leaned forward. 'No,' he said to the boy. 'These rebels are little more than bandits and deserters. They can call themselves whatever names they choose, call their leader "the General" and claim a mandate from the masses, but they are thieves and cowards and pose no threat to anyone who matters.'

At the mention of the General, the young man's charcoal-shaded jaw flexed and Siavash wondered if he might retort, but after a moment he gestured to the table with slim fingers. 'Shall we play?'

Qadib smile-sneered, an impressive feat in Siavash's eyes, and he sat back and signalled to the dealer. A hush fell immediately, no sound but the clicking and scraping of the tiles, and Siavash steeled himself to lose the rest of his coin.

THREE

Only three players were left in the game, Siavash's final coins long since swallowed by the central pot, when the man approached the table. He struck Siavash as an oddly shabby figure for the location, despite what appeared to be a fairly well-made robe of finespun wool, dyed an impressively deep indigo. But his hair was unkempt and his beard, if it could be called such, was wild and bristly, and he seemed to have sawdust on his fingers and down his front. He shuffled up beside the young man, who was debating whether to risk half his stack to stay in the hand, and coughed. At once Siavash took the newcomer to be the young man's attendant, which made him feel a bit better about Ulfat's less than dignified appearance.

The boy ignored the newcomer, who coughed again.

'What is it?' came the gruff, near-whispered response.

'Time to go, isn't it,' the shabby man muttered, close to the boy's ear, just loud enough for Siavash to eavesdrop. His accent was unvarnished Hindmarch; Siavash would have known it anywhere. Siavash wondered if the young man's attendant had been listening to the same kitchen gossip as Ulfat, and felt a little better once more.

'I am playing.'

'Can see that, can't I. But it is time to go.' The shabby man leaned in closer. 'Our bags are packed,' he said slowly, and with what seemed unnecessary emphasis.

Still the young man didn't look up, or around. Instead he pushed forward half of his coin, his eyes never leaving Qadib opposite. 'Sweep them,' he said in his gruff whisper.

The dealer swept the tiles, then each player laid out his hand, to groans and gasps from those around the table, Siavash among them. Siavash's yellow-clad neighbour threw out his tiles in disgust – his bluff had failed, and the last of his coin was gone. Now only the Guild worthy and the boy to Siavash's left remained in the game, and all of a sudden it was the young man who had the bigger stack.

The shabby fellow leaned in again. 'Strikes me as an opportune time for departure, it does. Shall I retrieve our coats, then?'

Qadib, who had been chewing at his lip with unaccustomed dissatisfaction at the way the game had turned, turned his gaze to the newcomer with hunger in his eyes. 'Retiring, are you, boy? I believe the terms of the game were winner takes all.' He glanced to the dealer, who offered a sweaty nod.

'Deal,' the young man grunted, and the dealer obliged.

The shabby fellow leaned in again. 'Not making myself clear, was I? We are in danger of *outstaying our welcome*,' he hissed. 'If we leave now, we'll *beat the rush*.'

The young man had barely lifted his gaze from his Guild counterpart across the table, but Siavash realised he wasn't staring the man down, so much as gazing at part of his outfit.

'Your brooch,' the young man growled. 'Fine-looking thing. Where did you get it?'

Qadib looked down, affecting surprise at finding the jewelled clasp at his shoulder. 'Would you believe,' he replied with a slow-moving grin, 'that I won it at the tables?' He ran a finger over the magnificent blue stone shining at the brooch's centre. 'A rider from the north, down on her luck. My own luck was in that night.'

'For fuck's sake—' the shabby man began, and at last the boy turned.

'Get our luggage on the wagon and make ready,' he snapped in his gruff whisper. 'I'll be right down.'

'Your funeral,' the man muttered, and sauntered away, leaving a gentle rain of sawdust in his wake.

The Guild man looked up from his tiles, his expression fixed in private mirth. 'Still with us, boy?'

The young man returned his attention to the table. He said nothing for a moment, then slid his entire treasury towards the centre.

'All in.'

'But you haven't even looked at your tiles!'

The boy folded his arms, lost in baggy sleeves.

'Then you'll probably win.'

Qadib's throat moved up and down, his eyes flicking to the men around him. Nobody spoke.

'You have the advantage in funds, should I choose to play, I would—'

The young man's voice was quiet, but it felt like the entire Den had fallen silent. 'Wager the stone, then. Shall we see if your luck still holds?'

Siavash was holding his breath, and his cheeks were getting hot, his heart thundering in his chest. He'd not even put down his empty brandy cup. Unsighted, he waved it towards where he suspected Ulfat still was, and felt it lifted from his hand. Blessed Ulfat.

The Guild man's brows were low. 'You haven't looked at your tiles.'

The boy lifted his shoulders. 'Win or lose, it's time I was off. Past my bedtime.' A few chuckles around the table at that, but they were nervous. 'Thought I'd make things interesting.'

'Are you cheating? Is this a rig?'

'What kind of question is that?'

'Because if you're cheating—'

The young man leant back in his velvety seat. 'You certainly talk a lot when you're afraid.'

The colour left Qadib's face. For a moment, Siavash thought he might try to strike the boy, or have his minders do it. It would be terribly bad form, of course, and he'd likely be barred from the *Den* for a goodly period, but it might restore some measure of the man's self-regard. Instead he reached a slow hand up to his shoulder and worked the brooch free, before tossing it into the middle of the table with a magnificent thud. His cloak slid quietly, as if ashamed, to the floor behind him.

The boy tilted his head, peering from beneath the brim of his hat. 'And the coin.'

'That stone is worth—'

'You're short.' A flash of grin from beneath the hat. 'What do you really have to lose?'

With a growl the man shunted his treasury into the brass circle at the table's centre. 'Sweep them,' he snapped at the dealer.

One by one, the tiles turned. Those around the table craned forward as the boy, his eyes still fixed on the man opposite, flipped his hand, one by one.

'You cheated!' Qadib was on his feet, cheeks dark, sweat plastering his hair to his brow, his heavy chair spinning away behind him. 'You fucking cheated!'

The boy remained seated, merely leaning forward to scoop up his winnings.

'There is no way under the *gods* you could have known . . .' the Guild man burbled. 'Get your hands off my stone, you thief!' He lunged forward and the young man slapped his hand away.

'This is mine, now.'

'He cheated! You all saw him!' Qadib turned to the dealer, then wheeled on his guards who stood sweaty and awkward in their Guild finery. 'Arrest him!'

A number of the house guards had made their way over, drawn by the commotion, their sashes reflected vividly in the breastplates of Guild minders. It was at once rather busy on the top table's dais, and Siavash felt a little hemmed in. He hoped Ulfat would soon be returning with another drink.

One of the house guards addressed the dealer. 'Is there a problem?'

'This little wretch, this piss-licking swindler, has attempted to rob me through treachery and deceit!' Qadib bellowed.

'Prove it.' The young man had tucked the brooch into his robe, and was making the mound of coins into neat piles. 'You think I ran a rig – how did I do it?'

'I don't know!' the Guild man shrieked. 'You bribed the dealer, you hid tiles in your sleeves, you . . . you . . .'

The young man stood, adjusting his robe. He seemed small and slight before all the burly, looming heavies. 'Never met the dealer,' he said, 'and nothing up my sleeves.' He rolled up the capacious arms of his robe, revealing slim forearms that were nonetheless corded with muscle, and featured a number of interesting scars. Siavash was impressed. 'A box for my coin, please?'

'Your *hat*,' Qadib crowed. 'You had something under it.'

'What could I possibly—'

'Look under his hat!'

'That is—'

'If it please you, sir,' said one of the be-sashed heavies, leaning forward, 'house rules do require players to submit outfits to inspection.'

He plucked the wide-brimmed hat from the boy's head, and revealed . . .

Nothing. Nothing but a cascade of thick, dark hair, that fell either side of a suddenly unshaded face. A face that, despite the charcoal bearding, looked at once unmistakably female. Siavash had been blessed with many nieces, and would confidently place her in her middle teens, with an outraged expression to match.

'He's a girl!' Qadib screeched. 'I told you he was cheating! Girls aren't allowed!'

'Shit,' said Javani.

The man holding her hat moved first. 'Rules are rules, young lady,' he began, reaching for her with his other hand. 'The game is forfeit, and you'll be returning all items to—'

'Will I fuck,' Javani snapped, and bolted for the end door, ducking under the man's grasping hand. She was past the next guard before he'd even registered her movement, sweeping around the table and the stunned players with her head low and shoulders hunched. Qadib's shrieks followed her, his triumph turned to fury at her escape.

She was within a few paces of the door when it swung open towards her, revealing the lumbering form of an onrushing house guard with more of his colleagues at his back.

'Shit,' said Javani, and threw herself feet first at the opening door. Her boots collided with its edge and smashed it back against the astonished guard, who clattered howling into the men following, blocking the hallway beyond in a bellowing heap of sash-clad indignation. They were large men, with large hands, and she would not pass them, especially not when supine on the smooth-polished floor with a thudding pain in her backside from her landing.

'Grab her!'

'Shit,' said Javani. She pressed her hands down and swivelled, kicking the legs from the guard bearing down on her and hopping into a crouch, then leapt past his bewildered colleague, who was still holding her hat, planting one boot on her now empty chair and up onto the gaming table. One wild foot sent her once neat coin stacks spraying like a silver fountain, the shocking noise and shimmering flight drawing the attention of every grasping chancer in the chamber who had otherwise been able to ignore the commotion thus far. Which had to include every house guard in the *Den* – they were pouring from the other doorways like striped ants.

She had no time to do much more than wince at the complaint from her silver-stung toes – her options were narrowing, and the two men in Guild breastplates were trying to get close enough to grab her legs from the table's edge. One even looked like trying to jump up himself, if he could lever the slack-jawed man in yellow brocade out of the way.

'Shit,' said Javani, and leapt for the chandelier. She grabbed and swung, hauling her legs up and out from the lunging grasp of the Guild minder, then at the apex of the swing she let go, arms flailing, dropping from above the dais towards the main chamber, where the chandeliers were just that little bit lower.

Her fingers snatched the rim of the lower chandelier and the swing continued, her shoulders screaming almost as much as the furious Qadib and the astonished gamblers combined. From behind her came a terrible crash, and the shrieks stepped up a notch, but she had eyes on one thing only: the high, shuttered window directly ahead. It opened outwards, and, gods willing, would not be barred. She was due a little luck.

As the chandelier reached the peak of its swing, and the screams peaked likewise, Javani hurled herself at the window.

Her luck was out when it came to the barring, but the force of her impact splintered the hinges and threw one shutter half off its fitting. Mercifully not every part of the *Illustrious Den* was kept in pristine condition. As the ruined shutter drooped, the only marginally less ruined form of Javani rolled from the thick sill and dropped to a heap on the wooden decking outside. She tried to say 'shit', but all that came out was a groan.

She pushed herself tenderly to her feet, blinking in the sudden and unwelcome light of the midday sun. It had been cool – and a little moist – inside the tiles chamber, but on the other side of the walls lurked the full heat of day. Sweat popped instantly on her back and forehead. It was enough to give her a headache to go with her grumbling toes and whatever it was she'd done to her shoulder. For a moment, she thought of Ree, but it was not the time for that. Not with an escape to make.

She put an unsteady hand on the railing before her. She was on the middle deck of the *Illustrious Den*, the protectorate's tallest and most fabulous leisure barge, and on the port side. The wrong side. The clear blue water of the River Dairis stretched before her, its gentle current lapping at the vessel, towering red rock pillars on the distant far bank shimmering in the haze, age-weathered and striped in rosy shades. The gangway was on the starboard, as, presumably, were Anri and the wagon. She needed to get to the lower deck, and the other side. That meant going around the bow, around the stern, or chancing it back through the tiles chamber.

From the dark of the window behind her came another crash and a bevy of screams, then the smell of smoke tickled her nostrils. Uh-oh. Not that way.

'She's up here!'

Shit. Two guards at the stern end of the narrow deck, thick batons in their hands. Sharp edges and weapons in general were forbidden on the *Den*, and she could quite understand why, but she had some first-hand experience of the effectiveness of a heavy stick in getting opinions across and had no desire to be on the receiving end. Bow side it was.

She ran, limping, towards the prow of the boat, throwing over barrels and crates in her wake, speeding past shuttered windows from which smoke was beginning to creep. A bell was ringing, possibly more than one. It was no good, the two guards at her heels were closing.

'You're fucking this up, Javani,' she admonished herself as she scatter-ran. 'Stop fucking this up, Javani.'

She rounded the fore cabins and nearly went head first into a guard coming the other way. The shock of it sent her skidding to a halt, scudding back on failing boots, then flopping to her bruised backside on the polished wood of the deck. The two chasing guards were on her immediately, crying triumph. Thick gauntlets seized her shoulders, giving her a sharp reminder of the bruising she'd already achieved, and the growing dread that it was just the beginning.

'Where do you think you're going, you little shit?'

'Know what we do to thieves and chancers on the *Den*? We'll fucking keelhaul you.'

Overhead, gulls wheeled. They sounded hungry.

The third guard, the man who'd spooked her at the corner, had caught up, slowing his jog to a walk as he approached. Something about the sway of the walk seemed familiar.

'Say, friends,' the third guard said. 'Would either of you happen to know what kind of bird that is?'

'What?'

'Where?'

The sweep of the baton caught the first guard under the chin, and he crumpled. The second man managed to get an arm up, but a kick caught his knee and then he was over the rail, screaming as he tumbled.

Javani looked up, blinking against the sun's glare, as the new man dusted his palms and extended a hand.

'Captain Manatas? What the fuck are you doing here?'

'I should be asking you the very same question. Up, young lady, and away we go.' He hauled her to her feet, and did not release his grip on her palm. 'And I do not care for your language.'

'Why are you dressed as a guard?'

'Perhaps we will save the questions for a more opportune occasion?'

He dragged her through a doorway and into a lavish cabin, kicked through the far door, then again through a hallway, another cabin, and at last out onto the shaded starboard deck. They passed at least one punter in a bath, and more in states of confusion and alarm besides.

'We need to get to the lower deck,' Javani urged, trying unsuccessfully to wrest her hand from his grip. 'The gang—'

'It is,' he replied, breath coming hard, 'a little late for such.'

She looked over the rail. The barge had cast off. They were already moving down the river, and at some pace.

'Shit,' said Javani.

'Language,' said Inaï Manatas.

FOUR

'When did we cast off?'

'Some time ago! You were not aware the vessel was underway?'

'My attention was a little occupied! What do we do?'

'In truth, I had aspired to locate you before the cast-off was complete. We are fortunate that this unexpected fire has delayed much of this enterprise's attentions.'

'Why aren't we stopping, then? We can't be the only ones who want out, given the . . . you know.' The smell of smoke was getting stronger, even at the front of the vessel.

Manatas shook his head. 'There's no jetty in this next stretch of river, too many rocks – the vessel's draught is too deep to get us close enough to the bank. There may yet be smaller vessels below, if we—'

'It's swarming with guards and displaced punters down there, we'd never beat the press.' Javani was leaning over the rail, eyes scanning the barge and the drifting water beneath. It shone crystal beneath the brilliant sun, lapping white against the tall red earth of the bank. 'The bank's high here, at least for the next stretch. And we're not yet that far away . . .'

Manatas was looking at her sidelong, lips tight with growing unease. 'What dark scheme gestates in your febrile cranium, young lady?'

She pointed. 'Cargo hoist. We can swing on it, should be able to make the bank if we release the locking wheel first and let it spool out.'

His mouth hung open for a moment. 'I . . . I foresee *many* dangers to this endeavour . . .'

'Beats getting stuck on a burning boat then getting beaten to death by the goons, doesn't it?'

'What if the spool is too fast?'

'Then we get wet. Fond of your little guard outfit?'

'I have minimal affection for this attire, and it has served its purpose.'

'Then let's get a fucking move on, eh?'

'Language.' He followed her limping run towards the hoist. 'You are far too like your mother,' he muttered.

'Don't know what you mean,' she snapped as she hauled back the lever locking the pulleys. 'We'll need to go together; once this thing reels out it may not stop.'

'While hardly replete with confidence already, I somehow feel it ebb.'

'Hold tight, on three we go.' The shouts and bells were everywhere now, black smoke thick in the barge's wake, the rush of footsteps thumping around them. They needed to hurry. 'Run up?'

'Run up.' He went to wrap the rope around him, then paused. 'We must be sharp on release, or we will simply swing back against the vessel's flank.'

'Well, yeah. Ready? One, two—'

'Hey now, I am still— Very well, proceed.'

'Three!'

They ran, side by side, their arms locked around the heavy rope of the hoist, and leapt for the rail. She planted her leading boot squarely on the brightly painted wood and launched herself, just as something snagged her trailing foot and yanked her back.

'Fff–aargh!'

Her foot slipped back off the rail and she slammed chest first into it, the rope ripped from her hands, then bounced breathless and gasping to the deck, her vision blurring. Through the ornate scrollwork beneath the rail, she made out the hazy form of Manatas spinning on the rope as he swung out over the water, the pulleys hissing away as he dropped. Her fall had pulled him sideways, and in the moment before he plunged from sight he did not look like he'd reach the bank. His expression looked hurt.

Groaning and sucking air, she tried to roll and found her foot still held tight. It was gripped by the prone form of the guard from the front of the boat, the man Manatas had cracked around the jaw. One of his hands grasped her ankle, the other was pressed to the side of his face, which already looked swollen and discoloured.

'Got you,' he spat through his broken mouth.

'Disagree,' she growled and with her free boot kicked him hard in the face. She kicked twice more, driving the heel of her boot right into the most painful parts, and he released her with a tearful wail. Cursing and huffing, she jumped to her feet, feeling every tender bruise, then kicked the cowering guard again.

'Dick. Look what you did.'

The hoist had wound out, the rope now trailing in the churning water below. No sign of Manatas on the bank, but a rising plume of dust from the road that ran along it. The barge was moving fast now, carried by the current, but catching it was an open-topped wagon, pulled by a pair of stout ponies, and driven by an enormous, muscular man with colourful hair and a lot of piercings.

'Attaboy, Tauras!' she called, waving her arms and wincing from the movement. 'Up here!'

To her consternation, the wagon slowed for a moment, then Tauras reached down with a thick arm and hauled something up from the roadside. It was, from the look of it, Manatas, who despite appearing unharmed seemed most agitated. A shaggy figure in the back of the wagon now stood upright amongst the crates and bundles packed within, a bow over one shoulder and hands on his hips: Anri, in full critical flow.

'Come on, you daft old bastards, this is not the time for an argument,' Javani muttered.

A volume of pointing and gesticulation followed, the two elder men on the wagon in visible agreement that it was precisely the time for remonstrations.

'Gods above, not again!'

The guard on the deck had stilled his whimpering, and despite both hands being clamped to his jaw, had the look of someone plotting something. Javani would know, after all. Without warning she smashed a kick between his outstretched legs, then punched his jaw as he doubled over. It really hurt her knuckles, but it made her feel better.

'You really buggered up my getaway, dickhead.' She turned back to the wagon on the roadside, which was now running parallel to the barge, about twenty strides across from where she stood and a further ten below. The old men had finished their argument, or at least postponed it, and had returned their attention to her predicament.

'Javani!' Manatas's voice was faint. 'The rope! Can you retrieve it?'

She strained at the hoist, but it was impossible to raise – the trailing rope was sodden and pulling away through the water, and she lacked the strength to haul it up. She cast around the deck and saw a spool of thin silken cord hanging beside a doorway, possibly intended for tying back heavy curtains. It would have to serve. She grabbed the cord and ran back to the rail, then considered her options. Her throat was dry and almost every part of her hurt. She did not know what to do.

'Throw us one end!'

Twenty strides to throw a loop of rope to a moving wagon. She could do it.

Six attempts later, she was no longer convinced. She was sweating through the robes, her body battered and exhausted, fingers and palms raw from hauling the cord back up from each failed attempt. Her heart was beating far too fast, the guard behind her might come after her again at any moment, and there was a hot feeling in her chest that told her tears were not far away.

I will not cry on a burning boat. I will not.

Her tears were reserved for private reflection, for mourning lost friends and lost futures, not for being a fucking idiot. She sniffed, hard.

Manatas was still waving. 'Like I taught you,' came his voice over the barge's commotion. 'Like we practised.'

One more attempt. Feel the weight in her hands, feel the flex, the heft. Lift and swing, swirl and sway. Get the rhythm, get the pace, and *release*—

The cord flew from her open hand, arcing over the gap like a swallow in flight, stretching over the water, over the drifting scrub and russet earth of the bank, almost to the lip of the wagon-side, then it dropped away, lost in a curtain of dust. Manatas lunged, Manatas grabbed, and only Tauras's restraining hand kept him from tumbling from the wagon, but when he stood he held the loop of cord triumphant in his hand.

'Yes!' Javani squealed, clapping her hands together with glee. Then a cold feeling began at the base of her ribcage and began to spread, the hairs on her arms and the back of her neck standing up as realisation dawned.

I let go of the other end.

The men on the wagon had realised it too, and she watched with her throat locked as Manatas swept up the rest of the cord and piled it onto the wagon, his face ashen. He was probably wondering what he was going to say to Ree about her daughter's loss. Had Ree sent him? How much did she know? She always seemed to know more than she should, yet it was never enough.

Anri shunted Manatas towards the bench and snatched the rope from his hands. He bent for a moment, rummaging, then stood, his bow in his hands. 'Duck,' he might have muttered, but there was no way Javani could hear it from there. An instant later, an arrow whistled past her head and thunked into the lacquered panelling behind her, quivering and producing a hilarious noise, at which she would definitely have laughed at any other time.

'Go on,' Anri bellowed, 'get to it, then!'

The cord was tied to the arrow, and now stretched out across the water and down to the wagon. Manatas had been ordered to the reins, and the cord's far end now rested in Tauras's sturdy grip.

She didn't hesitate. She threw off her oversized, sweaty robe, spun it twisted in her hands, then threw it over the cord. She took a shaky breath, gripped as hard as she could and once again leapt for the rail.

She lurched downwards immediately, the cord sagging with her weight, and for a heart-stopping moment she thought the arrow had sprung loose. Then her shoulders shrieked as they took her weight and she slid, the twisted robe squeaking along with her. She began to pick up speed across the gap, now seeing the wagon clearly as she approached, Manatas's desperate concern on the wagon bench, Tauras's quizzical expression, the cord wrapped tight in his fists, the look of absolute horror on Anri's face . . .

Wait, what—

The side of the wagon was approaching at speed, and every knot and seam in its bleached boards was suddenly available in extraordinary detail.

'Higher, meat-boy!'

Tauras lifted the cord and she slowed, her trajectory no longer quite so doomed beneath the wheels.

'Grab her!'

He only needed one hand for the cord; the other arm enveloped her, plucking her from the air and cushioning her landing onto the rattling, shuddering wagon. The feeling brought back way too many memories.

'Th-thanks,' she murmured to them all in general, grateful at last to be off the smouldering barge.

Anri cuffed her around the head. 'The fuck was that?'

'Hey! What? I thought I did that pretty well.'

'Supposed to re-tie the cord, weren't you, you salted lamb's cock! To something with some fucking heft!'

'Oh.' That explained the look of horror. She felt giddy and sick and very, very sore.

'Big man, let go the other end now, eh?'

'Right you are, Anri.' Tauras released the cord, and it vanished from view into their trailing dust. 'Nice to have you back with us, Javani. Did it go well?'

Javani pushed herself shakily to her knees. Across the narrow stretch of pristine river, the *Illustrious Den* burned. Sections of the upper deck were fully aflame, and thick black smoke roared in columns into the morning sky. The lower deck teemed, and small boats were being lowered into the water at the stern.

'Huh,' Javani said. 'Turns out it had lifeboats after all.'

Anri was peering over the tailboard, into their rolling dust cloud. 'We've got riders on the trail, boys,' he growled. 'I'd say we are pursued.' He leaned forward. 'Hoy, captain – don't spare the reins, we need to get back to our mounts pronto like.'

Manatas turned back on the bench. 'While I am fully in support of such efforts, my own mount was left tied at the jetty back there. Where am I supposed to be going?'

Anri gave an exasperated sigh. 'Piss of the gods! Budge off that bench, then. Looks like I've got to do everything myself around here.'

A moment later they were rocketing along the trail, and Manatas was crouched in the wagon alongside Javani, who was counting her injuries.

'Are you hale?' he asked, concern intent in his eyes.

'Mostly,' she admitted, wincing at every significant rut in the road.

'I hope this endeavour has been worthwhile,' he said quietly, not meeting her eye. 'But I cannot imagine what could possibly have justified such risk.'

Javani put a hand to the jewel that was pinned to her stained and ragged shirt, and wondered.

They peeled off the trail in the shadow of two great overhanging towers of rock, slung together like lovers, and barrelled into the narrow gully where they'd left the rest of the horses.

'Quickly, now,' Javani barked at the others, anxious to reassert some control over matters. 'Let's get our takings transferred. Captain Manatas, how far ahead do we think we are?'

'I am content for you to call me Inaï,' came the reproachful reply. 'We should have a little while yet. They had not yet crested the far bend when we turned, though our tracks will compel scant interpretation.'

'Come along, big man.' Anri slapped Tauras on the shoulder as he clambered down from the wagon. 'Faster we get these packs on the beasties, faster we're away into the yonder. Don't much fancy being chased across the desert in a wagon like some gormless pillock. Can you imagine?'

Javani ignored that. Manatas was beside her, following their lead and tightening straps.

'Would now be an appropriate juncture to ask just what in all the hells you were up to back there?'

'No. Anri, did you get it all?'

'Course I did. Hands chapped from all the drilling, they are.'

'Drilling?' Manatas released a sharp breath through his nose, teeth clenched. 'Drilling what?'

'Back of the strongbox, isn't it. Had to go through the wall to get to the goodies within.'

Manatas rubbed his palms over his face. 'Then why seat yourself at that table of iniquity, Javani?'

'You saw that?'

'I saw enough.'

'You saw me win.'

He dragged his fingers through his hair, leaving tufted wings. 'Why risk playing, if you were securing your spoils by other means?'

'I had to keep our mark playing long enough for the drilling. Everyone else was just letting him win, he'd have buggered off before we got through the first plank.' Javani checked over her string of ponies, and the now empty wagon-bed. 'Mount up, let's go.'

Manatas pulled himself into the saddle beside her. 'This strikes me as a considerable number of animals.'

'Four to each rider, plus spares. We planned ahead.' Javani clicked her mount into motion, the three ponies roped in a string behind it following along. 'And made a stop along the way.'

'Ree will be greatly displeased if she hears you stole unsanctioned from—'

'I think my mother will be greatly displeased no matter what, don't you?'

He was quiet a moment as they moved into a trot towards the gully's end. 'That may indeed be the case.'

'Did she send you?'

'Would matters be changed either way?'

Javani gave a bitter smile and straightened the bow at her shoulder. 'Point taken.'

Anri rode alongside them as they cantered out of the gully and onto open ground, winding back along the trail before cutting away from the river. Buzzards shrieked overhead. 'How come you wouldn't leave when I told you, then? Obsessed with winning, or what?'

'Not exactly. What we came for wasn't in the box.'

'Oh.' They cantered up a narrow switchback and onto a rugged, scrub-thick mesa punctured with tiered columns of baking red rock, Tauras bringing up the rear on his larger mount. Anri remained perplexed, thick brows almost covering his eyes. 'We don't want what was in the box, then? I'll chuck it in the dust then, shall I?'

Javani flicked him a gaze. 'What was in there?'

He shrugged with his mouth, silver bristles stretching. 'Bunch of documents and ledgers and whatnot. Load of crap, I thought. Nothing shiny.'

'We'll keep them for now.'

'Where was it, then? Our target.'

Javani smiled, to herself most of all. 'He was wearing it. And that's why I had to win.'

Manatas was at her other flank. 'And how, exactly? You didn't even look at your tiles.'

'You *did* see.'

'The fellow made quite the scene, but you were gone before I could intervene. His complaint seemed well-founded, nonetheless. How did you best him?'

Her smile grew, a tight, close-lipped thing, a manifestation of a sense of satisfaction that glowed within her chest now the immediate peril was passed. 'Well, for a start, I did look at my tiles. I just did it quickly, when everyone was looking at the brooch and nobody was looking at me.'

'Ah.' They swung towards a pair of jutting columns, ridged and top-heavy, casting shadows like hammers across the mesa. 'But to know you could beat him, to play like that?'

'Oh, that.' The smile was a grin now, feeling the air on her teeth. 'That was just a question of character.'

'Yours?'

'No, his.'

'In what fashion?'

'Well,' she replied, her grin broad, easing her horses back into a walk as they began to climb, 'in the fashion of: "What kind of dickhead plays tiles with two men in very, very shiny breastplates standing right behind him?"'

'Behind!' Tauras's shout came up the slope, and they wheeled. Two riders, no, three, travelling across the mesa at a full gallop, throwing great chimneys of dust into the morning sky.

'Shit. Not ahead by enough.' Anri was already moving to dismount.

'No, Anri, keep on with the others. Get down into the gully and back along the back-trail. That ought to do for our sign.'

He looked at her, long and hard. 'Don't fuck it up.' Then he geed his horse, and he and his string were off up the hillside at a gallop, Tauras and the other ponies right behind him.

Javani turned to the lingering Manatas. 'You, too, captain.'

'I cannot in good conscience—'

'I ride faster than you and I'm a better shot.'

'That is unproven at this—'

'Fucking *ride*! I'll catch you up!'

'Language,' he sighed, and set off after the others, with only two looks back.

She paused a moment, retrieving her arm-brace from her saddlebag and lacing it tight. Three riders, coming in hard, maybe Guild, maybe not, but all with weapons in hand and aspects of murderous intent. This would not do.

Javani let the pursuers come close enough to see her, then she rode at them. Not fast, not hard, but downhill with three other ponies at her back, a sudden reversal. The pursuers slowed, their horses already tired and grateful for the break, and as they bunched to confer she sent the first arrow off the helmet of the man in the centre. The second winged the man to her left, and she was close enough to see the panic in their eyes as she loosed the third. As the man on the left dropped his sword, an unexpected arrow jutting from his arm, she began to steer the pony in a turn, keeping her knees tight as she nocked another arrow. The final rider had been wheeling to flee, but read her turn as retreat.

It was not.

Her final arrow, delivered at the apex of her turn, took the man full on the forehead, sending his helmet spinning into the air and knocking him half-senseless, and a moment later all three riders were little more than a receding dust cloud, only spatters of blood and discarded weaponry in their wake. Javani reined in, satisfied at a job well done, took a long breath, then froze, her eyes scanning the landscape.

The mesa was empty, but for the increasingly distant fleeing riders. There was nobody else, no sound but the cacophonous buzz of insects, the distant cries of soaring birds. She stayed immobile a minute more, eyes tight on the bright and shimmering landscape, then shook her head and set off back up the trail. But as she rode back up the climb, she still could not shake the feeling that she was being watched.

Siavash watched the smouldering ruin of the *Illustrious Den* slide hissing into the frothing water from the relative comfort of one of the small boats its staff had so kindly prepared. Beside him on the narrow bench, Ulfat was shaking his head and muttering.

'Ulfat, what is the matter?'

'The rebellion, master, they came for us. Just like they said in the kitchen.'

'I don't think that was the rebellion, Ulfat. It looked like a young lady asserting her right to play at the top table to me.' He nodded to himself. And why not? She had beaten every man jack of them, hadn't she? And she'd also kicked a handsome volley of silver straight back into Siavash's lap, which had more than made up for his somewhat damp and singed exit from what should have been a pleasant excursion.

And the fruition of his new investment was not far away now, not far away at all. The gods were once more smiling on Siavash Sarosh.

'Master, I think your laughter is upsetting some of the other passengers.'

'Apologies, dear Ulfat. Apologies.'

FIVE

The woman whom others called the General watched the approaching feather of dust from the high post on the bluffs above the camp. Getting all the way up had been murder on her leg, but it was the best place to keep watch over both the workings of the camp and the approaches through the ravine. The allocated sentries did their best to ignore her. She knew her presence made them uneasy, but she did not care.

Signals confirmed the approaching group were recognised and friendly. Ree sucked her lip against her teeth. Their reception would be anything but.

Now all she had to do was get back down.

Javani spotted her mother before they'd even reined in, posed outside her yurt, leaning heavily on her stick, her expression impossible to read with the sun behind her. Around them, the camp teemed with activity – it looked like another raid was about to go out, but the larger supply caches were already being loaded onto travois and they'd seen the outer perimeter being struck as they passed.

'Hey,' she called down to a passing rebel, a man she knew as Rozs. 'Are we moving on already?'

He wouldn't meet her eye, and instead glanced in Ree's direction before hurrying away, a bundle of horse bows in his arms.

She nosed her pony into the nearer corral and slid from the saddle, looking around for a groom. Manatas was nearby, already rubbing down his most recent mount. 'We're striking camp?' she demanded.

'Did you know about this? What if we hadn't got back in time? Is that why you came after us?'

'Don't talk to him, talk to me.'

Somehow Ree had crossed the intervening distance in an instant, and was standing on the other side of the corral posts. She looked gaunt and pained and simmered with barely contained fury. Javani swallowed.

'I was just—'

'You'll answer before you ask, Javani.'

Javani pursed her lips, feeling heat burn her cheeks. 'Very well, Ree.'

It had been Ree's idea for her to stop calling her 'Ma'. Operational security, and all that – the camp was large now, their raiding force expanded, and while their relationship wasn't exactly a secret, it was no longer something they advertised. The suggestion had stung like a slap at first, but given she'd spent the bulk of her early life thinking Ree was her aunt, going back to calling her by name had, in time, felt like slipping into a pair of comfortable old boots.

On the other hand, Ree had stopped calling her 'kid', which she knew she should be glad of, but that . . . that was proving harder to get used to.

'Before anything, are you whole? Are you injured, damaged, hurt in any way?'

Javani shuffled her arm against what was going to be a magnificent bruise across her abdomen and angled the battered side of her face away. 'I'm fine.'

'Good. Yes, we are moving out.' Ree's white hair was long now, longer than Javani had ever known it, tied back and bound tight behind her neck. Without it framing the lines of her face, she looked thin and haggard and raw. 'We're going on to the next post early.' She nodded to where Rozs and the other raiders were forming up at the second corral, passing out sabres, armour and quivers of arrows. It still tickled Javani no end to see Guild breastplates strapped to their comrades, their crests hammered flat and sheen tarnished, but no less effective for it. 'They know where to meet us.'

'But why?' Javani said before she could stop herself.

Her mother was, it seemed, prepared to allow her one answer.

'Because a collection of dunder-headed fuckwits rode out from this camp and set the pride of the province ablaze, then made a very public getaway back in this direction.'

'We weren't—'

'Shut your mouth, girl, until I ask you a question.'

Javani recoiled as if struck, but fell silent.

'This is serious business, Javani. This is military business. We are waging a war on the Guild. Don't roll your eyes – this is a fight for not just our lives, but the lives of everyone in the protectorate. We have a chance to free tens of thousands from the diggers' bondage, and we are winning, girl, do you understand? We are winning. But we must move as one. We must fight as one. We cannot have people galloping off on a whim, indulging themselves in a little freelance piracy! You've got to follow orders, you of all people.' Ree's expression softened, the flint fading from her eyes. 'Do you understand me? Do you understand how important this is?'

'Can I speak now?'

Ree closed her eyes hard and gave a small nod, her mouth tight. When she reopened them, the flint had returned. 'Well?'

'I liked it better when I had a mother, not a general.'

'We've been through this all before, Javani. I know you understand.' Ree took a long breath. 'What were you thinking?'

Javani's hand had strayed to her shirt, where the brooch and its gleaming blue jewel were pinned safely out of sight. 'It was a gambit,' she said in a low voice. 'And it was planned and executed completely under control.'

'Really.' It wasn't even a question. 'Who was there to look after you? Anri? Don't tell me you put all this on poor Tauras.'

'I don't need anyone to look after me.'

'That very much appears not to be the case.'

'You didn't need to send a minder after me.'

'I didn't.'

Behind Javani, somehow hiding behind a pony that only came up to his chest, Manatas coughed in embarrassment.

Javani planted her feet, hands on hips. 'You don't need to move the camp yet. We weren't followed.'

'You can't be sure.'

'I can! We took the old trails, we took the nomads' paths, the shady places. Nobody else knows where the water is, they *can't* follow.' She thought for a moment of the feeling on the mesa, the certainty that she'd been watched, and felt a prickle of unease. 'They can't follow,' she repeated. 'Besides, I took care of the riders who came after us on the road.'

'You killed them?'

'I gave them something to think about. Then we kept to the trails, and here we are, *unfollowed*. So you can tell everyone to stand down on the camp-striking.'

Ree took a long breath, then edged herself painfully into the corral, each step on her bad leg reflected by a silent twitch across her features. 'Javani, we stay ahead of the Guild one way, and one way only. We ape the nomads, we ape the Mawn. We melt into the plains, we keep moving, we take nothing we can't carry or use. You've seen the coin we leave, the fortunes in ore – let others sweep up in our wake, yes?'

Javani nodded reluctantly, her bottom lip projected. 'Ced Wins us local friends.'

'Exactly.' Her mother's eyes were intent, searching hers for an understanding that she refused to grant easily. 'There are a lot of stories about the Mawn – how they kill their old, eat their young, wear the skins of their captives, you know the ones – and some were invented, some had a basis in truth. They owned these plains, and they were feared. But it did them no good in the end.'

'People still fear the Mawn.'

'As ghost stories, maybe. But when did you last fear meeting one? Despite their reputation, despite the hidden trails and watering spots that we now travel in their echo, they were hunted and they were scattered and ground to meal. It only takes one mistake, one stroke of misfortune, to trigger catastrophe. Obscurity does not guarantee security, remember?'

'Whatever.'

'Nine hells, girl—'

'For how long, though?' Javani still hadn't even got the saddle blanket off her pony, and was itching for this interaction to be over, but something was burning within her and she would not stop now. 'You call this a war, but how are we ever going to win if we just keep running away? How is this any different from our escape from Kazeraz? You want to just keep running until we exhaust them, is that it? We flee our way to victory.'

'You know how you win a war, Javani?'

Her arms had folded themselves. 'Why don't you tell me.'

A flash of teeth from Ree, not a smile. 'Not battles. You win by destroying your enemy's ability to fight. Look at what we've been doing: raiding them, robbing them, humiliating them, denying them peace and comfort, the chance to rest and rebuild. They never know where we are, or where we may strike next. They are at breaking point across the expanse, and it's being noticed. We just need one more push, one shock to tip them, and they will start to crumble. We are so close and I cannot have you *fucking it up*!'

'Oh *really*? We wouldn't even need a rebellion if Arowan hadn't let them grow so powerful in the first place. We could have been in Arestan by now, enjoying paradise.'

'Arowan's . . . capabilities . . . suffered greatly in the—'

'Rice and wine and water as blue as sapphire,' Javani went on. 'That could have been us. But instead, it's *this* . . . dust in my pits and never-ending war.'

Ree's eyes seemed to glow in the light. 'I just told you we are a curled hair from victory.'

'Then you can hand it over to someone else, right? The hard part's done. Let someone else take the reins. Hells, let Arowan finish the job.'

'You can't always look to other people to fix your screw-ups, Javani,' Ree said with a coldness that would have shocked her were she not already fizzing with rage.

'What?'

'The end is in sight, and I will finish what I started with this rebellion, if no one else has what it takes to get it done. And as for you . . .'

Manatas slid between them, arms piled with tack, his expression a crafted study in oblivious neutrality. 'If, uh, you ladies would care to speak in a more intimate setting, I could perhaps—'

'If the General has something to say to me,' Javani snapped, 'she can say it in front of the camp. I'm just another soldier, after all.'

The captain withdrew as if pulled away by ropes.

'Well,' Javani said, arms folded and head to one side. 'What is it you want to say to me? What are my orders?'

She expected Ree to shout again, but when her words came they were quiet and cold.

'You never think about what might go wrong.'

'That's not true, I—'

'You never think of what might go wrong, and what you'll do if it does. You are risking more than just yourself, Javani. You're risking too much.'

'What does that even mean? Gods, it's like you've forgotten what it's like to be young.'

'Quite the reverse, and you should count yourself lucky you have someone with your best interests at heart, not parents like mine.'

'Hells, not this again. "Do you know what my parents did to me . . . ?"'

'Do you think I got to make choices when I was your age?' A hot edge had entered Ree's voice. 'I am trying to keep you safe!'

'Oh, so I do get special treatment, then? But you're happy to send others to die.'

Ree took a sharp in-breath, her eyes wide, and Javani wondered if she'd pushed it too far.

'Where do you want all this bollocks, then?' Anri came swaggering over, arms laden with the proceeds of Javani's gambit. 'Bunch of declarations and so on, a fancy ledger with a little lock on it, a booklet of enthusiastically anatomical sketches that I'll be keeping . . .' He looked up. 'Oh, in the middle of something, was you?'

Ree extended a hand. 'Let's see it.'

'You can have a look, but I'm keeping it. Quite skilled penmanship, it is, impressive shading on the curves—'

'Not the smut, you galloping piss jug! The ledger. Thank you. I see you already broke the lock open.'

'No point hanging around, was there.'

'Indeed.' Ree peered at the ledger, blinked, then, holding it at arm's length, she flicked through the pages with conspicuous uninterest. Despite herself, Javani felt pricked.

'See, it's useful stuff, right?'

Ree tossed the ledger back to Anri. 'Schedules and rotas. Nothing we haven't taken before, and rarely useful – just bureaucrats and functionaries sashaying between outposts. How often do we need to know that a given Guild auditor is planning to inspect the accounts of a given Guildhouse when we can track their shipments and deliveries from the source?'

Anri looked down at the bundle in his arms. 'What should I do with it, then?'

'Whatever you like.' She leaned over and pressed a finger against his arm. 'And I expected better of you, Anri. No, *hoped* for better.'

'Just trying to keep the girl out of trouble, wasn't I.'

'Improve.' She gave her head a grim shake. 'Is this it? The sum total of your bonanza?'

Javani kept a tight hand against a bunched wad of shirt. 'Yes.'

'I see.'

Javani's cheeks were hot, her fist rigid around the jewel. 'I can contribute, you know. I can do things.'

'The best thing you can do right now is stay out of the way.'

'Am I an inconvenience to you?' She was nearly shrieking.

Ree shook her head, mouth tight. 'Right now I am trying to bring about the downfall of a militarised organisation of staggering heft, and I am old and tired and in considerable pain. Everything is an inconvenience to me.'

'Well, I'm sorry I'm making the General's great campaign harder.'

Ree held her glare, her voice flat and final. 'You can train with the others but that's as far as you go. You're confined to camp until further notice, and will be travelling with the cargo.'

'*What?*'

'Anri, this is on you – if she crosses the picket, I will castrate you and feed you a protein-rich lunch.'

'How is this my fault now, then?'

A runner scampered up, flashing anxious glances at the group before approaching at Ree's nod. 'Messages, General. Latest collection.'

Javani looked up, her fury momentarily forgotten. 'Anything for me?'

Ree barely raised an eyebrow. 'Are you joking?'

'What? I write to people. And Mariam sets me reading assignments.'

Ree turned without another word and set off back across the camp with the runner at her heel, her steps slow and radiating pain. After three paces she called back over her shoulder, 'And rub your own horses down, you're not a princess.'

Javani's lips were pinched together. 'But I could have been,' she muttered, and turned back to the animals.

SIX

Ree had barely made it halfway to her yurt before Manatas caught up with her, one elbow proffered. 'May I offer you an arm?'

She didn't look up, just concentrated on putting one foot in front of the other, placing her stick carefully in the broken ground. Sweat was thick on her back and her head hurt. She hated arguing with the kid, hated it, yet of late it seemed to be only that or silence. 'Our people need leadership, Inaï,' she breathed, 'they need an example. Seeing me dragged across camp is hardly going to inspire.'

'And how inspiring do you imagine the sight of you sprawled lowing and incoherent in their midst will prove?'

Ree released a slow, hot breath, then took his arm. 'You win, this time.'

He offered her a gentle smile to match the arm, deep affection in his gaze. 'I like to think our victories can be shared.'

She almost managed a smile in return, but the pounding in her head stymied the effort, and his own faded. 'Is the runner still with us?'

'She has, of all things, run off. The messages are within your yurt.' They continued for a few more steps, him taking more of her weight than she wanted. 'Do you . . .' he began, then licked dry lips, swallowed. 'Do you wish to speak of what ails you?'

'What ails me, captain, is that we need to move our camp on ahead of schedule and in a great hurry, or risk capture and annihilation. What ails me is the bevy of townships who still cling in fear to the Guild's teats, despite years of grind and exploitation, and refuse every entreaty to rise up and throw them off – in defiance of every rational notion. What ails me is feeling like I am the only one who wants to bring down the Guild, and is willing to make the sacrifices that entails.' Her words came in a hot rush, and the pounding in her head only increased. 'They fight against their best interests, and those of everyone else.'

'And that's all?'

'That's all.'

They were almost to the yurt. It would be cool and shaded inside, for the short time before it was collapsed and prepared for travel.

'In my experience,' Manatas said, his words slow and careful, 'no matter the rightness of our cause or stance, there remains something to be said for, uh, endeavouring to bring others to our side through more positive means, over, perhaps . . . scolding.'

'I'm her *mother*.'

He swallowed again. 'I was, in truth, referring to the townships.'

Ree harrumphed.

'. . . but that is not to say that there might not be principles that could apply to both situations.'

They were inside the yurt at last, and Ree flopped down onto the cot, bad leg extended, and released a mighty sigh. 'You've seen how she is.' Ree threw up one hand, the other resting her stick against the canvas wall. Manatas remained in the doorway, head bent by the height of the awning. They still had separate yurts, if only for practical reasons. Even after a couple of years, their relationship remained hazily defined but mutually satisfactory, at least as far as Ree was concerned. 'How am I supposed to bring her to my side when she won't fucking listen?' Ree forgot whose idea it was that she and the kid should stop addressing each other in familial terms, but it had done little to boost their communication.

Manatas shook his head. 'It is not to say—'

'She hates me.'

'She does not.'

'She does. Don't misunderstand, I've made peace with the notion, Inaï. It's a normal and natural thing for a girl of her age to hate her parents, especially her mother. Gods know, at her age I was scheming the downfall of my own progenitors, and would happily have seen them thrown from a tower window, so the fact she deigns to bandy words with me even occasionally I'm considering a bonus.' She sighed again. 'She needs some friends her own age, though. It can't be good for her to be hanging around with a bunch of old people all the time.'

'Anri isn't *that* old.'

Ree ran her hands over her face. She felt coarse and sore. 'I just . . . I *care* about her, and I can't get her to take her own safety seriously, let *alone* anyone else's. I cannot bear to see her hurt. How can I make her understand when she just won't listen to me?'

Manatas said nothing for a moment, his mouth tight and eyes downcast. 'Perhaps, should chance dictate, you might voice some of that sentiment to the young lady in question under less-charged circumstances? The caring for her well-being aspect, and the profound affection likewise, might see a—'

'You can talk to her. She'll listen to you.'

'I, uh, that is . . . up to a point perhaps, but—'

Ree sat forward, feeling a plan coalesce at last. 'Take her for a ride out, somewhere safe, tell her it's a training assessment. She'll like that; little weed loves a challenge. Then along the way, when it's just the two of you, you can expound on the merits of following orders, making reasonable assessment of personal risk and keeping the fuck out of trouble while your mother is trying to unseat a quasi-governmental organisation.'

Manatas didn't raise his gaze, still lost somewhere on the baked earth floor of the yurt. 'My lady Ree,' he began.

'Uh-oh,' she replied, half a smile on her lips, 'you get formal when you're uncomfortable. More formal.'

Colour indeed darkened his cheeks. 'My lady Ree, I fear I cannot, in good conscience, act as intercessor in these matters.'

'Why not?'

He ran a hand up and down the side of his face, palm rasping at stubble. 'Do you remember what I said to you? When we embarked upon this grand endeavour?'

'Which bit? You said a lot.' She smiled again. 'And continue to do so.'

He didn't match the smile. 'When you named it as a joint adventure, an undertaking for us both.'

'Ah. I think I remember.'

'"I can serve you as a lieutenant or as a lover, but not both, not to the fullest extent."'

'I'd say you've done a decent job so far, in spite of that.'

He ran a hand through his hair, scratched at the back of his head. 'If I am to be your lieutenant, I must on occasion tell you things you do not wish to hear, I must challenge you, I must make you argue and justify in pursuit of our goals. If I am to be your partner and companion, I must stand beside you come what may, I must be your rock and your shelter, and be the platform from which you launch yourself in flight.'

'My what now?'

'Forgive my lack of poetic acuity. I mean only that I must support you without question, to enable you to be the greatest version of yourself.'

'I'm not seeing a contradiction here, Inaï. The greatest version of myself gets this rebellion done.'

'But at what cost, Ree?'

'What do you mean?'

He shook his head, eyes back on the floor. It infuriated her when he was meek. A man of his experience and capability should not be fucking meek.

'What am I, to you?'

She arched an eyebrow. 'Good company, and frequently useful.'

'That's not what I mean—'

'I know what you mean, Inaï, and we will have this conversation, but please the gods, not now. Not with everything else going on.'

'I . . . I just . . .' He fell silent.

'What? Spit it out, man.'

'It is nothing. I have said my piece. I only ask that you ponder, and consider where you would have me devote myself – for devotion is the word. I can be your right hand, or your shoulder, but not both, and you must choose.'

'Really.' She took a breath that was suddenly hot and shaky. 'Somehow I don't think that'll be as hard as you seem to think. Now pass me those messages.'

The flinch showed only in the lines below his eyes, but he did as ordered, along with the recent ciphers, then withdrew to the doorway. Ree leafed swiftly through the sheaf of dispatches, collected from dead drops and agents across the expanse, parcelled and carried in secret, transferred and smuggled, hidden and retrieved, until finally they reached her hand. It was not, it had to be said, a rapid means of communication.

She found what she was searching for and held it up in the occluded light from the doorway, just far enough away that she could focus on it. Her eyes widened in triumph. 'About fucking time.'

'I can contribute.' Javani paced to the south end of the ravine, where it forked into an area of open earth that the camp had been using as training grounds and had probably once been the site of a nomad winter village. Already gear was packed and stowed, and the air thronged with clatters, clangs, calls and shouts, and the occasional snort of a put-upon animal. The posts were still up, though, and she made straight for the first, leaping onto it with barely a wince from her bruises. 'I can do things.'

Standing on one foot, she whipped the recurve bow from her shoulder, pulled an arrow from the quiver and sighted at the first target at the range's end. She loosed, and hopped to the next post. 'I'm fifteen!'

She loosed again, as in the distance her first arrow thunked home. 'And a half!'

She leapt onto the crossed beam, matching its sway, then sprang along it with swift and careful steps, loosing her third arrow as she went.

'Would it kill her, just once, to say "well done, good work, I'm proud of you"? I can—'

'Missed it.'

She slid off the beam's end before her balance went. 'I did not.'

'Totally missed it, you did.'

'Fuck off, Anri.'

'Nope.'

She marched off towards the targets to retrieve her arrows, straying from the shade of the ravine walls into the heat of the afternoon sun. She was sweated through in moments. 'Stop following me.'

'Can't do that, can I? Not partial to a bollock banquet, especially not my own.'

'She won't castrate you.'

'Risky taking your word for it though, isn't it.'

'She was joking.'

'General doesn't seem much inclined to gags these days, does she. Not since becoming all . . . General-y.'

'Huh. Maybe not.' Javani yanked out the first arrow with a grunt. It was dead in the target's centre. 'I'm a better rider and a better bowshot than anyone in this camp,' she hissed.

'Are you now, then.'

'You know I fucking am. Edigu says I'm the closest thing to a true horse archer he's seen since he left the plains, and he knows a thing or two.'

'Old fellow's Mawn, is he?'

'Well, no, but he seems to have had some first-hand experience.' She yanked out the arrow from the second target. Also dead centre. 'I can run, I can ride, I can climb, I can shoot, and I can plan. The only thing I can't do is sword fight, and that's because she promised to show me sword forms and never did – always said she didn't have the time. Now I'm too old to learn properly! Edigu said if I was Mawn I'd have started before I was five.'

'Don't need a sword if you can stick an arrow in a bugger, do you.'

'I can contribute! But, gods, she just won't let me *do anything*.'

'Doing a good job of scuffing these targets, aren't you.'

The third arrow was not dead centre, for which she blamed Anri's unsettling aura. She checked the arrowheads and replaced them in her quiver, then began the slow, hot walk back. The heat seemed to sap her rage, her words slowing with her steps. 'It's like she's changed. I mean, she was hardly Mistress Cuddles before, but she's so . . . so harsh, now. Like the pain sharpened her.' She wiped a hand across her brow. 'I begged her to rest that leg, but she never did. She never would. All she had to do was stop for a little while.'

She sniffed. The air smelled very strongly of a lot of animals in close proximity, and their accumulated digestive output. 'The only times I see her now are when she's telling me off for something. And it's not like I . . . like I . . .' She sniffed again, wiped her nose on her sleeve. 'I suppose you can love someone but not actually like them very much,' she said quietly.

'We burning all this stuff from the barge, or what? Oh, were you talking to me then? Miles away, I was. Wondering what colour flames this little book might give off.'

'Just leave me alone, will you? And don't burn anything.' She stowed her bow and quiver and unwrapped one of the ropes from the rack. She'd embarrassed herself on the *Illustrious Den* and that would not happen again. Next time, she'd land the rope first time. Whenever next time was.

'Look tidy, your new daddy's coming over.'

'Fuck *off*, Anri!'

'Nope.'

He went anyway, albeit not far, exchanging an uneasy nod with Manatas as the captain swayed past.

'Anri.'

'Dickhead.'

Shaking his head in injured bewilderment, the captain reached Javani as she tied a rusted horseshoe to the rope's loose end and began to swing it in a loose circuit above her head.

'You're practising, good.' He chanced a smile. When she didn't respond, merely continuing her grim-faced swinging, he pressed on. 'On the matter of your exit from the barge . . . There was no dishonour in your attempts, and in truth the circumstances were extreme.'

She let the rope swing longer from her hand, then drop and begin to wrap her torso.

'There is strength in training, and while no exercise can truly prepare you for life's vicissitudes, they can at least leave you best placed to face them.'

A flick of one shoulder sent the rope travelling in a diagonal parabola, criss-crossing before her in a menacing figure of eight. Manatas took a small step back.

'Thus,' he went on, a little less steadily, 'I applaud your determination to—'

'Captain Manatas?'

'Yes, Javani.'

'Shut up.'

To his credit, he did so, but she caught the tightening of his eyes, the twitch of his lips. He was allowing her this, but the man had limits.

She swung the rope off her body, unwinding it with a tender flex of her abdomen, flicked it under one leg, then the other, then finally let fly. The rope sailed across the dusty ground and thunked against the first post, wrapping it three times before the horseshoe dangled.

She checked the other end was still looped once around her waist.

'Just needed more weight on the end,' she muttered.

'I am impressed.'

'I'm not doing this for you.'

Again, the tightness beneath his eyes. She didn't care. 'Nor should you. Your strength is your own to command.'

She set about untangling herself. Her injuries hurt more than she was keen to admit, and she was beginning to regret some of the more ambitious circuits.

'Would you care to hear any pointers at this time?'

'No.'

'That was, in truth, my expectation. But, please, if you intend to work the high posts in future, consider stringing the net beforehand.'

'I don't need a safety net.'

'The net's attachment need not signify a lack of faith in oneself. Consider it merely . . . insurance against the unforeseen.'

'Hm.'

They stood in awkward silence for a moment. Javani had nothing against the man – he seemed, in many ways, more sensible than her mother, and had a bit of humour about him – but their relationship, even years in, was defined entirely via Ree. And when not in her presence, neither seemed to know exactly what to say. Commonly, Javani preferred to say nothing, but this time the captain seemed to have something on his mind.

'Did she send you to see me?'

'Emphatically not. In fact, I made something of a point in that regard.'

'Good for you.' She finished wrapping the rope. It was hot, and her enthusiasm had waned as her aches had grown. If she was confined to camp for the duration of their move, she'd have little to do in the near future beyond rope practice, riding and shooting anyway. There was no sense in rushing it now. She wandered back to where she'd left her waterskin, and he followed.

'Then why are you here?'

He shook his head as if puzzled, a half-smile pulling at one side of his mouth. 'Can we not simply converse, as . . . uh . . .'

As whatever we are, she mused. He isn't sure either. Manatas and Ree had been a pairing since before they'd left Ar Ramas and the mountains – some said since the day of the battle, if not even before, which seemed unlikely to Javani – and for the most part, Javani had been content with that. Happy, even – his nature appeared placatory by default, and seemed to serve to regulate Ree's more aggressive excesses, for a time, at least. But since the rebellion had gone from a shared whisper to a multi-pronged insurgency over the months that had followed, Ree had thrown herself into the destruction of the Miners' Guild, and her ostensible partner had been dragged along in her wake. As had Javani.

Maybe they had more in common than she realised.

'Why did you come after me, Captain Manatas?'

'As I averred, is it impossible that I might simply wish to converse—'

'No, on the boat. If Ree didn't send you, why did you come after us? After me.'

He pressed his lips together, mouth stretched wide in consideration. 'I was, I believe it fair to say, concerned for your collective well-being, and that of my man Tauras.'

'You came for Tauras?'

'For all of you.'

'Why?'

'You really want me to say it?'

'You think?'

He released a heavy sigh and wiped the back of his hand across his forehead. 'Because I care for you, young lady. I care for all of you, but you are – that is, your mother is, and by extension, you are . . .'

'Water?'

'Thank you.' He took a modest swig, which seemed to calm him, and when he spoke again some of the fluster was gone. 'While I understand we have no familial relation in the formal sense, I have, in our time together, come to think of our fellow travellers in this grand endeavour, and, yes, you in particular, as a manner of family. As such, it falls incumbent upon me to maintain what layers of safety and security I may over those to whom I am bound.'

She rubbed her fingers against her cheeks. 'Come again?'

'I want to protect those I care about, for as long as they'll permit.'

She looked up at him, head tilted. 'What do you mean? Like, I could tell you to back off, and you would?'

He nodded. 'If that was your wish. I only ask that it be considered.'

'Huh. Why?'

'That is for another day. Besides, there has been a development, and you may wish to attend.'

'What? Don't you think you could have led with that?'

'I apologise, I became . . . distracted.'

'Huh.' They set off back towards the centre of the camp in the body of the ravine, red rock walls climbing either side, falling once more into awkward silence. Whatever this development was, it had concentrated the camp's upheaval, drawing it to the assembly ground beyond Ree's yurt. Something was afoot, and Javani realised with crushing disappointment that whatever it was, she was unlikely to play any part in it.

'Captain Manatas?'

'You truly may call me Inaï.'

'Does Ree ever talk about Arestan? Finally going there, all of us, or . . . ?'

'I have heard her express sentiments in that direction, in the abstract.'

'But not now.'

He sighed. 'Not now.'

They walked a few more paces in silence.

'Could you talk to Ree for me? About this ridiculous confinement?'

His bitter laugh echoed from the rock and sent a roosting jay squawking into the air.

'I'll take that as a no.'

Anri was loitering at the edge of things, as he tended to.

'What's going on?' Javani asked, as Manatas slid quietly off towards where Ree sat outside her yurt, staring at some documents spread across the ground before her.

'Camp's moving out.'

'I knew that already. The captain said there was a development.'

'Should probably have asked him, then, shouldn't you.'

She let out an exasperated growl then stalked over towards her mother, trying to approach sidelong so as not to attract Ree's ire before she'd found out what was going on.

'. . . just what we needed,' Ree was saying. 'If it goes well, we can start turning the screw on them for good.'

'Who do we send?' The question came from Edleon, another of the rebel captains.

'This one,' Ree said with a gleam in her eye, 'I will need to handle myself.'

She snapped her attention up to Javani as if she'd been tracking her by scent. They locked gazes, neither speaking, neither looking away, Ree's expression oddly calculating, not the hostility Javani had expected.

'What's going on?' Javani said at last, unable to hold the wordless stare forever.

'A change of plan, soldiers,' Ree replied briskly, apparently to the audience in general. 'The camp will be moving on, but I'll be taking a small delegation south. At long last, we've got our meeting.'

'What meeting? With who? Where?' Javani felt her throat tighten. 'Can I come?'

Again, the calculating look returned. Ree chewed at her lip for a moment, her dark eyes unreadable. 'It occurs to me . . . that you can't be left unsupervised. Against my better judgement, you'd better come too. But Anri is to watch you like a hawk.'

Javani tried to keep the elation from her voice. 'Where are we going? When do we leave? Can I bring my reading? Mariam set me a test . . .'

'South, immediately, and by all the gods, no. We travel light, and fast, and – we pray to anyone who's listening – very secretly indeed. Prepare yourselves: we're returning to civilisation.'

SEVEN

Maral waited patiently in the shade of the doorway. It was a fine doorway, corniced in pale stone, a lip of glossy if dusted tiles beneath her feet. The door itself was sturdy, thick planks of blue-painted wood bound in iron, and stoutly locked. Maral did not care. She had no intention of trying to get through it. Her attention remained on the other side of the side street – too wide to be called an alley, and alive with enough foot traffic to cloak her presence – and on the small door embedded in the high wall opposite, the wall fashioned from fat blocks of engraved sandstone and topped with curlicued spikes that were no less vicious for their craft.

This part of the Heribah township had made strides since her last visit. The street thronged with citizens, successful merchants and grandees in finespun, lightweight fabrics and silk affectations, artisans in more hard-worn garments, many carrying or carting bales of merchandise, moving between the wealthier quarters and the open squares and bazaars in time for the day's fiercest hours of commerce. The street was a cut-through, a chequered shortcut for those in the know, and happened to feature her interesting little door at its heart.

The door remained closed, immobile, inert. Maral did not care. She was patient. She was steadfast. She was barely even distracted by the improvised stall on the street's far side, a little way down from the doorway, a handcart strung with loose and flowing garments of shimmering silk that were almost certainly stolen, the enterprising vendor proffering swishing sleeves and scarves to any who passed close enough, one eye always on the next potential customer. Maral had studiously avoided his gaze. But the clothes . . . the clothes were . . . nice.

Sound, at the edge of her hearing. Could it have been a shout from within the high walls? A cry of alarm, or distress? She shifted her weight, coming away from the cool stone, readying herself to move. She needed to be closer. Shaking out her shabby robe, she slipped into the sunny street, threading carefully between hurrying denizens. Always she kept her eye on the doorway: on the gleaming rivets in its panelling; on the little grille at its top that remained locked shut; on the stout, oiled hinges. She barely looked at the silk until she stood before the handcart, looking past it towards the doorway, but her hand was somehow on a fold of a lustrous dress. It was blue, the blue of a pre-dawn desert sky, a blue of unfathomable depth. Gold stitching marked the hem and worked in patterns like water up the side, flowing with—

'Hoy! Get your filthy hands off, that's not for you.'

The vendor swished a stick at her, a length of polished hardwood no doubt as stolen as the garments, with no real intent beyond shying her away. But he saw her – beneath the hood of the sackcloth, he saw her face – and his eyes widened, his lips stretching wide in horror. In a flash he had levered up the handcart and was dashing off down the street, weaving between surprised locals, his wares flapping like rainbow sails. Such was the reaction she inspired, Maral rued. The man had been right. Such things were not for her.

She dragged the festering hood lower and turned back to the little doorway in time to see it swing open and a figure in porter's robes hurry into the street. The man was likewise hooded, casting furtive glances each way as he pulled the door closed behind him with exaggerated care. The robes were not a perfect fit, Maral noted from beneath her veil of mottled sacking: too short in the leg, too tight across the torso, and the glimmer of half a dozen rings on the hand that clicked the door into place confirmed her assessment.

'Going somewhere, Guildmaster Raad?' she murmured to herself, and set off at a shuffling, stumbling walk towards him. Raad had tucked his hands into his robe and was walking swiftly in her direction, his head down, attempting to look to all the world like a kitchen servant dispatched on an errand.

Maral stumbled and staggered, bouncing a loose hand from the sandstone wall before veering straight into Raad's path. She flopped against him then reeled away, muttering incoherent apologies as he sent idle curses after her, brushing one hand over his robe as he hurried on. Maral continued on her way, her lurches declining, until she reached the corner of the wall and tucked around it and out of sight. In the narrow channel between the great blocks of sandstone and the hefty timbers of the neighbouring stockade, she threw off her stinking sackcloth and stuffed it out of sight. She then edged back around the corner, alert to any watching eyes, before stepping back out into the street and sauntering back the way she'd come.

As she did so, she heard the first of the screams from ahead, saw the scatter of denizens as the man collapsed in their midst. Her blade had been razor-sharp and very thin indeed; there was a good chance he'd felt nothing more than her thumping against him, then wondered idly as he went on his way why his side had started to ache and his leg felt hot and wet, but even that was no guarantee in this sweating heat. His first realisation that his liver had been fatally punctured might have been a flutter of light-headedness, then a sudden feeling of desperate panic as the strength left him and he collapsed into the road. She could see him now, spreadeagled in the dust as townsfolk scampered away, his blood sticky in a slow-oozing halo around him. No one had dared approach him yet, but when they did it would not be to lend assistance. Not even in this salubrious part of the township would anyone be looking at anything more than the rings on his fingers, then risking a rummage in the dying man's sodden robes to see what further treasures might lie within.

He wouldn't be dead, not yet, but he would know it was not far away, and that it was inevitable. Maral was tempted to wander all the way over and pass on a verbal message, but Raad would be under no illusions as he lay gasping and gurgling in the baking street as to the cause of his killing. Once his identity was revealed, possibly very soon if the man had his guildmaster's seal stashed beneath those porter's robes, everyone else would be reminded, too.

The Guild brooks no dissent.

Maral lingered by the little doorway. A scrap of material was lying in the powdery ruts where the handcart had stood, an off-cut or kerchief or sash. She flicked her gaze each way then darted to snatch it up, blowing and scrubbing the dust from it with one hand. She had blood on her fingers, and swapped hands for fear of staining the cloth. It was a little rectangle of blue silk, one side edged with gold thread.

The little door burst open, and Maral tucked the silk away in her belt in a rush.

'Maral, you made it!'

Kuzari stood framed in the doorway, hands on the doorposts, a broad grin illuminating his sculpted features, his hair thick and gleaming in the fierce light of the midday sun. He was spattered with gore.

'Hi, Zari.'

'Did our mutual friend come this way, by any chance?'

She nodded, feeling her cheeks burning. She knew she should not have the little rectangle of silk. It was not for her. 'Over there.'

He followed her nod to where the more enterprising members of the township's mercantile class had overcome their initial wariness of a man dropping dead in the street to advance on his cooling corpse with an eye for repossession.

The grin redoubled. 'Marvellous. How did your thing up north go?'

The chamber behind him exploded with shouts, echoing from the flat stone within. Kuzari's grin became a grimace of pure excitement, a little boy delighting in the effects of a prank with no regard to the immediate consequences. Maral loved him, but even she knew he was quite mad.

'Time to go!' he trilled, and they bolted, charging down the street in unison, whipping between alarmed passers-by who had not yet spotted the gathering crowd up ahead, or were approaching it with a mixture of curiosity and avarice. Behind Maral, shouts filled the street, and she didn't need to look behind to know they were pursued.

'The quiet approach didn't work?' she asked Kuzari as they fled.

'It was taking too long.' They rounded a corner into one of the main squares, the market in full swing, slid between confused punters and back into another side street. 'And?' he went on as they resumed their run.

'And?'

'Your thing in the north.'

'Oh.' They leapt a broad-wheeled oxcart that blocked the street, Kuzari with great springing strides, Maral with a solid thump of her palms leading the swing of her legs. 'Fine. Reported back already, I'll be back on it soon.'

Kuzari snatched a hanging rug from a stall as they rounded another corner, sliced a hole in it as he ran, then strung it over his head. He grinned again. 'Disguise.'

Maral tried to match the grin, but found the effort beyond her. Her day was hardly boring, but she still wasn't convinced joy lay within it.

'Zari,' she began, but he tapped her arm and she followed him into a narrow courtyard. He put one finger to his lips and tucked back against the wall beside the courtyard entrance. Maral matched him on the entrance's other side, her breathing coming hot and hard, sweat pooling in her boots. He reached beneath the ravaged rug and produced a smallish knife, holding it close to his body, and again Maral matched him. The sounds of pursuit were getting louder, footsteps and shouts, the jingle and shunt of equipment at speed.

Kuzari met her eyes. 'Three,' he mouthed, 'two, one—'

They moved in synchrony as the guards charged into the courtyard, lunging as one and driving their blades into the necks of their pursuers. Maral's went down immediately, Kuzari's managed a gurgling shriek before he was irretrievably cut. They pushed the flailing men away and into the dirt. Maral was conscious that above them, beyond the spread of the citrus trees and climbing blooms, were gantries and railings and darkened windows and doorways, and she felt eyes upon them.

She looked down at the juddering, spasming men, their swords fallen, their grand armour fouled and useless. 'Zari, if these men worked for Raad, and Raad worked for the Guild, and we work for the Guild, does that mean we're on the same side?' She poked one with a toe. His movements were fading. 'Shouldn't we just have told them to stand down?'

'Think so?' Kuzari hefted a kick at his, who produced a sickening, bubbling groan. Well, it would have been sickening to anyone else, no doubt, but in Maral it produced no reaction at all. 'Look at their colours, these were his private guard. They weren't standing down if he wasn't.' He looked up at her, eyes dancing, wiping his knife on a fold of the unfortunate rug. 'Besides, where would the fun have been in that?'

'About that—'

A third man charged into the courtyard, sword high, and swiped a lethal cut at Kuzari's head. Kuzari threw himself backwards, the knife gone from his hand, stumbling over the dying man at his feet and crashing to the ground. The new guard seemed oblivious to Maral, his eyes only on Kuzari, and he charged at him, sabre wild above his head, a bellow of murderous rage booming from the courtyard walls. Maral was paralysed, for the first time in her life rooted to the spot, seized by shock, rigid in the grip of seeing someone she cared about cut down.

No, not for the first time in her life. The feeling was . . . familiar.

Kuzari's boots came up as the guard loomed over him, crashing into the man's breastplate as he swung. The stroke went awry, the sabre wide and flailing as the winded man staggered back, then a throwing knife took him in the eye and it was over. Kuzari climbed casually to his feet as the collapsing guard screeched himself hoarse, took his time collecting the sabre, then brought an end to the stricken man's screams.

'You were saying?' he said, plucking the knife from the gushing guard and wiping it on the rug. The rug was not looking good.

'Mm?'

'Before.'

'Oh.' The feeling haunted her. Paralysis. Fear. Terror of death. She had felt this before, but not any time she could remember. 'What were we talking about?'

'I said where would the fun be if Raad's guards had stood down.'

That was it. She put away thoughts of limb-freezing terror. 'You said before that work brought you joy. Was today fun?'

He considered, then nodded. 'Definitely. You didn't enjoy yourself?'

'I don't know. I feel . . . satisfied.'

'That's it?'

She pondered, bottom lip jutting. 'Yes. I'm pleased that the job's done, that we did what was asked, but . . . that's all.'

He gazed at her, gloriously blood-streaked, his brows jaunty with disbelief. 'What about resolving Raad? Not a little thrill?' At her headshake, he reached over and slapped her on the shoulder. 'Then there's your trouble, sis. It was too easy.'

Now it was her brows that climbed. 'Too easy?'

'You've got to make things interesting! Like today – I could have gone softly softly in flushing Raad, but I wanted to liven it up a bit.' He pulled the sad remains of the rug over his head, then tossed it onto the crumpled form of the third guard. 'Or with this fellow, dropping my knife, giving him a chance, letting him take a swing.' He nudged the body with his foot. 'Sometimes we need to challenge ourselves, you know?'

'You knew he was coming?'

Now his incredulity was tinged with concern. 'Heard him huffing a street away. You didn't?'

'I was . . . I was thinking about something else.'

The concern deepened, his head tilted, his eyes earnest and shining. There was so little behind them. 'No more of that, sis. Thinking's not for the likes of us.' He tucked away his throwing knife, then stooped to retrieve the one he'd dropped. 'Time we were off. Things to do, eh?'

She nodded, giving one last glance around the blood-slick courtyard. She could feel the eyes watching from above, their horror, their disgust. She did not look up to meet them.

Kuzari was whistling as they sauntered into the scorching glare of the street beyond, his sullied hands stuffed into his jacket. 'You back on your thing now?' They could have been a couple of abattoir workers out for a lunchtime stroll.

'Yeah.'

'Lots of chatter about the Swan back at the palazzo. Think we'll be asked to resolve her?'

'Hm? I doubt it. She's off-limits, remember? Too sensitive, risks rallying support, something like that.'

'Would be a challenge, eh? Even if she is a doddering stumper. Bound to have lots of guards.' He laughed, although Maral struggled, once more, to see the humour. 'You know, years ago, there was a fashion for plague beggars down south. Send some pox-riddled unfortunate to give your target a hug, let nature take its course.' He rolled his eyes. 'Not exactly efficient. Might as well use poison, at least there'd be less waiting around.'

Now Maral managed a smile. 'And what do we say about poison?'

'Poison is for cowards!' they chorused as they reached the square that led to the gate.

Kuzari nodded towards one of the livery stables. 'This is me. Look after yourself, sis.' He clamped his soiled hands on her shoulders. 'And remember what I said – find ways to make it interesting, then you won't waste yourself on all this –' he twirled a finger beside his head, '– thinking.'

'I'll try, Zari. See you soon.'

'It's not for us, sis.' He strode away, swaggering through drifting dust.

Her hand crept unconsciously to the scrap of silk at her chest. Not for us. Not for her.

But what was?

EIGHT

Night was falling across the plains, the sun swallowed by the distant blue ridges of the western horizon, its lingering band of golden fire casting the tattered blanket of clouds beyond in vivid hues of amber and rose. The darkest clouds loomed directly overhead, their edges blood-hued by the dying sun like cleaving blades. Ree hoped it was not an omen.

The ride had been long, and hard, and at one point they'd had to veer to avoid what might very well have been a slaving party, but their pace was slowing now they were at the fringe of civilisation – they had passed farmsteads and villages, and were now on a recognisable road, along with an increasing volume of foot and horse traffic, as they wound between walled estates and expansive terraced holdings. They'd left the bulk of their spare ponies with a skeleton crew at the edge of the wilds; this close to the urban centre, the volume of their mounts would have telegraphed their identity from a thousand strides.

They were close now, close enough for the wind to smell of smoke and effluent and charring food and caustic industry, a nauseating cocktail after so long in the fresh, untainted air of the plains, where the worst thing that might assault your nostrils when the wind changed was the rich combination of tanning leather and horse apples, or the occasional sheep-biscuit fire. The air this close to the city was heavy and thick with population, and they remained many miles from the gorge at the city's heart.

She tried to focus on the meeting to come, what she'd need to say, what she must not, but her mind kept dragging back as if anchored. To her last conversation with Manatas, the look on his face when she'd told him he should stay. She shook her head again, blinking hard, trying to frown the memory away. It was as if he'd . . . crumpled. She knew it was the right choice, she was adamant, inviolate on that. Someone needed to move the camp on to the next location, someone needed to keep their plans moving, keep the raids organised and controlled. Someone capable, someone trusted. Manatas was the obvious choice. Yet his reaction . . .

His reaction infuriated her.

Then I understand your decision is made.

How dare he? How fucking dare he act like a kicked spaniel when asked to step up and lead? How dare he look at her with hurt in his eyes, as if she'd banished him? She was trying to win a fucking *war*—

'General?'

'*What?*'

The force of her reaction took the scout aback. His eyes flashed to Javani, who rode beside and a little behind her, who merely shrugged. Of course she did. The kid had barely spoken on the ride down, concerning herself only with performative displays of indifference to all that surrounded her, and evidently saw no reason to break the habit now.

'Uh, that is,' the rider, a youngish man named Sarian, stammered, 'we are within sight of our destination. The way looks clear, all signals are present.'

'Good,' she snapped. 'And don't call me General in these parts. "Ree" is fine.' She flicked a glance at the kid, who was pointedly Not Looking.

'Understood.'

Their small party crested the rise together, and before them lay civilisation.

Ree reined in, without conscious thought, pulling her mount to the roadside where it began tearing at the wiry grass that sprang from the edge of the drainage ditch. The rest of the party reined in alongside, allowing the road's dwindling traffic to pass by.

By the gods, things had changed. Ree tried to think, tried to calculate. Fifteen . . . no, sixteen years since the siege. More than a decade and a half since she'd ridden over the Martyrs' bridge with a child in her belly and out into the plains, as the city in her wake was near blasted into the gorge. She'd ridden through these lands, these dotted settlements and smallholdings, these widely spaced attempts at agriculture in the face of persistent threat from Mawn, nomads, bandits, slavers and who knew what else. The Serican protectorate had amounted to little more than a network of terrified farmers, begging relief from the ravages of both the elements and human predation from a preening city state with an inflated sense of its own invulnerability and a hunger to consume. But things had changed.

'This is Arowan?' The kid was alongside her now, her face curdled in a dismissive sneer. 'I thought it was supposed to be all glittering architecture and towering buildings. I can't even see the gorge, is that because it's getting dark?'

'That's not Arowan, kid,' Ree replied, forgetting she was no longer supposed to refer to the kid as such. She pointed over the spread of glimmering lights before them, the vast sea of small fires, lamps and lanterns that twinkled from windows and doorways across the blue twilight. 'See that? Past the next ridge, and those beyond it. That pillar of light on the horizon. That's Arowan.'

The kid peered. 'Oh. Whoa. So . . . so what's all this?'

Ree shrugged. 'I guess this is Arowan, too.'

This far out, there were no walls or towers, just growing accretions of dwellings and workshops, strung and clumped together, inadvertently contiguous, until the land between settlements was little more than strips and enclosures. Hamlets were villages, villages townships, townships districts of the ravenous whole. Arowan had maintained its hunger, but where once the city had defined itself by its pure verticality, its bounds contained by its walls and the landscape of the gorge on which it sat, it seemed somewhere in the last decade-plus a figurative dam had burst and the city had flooded onto the plains in an urbanising deluge. Now the city was eating the expanse.

'Are we going all the way to, uh, old Arowan? The bit on the horizon?' Still riding *nearly* beside her, the kid sounded excited but tired, as if balancing the appeal of the bright lights of the old city against the thought of having to ride on for what was potentially days more through the winding mass of new settlement.

'No. Our stop isn't far.'

'Oh.'

'It wouldn't be safe to get any closer. In truth, I had no idea the city had spread so far, or I would have thought twice about coming even this far.'

The kid scoffed. '*We must be prudent,*' she carped under her breath.

'*At least,*' Ree growled, 'we should be unlikely to encounter any of our digging friends around these parts. Every township has its own jurisdiction and allegiances, and if our reports are right – and they damned well should be – our destination falls between claims. No Guild, no City, this far out.'

'Some townships have allied with the Guild? Why would they do that?'

'Piss of the gods, girl, have you not been paying attention?'

'What do you think.'

Ree took a long, hot breath, trying to control the muscles of her face. She knew the kid wasn't stupid, she knew she was curious and insightful and exacting, but sometimes she was just so fucking *exhausting* to deal with. Through teeth that were not un-gritted, Ree said, 'Why do you think we're trying to destroy the Miners' Guild, Javani?'

'I dunno. Because they're bad.'

Ree fought the urge to press her hands to her face, run her fingers over her eyeballs and push until something popped. 'Why are they bad, Javani?'

The girl shrugged. 'They push everyone around, I guess. Which is bad,' she added, pointedly. Ree ignored it. 'So I don't get why anyone would make friends with them if they had the choice.'

Ree allowed herself a small out-breath. 'There you go. A lot of them don't have any choice, or don't think they do. They're small – in the grand scheme of things, compared to tribes or nations – and isolated. And the Guild are large, and they're everywhere.'

'We fought them off, when they tried to claim Ar Ramas. We sent them packing out of the mountains.'

'Not everyone is willing to fight, kid. Not everyone is able – Ar Ramas should have been instructive on that score. Most people just want to live in peace, and are prepared to pay for the privilege.'

'Until they hit their limits. Like in Ar Ramas.'

'Right.' Maybe the girl had been paying attention after all. Perhaps she'd even read some of the books, documents, scrolls and texts Mariam had been sending her to boot. 'Why do you think states exist? States like Arowan and the protectorate, like the kingdoms down south, like all those wild places across the sea. What are they?'

The kid frowned. 'What are they?'

'What's the point of them? What's their purpose?'

To her credit, she seemed to give the question genuine thought. 'Like . . . mutual protection? Banding together? Or, or organisation. Food, and roads and things. Stuff people can't do alone.'

'That's . . . that's not a bad answer.' Ree found she was smiling with one side of her mouth, a warm, proud feeling at the centre of her ribcage. There was hope for the girl yet. 'Let's say, in theory at least, a state exists to look after its people. Most end up enriching those at their centre at the expense of those at the fringes, but the question is one of degrees.'

She leaned forward in the saddle, shifting in a quest for comfort. Despite the sedate pace of their ponies through the city's fringe, her leg was beginning to give her serious grief. 'For many of the townships, the Guild has the trappings of a state – it manages things like taxes and transport, provides security and rule of law, guarantees the flow of commerce. It looks like it's doing everything a state would. But it's an engine of extraction, you understand? However flawed the current governance of Arowan, it at least has a pretence of caring for its citizens. All the Guild exists to do is squeeze everything it can from those within its sphere, squeeze until they are husks.'

'Or until they hit their limits.'

'Assuming there's anything left to fight back with at that stage, yeah. So that's our objective. Turn the townships before they're too crushed to rise by themselves. Demonstrate to them, beyond doubt, that the Guild is not their protector, not their state, that it is a mirage, an artifice in the shape of bulwark against chaos. Expose it.' Ree realised she was smiling again, a tight smile of grim purpose, but a smile nonetheless. This was the most engaged the kid had been in months. It was their longest conversation likewise. Perhaps they were turning a corner.

'And how are we doing that?'

'With a meeting.'

The kid whistled. 'That's going to be some meeting. I look forward to seeing it.'

'You won't be there.'

Her outrage was instantaneous. 'What? Are you telling me I rode all this way to be—'

'I brought you to keep you out of trouble, not put you in more!'

'It's a meeting! Are you worried I'll get splinters in my bum cheeks?'

'This is the most delicate political operation of our lives, I cannot risk—'

'Oh by the gods, what do you think I'll do, shit in my hand and draw on the walls? You won't trust me—'

'Don't want to interrupt or anything, do I,' came Anri's voice from behind, 'but there's some boys over there wearing Guild breastplates, looking like they might come riding over by here.'

'You said there'd be no Guild around here,' the kid hissed.

'Well, there fucking shouldn't be,' Ree hissed back.

'Keeping our voices down, perhaps,' Anri went on, 'is all I'm saying.'

They rode on in silence, heads down, as the Guild riders set off along another road. The warm feeling in Ree's chest was gone, and in its place was pain.

'This can't be right. We've erred somewhere.'

Ree blinked at the structure before them as the scout, Sarian, quietly recited the directions, brow beetled in concentration. The building stood on a corner of two streets, and was tall, panelled in hard timber. Coloured lights glowed from its windows, and paper lanterns in a rainbow of hues hung in strings along and before it.

The kid was peering alongside her. 'It looks friendly. Is that music I hear? What does the sign over the door say? I can't read it.'

'This is a bordello, Javani.'

'A what?'

'A house of ill repute.'

'People seem to be going in happily enough. They're queuing up.'

Ree shook her head. The headache was back, and her leg throbbed. It was full dark, the sharp cold drawing around them after the day's fierce heat, and they were late. They were too far behind schedule to be backtracking, flailing around in the dark trying to work out where they'd gone wrong. Her chest tightened, sweat at her back. She could not miss this meeting. It had been months in the making, and had taken more than two years of campaigning to create the possibility. She could not miss it.

The kid straightened in the saddle. 'Nine hells, isn't that . . . It is!'

A figure stood inside the colourfully lit double doorway, towering over the queuing punters, inspecting each and nodding them through if muster was passed. A looming, pale figure, thick braids of hair shining polychromatic beneath the lustre of the lights.

The figure noticed them at last, still mounted in the dark of the street, and raised a massive hand in greeting. Down one pale cheek was a tattoo that looked a lot like a spear.

'By the gods . . .' Ree whispered in disbelief.

'Maybe it's the right place after all, eh?' the kid replied.

NINE

The White Spear looked wrong without her armour, diminished somehow, despite her prodigious height. There was still no shortage of the woman, and she loomed and menaced in equal measure just the same, but without the great featureless shell of black steel, it felt like part of her was missing. Aside from that, she was unchanged since Ree's last sighting of her in Kazeraz and its aftermath, when the vast mercenary had come to claim the kid as a long-lost heir to a distant land. What a waste of everyone's time that had been.

'Come,' she said, beckoning them inside, their horses retired to the stable at the building's rear in the care of Sarian the scout. Control of the queue had been delegated, and Ree, Javani and Anri followed the giant Horvaun past happily chattering punters as she ducked through a succession of doorways and into the building's main chamber.

'I told you there was music,' the kid muttered, although Ree had never disagreed.

The room was larger than the building's exterior had suggested, its high ceiling supported by regular pillars across the wide timbered floor, itself crammed with tables lit by delicate lamps around which cheerful patrons crowded. Tasteful chandeliers hung from beams overhead, although Ree did not like the way the kid was looking at them. At one end of the long room stood a bar, thick with clientele, while at the opposite end was a raised stage where a band played something fairly upbeat, and a woman sang along, her voice powerful over the prodigious background level of sound. The White Spear led them away from the stage, towards the room's far corner, where a section of tables stood on a step-raised plinth beneath the shadow of an ornate staircase that wound up from the corner to the floor above.

The White Spear made directly for the corner-most table, and indicated to those currently seated there that they should vacate at their earliest convenience. This she did with a look and a nod of such intensity that the table's occupants scrabbled away without protest or hesitation. The White Spear gestured to the now empty table.

'Sit.'

Ree risked a hand on the woman's thick arm. 'Are we still in time?'

'There is time. Sit. I will bring drinks.'

Ree sat with a hiss, grateful to relieve her leg at last, her walking stick resting against the comfortably upholstered chair. 'Nothing boozy for her – she's still a child.'

The White Spear followed Ree's jabbing finger, and looked again at Javani, her eyes widening. The kid was too busy blustering in return to notice, but Ree was chastened to realise the Horvaun had not recognised the young woman sliding along the bench to Ree's left as her former protegee.

'What'd you say that for? I'm basically an adult now!'

'You can be an adult when you act like one.'

'What, be a massive hypocrite? Keep telling everyone that everything I do is too important for them to understand? Lie all the time? I can do that now.'

'Watch yourself, girl.'

'Or what?'

Anri lowered himself into the seat opposite. 'Needed for this, am I? Seems you two would be just fine if I made my way to the bar.'

Ree turned her glare on him. 'In a moment, gods willing, I will be going to the meeting, and it will be your mission to keep this *child* out of trouble.'

'Give me the hard jobs, why don't you,' he muttered as the kid glared daggers.

On the stage, the band reached a crescendo, then with a single prolonged and piercing note, the singer brought the song to a close. The long room erupted into whoops, stamps and applause. Anri sniffed. 'Fair play, they're not bad, that lot. I suppose.'

He sat up a little straighter. 'Look lively, singer's heading this way.'

It took Ree a painful, giddy moment to recognise the woman reaching their table, an incongruous grin of utter delight plastered across her features.

'Ree? By the Goddess, Javani, is that you? Come here, child!'

The kid bounced from the bench as if on a spring. 'Anashe?'

Anashe seized the girl in a bear hug, then projected her at arm's length, raking her with her gaze, taking in every aspect of her appearance as the kid squirmed in her grip. 'You have grown, little one! You are so tall, and blessed with hips! And what charming spots!'

As the kid writhed, Ree felt a sudden lurch, a moment of externality, seeing the girl at once as Anashe did, the changes of years delivered in a compressed instant. Vida and Mariam had been right, the girl had bloomed – or had it been blossomed? – and despite the creep of changes, it had been quick, and quicker than Ree had been ready for. The kid was a kid no longer, despite her perennial idiocy and asinine decision-making. It wasn't true to say that Ree had missed it, she'd been with the girl the entire time. But her attention had been elsewhere. They had a war to win, for the sake of the gods. Was it too much to ask to deal with just one thing at a time?

Anashe was hugging the kid again, then holding her out. 'And do you still go by Javani? Do you have a new name I should use?'

The kid was hunched and staring floorwards, cheeks flushed, but Ree caught the tiny smile that tweaked her scowl. 'Still Javani. For now.'

At last, Anashe released the girl. 'And Ree, how do you fare?'

Ree managed an upward-turned grimace. 'I abide. Mind if I don't get up?'

'Your leg troubles you still?'

Ree paused, waiting for the kid to chime in with 'Because she never rests it!', but it never arrived. Apparently even she was tired of their routine.

'It does.' She tried to sit up a little straighter, suppressing the urge to wince as she shifted the leg. 'You look . . . serene. That was you singing up there?'

Now it was Anashe's turn to blush, and she covered her mouth with one hand as she smiled in a manner that reminded Ree so much of Anashe's mother that she almost gasped. She had not been prepared, mentally or emotionally, for the intensity of this reunion, and there was far too much to do to wallow in her feelings.

'I have . . . I endeavoured to take your advice,' Anashe said, not meeting her eye, as if confessing a double life as a grave robber. 'I went in search of my . . . prospects.'

'Nashi, these are your friends?' One of the musicians had made her way over, weaving between tables with a confident sway of her hips, a sturdy young woman with a cascade of tall braids and a ring in one side of her nose. She slung an arm around Anashe as she reached her, revealing an impressive set of regimental tattoos along its length.

Anashe's blush deepened. 'This is Sefi,' she mumbled. 'A friend of mine. This is Ree, and Javani.'

Sefi waved a calloused hand and offered a brilliant smile.

'Hoy!' came Anri's surly voice from the bench. 'Nobody going to introduce me, then?'

The White Spear returned, bearing a large clay jug in one hand and a tray of mugs in the other, bafflingly small in her hand. She placed them on the table and instructed everyone to sit, which they did, Sefi included, she and Anashe piling onto the bench beside the kid. Sefi's arm was still around Anashe's shoulder, and Anashe seemed in no hurry to remove it. The White Spear doled out the mugs, then placed a taller wooden vessel in front of Javani.

'What's this?'

'Goat milk.'

'What's in the jug?'

'Wine.'

The kid made a face like she was being denied sustenance for a week. 'I can drink wine! I'm old enough. Is this goat milk even fermented?'

'No.'

'This is so unfair.'

Ree chuckled as Anashe poured wine into the other mugs and passed them out, then took a small sip herself.

'You drink wine now, Anashe?'

'I am trying.'

'She still makes the face,' Sefi laughed. 'See? But she's trying.' She gave Anashe a squeeze, and Anashe smiled through The Face.

'Is there anything to eat?' the kid piped up. 'I don't care what, I'll just be happy to eat something that hasn't been tenderising under a saddle for days.'

'We will remedy,' rumbled the White Spear, and signalled to a passing member of staff.

'Don't mind me,' Anri muttered, 'just sitting here like a plum, I am. Hairy fucking gooseberry.'

'Oh yes.' Ree shifted in her chair again, trying to find a comfortable position for her foot that didn't involve bumping it against the forest of legs now crowding under the table. 'This is Anashe, a friend of ours, and Sefi, a friend of hers.'

'Heard that part, didn't I. Not bloody deaf.'

'. . . and the large lady to my right is the White Spear, the famed mercenary.'

'No. I am a mercenary no longer. I am retired.'

The White Spear reached into a satchel and withdrew a ledger, a stack of documents and a pen and ink set, then laid them out on the table before her. 'Please pay no mind. I have accounts to tally.'

The kid's jaw swung open. 'You're an accountant now?'

One corner of the White Spear's mouth tweaked upwards as she dragged the table's lamp closer and focused her attention on the columns of numbers before her. 'You think this place manages itself?'

'What about your armour?'

'Sold. To fund this place.'

'You own it?'

Anashe turned in Sefi's grip to face her. 'We both do. Whitespear settled her business interests, and I used Aki's gift.'

'Huh.' The kid gave Ree a pointed look. '*We* used our share of the gemstones on armaments and supplies.'

'And it's a good thing we did,' Ree growled. She cocked her head at Anashe. 'No more freelance retrieval?'

'We are both retired. This place occupies our time now.' Sefi wrapped her hand over Anashe's, and their fingers twined.

'And you sing.'

'I do. The words belonged to my brother. I only give them voice. Hence the name of this place.'

The kid shuffled around. 'What is it called? I couldn't read the sign.'

'Aki's Rest,' Anashe replied with a sad smile.

Ree felt the tightness return to her chest, hot and squeezing. Her throat was locked, unable to speak, unable to swallow. It was too much. Too much had happened. Too much was happening. And she couldn't pay attention to everything.

'If it's not too much fucking trouble,' Anri bellowed, 'perhaps someone might care to introduce me?'

Anashe's eyebrow went up, razor-edged, her mouth puckered, and for a moment things were back as they should have been. Then her wry smile returned.

'Sorry, sorry,' the kid laughed. 'This is Anri, my sort of, uh . . .'

'Wise mentor,' Anri supplied.

'Weird uncle,' the kid finished.

Sefi inclined her head. 'Are you two . . . ?'

'Eww!' the kid near gagged. 'Gods, no.'

'Not fond of the strength of that reaction,' Anri muttered. 'Quite the catch, I am. But no, pest here is my ward.'

Anashe gave Ree a look of cautious expectation. 'You did not bring your gentleman friend? I was looking forward to meeting him, from your letters—'

'No. He had to stay behind.' Ree couldn't take any more. She had to focus on what mattered. 'Anashe. The meeting?'

Anashe's smile vanished as the familiar look of cool competence returned. 'All is prepared. The Commodore will be waiting upstairs.' She nodded to the stairway behind them, then her eyes tightened with concern. 'How are you on stairs?'

'I'll manage.' Gripping her stick and trying not to grunt, Ree pushed herself to her feet.

'I should go with you.' The kid was rising too. 'To help.'

'Don't need it. I'll be fine.'

'Can't I meet this old friend of yours? I want to hear some stories of your misspent youth.'

'Old colleague. Never said friend.' Ree tried to offer a smile to the table, but she knew it was little more than a rictus. 'You all sit, catch up. I won't be long.'

Anashe held her eye. 'I hope things go well.'

'It'll be fine.'

By the time she reached the top of the winding stairway, Ree was more than aware she was gasping and sweated through. She paused at the top, leaning on the thick banister, fighting for breath, resisting the urge to collapse to the floor and spend an hour rubbing her accursed leg.

'Fucken hells, man,' came a voice from the gloom. 'What happened to you?'

TEN

'It's so unfair,' Javani grumbled, turning her wooden milk cup in both hands. 'I'm never allowed to do anything.'

Anashe offered her an indulgent smile. It seemed wrong on her face. Happy Anashe was not the Anashe Javani knew. 'Your time is coming. The years pass so fast, one day this time will be little more than a blur.'

'My time seems to be taking its own sweet time.'

'Keep caution in your desires, little one. Life can turn in an instant, and not in a way you might have wished.'

Opposite them, the White Spear rumbled in agreement.

'Wine seems to have gone,' Anri muttered, holding the jug up to the light. He'd been curt and standoffish, or more so than usual, which had annoyed Javani, and parts of his beard were shining with drops. 'Go to the bar then, shall I?'

Sefi jumped up. 'I'll come too – show you where she keeps the good stuff, not the swill they serve to cattlers.' She leaned down to plant a kiss on Anashe's cheek. 'Take your time catching up,' she whispered, then led Anri off into the tumult.

Javani and Anashe sat in relative silence, disturbed only by the White Spear's mutters and mumbled calculations. After a moment, the big Horvaun looked up. 'We will never turn profit if you give so much away.'

Anashe bristled. 'We give what we can spare to those with greater need.'

The White Spear shrugged. 'Is your decision. But no path to profit.'

With a sigh, she packed up the ledger, documents and ink set, replacing them in her satchel, then lifted a previously unseen basket from the floor up beside her. In the basket were several balls of dyed wool and a selection of long wooden needles of varying lengths and thickness. The clicking of needles began shortly afterwards.

'Are you knitting?' Javani asked.

The woman did not look up. 'We still need socks.'

Javani turned back to Anashe. 'Is that what you give away?'

'Our surplus,' Anashe replied, still a little prickly. 'Food, clothing, whatever is more than we need.'

'I wondered if it might be songs. Or poems.'

Anashe laughed, her rigidity dissolving. 'Aki would have liked that.'

Javani's smile was small and sad. Anashe's brother had styled himself a warrior-poet, possibly the only one of his kind ever to stalk the continent, but for all his bluster and grandiloquence had given his life to protect his sister, and Javani and Ree in turn. 'Do you miss him?'

Anashe held her gaze. 'Of course. Every day.'

Javani sniffed, nodded. 'I miss him sometimes. And I only knew him a few days.' She realised, uncomfortably, that aside from their infrequent letters, she'd only known Anashe a few days likewise. She decided she did not care.

'He could certainly make an impression.'

Javani's smile was a weak thing. 'He could. I miss Moosh too, and . . . well, you didn't know him. But sometimes . . . sometimes I cry, you know? I just, I cry a little, or a lot.' She felt tears pressing at the corners of her eyes. 'I just cry.'

'As do I, little one. It is normal, and healthy, I think. What is the mercenary saying? So long as the story is told, the life remains?'

'It was Aki who said that,' Javani said with another sniff.

'Then it remains a common sentiment. These tears,' Anashe said, wiping at Javani's cheeks with a cool, tender thumb, 'these are a reminder to ourselves. Our love remains, and like this, it is real.'

'I see him, you know, sometimes. In the sky.'

Anashe's brows lowered, her head tilted and wary. 'His face in the clouds?'

'No, there's this hawk, I call it my lucky hawk, and it followed us into the mountains. Ree says it was a load of different hawks, but I'm sure it was the same one. I still see him sometimes, out on the plains, but he stays away from the towns.'

'Then you must wave to him from me. And tell him he remains useless.'

'Ha, I will.' Javani wiped her nose on her sleeve.

'And your time in the mountains, it ended happily? Your letters mentioned the defeat of an entire mercenary company . . .'

'Ah, yeah, well, not exactly. Once their leaders were gone, most of them ran off, but a bunch stayed in the village.' She sniffed again, then lowered her voice. 'Some even joined the rebellion.'

Anashe gave a knowing nod. 'Do you cross paths with anyone else from the north? Whatever happened to that bandit you sent packing? The bearded, limping gentleman whose wagon we . . . appropriated.'

'Oh, Movos Guvuli? I hear he found a new job, is doing pretty well for himself.' Javani pushed herself upright. 'But what about you, Anashe? Apart from missing Aki, you're happy now? With this – amazing – place, with your singing, with Sefi?'

Anashe's smile very nearly reached her eyes. To her shock, Javani caught the flash of hesitation that preceded it, the fabrication behind the expression.

'I am.'

'Are . . . are you sure? Because—'

Anashe's gaze flicked towards the bar, where Anri and Sefi were still milling. They looked to be arguing about something, Anri dark-faced and belligerent, Sefi mocking and gleeful. Beside them, the White Spear click-clacked on. 'Perhaps we can talk more when your mother returns.'

Javani shot a look to the White Spear. The old mercenary wasn't supposed to know that Ree was Javani's—

'Continue,' the Horvaun rumbled, without looking up from her knitting. 'I am not a fool.'

'Oh.'

Anashe's brows were lifted. 'And . . . how are things between the two of you?'

Javani sat back against the bench and released an exasperated groan.

Anashe said nothing.

Javani groaned again.

Anashe said nothing.

'You've seen how she is.'

Anashe said nothing.

'I just . . .'

Anashe continued to say nothing.

'Now there's the whole . . . thing . . . going on, and she's at the heart of it, she doesn't have time for . . . for anything. And she keeps me out of it all. I can ride, I can run, I can shoot, even Edigu says so – you don't know who that is, but trust me, it means something coming from him – and she won't let me get anywhere near anything she's doing.' Javani reached a hand to her chest, where the blue stone remained pinned, secretly and uncomfortably, inside her shirt. 'She doesn't have space for me any more.'

'While I do not know the details of everything, it is my understanding that matters are at something of an inflection point. Once this moment passes, I am sure these pressures will ease.'

Javani flopped forward, elbows on the table, hands under her chin. Without looking, the White Spear reached out and stabilised the wobble of the table lamp from her impact.

'It's not like that,' Javani sighed. 'She had a life before me, you see? She lived a whole lifetime before I even showed up, before I interrupted her. And now she's getting back to what she always wanted, what she always was. And I'm just in the way.'

'You cannot believe that.'

'Why not? She only agreed to try crossing the mountains with me because we ran out of other choices. We could have stayed in Ar Ramas and lived quietly and happily, but then the Guild . . . The Guild fucked everything. And once she got the scent of their blood, it's like she's living her life again. The life she wanted, before I ruined it.'

'Little one, do not say such things. You must talk to her about this, before things escalate beyond repair.'

'It's fine. It's fine.' Javani sniffed again. 'I'm going to ask her, flat out, if she wants me around. But I can tell you the answer now. It'll just be dressed up with "duty" and "the needs of the many" and other sophistry. But it's all the same in the end.'

'Sophistry?'

'What? I read. Now.'

'Javani, listen, you must—' Anashe paused, her attention caught by the wide doorway at the long room's far side. 'Hmm.'

'What? What is it?'

A group of riders had entered, hard-faced types in dark and heavy cloaks, but Javani caught the gleam of mail from cuff and collar, the dangle of weapons at their hips. They were scanning the room, and Javani's heart leapt into her throat. 'Oh shit, is that the Guild? Are they here for us?'

The White Spear had already turned to regard the new arrivals. 'No,' she said. 'Not Guild.' She paused. 'But not not trouble.'

The riders located a free table by the stage and made their way towards it, and Javani's pulse began to slacken. 'Are they slavers?'

'No. Members of the Brotherhood have tried to enter, once or twice, but we will not permit them. Ever.' The Horvaun's knuckles whitened as she spoke.

'But you let the Guild in?'

'They are not proscribed.'

'Do the Guild riders come around here much? We thought we saw some a few streets away.'

Anashe pursed her lips. 'We see more of them than we used to, and far more than we would wish. With the Goddess's favour they will stay away tonight.'

Javani watched the new riders settle themselves around the table, displacing some nearby punters in the process. 'Who are they, then?'

'From the city. They come this far out to . . . relax.'

Javani frowned. That didn't sound so bad. She wondered how Ree was getting on upstairs.

Ree waited for her pulse to drop back into vaguely normal range before responding.

'Time.'

'What's that?'

'Time happened to me.'

'Aye, right, sorry. You were so tardy with your response I mayhap forgot the question.' The figure in the darkened hallway twisted the hood on a lantern, and slivers of light squeezed onto the walls. Doors down one side, a storage area to the other. And between them . . .

'The Commodore, I presume.'

Ree could make out little beyond a pale, freckled face and a mountain of curls, cast copper and blue from the wandering lights.

'Aye, if you like. And you'd be the General, eh?' The voice was lower than she remembered, a little roughened around the edges, the accent perhaps softened a touch. Not much, though, not by a long shot. 'Am I calling you Genny for short?'

'If I can call you Commode.'

'Nothing wrong with the name Genny, mark you, it's a fine Clydish name. I knew loads of Gennies and Gens back home, top bunch of bastards they were, no exceptions.'

'Still no. Are we doing this at the top of the stairs?'

'Ah, course not. Step this way.'

Ree followed the Commodore and her feeble lantern to the hall's end, where she unlocked a small door and stepped through. The room beyond was another storage space, stacked with crates and cases and coated in a layer of dust. A small shuttered window looked out over the stables, and the smell of horse and horse product came strong through it.

'Take a load off.' The Commodore gestured to one of the crates, and Ree was not too proud to flop onto it.

'Your Serican improved, I see.'

'Aye, did it fuck. I was always this fluent. Where's the boyfriend, then?'

'He had to stay behind.'

'Oh. Great shame, great shame. Would have been nice to meet one that had lasted more than an afternoon in the flesh, so to speak. What's his story, then?'

'What?'

'Well, he can't be so awful if you've been dragging him around for a couple of years. What's your type these days, Genny? Someone in the profession of freelance soldiery, no doubt, perhaps a former fort-line ranger caught short by Arowan's post-siege collapse, forced to mercenary work by pecuniary necessity, then met his match across a misty valley when his company attempted to assault an innocent village and found Serica's own rebellion brewing within it?'

Ree sucked at her lip, eyes narrowed. 'You did your homework.'

'Who said anything about homework, it's all educated speculation and deductive reasoning. You always had a type, I'm saying.'

Ree ignored that, casting her gaze around the musty storeroom. 'This wasn't what I was expecting.'

'Should hope not. This isn't yet the meat of the dinner – we're merely biding here.'

'What are we biding for?'

The Commodore was pressed against the wall, peering out through the shutters. 'Just a wee signal, that's all.'

'I see.'

Ree's eyes were adjusting. The Commodore seemed almost exactly as she remembered her in the half-light, perhaps some coils of silver in the hair, perhaps a hint of lines at her eyes, but in all other respects she seemed stunningly unweathered.

'You look well.'

'Aye, I'm upright, if that's what you mean, you know, considering. You look . . .' The Commodore glanced back, then returned her gaze to the window. 'Stopped colouring your hair, eh?'

Ree ran a hand through her sweat-dampened mop, abruptly self-conscious. 'I've been thinking about doing it again.'

'Suits you like that.'

'Fuck you.'

'Ha, there she is.' She was quiet a moment, her concentration back at the window. 'You know, I always wondered how the old girl became a general.'

'What?'

'Aki and Anashe's mam, when we rode with her in the beforetimes. They always said she'd been a general, back east. Could never square it at the time, but, well . . .' She glanced back again. 'Here we are, with another general in our ranks.'

Ree leaned back against the crate. 'Some of us are born to generalcy, others have it thrust upon us?'

'Aye, no doubt. I heard you were a farmer.'

'I kept some horses, for a time.'

'Being honest, I had trouble squaring that one, and all.'

'You knew where I was, then? Before you sent Aki and Anashe my way?'

'Not exactly, no. Continentally, perhaps, but it was only when I saw the tender for wee sprog's collection that I put the necessary together.'

'And you didn't look for me before that?'

'Well, likewise, eh? Figured you'd prefer to be left alone. Was I wrong?'

'Not entirely.'

'You never fancied coming south again? I'm telling you, the city proper's changed since you last, er, passed through. I've got a nice little office, plush wee place with a view of the gorge. It's not like it was, gates are wide open now, a real hive of entrepreneurialism.'

'I'm not sure that's a word.'

'Sure it is – told you, I'm fluent. Anyway, it's a town of opportunity for the opportunity-minded, like me.'

'I can imagine the eradication of its ruling class in the siege might have had that effect.'

'Aye, for a time, certainly. And it will again, once our digging parasites are removed.'

'Which is rather why we're here, isn't it? Where's this signal of yours?'

The Commodore waved a hand. 'It's coming, man, relax. You never used to be this uptight.'

'I think you'll find I was exactly this uptight.' Ree looked around the dusty storeroom. There was absolutely nothing of interest in it, and nothing to drink. She regretted leaving her wine downstairs. 'You're still working, then? Keeping your agency going without . . . with a smaller headcount?'

'Aye, well, I like to keep a roster on rotation, so to speak.' The Commodore swivelled, looking along the outside wall for a moment, then back to her original starting point. 'And you, got a little crew together again, eh? Like the old days?'

'Hardly. I'm leading a rebellion, L— Commodore, not trying to start a free company.'

The Commodore shrugged. 'Not like we got much off the ground with our efforts back then. But some shenanigans, eh? You can't forget the shenanigans.'

'No matter how I try.'

'We were a kind of family though, eh?'

'We were colleagues.'

'Aye, that's right. I'd forgotten you made yourself hard to like.'

'What's that supposed to mean?'

'Not like we didn't persevere, of course, noble souls that we were. And look at you now.'

'Look at me how?'

'In the family way.' The Commodore shook her head, the mass of curls dancing. 'That was the other thing I found un-squarable. You always hated kids.'

Ree shifted on the crate. 'Maybe I thought differently before I had one of my own.'

'Well that's disappointingly solipsistic, even for you.'

'Is this signal really coming, or is this just an excuse for you to insult me in a storage cupboard?'

'Merely happy coincidence. She well, then?'

'What?'

'Your offspring. Is she content, healthy, well-adjusted? You know, considering. Anashe told me about her, see. How, well, alike you may be.'

'She's . . .' Ree took a breath, let it sit a moment. 'We're not getting on.'

'Oh no, this is a devastating shock.'

'Fuck off.' Ree straightened her shoulders. Everything ached. 'She'll come around. There's just a lot going on at the moment and I need her to get off my back for a while.'

The Commodore sniffed. 'I may not be a parent, nor even much of a parental proxy, but is it just possible that you're maybe allowing your relationship to wither while you throw yourself into other pursuits?'

'Those "other pursuits" are the restoration of free existence to the whole expanse. For now, she needs to grow up and get over it.'

'Fair boggles the mind as to why you might not be getting on, so it does.'

Ree ran her fingers through her hair, laced them behind her neck and squeezed. Her neck ached, too. 'Is this signal coming or not?'

The Commodore met her glare with a withering look of her own. 'Course it's coming. I'm far too old to be staying up this late without cause.'

'Don't you dare say you're too old – you're younger than me. Right?' Ree paused. 'How old are you?'

'You know what? I'm not even sure myself these days. What year is it?'

'I think there's a six in it.'

The Commodore stiffened. 'Aye, fuck. We're on.'

Ree forced herself upright, the world a weight on her shoulders, and a feeling like hot blades in her calf. 'About fucking time.'

'And there I was thinking we were having a nice wee catch-up.'

The Commodore held up the hooded lantern to the window and twisted it back and forth in a return signal, then doused them in darkness once more. Settling the lantern on the ground, she set about moving a set of crates away from the wall, revealing a small hatch behind.

'Feel free to help at any time.'

'You look like you're on top of things. I'd just get in your way.'

'Fucken hells, man. This way.'

She had to crawl through the hatch, which led to a low, dim tunnel that stank of horse, the ceiling pitched just high enough for them to walk hunched. 'Runs through the stable roof,' the Commodore whispered back over her shoulder. 'Step quiet, like.'

Ree did her best, although the clomp of her stick might well have alarmed some dozing ponies.

'What is this?' she hissed. A small square of flickering light beckoned ahead, the only brightness in the claustrophobic tunnel.

'Cheeky wee bit of access to the fancy rooms next door,' the Commodore whispered back, 'for those who like to enjoy some music, booze and dancing, and don't want to be seen coming and going.'

Ree was impressed.

The Commodore ducked through the far hatch and offered a hand to help Ree through, which she grudgingly accepted. They were in another storage cupboard, which the Commodore unlocked, then turned to face her, the lantern at last unhooded.

'Gods, you look exactly the same. Your hair's barely even—'

'Aye, right, never mind that.' The Commodore reached out and brushed some of the dust and cobwebs from Ree's clothes. Ree thought she saw concern in her eyes. 'Are you feeling . . . that is, beyond this door, well, there's another door. But beyond that door . . . Are you ready?'

Of course I'm ready, she went to say, I've been waiting on a crate suffering your barbs for an age, and I rode across the plains with barely a stop to piss for days before that. I've been trying to secure this meeting for months, and it's taken the work of years to get this far. I have been ready for this moment since Ar Ramas, since Kazeraz, since I rode over the Martyrs' bridge and left Arowan behind. Of course I'm fucking ready.

'Probably,' she mumbled. 'I may not be on good terms with the Exalted boss, but I can browbeat a flunky into doing the necessary.'

'Grand. Let's do it.'

The Commodore opened the door and stepped into the lamplit hall beyond, then walked smartly to a wide, ornate door and rapped out a complex tattoo. The door swung open an instant later.

The Commodore ducked her head and stepped back. 'After you.'

Ree squared her shoulders, steeled herself, and walked stiffly into the chamber beyond, her stick tapping echoes on the polished floor.

The room was dim, lit by lamps and beeswax in the corners, illuminating a single, hooded figure standing beside the tall, heavily draped windows. The figure turned and stiffened at Ree's approach, then reached up with one slow hand and pulled back the hood.

It was not a flunky.

Ree came to a halt, and met the dispassionate gaze of Exalted

Matil, Keeper of the City of Arowan, Guardian of the Protectorate and Shield of the Expanse, the Serican Swan.

'Ooh bollocks,' whispered the Commodore from behind her.

Ree had not been ready.

ELEVEN

Anri and Sefi had finally returned with more wine, while still engaged in an acerbic argument that Javani couldn't follow in the slightest, and Javani realised she was getting sleepy. It had to be approaching midnight, and the long ride and hard camping hadn't helped; nor had two big mugs of goat's milk, the second warm. She tried to suppress a yawn and failed, and Anashe patted her shoulder. 'As soon as your mother returns, we will make up your beds. I imagine she is just as tired as you.'

Javani nodded, still finishing the yawn, its intensity making her eyes water. 'You have beds here?' she managed at last.

'Yes, upstairs.'

'Anashe, what's a bordello?'

Opposite them, the White Spear lifted her head, sniffed, and stiffened. With care she placed her knitting back in the basket and turned in her chair to observe the long room's doorway. Her fatigue forgotten, Javani looked past her to the source of her disquiet.

'More riders?'

The White Spear grunted in assent.

Javani swallowed. 'Same group as before?'

The second grunt disagreed.

Anashe was halfway to her feet. 'By the Goddess, the foulest luck . . .'

The new group entering the long room cut enough of a menacing swagger to clear a path before them. Long split-tailed coats, burnished breastplates gleaming beneath the coloured lights, bracers and greaves shining. Sabres swung brazen from their belts as they advanced into the room.

'We must start enforcing the no-weapons rule!' Anashe hissed to the White Spear.

The Horvaun shrugged. 'Is administrative burden. Will increase costs. Diminish . . . surplus.'

Anashe pressed her palms together. 'Perhaps they are merely here to enjoy some music and a convivial atmosphere. Let us not leap to conclusions.'

The Guild riders had decided which table they wanted, and were making this clear to its current occupants. Somehow their approach lacked the charm of the White Spear's technique, and seemed to involve a lot of sneering and gesticulation. When one of the punters proved too slow in moving away, a Guild man kicked him to the ground. Needless to say, his comrades burst out laughing at the unfortunate client's pratfall, then glared around to see if anyone dared challenge them for their antics.

Javani sat up, mouth dry, palms sweaty. 'Do we need to leave? Should I get Ree from upstairs?'

Anashe put out a restraining hand. 'An attempt to leave might risk their attention. For now, at least, unpleasant as they are, they may be humoured by—'

The long room fell silent at the heavy scrape of a chair against the timber floor. One of the first group of riders had stood, shoulders squared, heavy cloak swaying, and turned to face the Guild mob. Within his cloak, he rested a comfortable hand on the pommel of a straight sword.

'I believe that table is already occupied,' the cloaked man said. His hair was streaked grey and tied back in a ponytail, and his thick moustache was likewise peppered with silver. Javani noted substantial differences between the two groups. For a start, all the Guild riders gleamed with polished metal, new and unblemished, while the dark-cloaked bunch had a far tattier, more lived-in look, and second, the dark-cloaks were either middle-aged or very young: the Guild riders were of all ages, and some of them looked like they'd come from distant parts. Presumably, she hazarded, this had something to do with the war.

The Guild man who'd done the kicking, a square-jawed, black-stubbled type who could have been Acting Guildmaster Kurush's squat cousin, turned to face the cloak-wearer. 'I believe you are mistaken,' he said, folding his arms across his shining breastplate.

The cloaked man took a casual step forward, eliciting a flurry of further chair-scrapes as the club's patrons tried desperately to get out of the way. 'The mistake is yours, digger. You're not in mining country here.'

The Guild man rocked back with feigned laughter, hands now placed on his hips, and that much closer to the hilt of his sabre. 'Didn't you hear? Everywhere is mining country.' He took a step forward himself, as behind him his comrades flexed and shuffled. 'Do you know what the Guild does to those who fail to show the proper respect? Just who do you think you are, worm?'

The moustached man threw back his cloak, revealing a silver breastplate beneath, stamped with the sigil of the butterfly.

'The hand of the city says it's time for you to leave.'

At that, the other cloaked riders left their seats. They faced each other, six Guild men to five in cloaks, a narrowing stretch of empty floorboards between them. The Guild riders did not move.

'You're a long way from the city, fancy man,' the Guild man snarled. 'Your jurisdiction ends, oh, about seven miles that way.'

The other cloaks went back, revealing matching mail and breastplates and a lot of weapons. 'And your jurisdiction never began. Get out of here, lackey. Now.'

'Make us.'

'Goddess have mercy,' moaned Anashe. 'Not again.'

'Should we intervene?' Javani hissed. 'What do we do? Should we warn Ree? I feel like we should warn Ree.'

'We should not . . .' Anashe began, her attention locked on the bristling riders, while across from her the White Spear rose hugely to her feet with a sigh, her thick knuckles cracking.

'Anyone? Well, I'm warning Ree,' Javani snapped, and scurried for the stairs, deaf to the calls that came after her.

The woman before Ree remained tall, barely stooped with age, her short hair almost as white as Ree's own, and the years heavy on the flesh of her face: her cheeks hollowed, the carved lines around her eyes and mouth stark in the lamplight. Ree was stunned by the echo in Matil's features of her late mother, the preceding Keeper when Ree had last ridden through the city.

'Commodore,' Ree hissed from the corner of her mouth. 'The fuck?'

'Aye, right, sorry, wasn't expecting your sister-in-law to show, in her own self.'

'She's not my fucking sister-in-law.'

'Sorry, ex-sister—'

'Shut up!'

The Keeper arched a silvering eyebrow. 'I take it you were expecting someone else?'

Ree shook off her surprise with rigid intent. 'Not at all. Turning up in person seems the least you could do, in the circumstances.'

'I'm here solely as a courtesy to the orange one, who has occasionally been useful in the past.' Exalted Matil spoke softly, without emotion. Ree imagined the Keeper of Arowan rarely needed to raise her voice. It was something of a feature of absolute rulers, in her experience.

'Aye, well, cheers.'

'It's true, then.'

Ree tried to match the Keeper's tone and volume. 'And what's that?'

Matil lifted her head, cheeks drawn in a vague smile. 'The engine of rebellion that stalks the plains is . . . you.'

'Disappointed?'

Matil didn't reply. Instead she walked slowly towards a narrow table by the window and lowered herself to the only chair. She sat for a moment, head on one side, regarding Ree dispassionately, inspecting, assessing. Ree felt heat in her cheeks, tension in her jaw, and pain in her leg. The corner of Matil's mouth twitched, ever so slightly, as she looked Ree up and down.

'You know why I'm here,' Ree growled, trying to steer matters back under her control.

'You said you'd never come back. Twice. You remember that, Rai?'

'It's Ree. And I'm not back. We're a long way from the marble spires here, and this is as close as I'll ever get. Will you *stop* looking at me like that?'

'Forgive me . . . Ree. It seems the years have been less than kind to us both.'

Ree eased her shoulders back, attempting to shift some of the weight from her stick. Why was there only one chair in the room? She should be berating the Commodore for this, but there were more important things at stake.

'I said, you know why I'm here, yes?'

'Truly, none of us is spared.'

'Do you have something you want to say, or can we get on with it? I came a long way for this.'

Matil leaned back in the chair, high backed and well-upholstered as it was, and put her hand to her chin. Still the look of assessment remained in her eyes, along with something that was not contempt, but far worse: pity.

'If my brother could see you now—'

'Well, he can't. Death tends to get in the way of that kind of thing.'

'. . . How different things might have been.'

'*No one* wishes that more than me.'

Matil scoffed, and when she spoke again it was with every ounce of regal force. 'You bewitched him.'

'I was a *child*.'

The Keeper of Arowan shook her head, the heat gone from her voice. 'To think they wrote songs to your beauty.'

Ree's fists were balled, the head of the stick creaking in her grip. 'Fuck this. What was I thinking, expecting logic or sense from your family.'

'Whoa there, hey hey hey, let's not be overly hasty in the departure department, eh?' The Commodore was still inside the door, shuffling forwards with her palms raised. 'This audience possessed merit enough in the abstract to draw the pair of yous here, so perhaps let's be digging back towards realising some of the aforesaid before further river crossings go up in flames, yes?'

Ree took a long breath through her nose. 'Still talking utter bollocks, then?'

The Commodore winked. 'Tactical bollocks, aye.' She gestured back towards the table and the window. 'Shall we?'

'One more chance.'

The Commodore leaned in close as they turned. 'Old girl's under more strain than she lets on. Let her vent, eh?'

'One more chance.'

Matil was standing when they turned back, her long outer robe shed and draped over the chair. Beneath it, she wore simple silks, their quality obvious, but had not been able to resist a jewelled swan at her chest. Her left sleeve was pinned where she'd lost her forearm during the siege sixteen years before. Ree ignored it.

'I seem to remember you were the one agitating for this audience,' the Keeper said, leaning against the chairback with her elbow. 'Was there any purpose to it beyond reminiscence?'

Ree shot the Commodore a warning look. 'You're going to make me spell this out?'

'Assume I'm ignorant of your intentions.'

'Very. Well.' Ree balanced her stick against her leg, interlaced her fingers, and cracked her knuckles. 'We have the same enemy. The Chartered Miners' Guild of Serica.'

'I wasn't aware I had enemies.'

'Aside from everyone who's met you? You know very well they're working against you. The Guild have supplanted Arowan across half the expanse, and they're working on the other half. It's only down to *our* efforts that they haven't succeeded. And it's time you and the city started pulling your weight.'

Matil leaned back against the wall, index finger to her chin, the heavy curtain rippling against her. 'Are you asking for troops? You know very well we cannot have open warfare between the Guild and the state.'

'I'm well aware,' Ree snapped. 'You know what I'm going to ask, because you should be planning for it already. I'm just here to remind you of what commitment looks like.'

Matil placed her hand on the chairback, inclining her head. 'You're talking, I presume, about renewal?'

'Of course I fucking am. The Guild cannot be destroyed until the protectorate's population sees them that way. The settlements of the outer ring – those you abandoned, remember? – chafe against them, they are desperate to turn but they fear isolation and the diggers' wrath. None will move until another does, so they stay paralysed and suffering. My raiders have *hammered* the Guild across the expanse, we have hamstrung and drained them, but they can rely on slurping from the protectorate's teats to keep themselves fat. They have a monopoly on mining, on refinement, on trade, on taxation across the expanse, sole access to the product of Arowan's workshops, and you have allowed it to happen. It's time to correct that mistake. The term of their charter ends in a few weeks. You must block its renewal.'

Ree leaned forward on her stick, gaze intent on the other woman. 'The instant it expires, they no longer control trade from the ports, the food, the ore, none of it. They can no longer claim domain over new lands on behalf of the Serican throne. No more monopolies, no longer able to crush competition. It's open season on the Guild, and the whole of the expanse will see it.'

Matil was no longer passive. Instead she looked pained, the hand on the chairback tight, the knuckles pale.

'I don't know if I have the votes.'

'What are you talking about? You're the Keeper of Arowan. Issue a decree.'

Matil grimaced, a flash of lower teeth on a tight in-breath. 'You've been in the plains too long, little general.'

'Don't patronise me, old woman.'

'And don't presume to lecture me. I was playing the courtly game while you were still batting your eyelashes at my brother.'

'I did no such fucking thing.'

'Still wearing his sword, I see.'

'This sword is—'

'Aye, you know, ladies, I think we might perhaps be straying somewhat, once more, from our zone of productive discussion, and perhaps could find merit in inspecting said unploughed furrow, should it yield a bounty?'

'What did the orange one say?'

'That we should return to the point. What do you mean, you don't have the votes?'

Matil took another breath, long this time, through her nose. 'The siege wrecked Arowan. It destroyed half the city, the workshops, the bridges, it killed a quarter of the nobility and most of our soldiers, it scattered the populace, it annihilated our water and our silk. It claimed the life of my mother, and took my arm. The collapse that followed was predictable, and in truth it could have been far, far worse – and would have been, had the siege ended differently. Perhaps you would know this, if you hadn't fled.'

'I seem to remember being asked to leave.'

'Ahem, once again, ladies, if perhaps . . . ?'

Matil rubbed her fingers against the bridge of her nose, her passion spent. 'Either way, it's no secret that in the aftermath, the "protectorate" ceased to be, along with most of the Serican state. The Guild took root because it was that or greater suffering. You say I let it happen. I had no choice. The throne of Arowan became a passenger to events, but we endured. The city rebuilt, and revived, and now it flourishes, but it does so in a new image. Did you think we could suffer such tumult and not be changed?'

'What are you saying, Matil?'

'I am thirsty. Some tea would be welcome.'

'Aye, right, likewise. Oh, you mean . . . ? Suppose I'll be off then.'

The Commodore shuffled from the door, muttering about fruit and the height it hangs at.

'She's gone. What didn't you want her to hear?'

Matil spoke slowly, as if recounting rehearsed words. 'I will be the last Keeper. That I have no heirs is well known, and should surprise no one. My mother played a terrible game with the future of our city, dangling her succession like twine before kittens. I will not let another crisis overtake the protectorate when I have the means to stop it. The wheels are already in motion. Serica is to become a full republic.'

Ree's jaw fell open. 'You cannot be serious.'

'Amistreb is a republic, and it thrives.'

'They thrive because they are sea pirates! They plunder anything that's even vaguely damp.'

'Serica becomes a republic or our state fails. The throne is weak! I cannot impose its rule without the consent of the populace, and the only way to secure that consent is to give them a stake in its function.'

'You're abdicating?'

'Once things are in place, I will step back, and the senate will elect a new leader, but not yet.' Now Matil was becoming more animated, standing straight, and she began to pace before the window. 'Every settlement in the protectorate – including my failures, as you so helpfully outlined – will have representation in time, but for now the wider senate is populated by notables from both the city and the surrounding townships – those who deign to deal with us. Support for the Guild is . . .' She took a heavy breath. '. . . strong.'

'They're paying people off, presumably.'

'Not in the way you think. The senators in question, more than not, believe the Guild to be the best option for the people they represent.' Matil shook her head. 'There are rumours they'll put forward their own candidate for leadership when I go.'

'So you can't stop the renewal? Their kept senators won't vote against their own interests, and the townships won't turn against them until they know everyone else will? This is absurd. There must be something you can do. You're the fucking Keeper!'

Matil met her glare. 'I am not completely without power. And once representation expands, once the outer townships have their own stake in the management of the state, they may pull away from the Guild and—'

'Nine fucking hells, they *may*?'

'Do you think I don't care?' Matil roared. 'The Guild are stifling trade, choking food shipments in the north, because you have forced their hand! Your rebellion has made them desperate and dangerous.'

'They were already dangerous, you daft cow.'

'Now they are dangerous to the continent! You want me to cut their access to the workshops of Arowan, but it will be futile: they have begun their own negotiations with the Iokara. They're planning to open new trade routes across the Borabod, and they're trading straight from the sea corridor. Serasthana hungers for ore . . . and much besides.'

'What? How?'

'You've heard of the Iron Road?'

'I have.'

'They will use it to transport ore across the plains, direct from the mines to the port. It will be loaded straight onto Iokaran black ships and carried away, and Arowan will see nothing from it. They would never have embarked on so outrageous a course of action were it not for—'

'Cast-iron bollocks. At worst we've flushed them into the open, but pressure doesn't change people, it reveals who they were all along. You should know.'

'If you cannot win in the field—'

'That's what you want? A crushing military victory?'

Matil glared back. 'You said it yourself: the expanse must see them beaten. The co-opted senators must know the landscape is changed, the townships must see it is safe to reject them. You must rout their forces.'

'That is . . . impossible. We can't face them in open battle.'

'How can you ever hope to win?'

'Are you seriously telling me that you cannot block the renewal of their charter somehow? What is your legal capacity now, in this modern age of political representation?'

Matil scowled, her breathing slow and audible. 'All laws are still recorded and sealed in the Keeper's name, and executed by extension of her authority. But everything is done with the consent of—'

'There you have it! Refuse to stamp the new charter. Hide the seal, say you lost it. Delay long enough for expiry, then it's out of your hands.'

Matil swallowed. Spots of colour had appeared on her cheeks. Ree's mouth went dry.

'Matil, where is the Great Seal of Arowan?'

The Keeper could not meet her eye. 'They have it.'

'You fucking what?'

'It was taken as . . . collateral . . . in the early days. When I did not have the power to stop it.'

'Are you telling me the Guild have been stamping Arowan's laws this whole time? Blessed fuck, no wonder they've accumulated monstrous power!' Ree stormed towards the taller woman, her finger wagging. 'Where is it? Where do they keep it?'

'I don't know.'

'You have spies, Matil, even weak-throned as you are. Don't tell me you haven't been looking.'

'They move it around. It travels with their functionaries. We've never been able to pin it down.'

'But they'll have to bring it out for their renewal. Out in the open.' A sudden feeling of certainty settled over Ree, a sense of absolute purpose. 'Then that's the play. We find the Great Seal of Arowan, and we take it, very, very publicly. That can be our message – without the seal, the Guild are on borrowed time.' She fixed Matil with a wide-eyed stare. 'Well? That would work, right?'

The Keeper seemed to reel before the force of the stare. 'I . . . I . . . Maybe. Maybe so.' She swallowed, composed herself. 'That or destroying the Iron Road, of course.' She offered a weak smile to match her joke.

'Perhaps this wasn't a complete waste of time after all.' Ree almost matched the feeble smile.

'Perhaps not.' Matil's smile faded, replaced by something colder, more calculating. An expression Ree recognised a thousand times over. 'You know, I wondered, when I heard the reports. I couldn't imagine it, I couldn't conceive of . . . of why. What in all the hells you'd be doing it for.'

'Bringing down the Guild?'

'You want back in, don't you? A seat at the table, your old crest? I can't make promises, but you see this done, and—'

The door creaked, and both swivelled, Ree's hand on her sword, stick clattering to the floor. She whipped the blade free, moving softly and painfully towards the doorway as the Keeper swept back behind the chair, then yanked the polished door aside.

The kid stumbled into the room, landing heavily on a thick and glorious rug. She looked up, eyes darting from Ree to Matil and back. 'I, uh . . . I can explain!'

TWELVE

'You little shit!' Ree snapped. 'I told you to wait downstairs. Were you listening at the door?'

'Is this yours, R—ee?' Matil's brows were pinched, her head tilted, fascinated by the embarrassment picking itself up from the floor.

'How did you even find us?' Ree growled. 'This is a secret rendez-vous.'

The Commodore came around the corner behind the kid, tray in hand. 'Here we go, brew's up . . . Ohhh bollocks.'

The kid brushed herself down. 'Your trail wasn't exactly hard to follow. And you left all the doors open and unguarded.' Ree flashed a glare at the Commodore, who was looking off into a corner, lips pursed in a pretend whistle, the steaming tray still in her hands. 'Anyway, listen, there's trouble downstairs. Bunch of Guild types, squaring off with some city guards, could get fighty.'

'So? Let Anashe and Whitespear handle it, it must happen all the time. This is why you interrupt us? Get out of here. Now.' Ree could feel the heat in her face, the indignity of her daughter's appearance before the Keeper infuriating her beyond measure, beyond sense. 'Now!'

'Don't rush on our account,' Matil said airily. Her heavy robe was already back around her shoulders, and she dragged the hood over her head with impressive ease. 'I believe our business is concluded for now. I will watch for the effects of your work, but we will not speak again until this is over. One way, or another. Orange one, I am leaving.'

'No tea, then? Aye, right you are, let me just stash this and get the door, there. I'll, ah, I'll walk you out, eh?' The Commodore shot a guilty look over her shoulder. 'Just to check the way is clear, like. I think your lads are downstairs somewhere.'

The door thumped closed behind them, leaving Ree and Javani alone in the lavish room, the discarded tea tray left on the floor. Ree's breathing was coming hard and hot, still gripped by a fury she could not explain, could not justify. The meeting had gone well. She knew exactly what was required. Seize the Great Seal and the Guild would fall. It was simple, it was clear. So why was she so angry?

'Was that really the Exalted Swan? What's the Iron Road?'

'Shut your fucking mouth.'

'Excuse me?'

Ree sheathed her sword, her palm slick with sweat, trying to ignore the tremble of her hand, the struggle to place the blade smoothly. She knew she was tired. She'd come so far. And the way was clear. She just needed to—

'I said, excuse me?'

'And I told you to shut your fucking mouth. Why couldn't you stay where you were put?'

The kid took a step back, head cocked and eyes wide, her hands loose at her sides. 'I was coming up here to warn you! I thought you might be in danger, you and your little secret meeting friends.'

'Don't lie to me. You were looking for an excuse to come up and involve yourself.'

Now the kid's jaw jutted, her nostrils flared. 'And what if I was? Would it have been such a crime to involve me in something? You let that person with the hair join in. Was that the Commodore? What kind of outrageous accent was that?'

'Just how long were you listening in, you damned-by-gods little spy?'

'What choice did I have? How else am I going to find out what's going on? You never tell me anything, you never involve me.' She took a sharp breath through her nose. 'You never involve anyone. Manatas trails you like a duckling, surviving on . . . *crumbs* of your attention, but at least he's chosen. Where's my choice, Ree? You won't let me near you, won't let me leave, what can I do?'

Ree tried to push out her anger, to breathe it away. It almost worked. 'Javani, listen, it's been a long day, we're tired—'

'For the sake of the gods! I'm not a kid any more, stop talking to me like I need to be put to fucking bed. You keep saying we'll be partners one day, keep telling me to wait, so when's it going to be time? When will I count? When I turn sixteen? Eighteen? Twenty? Thirty-five, the age of wisdom? When I'm your age now, old and fucked as that is? Or are you going to keep finding reasons why you need to make all the decisions for both of us? *Why do you always have to be the one to decide everything?*'

The kid's chest was heaving, sweat proud on her brow, but her gaze didn't waver. Her eyes bored into Ree, and despite herself, despite all she knew, all she told herself, Ree could not back down.

'Listen—'

'Stop telling me to listen!'

'Then open your fucking ears!' Ree reached down and snatched up her fallen stick, teeth gritted against the sharp flare of pain up her leg, gripping the wood with livid fingers. 'This is a war, and you should not be part of it. It's not fair to you.'

'And it's fair to you?'

'I can't give you orders! How can you fit into a command structure when you're my daughter? Without clear command, without cohesion, we cannot function, we cannot fight. We cannot win, and all this will have been for nothing.'

'Yeah, heavens forbid there should be more than one opinion that matters. We'll never be partners, will we?'

'Not in this! How could you . . .' Ree gestured with her empty hand, futile, grasping, '. . . in war?'

The anger had left the kid's voice, her face slack, her eyes hard. 'I see.'

'Javani, I am trying to protect you. You never think of what could go wrong! When I was your age, my parents—'

'Oh no, did they sell you? Was it for political advancement? Did it make you sad? Nine fucking hells, Ree, it's been thirty years. Is this all you've got?'

Ree swallowed hard, heat in her throat. 'Maybe it's hard to get over that kind of betrayal.'

'Tell me about it.' The kid's mouth was curled, the outline of a sneer. One hand went to something bundled in her shirt. 'You know, I had something to . . . but what's the point? You've made yourself clear: you don't want me around. I'll make my own way from here.'

'Javani, no—'

The door slammed before she could even take a step.

Ree stood, alone, in the lamplit room, feeling every thump of her pulse in her ears, the rasp of her breathing, feeling the polished wood of her walking stick in her sweat-slick grip. The kid wouldn't go far, she told herself. It was late, somewhere in the small hours by now – the shutters had been closed against the chill of the night before she'd even arrived in the room. Sweat clung to her, her hair hanging lank across her brow, thick at her neck, and she thought again of Matil's words.

To think they wrote songs to your beauty . . .

It stung. It stung her in a way she had not expected. In the corner of the room was a set of drawers, glossy with lacquer, and on top stood a pewter pitcher and basin. She should at least wash some of the dust and travel grime away before she descended and tried to make peace with the kid once more. The girl was exhausting, and had been from her first days. Ree half-smiled to herself, a rueful shake of the head. Fifteen years of being tired, no wonder she didn't look her best. She slept so badly these days, months of shattered rest, and she broke out in sweat even in the cold of night. Her body was already betraying her.

A mirror of polished bronze hung above the basin, and she did not look into it. For a time, at least. But she couldn't fight it forever. Years ago, mirrors had been her friends. Any highly polished surface would have warranted a peek, a quick check-in, an adjustment of hair or wardrobe. Ree had worn her looks as armour, wielded them as a weapon. She'd been punished for them enough before she'd had the strength to fight back – it was only fair she should turn them to her advantage in her freelance career. She had claimed herself for herself, and it had been no small thing. Then the kid had come, and she had put everything to one side, fled into the plains with a babe on her hip, her old life forgotten.

For a time, at least.

Had the girl's petulant refrain been right? Had her diversion into parenthood been just that? Had she truly been biding her time, spinning her wheels, lying in wait for the chance to resume her former existence at the first opportunity? When hunters had come to Kazeraz, she'd acted by instinct, but in Ar Ramas, she'd laid her first plans. The kid had accused her then of lying to her, lying to herself, about her motivations, and Ree had brushed it off. But then their rejoinder to the Guild's encroachment into the mountains had snowballed into the rebellion she led today, and at no point had she felt like stopping it, like stepping aside. Who else could lead it, after all? Who else could have achieved all she had? Manatas? Camellia? She laughed at the thought, and her gaze settled on the mirror.

For a moment, she was frozen, baffled by the face of the woman before her, hunched and lopsided from the stick. The gaunt, sallow cheeks, the deep ruts around her mouth, as if carved into the blotched teak of her skin. The scar at her temple somehow enlarged, livid and shining, as fierce and fresh in the lamplight as it had been in those first weeks. Her hair, stringy and thin, no longer the compelling brilliant white of her youth but the tired colourlessness of age. And her eyes, shorn of lustre, their shape shifted somehow, one bigger than she remembered, if only by a lash, and encompassed by a spider's web of cracks and furrows, sand-blasted and sun-baked, four and a half decades of wear.

Had it been so long?

Was she so old?

How much did she have left?

The thought rooted her, a lance of jolting emotion, a spear of panic. She had burned more than half her life, far, far more. She had scoffed at Matil's geriatric appearance but the Keeper was less than a decade older and lived in far greater comfort, despite her protestations of republican certainty. Ree lived close to the knuckle, hard on the plains, and though she'd always known there would be limits she was not ready to face them now.

How much longer could she do this? And what would she leave when she could not?

Over her shoulder, reflected in the gleaming bronze, the heavy curtain shifted in a breeze from the window.

Ree's digressions scattered. Keeping her hand close to her body and her movements slow, Ree reached for her sword.

Javani seethed. She paced in the grand hallway outside the heavy door, kicking out with every step, scuffing the gleaming boards beneath her boots. Her cheeks burned and eyes stung, and her chest was hot and tight, her ribs too small. Every sob was fought back and crushed, she would not cry, she would not wail. She was too furious for that. Ree had confirmed all her worst suspicions, and she'd done so to her face. She'd outright declared her daughter useless, a distraction, a dead weight, a drag on her great campaign. How much better for them both if she no longer had to worry.

So be it. In the back of her mind, for some time now, Javani had been planning, compiling a mental inventory, a worst-case agenda. She had all the gear she needed downstairs in the stables, and although she wasn't exactly flush with coin on a personal level, she had no concerns about her ability to earn. The *Illustrious Den* might have sunk flaming beneath the waves, but there was no shortage of other venues to ply her trade should she wish to take up the life of a professional sharp. She had a couple of good knives on her, and her bow and quiver were downstairs, so hunting wouldn't be a problem until she had enough means to saddle others with the labour of feeding her. And then of course, there was the blue stone . . . Perhaps Anashe might be open to taking her on as a third partner in her venture? They were right on the edge of Greater Arowan here, the closest Javani had been in her short life to the hub of Serican civilisation, and who was to say there weren't opportunities teeming—

A crash from the other side of the heavy door, something heavy hitting the ground with force. Javani came to a halt, incredulous. This was rich. *Ree* was throwing things? After everything she'd said? If anyone had a right to be angry, it was—

Another crash, and a thump that wobbled the lamp-sconces in the hallway. Something had hit the wall then. Javani's ire stalled, replaced by a narrow, sharp-edged curiosity. Either her mother had hurled a table across the room, or . . .

A cry, that was definitely a cry, strained and muffled. Now Javani's rage was gone, the hot feeling moved to her throat, a sudden rush of constricting fear.

'Ree?'

She leapt for the door, threw it open with her shoulder as she burst into the room, and came to a puzzled halt. The lights were out in the room, the lamps extinguished – one of them splintered beneath her boots – and in the sliced amber light from the doorway behind her, the room was painted with indigo stripes. At last, movement drew her eye to the far corner, where Ree appeared to be wrestling with the curtains.

'Ree?'

Ree and curtains staggered back, huffing and thrashing, bouncing from the back wall and knocking over the narrow table beside the tall chair, finally caught in the light from the doorway. Now Javani saw the extra pair of legs beneath the curtains, and Ree's arms wrapped tight around the bundle, pinning the owner of the legs within the thick folds. She turned her head to the doorway, eyes narrowed, teeth gritted.

'Get . . . help!'

'I can—'

The bundle jerked and twisted, and Ree's bad leg gave, sending her reeling. She hit the tall chair and spun, only keeping her balance with a desperate grab of the chairback. Javani had a knife in her hand, poised to throw, but in the half-light had no idea what she was aiming for.

'Javani!'

The owner of the legs tore off the curtains and flung them to the floor. Suddenly there was a figure before Ree, squat and wide-shouldered, its hair wild and clumped. Its hand blurred, then something gleamed in it. Ree was the other side of the chair, one leg bowed, hands gripping the chairback. Her scabbard was empty at her hip, and her eyes were locked on her assailant.

Ree's voice was quiet and slow. 'Javani, get help.'

'Hey!' Javani shouted. The figure did not respond. It was closing on Ree, moving crab-wise around the chair along the window side.

'Hey!' Javani repeated, and as the figure moved past the now un-shuttered window, she threw.

It was a glorious throw. She knew as soon as the knife left her hand that her aim was true, and she wished Manatas could have seen it. The number of times he'd chided her – gently – for sloppy throwing during their informal training sessions, when this time, when it really mattered, she'd—

The knife whistled through the air and thumped, hilt-first, into the attacker's shoulder, then dropped to the rug with a clunk.

'Ow,' growled a low voice.

'Shit,' said Javani.

'Javani, get fucking help before you get us both killed!'

'I can help! For the sake of the gods . . .' Her second knife was in her hand. 'You like that?' she called. 'Next time it'll be the sharp end. Now back off!'

The figure didn't move, still silhouetted by the murky indigo of the window, only the lower legs lit by the stretched glow from the doorway. For a moment, it was completely static, and for one glorious instant Javani thought that perhaps her threat had worked.

Then it moved, darting forward with inhuman speed, one arm whipping towards Ree. The glint in its hand hissed at Ree's warding forearm as she reeled back behind the chair, making only the barest contact, then the figure pivoted, wheeled away, and leapt from the window into the night.

'Huh?' Javani said. Perhaps she was intimidating after all. Knife still in her hand, she crossed the room, debris crunching beneath her boots, to where Ree panted against the chairback. 'Are you hurt? Did . . . it . . . get you?'

Breath coming hard, her mother inspected a slim red mark on her arm. 'A scratch. I'm . . . fine. It was a she, and she was . . . quite possibly . . . Mawn.'

Javani's skin went cold, the hairs rising on her neck. Mawn had killed her parents, so the story went, and although in the end that had been one of Ree's tales, Mawn had certainly killed enough of other people's parents to make it believable.

'But . . . But why? I thought the Mawn were gone, scattered to the farthest reaches of the plains?'

Ree was dabbing at her arm with her other sleeve, her sweat blue in the moonlight as she recovered her breath. 'Who's to say? The tribes may be scattered . . . but the individuals are— Javani, what are you doing? Javani? Javani!'

'I'm going to get some answers.'

'Don't you . . . fucking dare. I forbid it. Get back here . . . right now.'

'Did you forget?' Javani said. 'You can't give me orders.'

'Javani, listen to me . . . I swear to all the gods that if—'

'Don't you get it?' Javani spat. 'You can't hold me back any more.'

She leapt from the window and into the night.

The Commodore came bowling through the door with an axe in one hand and a mug in the other. 'What in ruckety-fuck are yous doing up here?' She took in the upturned furniture, shattered lamps, torn-down curtains and the wide-open window, its shutters creaking. 'I've got to pay for this room!'

'I was . . .' Ree was still by the window, although the kid had long since been swallowed by darkness. 'Attacked.'

'You what?'

Ree tried again. Words were hard to form. Her fatigue was claiming her, settling like a fog over her brain. 'Assassin. Mawn. Came through the window.'

'When?' The Commodore's head tilted, sending her hair mountain bouncing. 'How much did they hear?'

'Can't . . . say.'

'Are you doing all right? You're starting to look a mite peaky there, Genny.'

'Fine.' Ree shook her head. The world wobbled. 'Just a scratch.' She gestured towards the window with her uninjured hand. 'The kid went after. The Mawn.'

'You what? Your infant? The wee scrote that came bumbling in here?'

'I can't . . . give her orders.'

The Commodore tried to rub her hands over her face, realising in time that one held booze and the other a sharp edge. She downed the mug and flung it aside, then hefted the axe over her shoulder. 'Fucken hells!'

She barrelled from the room, leaving the door swinging.

'Thanks,' Ree murmured, resting heavily on the chairback and closing her eyes. The cut on her arm was starting to burn.

THIRTEEN

Javani ran. The initial trail had been easy to follow across the stable roof, and the moon was strong – more so in the deep of the night, the candles and lamps of the buildings beneath her feet dwindled and spent. From the strength of her sign, the Mawn assassin had not expected to be followed. Javani was grinning as she leapt from the sandstone ridge of the narrow temple beside the stables and onto the sloping roof of the bakery beyond, its stones already warm from the banked ovens within. Twin streaks through the dust marked the Mawn's progress, and Javani slid down alongside, eyes searching in the darkness for the next sign of her quarry.

Movement on the roof across the alley, a loping blur in the murk. The Mawn was heading north, away from the city and the meat of the conjoined townships that made up this area of sprawl. They'd ridden in from the north, and that way lay farmsteads and estates, then the open plains. Javani realised it was likely the assassin had a horse waiting. She needed to stay close.

She would not lose the Mawn. She was owed some answers.

Teeth gritted, Javani ran.

Maral was making good time at an easy pace, but she could not shake the gloom that plagued her. *Make a challenge for yourself*, Kuzari had said. *Find the joy in your work. Make it fun.* She had followed his words, their sentiment and instruction clear, but she'd felt no delight, no sudden rush of jubilation at what had unfolded in the grand room. It had been unpleasant and shameful, and now here she was, scurrying over rooftops in the moonlight, knowing that Beralas awaited her report with ravenous anticipation.

She so wanted to tell him everything he expected to hear. She yearned for his approval, to see the controlled disdain in his eyes melt away, replaced by that same gaze of affection he bestowed upon his daughters, his wives. Upon Kuzari. Maral had once heard scullery gossip that Kuzari was Beralas's own bastard son, that his mother had been one of the girls in the early, pre-Guild shipments who had not survived the birth. Maral was sceptical. There were plenty of other reasons why Kuzari might be blessed with Beralas's exotic wardrobe, while Maral herself wore whatever she could scavenge along the way, as befitted her station and heritage.

No, she knew why Beralas regarded her with checked contempt while Kuzari dressed in robes that would be fine were they not spattered with greasy droplets of everything he ever ate, and it had nothing to do with familial relations. Maral knew what she was: a means to an end; a necessary evil. But she remained grateful: as base as she was, Beralas had showed compassion in taking her in at her orphaning, and in raising her, if not exactly as one of his own daughters, then at least along parallel lines and only two floors below. In return, she performed the duties that only she could, the duties that Beralas required, for him, his family and the wider Guild. She did what came naturally.

And now she had to return to him, her benefactor, her saviour, and report her cowardice. It was enough to make her cry, were she capable of tears, which she knew she was not. She had not even cried at her orphaning, her family butchered by marauders. Beralas had told her so, with something akin to wonder in his voice, not pride but within sight of it. She had not cried; she had walked, alone and bloodied, soot-streaked and stinking, the lone survivor of the slaughter of her clan, out into the plains. A Mawn who had fled battle, who had hidden and skulked. A low, cowardly thing, barely deserving of his pity, let alone his largesse.

Her own memories were dull, fuzzy things, and he had been kind enough to enlighten her on her origin, but generous as he was, even he could not keep every drip of distaste from his voice in the telling.

A savage, ill-bred Mawn, good for little more than a brief and bloody existence in the kill-or-be-killed lands of the northern plains.

'Why didn't you hunt them down?' Kuzari had asked, in his airy way, as if all things are possible if only the idea is had. She supposed, in many ways, for him they were. 'The killers of your birth family? Didn't you want revenge? I'd have wanted revenge. If I found someone had murdered my kin, I'd feed them their eyeballs.'

She'd had no answer she could give. Fear and shame were her only companions. She didn't remember it, or anything before. Just the feelings.

'How old were you?' he'd said.

'Four or five,' she'd replied, bracing herself for his condemnation. She'd already been accomplished in the saddle, Beralas said, and with bow and blade – according to the few works in his library that deigned to touch the subject, Mawn learned to hunt as soon as they could walk, as soon as they could stand. They learned to kill, or they starved. Yet she had fled from vengeance. She had turned her back on what had to be done, and run from the plains, directionless, hopeless, honourless.

She had not cried, not even when the Guild caravan – a relative rarity that far north in those days – had spotted her, with Beralas at its head. He'd been younger then, his beard still thick and dark, his hair glossy with curls and only yet one wife to his name. But he'd taken pity on the wretch that had stumbled out of the tall-grass before them, this squat and filthy creature that his riders had been keen to ride down and scrub from the earth, as the heavens had intended. Beralas had stopped them and saved her life, and despite his natural distaste had taken Maral into his care. Cleaned, clothed, and cared for, offered education and opportunity. In return she knew what was expected, and the performance of that duty was as close to contentment as she experienced.

She swallowed, maintaining her loping pace, hurdling from one rooftop to the next. He would not be angry, she knew that. He was so good at controlling his emotions, his expressions – after all, he'd spent the better part of fifteen years disguising his abhorrence of the creature in his midst, and almost managing it. It was only the eyes that gave him away, and this time they would show justifiable disappointment. And behind it, lurking in perpetuity, the repulsion.

Maral cast a quick look over her shoulder. The girl from the rooming house was still following her, although what she hoped to achieve was anyone's guess. It had been hard to assess her in the confused light of the chamber – especially with her attention elsewhere – but she pegged the girl at a good few years her junior, still not fully grown in any capacity, despite the two of them being of similar heights. In their brief encounter, the girl had failed to do more than bruise Maral's shoulder, despite having had two knives and all the advantages she might have wished for in the situation, and now gave chase with a degree of crashing unsubtlety that would have made a shock trooper blush. It was only Maral's sense of self-recrimination that had allowed her to keep on the trail; she knew she needed to be punished for her failings.

Still, in short order she'd be out into the plains, and leaving this little flea in her wake. It seemed spiteful to turn and resolve the girl now, especially after all that had transpired in the rooming house and, despite her daily engagements, Maral was not a spiteful person. She would shake the girl and melt into the plains, and fulminate on her flaws on the long ride back. There would be plenty of time then.

The girl was still there, and Maral was beginning to reconsider her choices. She'd slid down the outer canopies of the souk at the township's edge and doubled back, this time with care to hide her trail, but the girl had stuck to her like a tick. Now they were close to the edge of what passed for town, the last cluster of buildings before land stretched away towards the horizon, dusted silver-blue in the moonlight. Time was getting on, dawn no longer a distant prospect, and she was being forced to give serious thought to cutting the girl and leaving her in an alley.

No. The girl was persistent, and she was lucky, but nothing more. Maral would lose her on the flat. She'd left her horse in the care of a farming family the far side of the next ridge – she had no trust in livery stables and hobbling the creature out in the wilds was no kind of plan at all – and two ducks and a shuffle between here and there would shake her tick. Then she could return to considering what she would report back to the Chairman.

Javani moved slowly and quietly through the tall-grass, keeping low. Her quarry was ahead of her, her pace slowed, climbing now towards a low cluster of buildings that stood at the centre of what had to be a farm. Her legs and chest burned from the speed of her pursuit, arms aching in tandem, and although the night was biting cold she was drenched in sweat, which was now beginning to cool in sharp and unpleasant ways. That was the longest she'd run for as long as she could remember, longer than anything Manatas or Edigu had set her, and she was very, very thirsty.

She'd pursued the oblivious Mawn for hours, across the roofs of the township, down through the alleys and out into the plains. The moon was lost behind streaks of silver-edged dark cloud, but already an auburn glimmer nibbled at the eastern horizon, the sky above it washed pale. Now her target had slowed to a walk, satisfied that she was alone on the plains, Javani was content to allow the distance between them to stretch in the interests of maintaining her cover. No sign of a horse yet, or any other mode of transport, but if that was a farm at the top of the ridge then one might not be far away. Javani wasn't going to blow it now. She was going to get answers. She was going to prove Ree wrong.

FOURTEEN

Maral approached the farm buildings slowly, but only because she was furious. How in the light of the heavens had she not lost the little weed currently skulking through the wildgrass behind her? At this rate, she was really going to have to kill the girl, and that had been no part of her instructions. Not that she was averse to showing initiative and making operational decisions as situations dictated, but she'd come this far without gutting her pursuer and it seemed like an admission of failure to do it now. Another one.

That said, if she made her way to the timbered barn before the girl had the wit to close, she could be up and away on her horse before there was any danger of intervention. There were no other horses on the farm – she'd been careful about that – and only one mule, and she trusted the owners to abide by their side in the interests of collecting the second half of their payment. This approach worked more than it didn't – that of trusting people to adhere to a deal – and Maral was more than confident enough to handle any attempted double-cross should it arrive. After all, one look at her features below the cowl of her cloak was generally enough to set them backing away. Sometimes, she supposed, it wasn't all bad that you horrified those who crossed your path.

Something was wrong.

Not with the girl squatting in the grass behind her, but with the farm ahead. This close to dawn, lights should already be lit, lamps in a window, the sounds of activity and preparation. The sounds of roosting chickens, shuffling cattle . . . the dogs, where were the dogs?

A door stood open on the low half-timber building ahead, a black rectangle against the fading blue of pre-dawn. Nothing, and no one, was stirring.

Maral slid to one side of the trail, thoughts of pursuit forgotten, and slipped the hog-slicer into her palm. She crept up towards the building, eyes darting in the crepuscular gloom. What about the barn? Was her horse still there? Had the farmers absconded with her property after all . . . and all of theirs too? It seemed . . . unlikely. She needed to get closer.

Dawn was imminent now, a red wash in the eastern sky, the wisping clouds above it painted in gold and pinks against the paling blue. Beralas had once gifted a dress to his previous wife, a marvel of lace and silk, somehow dyed in drifting shades like a sunrise. Maral had watched its presentation with hungry eyes, alert to every rattle of its beads, every tinkle of the dancing pearls of silver woven at the cuffs. The wife had stormed out shortly afterwards, as they tended to, and Maral had never seen the dress again, but she dreamed of it, sometimes.

This was not the time for such things. She stepped carefully around the low house, the building dark and cold at her back, keeping to the gloom of what would soon be the shaded side. She sniffed. The air was thick with animal smells, both before and after, but there was more here, buried by dung. She rolled her shoulders, slid another few steps to the corner. From here the barn was in view, its puckered timbers misted in the crisp air. Hollow. Dark. Motionless.

She moved to the barn's side with quick, silent steps, every sense alert, the hog-slicer angled and ready in her hand. Tracks in the central yard, the earth rucked and churned, the light still too weak to allow for any kind of assessment at distance. The smells, too, were stronger here, and a theory began to form in Maral's mind. Her pulse quickened. She needed to know for certain, needed to see for herself.

Lungs locked, she listened at the barn-side, ears straining for any kind of breath or movement. Nothing. She ducked around the corner in a sinuous twist then held still once more, lost in the shadow of the hayloft above. She was good at finding shadows; Maral was not meant to be seen. No sign nor scent of her horse. She had no particular attachment to the animal – just another of the stable that Beralas kept in the region – but the thought of proceeding from here on foot was not a welcome one. There were supplies in the saddle-bags, and – her blood ran cold – the little rectangle of silk she'd collected from the alley where Guildmaster Raad had met his fate. Her mouth was dry. It could not all be gone, not now. It was a sign from the heavens: she had not deserved it.

She moved softly through the darkened barn, past the low benches laid out with tools, past the coils of ropes hung from pegs on stout posts. She swallowed, her tongue against dry lips. She heard nothing of her horse, saw nothing, smelled nothing, not of the horse or indeed anything else. Certainty grew within her as she rounded the loose boards that formed the partition where she'd last seen her mount. Not only was her horse gone, but so was everything – and everyone – else. The farm was empty. It could only mean one thing.

Maral put her hands on her hips, hog-slicer resting against her thigh, and released a long, frustrated breath, just as a thick loop of rope dropped over her shoulders and yanked itself tight.

Javani moved fast. She leapt from the hayloft, both hands and her thighs wrapped around the rope, and found herself dangling, swaying a little over the head of the struggling assassin.

The woman looked up.

'What are you doing up there?'

Her voice was low, raspy, and tinged with obvious amusement. Javani grunted and yanked on the rope. This was not the plan. She was supposed to be hauling the Mawn up off the ground as she descended, not swinging three feet from the groaning pulley with increasingly tired arms.

'Did you think you would pull me up? I am heavier than you.'

The Mawn bounced up and down on her toes, sending Javani lurching on the rope.

'Cut that out!'

'See? Would you like me to jump?'

Javani gripped the rope pale-knuckled, her teeth gritted as the swaying subsided. 'You're pretty mouthy for a prisoner.'

'A prisoner?'

'Did you miss the part where I incapacitated you?'

'This is what you call this?'

'I can find something heavy to tie this to. Let's see how chatty you are then.'

The Mawn shook her head. In the growing dawnlight, ruddy gold through the gaps in the barn timbers, to Javani her hair looked like a mass of briar, thick and thorny. She'd dropped the wicked-looking knife at her feet when the rope had gone taut, and despite her back-chat had to be in considerable discomfort from Javani's body weight squeezing her arms against her innards. With one careful toe, Javani steered herself back towards the hayloft, scrubbing back an inch at a time to solid ground.

'What is your plan here, girl?'

'Prisoners are generally silent until interrogated.' She'd got one good foot on the loft now, and a swing of her hip brought the other alongside. There were plenty of solid posts along the barn, and she'd tie the rope to one. There might even be another pulley around – with a bit more leverage, she could send that gobby Mawn up to the rafters and out of harm's way. She smiled to herself. Mariam would be so proud to see her applying her education.

'Prisoners,' came the Mawn's voice from below, 'are generally imprisoned.'

Javani heard a noise like sawing, and had an instant to lunge for the loft before the rope pinged and fell slack. She dangled, one knee over the loft-edge, one leg hanging free, her fingers scrabbling for purchase. Beneath her, the Mawn was shaking the shorn coils of rope free. Of course she'd had another bloody knife.

'Now what,' the Mawn began, sheathing a small knife and reaching for the long and ghastly blade on the barn floor, 'little gir—'

Javani landed on her.

Maral spat old straw and earth, and something that in the name of the heavens had better not have been guano. The girl had flattened her and rolled, impressively quick, and once again the hog-slicer was gone from her hand. Maral pushed herself up on her hands and knees, blowing musty grass from her face. Where had the girl got to? When she got the—

The kick caught her in the ribs, but she was already rolling, professional instinct sending her sideways. She tumbled away into the filthy corner, hand already closing around her small blade, coiled to strike before the killing blow landed. But no follow-up arrived – the girl had fled. It was, she reflected, no great surprise. Maral got slowly to her feet, brushing away stable-muck, wincing at the jar to her shoulder. That had been . . . unusual. She was almost . . . disappointed?

She went to rub a hand over her face and caught a whiff of what was on it, spent a futile moment rubbing the hand against her clothes. She was filthier than Kuzari, and had none of his poise. The hog-slicer was somewhere in the dirt, assuming the girl hadn't run off with it, and the light was improving as the distant red sun made its cautious way over the eastern horizon.

She could, at last, return to the matter of her horse, and what had happened at the farm. All the signs pointed to only one thing, and now the light was improving she'd at least be able to follow what tracks—

Maral ducked as a horseshoe whipped past her head, scarring the post beside her. The horseshoe slipped off into the gloom, then came flying back past her as she swayed clear, snapped back on a rope.

'What in all the hells are you doing, girl?'

'Bringing you in.'

She was twirling the rope, the horseshoe at its end, and Maral was not entirely comfortable with her facility.

'By yourself? What are you, fourteen?'

The shoe fizzed past her chest then sang out at her knee, and Maral was forced into an unplanned backward step.

'I'm fifteen. And a half.'

Maral continued to edge away. In a moment, she thought, I'll be in the light. She'll see who I am. She'll see what I am. Maybe that will be enough to send her running.

'And you're bringing me in? To what?'

Another back-step as the shoe lashed at her. She wasn't convinced the girl was trying to brain her, but she was getting closer to serious head trauma than she'd have preferred.

'You tried to kill someone important.'

'Did I?' Almost into the light.

'You're going to answer for it.'

'To you? By yourself?' She could snatch the rope or rush the girl when a swing passed, she'd never be able to get the rope around in time. The small blade remained in her palm, her fingers loose. It could be over very quickly, if she chose.

The girl's chin jutted. 'Don't be an imbecile. My reinforcements are going to be arriving imminently. I told them exactly where I was going and left a trail a mile wide. All I have to do is keep you here.'

Maral's brow twitched. Invention? Possibly. The girl had hardly displayed exemplary tactical discipline, but her overconfidence could well be explained by a realistic expectation of backup. She flicked a glance at her feet, and realised as she did so that she had moved into the light; her face and upper body were bathed in the ruddy warmth of the dawn.

But the girl's expression hadn't changed. Intent, determined, pugnacious . . . but where was the revulsion? Had the girl not noticed? How could she not?

'You're pretty confident in your abilities. Do you know what I am?'

'You're my enemy.'

To her right, a loose and rusted piece of iron, a dismembered plough-head. It was perfect for her purposes. Maral flicked her gaze over the girl's shoulder. Was that distant hoof-beats? This affair had gone on too long already.

'Are those your friends?'

The girl turned, and Maral lunged for the plough-head. She snatched it up and swivelled in time to meet the girl's furious lash, the metal ringing in her hands as she battered the horseshoe away. That should have been the end of it, but the old iron was heavier than she'd bargained. She was thrown off-balance, too slow to stamp down on the rope, and the girl had the shoe back in her hand an instant later.

'That was a shitty trick,' the girl growled.

'What, exactly, were you expecting?' Maral continued to edge, now making slow progress out from the barn and into the wider yard. If she moved in an arc, she could pin the girl in the barn's corner where her range and elbow-room would be sorely diminished. And then she would put an end to this in the manner she pleased.

The girl tracked her movement and stung at her with the horseshoe, setting the plough-head ringing. Maral took half a step back. Patience was the key. The girl would tire soon, after their run through the night and physical exertions. A stringy thing she was, five years Maral's junior. Five years of professional bloodletting, to go with the years before that. It was, in many ways, impressive that she'd delayed Maral so long already. She was proving to be quite the unexpected challenge.

'Stop grinning, you fucker! This is serious.'

Maral blinked. She'd had no idea she'd been smiling. Curious.

'Why are you trying to bring me in, girl?'

'Why do you think?' The shoe sang out once more, and Maral batted it away with a clang and a shower of rust. 'You tried to kill my ma!'

'I tried, did I?'

This time the girl went low, and Maral leapt over the stinging arc of the rope. She made to close, but already the shoe was around and launching like an arrow towards her forehead. She got the plough-head up just in time.

'Who are you working for? I know you're Mawn. Are the Mawn in on this?'

Maral hadn't realised she'd paused until the shoe glanced off her elbow and made her fingers go numb. With a yowl, she dropped the small blade, then loose-armed met the next two swings with the plough as she backed into the farmyard. Her mind was unquiet, unable to focus. The girl knew. She knew what she was, what she did, and could see her plain in the open space. But there was no disgust, no repugnance, only her boggle-eyed determination to bring Maral down like a festival hog.

'You know,' Maral hissed through gritted teeth, the pain from her elbow surprising and raw, 'who sent me. It's hardly a mystery, is it?'

The girl's brows lowered, her face hard. 'You work for the Guild, then. You're going to tell everyone what they tried to do.'

Somehow she got the horseshoe arcing up, then cracked it down on Maral's foot. Maral stumbled, cursing. How in the sweet light of heavens was this infant getting the better of her?

'Better to kill me, surely, stop me coming back for more?' Maral hopped back, trying to shake the pain from her foot, one forearm still numb. 'Why take the risk?'

'So you face justice! To send a message! To prove a point.'

Maral was smiling again, despite the pain. She could feel her lips pulled back from her teeth, and somehow it wasn't a grimace. 'Justice? Remind me who the outlaws are here.' She dodged a sharp lash of the shoe and stepped in, plough-head raised, but the girl was fast enough to preserve the distance. 'The Guild are sanctioned by law. It's the rebels who will be facing justice.'

'Since when—' *whoosh* '—was attacking from the shadows—' *swish* '—an official part of the Serican—' *clang* '—justice system?'

Maral risked another dart forward, grumbling foot be damned. 'You don't read a lot of history, do you?'

'Horseshit! I read loads.'

Maral sidestepped a lunge and almost got a foot on the rope. 'Is that so? Favourite accounts?'

'Wait, a Mawn assassin reads history?'

Maral ducked the next lash. 'Everyone should have a hobby. Do you have a favourite or not?'

'Ilay of Whitestone's *Histories*. Although I read the translations, everyone knows the original is gibberish.'

Three sharp clangs as the rope whirled and Maral met it. 'Ilay is a bit gauche, isn't he?'

'I didn't say I agreed with it all! It's seventy-one volumes, there's a lot of variety.'

Maral hesitated. 'There are forty-three volumes.'

'Huh?' For a moment the assault wavered. 'You're not one of those people who just learn a few quotes to toss out here and there and pretend to have read the rest, are you?'

Now Maral blinked, the iron heavy in her hand. 'Why would someone do that?'

'I don't know, to seem like they've done more work than they have? My ma and I, we used to . . .' The girl tailed off, throat bobbing, something hard in her shining eyes. Maral felt something then, at the mention of the girl's mother, the woman Maral had laid the blade on in the rooming house. It came rolling back like a wave, her cowardice, her shame, and a fresh, bitter stab of something that could only be guilt.

'Girl, you should know . . .'

'Shut up.' The rope was moving again, and Maral was too slow to turn. 'You're coming back with me.' It lashed around her, wrapping tight, catching her square on her injured side. 'That's all there is to it.' The shoe thumped into Maral's chest with a vindictive sting as she staggered, half-bound and off-balance, then the girl yanked the rope and sent her crashing to the earth. Close enough to get another look at those tracks at last. Close enough to feel the tremble of approaching footsteps, get a noseful of that familiar smell.

They were not alone.

'Girl,' she groaned. 'You need to—'

'Shut up!' The girl was on her, hauling the rope taut, stuffing a rag into Maral's mouth before she could say more. 'That's all there is to it!'

Girl, Maral mouthed through fabric – little improvement on the dung-earth of the stable – *you need to look behind you.*

As if reading her eyes, at last the girl looked, and her reaction made it clear that the new arrivals were not her backup.

'Behold, Ferenz,' said one of the men. 'Was I not veracious in exhorting our return?'

'Incontestably, Berant,' replied his colleague. 'Incontestably. Another pair for the market!'

The Brotherhood had found them.

'Shit,' said the girl.

FIFTEEN

It was getting hot, and face down over a stinking mule was not a comfortable way to travel even in temperate weather. Javani twisted fruitlessly against her bonds, her arms tight behind her and her balance precarious. Should she slip from the mule's back and onto the trail, she knew she wouldn't get far; her ankles were roped to her wrists, and the fresh bruise on her cheek was testament to her captors' disapproval of impromptu attempts at navigational divergence.

Beside her, uncomfortably close and with a reek the equal of the mule's, was the Mawn. The woman was facing the other way, her stained and perishing boots bobbing not far from Javani's head, trussed with an extra helping of thick hemp beyond the shoe rope Javani had wrapped her in, the mouth rag buttressed with a rancid strip of cloth like the one that pulled at Javani's cheeks. And unlike Javani, who had struggled and wriggled and snarled and hissed from the moment they'd roped her, the woman was completely immobile, inert, as floppy as a grain sack. She'd put up no fight, said nothing, acted with pure compliance in stark contrast to Javani's own futile defiance. It was insulting, really.

Javani let her head fall, pushed her face against the mouldy, bobbing blanket draped over the mule's back. Where were her reinforcements? She knew Ree would come after her, there was no way she'd have let Javani do anything on her own after last time. She expected her mother, Anri and Anashe and who knew who else at her back, to come riding over the southern horizon at any moment.

Any moment now.

Gods damn it all, she'd planned it, hadn't she? Ree had accused her of a lack of foresight, well *fuck her*. Javani had thought this one all the way through, tracking the Mawn, isolating her, immobilising her, and doing a thrice-damned good job of it, right in time for her backup to come rolling in. The only thing she hadn't banked on was her quarry making for a slaver-raided farm, and the slavers not being entirely gone.

If anyone was to blame for this, it was Ree. Even after taking the time to rouse the rest of the party and fetch the horses and everything else, there should still have been plenty of time to follow the extremely unsubtle trail Javani had left *while moving on foot* and catch up by dawn. Plenty of time. So where the fuck was she? If she'd turned up when she was fucking supposed to, Javani would currently not be roped and gagged on the back of a sour and overworked mule, wobbling their way to gods knew where. Instead she'd have achieved the recognition she deserved: assassination attempt foiled, perpetrator tracked and captured, interrogation to follow, medals and plaudits all round. One in the eye for the General, who claimed she always knew best.

She knew, she just knew, that if she somehow got out of this mess, her mother would never let her forget it. It was so like her. Even when she was the one at fault. She'd accuse Javani of not planning, again, even though her plan had been rock solid. Who knew there were slavers operating this close to the fringes? Apart from Anashe mentioning it, of course, but that was hardly a formal briefing, was it. How was she supposed to have known? And the Mawn, what was she thinking, coming to a place like that. It was her fault just as much as Ree's.

They'd stopped. She turned her head to see where, but the Mawn's reeking boots blocked her view. An impression of blocky shapes and a hint of shade, at least. Buildings, maybe another farm, maybe a trading post. She swallowed. What kind of trading, exactly?

'Salutations, frater,' called one of the men who'd captured them, one of the first two, an ugly pair with an oddly florid manner of speech that set her teeth on edge. 'Come witness the fruits of our serendipitous bounty!'

'Frater, what fortune!' a voice replied, another man, obsequious, hungry. 'Whence did you discover such harvest?'

'By sheer happenstance, we were returning by way of that charming farmstead we passed yesterday, when our ears were assailed by the sounds of combat. Imagine our stupefaction when investigation yielded these fair specimens in the raw, one already shackled by the other. The gods have offered us providence!'

'Providence indeed, frater. Bring them inside, and let us discern what lies beneath their odium. The standard quarters are at capacity, but there are bars in the stores.'

Javani wished to yell many things through her gag, among them a demand to be released, coupled with copious threats and vows of retribution, and a warning that as soon as her mother showed up they'd all be turned inside out. A little further down the list was an enquiry as to the reasons for their baffling diction, and what it would take to get them to stop. She'd spent plenty of time around those, mostly men, afflicted by a degree of verbosity – Aki, gods rest him, and Manatas had both suffered no shortage of vocabulary – but there was something so confected, so manufactured about the way the slavers spoke that it had to be meaningful. Oh well. It wouldn't matter once they were inside out.

SIXTEEN

The store was a low and thick-walled sandstone and mudbrick building that stank of sick animals and offal, but was at least mercifully cool. The bars the slaver had mentioned were animal pens, individually partitioned, that ran along the back wall, separated by low walls topped with more bars, fronted by heavy iron gates. From their thickness, the animals held in them must either have been large and powerful or dangerously mad. Javani was pushed into the first, the Mawn the next, and then they were washed.

Javani went first, buckets of cold and unlikely-to-be-clean water emptied over her head while a hunched and narrow man scrubbed at her face in an attempt to shift her latest coating of grime. She growled at him, but any movement beyond tilting her head for his ministrations triggered a sudden cuff from the unsmiling man lurking behind her. The blows weren't hard, not like that first punch had been, but they were a reminder that a man she couldn't see was perfectly relaxed about causing her harm.

At length, endeavours complete, the narrow man removed the gag and inspected her teeth, and Javani lacked the fortitude to spit at him. Her righteous fury was subsiding now, in the hours since her capture, and doubt was beginning to creep in. Would Ree be able to track her to this new location? Were the slavers adept at hiding their tracks, mules and all? The Mawn's passivity worried her more and more – what did she know? Rumours abounded that the Guild and the slavers worked hand in glove, especially in the east . . . Could the Mawn know some secret code-word that would spring her free? Javani had muzzled her with the rag before the slavers arrived; she'd never even had the chance to speak. Javani swallowed. She didn't know how many people were in this slaver enclave, excluding the unwitting merchandise, but it was at least a dozen from those she'd seen on the way in. Suddenly, the chances of rescue began to feel somewhat remote, and a sick feeling roiled in her stomach.

Satisfied, the slavers moved on to the Mawn's pen, leaving Javani standing wet-haired and shivering in dripping clothes. She supposed she should be grateful for the cooling, but it didn't feel like it. At least these two bastards didn't talk. Through the bars above the partition, she watched as they unlocked the gate and moved inside, buckets and cloths and all, and set about the compliant Mawn, soaking her thicket of coarse hair, slopping it out of the way of her face and—

Tumbling backwards with a yelp.

The narrow man scrabbled backwards, kicking empty buckets, then leapt to his feet and made for the door. The other slaver was right behind him, slamming the gate and thumping the lock shut with desperate haste, and a moment later Javani and the Mawn were alone in the low building, quiet but for the sound of an empty bucket spinning gently on the earthen floor.

'What in hells was that about? Did you say something to them?'

The Mawn didn't react. They hadn't even untied her, and Javani realised her gag was still in place beneath her sopping curtain of dark hair. The woman remained unmoved, standing at the centre of a dark star of frothy watermark.

'If . . . if you move this way, I'll get the gag off you. Then at least you can explain yourself.'

The woman didn't move, her breathing steady, then with what could have been a sigh of resignation she shuffled towards the partition. Her hands and ankles were still bound, tied to each other, and her progress was slow and careful.

'Face away from me. I'm not risking a bite, gods know what kind of infection you'd give me.'

Had Javani imagined it, or had the Mawn's shoulders slumped a fraction at that? Surely not? For a moment, she felt a pang of guilt at her remark, then reminded herself of how she'd come to be imprisoned in a stinking animal pen in the first place.

'There. Now you can answer my questions at least.'

Maral flexed her jaw, opened and closed her mouth, ran her tongue over her lips. 'Hm,' she said. She still faced away from the girl, whining mosquito that she was.

'Why did the slavers run away like that? What did you do?'

'Nothing.'

'Why are you being so . . . so . . . feeble around them? Why aren't you fighting them?'

A puff of chuckle. 'Like you did? And how well you're doing by comparison.'

'You're in league with them, aren't you?' Anger in the girl's voice, but controlled. 'You work for the Guild, the slavers have an agreement with the Guild, and they're going to let you out any moment, aren't they?'

'I know nothing of any agreement.'

A pause, the sound of scratching. 'Then why did they run?'

Maral turned and looked at her, dead-eyed, through tendrils of dripping hair. Why had they run? Why did they always run? The answer was so obvious as to make the question almost . . . unsettling. 'Why do you think?'

The girl shrugged. 'I don't bloody know! That's why I was asking you.'

Maral's brows dipped, her eyes narrowed, not in suspicion but genuine surprise.

'I am Mawn.'

'Yes, we covered that.'

Maral gave her head a little shake. How could the girl not understand this? Had she been raised in an isolated commune, or been kicked in the head by a horse at an impressionable age? Maral spoke slowly, as if explaining to a child. 'They fled when they saw what I was.'

'Don't patronise me, you're barely, what, three years older than I am?'

'If you're really fifteen—'

'And a half!'

'—I am five years older than you. Probably.'

'Oh. Well, that's not that much. Compared to an old person.' The girl stood for a moment, arms wrapped around herself. She looked cold and damp. Maral was unbothered by the sopping chill, but the girl's attitude was making her uneasy. 'What do you mean, probably?'

'My exact age is uncertain. I was a foundling.'

'Who found you?'

Her saviour. 'Beralas Verdanisi.'

'The Chairman of the Guild? Ree's always going on about what bastards he and his brother are.'

'He found me on the plains, when my clan had been murdered, and he took me in, and raised me as part of his family. Does that sound like a bastard to you?'

The girl pondered. 'How did your clan die?'

'They were butchered by raiders. I was the sole survivor.' A refrain, not a memory. To remember would have been too much.

'Huh.'

Maral did not like the look on the girl's face. There was a note of something approaching . . . smugness. 'What?'

'Ree told me a similar story about my own origins once. Said I was the only one to escape a Mawn raid – no offence – and she took me in and raised me.'

'None taken.'

'Of course, that turned out to be bollocks.'

'Is that so?'

'So I guess I'm wondering . . . how long after this raid did your man Beralas say he found you?'

'It was a few days. I can remember it. He was heading north, I was heading south.' An image in her mind, waving grass, confusion, fear . . . then relief. Had it been relief?

'You think.'

Maral cast her memories aside, glaring through the bars at the girl beyond. 'What are you implying?'

The girl reclined against the partition. 'Beralas definitely killed your clan. He probably picked you up on his way home because he felt guilty, brought you home as a souvenir.'

Maral stiffened with outrage, forgetting she was still roped at wrist and ankle, nearly losing her balance in the process. Fury coursed through her, her blood thick with it, fury and a white-knuckled hunger to smash the girl's teeth from her mouth. How *dare* she? How dare she even suggest—

The girl chuckled. 'Careful there, killer.'

Maral's gaze was hard and cold. She had entertained this flea long enough, and it was time to remind her what she provoked. 'Why did you chase me, if you know what I am?'

'What kind of question is that?'

'You hate your mother. You scream at each other and vow to turn your backs—'

'You snooping little shit!'

'—then pursue an obviously dangerous killer, a Mawn no less, across the plains. Why?'

'Why do you think? Family's family. Even a lost little Mawn should know that.'

Maral felt a tightness in her abdomen that she immediately resented. 'Hm.'

'Well, what would you do if someone tried to kill your ma?'

Emptiness swamped her gut, hollowed by the girl's words, by the echo of Kuzari's – *If I found someone had murdered my kin, I'd feed them their eyeballs.*

'Nothing.' Her voice came out cellar-cold, flat with suppressed shame.

'You're a strange fruit, Mawn. You really didn't give those slavers some secret signal to let you out?'

Maral glanced down to her obvious bonds, and raised an eyebrow. She had not fought because she had deserved this fate. Why was this creature so incapable of drawing the most straightforward of conclusions?

'Right. You got a name?'

'Yes.'

'And?'

Maral said nothing. Her emotions roiled, bubbled like stew. She should not be speaking to the girl, that much was clear. She should have turned and resolved her at the first corner, back in the township. She should have made sure of the mother, too. She should have—

'I'm Javani.'

'I know.'

'Nine fucking hells, do you want me to keep calling you—'

'Maral. My name is Maral.'

'Huh.'

'Your name, it means "child".'

'I'm well aware! While yours means "tool", which as anyone knows is slang for a man's part.'

Maral snorted in genuine mirth. 'Nobody has called me anything like that before. Except Kuzari, perhaps.'

'Who's Kuzari?'

'My brother. Not by blood. Another foundling.'

'And he's another killer for the Guild, is he?'

'Yes.'

'By the gods, did your buddy Beralas just go around sweeping up murderous children as he toured the plains? I get that it's cheaper than mercenaries, but it's a hell of a long-term commitment.'

Maral paused. 'I don't know how to answer that question.'

'Yeah, nor do I.'

They were quiet for a moment, but for the dripping. Maral watched the girl's movements, her changing expressions, the cast of her eyes.

'I know why you keep looking at the door,' she said.

'And why's that, killer?'

'Your mother isn't coming.'

'I'm sure you'd like to think so. She'll kick the shit out of you when she turns up, bundled up or otherwise.'

Ordinarily Maral might have laughed. 'Girl, she is not coming.'

'She'll find us. You wait. We won't be here long.'

Maral sucked in her cheeks, the muscles of her jaw proud. 'She is not coming because—'

The outer door swung open with a bang, and a tall, rotund man came striding in, stifling the girl's cry of triumph before it was more than half formed. Like the other slavers, he was dressed in a curious sort of uniform – rich fabrics beneath tough, cured outerwear, dyed in bright colours. He had many golden earrings, and his teeth, when he bared them, were equally gilded.

'Which one?' he called over his shoulder. Behind him shuffled the narrow man, and one of the two who'd wrangled them at the farm, possibly Ferenz.

The narrow man indicated Maral, and the new man approached her pen, his tread cautious. He stopped well clear of the gate, peering in at her impassive form, tilting his head from one side to the other.

'Dear me, dearest dearie me. We can't sell this,' he sighed. 'Imagine if we traded it to our new confederates, fraters. Imagine the harm it could do. Cogitate and confabulate! We must move the cargo to Kilale with the greatest care and urgency, and the harm it could do outweighs any reward. Bury it.'

Ferenz nodded, his silver necklace jingling. 'And the other?'

The moustache turned to the girl. 'Some potential worth, perhaps, but our luscious transit is already packed, fraters. Attend it likewise.'

The man marched from the room without another word, Ferenz and the hunched man ducking from his path at his approach. They exchanged a nod, then followed in his wake, leaving the key to the pen gates hanging on a thick metal hook by the closing door.

'Shit,' said the girl.

Maral watched the gate key swaying on its hook, a heavy iron thing; no wonder Ferenz hadn't wanted to carry it out with him.

'Mawn. Mawn. Maral! Wake up, will you? Why are you being so bastard docile?'

Maral looked slowly over, and said nothing. What was there to say?

'I asked you a question. Why aren't you doing anything? They're about to murder us! Aren't you supposed to be a deadly killer?'

Maral lifted her shoulders, then let them drop. 'It is a fitting end,' she muttered.

'Shut up! None of that talk. Maybe Ree is on her way, maybe she's not, but we are getting out of this place right now, and you're going to do your bit. But first up, I need your word.'

'My word.'

'That if I get us out of here, you won't try to hurt me or mine again, and you'll come back with me to face justice.'

'Why would I do that?'

'Because otherwise they're going to kill you, and very soon. All I want is answers – tell the others who sent you, why and how, and maybe a few other things, make yourself useful, you'll be free. That's my promise. Beats dying here at the hands of these wankers, right?'

Maral considered. The odds were absurd. The girl was absurd. But something tickled at her, a sliver of delicate . . . hope? Impossible. What was there for her to hope for?

And yet . . .

'Fine. You have my word.'

'Good. Now shuffle over here, will you?'

'Why?'

'I need the rope, dickhead. They took mine away.'

Maral said nothing, but after a moment she began to shuffle towards the partition.

'No funny business. And don't you *dare* try to bite me.'

'I'll see how the mood takes me,' Maral replied, her back to the girl as she reached over the partition through the bars and worked on the ropes.

'Come on, come on . . .' the girl muttered, hands fumbling at Maral's back. She grumbled incessantly as she rummaged, lamenting her taken knives, and something about a hidden brooch pin that lacked the fortitude to tease the rope apart.

'Have you tried using your teeth? Or do only subhuman Mawn bite?'

'Gods, I never called you subhuman. Will you let me work on this in peace?'

'You don't need to say it, girl. It's no secret. A Mawn is a vile and wretched thing, deserving only contempt and horror, and perhaps, in the rarest cases, pity. You don't need to pretend otherwise. I've been conscious of it my entire life. I know how lucky I was that Beralas took me in, sheltered me, protected me. And I, in turn, have protected him. Until now.'

'Will you . . . kindly . . . shut up.'

'You hide it well, girl, but nothing is changed. I see it in faces every day, in checked revulsion, cloaked disgust. You asked me why those men recoiled. They saw my face. They saw what I was. And they were horrified.'

'Oh, shut up! Shut the fuck up!' The girl tore at the knot with a roar of frustration, yanking Maral's arms backwards. 'Those men weren't disgusted, they were terrified! They were *afraid*! Because Mawn are *scary*! They're not wretched subhumans, they're the terrors of the plains, the scourge of the expanse. Your people have a reputation as remorseless killing machines, and while you seem to carry that around with you like a fucking shield, you seem to be completely oblivious as to why! What in hells did your "protector" tell you? That he saved you from a short and wild life of savagery by spiriting you to civilisation? I'm telling you, that guy absolutely killed your family and kept you on the off-chance you might one day be useful, and it sounds like you've been doing his dirty work most of your life, so who got the better end of that deal, eh? A pet Mawn as his go-to killer – must have done marvels for his reputation.'

Maral had gone rigid, her mind a white-hot blank. The girl was finally silent for a moment, perhaps fearing a bite, headbutt or worse was coming, but when Maral made no move she fell back upon the knot, her verbal torrent undammed.

'By the gods, you really thought – come here, you bastard – that those men were repelled by you? They were shitting themselves! Probably petrified you were going to – come on, come on, *come on* – cut their fingers off and stuff them up their arses – *Got you, you bastard!*'

The knot was undone, and rope spooled around Maral's ankles. 'Quick, get the rest off and pass the rope through. Come on. What the fuck are you doing? Get it off and pass it over, they could come back at any moment!'

Maral was still facing away, immobile despite the release of her wrists. The structures of her mind, of her memory, were wobbling, spiderwebbed with cracks. The girl was lying. She had to be lying. *It's seventy-one volumes, there's a lot of variety . . .*

What else had been kept from her?

'The things you said . . .'

'Yes, yes, very sorry if I upset you, but can we—'

'The fingers. My people did that?'

'What? Yeah, that and considerably worse, on a regular basis. I thought you read histories?'

'Everything in the palazzo library. He had me tutored with his daughters. Well, in the next room, behind a screen.'

'And the peccadilloes of your people weren't covered in great detail?'

Maral gave a slow shake of her head, the thicket of half-dried hair swaying with heft. Thirty volumes absent, and that from a single account. How many other histories had she been denied? 'Some records were . . . missing. The remaining accounts . . . perhaps gave a . . . slanted . . . impression . . .'

'And to whose benefit might that have been, I wonder. Look, I don't know what to tell you, I'm sure some historians are fine people, but some are jingoistic rot-cocks with an agenda to push. And much as I'd love to debate this in fruitful and mesmerising depth, as would Mariam, my own blessed tutor, you may remember we are in something of a hurry with regards to the impending death situation, so would you kindly pass me the fucking rope?'

Jolted as if shocked, Maral moved at last, stripping the rope from her waist and ankles, then finally turning.

'Here.'

'Are you all right?'

'Yes.'

''Cos you look like you might cry.'

Maral knew she did not cry, but inside she seethed. 'Are we not in a hurry?'

'Right. Yeah.'

The girl started swinging the rope, muttering under her breath. 'Here we go, Javani. Don't fuck this up. Remember the weight, remember the arc, feel the path, see it in your—'

'What other things did my people do?'

'Nine piss-reeking hells, do you mind?'

'Hurry up, then.'

'You think this is easy? You want to try—'

'Someone's coming.'

'Oh for fuck's—'

SEVENTEEN

The door swung open again, bringing with it a bright blast of daylight and the calls and cries of activity from the camp beyond. Javani stuffed the rope behind her back as Ferenz and his erstwhile colleague Berant came swaggering in. Both men were decked with dark-stained, full-length leather aprons over their fancy clothing, and Ferenz wore gloves. Maral was back in the centre of her pen, hands behind her back, head hung. Javani swallowed. Had the Mawn reverted to her passive state, resigned to some kind of deserved execution? If that was the case, Javani was fucked.

'The clavis, if it please you, frater,' Ferenz called, approaching Maral's pen. In one gloved hand was a hatchet, its haft polished wood, its head silvery sharp. Javani squirmed at the sight of it. The weapon's aura suggested it had never been used to split firewood, only skulls.

Berant scooped the key from its peg and stepped beside his comrade. 'Be fleet, frater. The sooner it rots in the pit, the sooner we shall be riding in the footsteps of our confederates.'

Ferenz hefted the hatchet. 'Attend to the gate, frater, lest it aspire to bolt.'

'Without question, frater.'

Berant unlocked the gate and dragged it open just wide enough for Ferenz to stride inside. Decked out as he was, the hatchet swinging in his hand, Javani still detected a shade of apprehension to his movements, even when faced with a Mawn who was unarmed and supposedly hog-tied.

Maral had not moved, and Javani's pulse had begun to thump, her palms greasy against the rope, her tongue tasting thunder. Her hands were trembling, her knees weak. Once they murdered Maral, they'd handle Javani without breaking stride, and she was facing her final moments confined in a stinking, dung-washed animal pen with nothing but a despondent Mawn and two contemptible slavers for company. Where was Ree? What was keeping her?

Javani realised, with a crushing certainty that sprang tears from her eyes, that she wanted her ma. She was immediately ashamed of herself, furious with herself, and then, as the notion crystallised that the reeking air of the pens might be the last she ever tasted, a realisation supplanted all else that she'd give anything to see her mother come charging through the doorway.

I'll be a better daughter, I promise, if you turn up now. I promise. I just won't tell you out loud.

Ferenz set himself and raised the hatchet over the inert Mawn, then hesitated. His eyes had finally adjusted to the gloom of the pens.

'You're supposed to be tied up,' he said in a puzzled voice, his florid speech momentarily forgotten.

Maral raised her head, and the eyes gleaming through the thick clumps of hair were terrifyingly alive.

'Sorry.'

'Gods!'

He swung, but she was already moving. Her hand caught his wrist as he tried to bring the hatchet down and they twisted together, her elbow in his gut, the bones in his forearm wrenched. He howled as the hatchet clattered from his grip, searching with panicked eyes for his comrade.

'Berant! Help!'

The man at the gate stared, wide-eyed, as the Mawn hurled Ferenz to the putrid floor, stepping around his still-locked arm to drive her foot into his throat and choking his cries. Berant did not rush to help. Berant slammed the gate shut, and began fumbling desperately with the key, the iron thick and clumsy in his hand, battling to lock the Mawn inside before she came after him.

Javani roped him on the first try, dropping a loop over his head and yanking his arms against his sides before he'd even registered what was happening. The key dangled, un-turned, as she braced one foot, then the other, against the bars and hauled, dragging the struggling man away from the gate before he could snake a hand back up.

A truncated scream from the next pen and a terrible splattering sound announced an end to Ferenz's tribulations, then as Berant strained against the rope, feet sliding through ancient filth, the gate swung back open.

'This one's under control,' Javani called, trying to ignore the stripe of gore that marked one side of the Mawn's face. Ferenz's hatchet was in her hand, and it was no longer shiny. 'Grab the key. Once we tie him, we—'

Maral swiped the hatchet at the incapacitated man's midriff, and his guts poured out in a sickening rush, spooling over the sullied earth. He couldn't even scream before she'd grabbed a handful of glossy, twitching viscera and wrapped it around his throat, yanking it tight.

Whether from the sight, or the smell, or the sound it all made, Javani vomited. The rope slipped from her hands, and the ruin of Berant fell with it, coming to rest in a shuddering, oozing heap. The Mawn stood over him, hand bloody, hatchet dripping, her breath coming hard and even.

'Was that something my people did?' she said, her voice low, a growl in the sudden silence. 'I feel like it might have been.'

'Gods, Maral . . .' Javani clung to the gate bars with bloodless fingers, working hard to keep her eyeline high and tasting bile. 'Was that . . .' She swallowed, wiped at her mouth. 'Was that necessary?'

The Mawn met her gaze. 'No,' she replied. 'But it was important.'

Javani swallowed again. The smell wasn't going away, and an errant glance towards the next pen had given her sight of the top of Ferenz's head a long way from the rest of him. She had seen violence, she had seen bloodshed and death, and she'd told herself that as battle-hardened as she was for her age, nothing could get to her. She had been wrong. 'Could you . . . Gods . . . Could you hand me the key? I don't want to spend . . . any more time in here . . . please.'

The Mawn looked around the room, taking it in from her new

vantage on the other side of the bars, then stuffed the hatchet into her belt and dragged most of Berant into the far corner. The trail he left was distinct, even against generations of caked stool. Once Berant was piled, the Mawn returned to her pen, and dragged Ferenz out likewise. This time Javani was careful to avoid looking above the neck, but she definitely heard Maral kick something along.

'Hello? Can I have the key, please?'

The Mawn crouched beside the two ex-slavers and with impressive efficiency rifled through their belongings. She removed a set of knives, two coin pouches and a few other oddments, then paused, Ferenz's silver necklace dangling from her soiled fingers. Somehow, it still shone.

'Hello? Maral? Gods, the smell . . . The key, please!'

The Mawn stood, the knives already disappeared somewhere about her, the necklace still shimmering in her grip. Then she shook her head and dropped it back onto its former owner's chest.

'Maral? Key?'

The Mawn yanked the hatchet from her belt and strode to the door. 'Wait here.'

'Hey! Where are you— You can't leave me, I got you out! Come back! Come fu . . . Gods!'

Javani was alone in the pen, but for the bodies of the slavers and their gathering congregation of flies. The key hung from the other gate, and the rope had followed Berant across the room's floor.

'Shit,' said Javani.

The sounds of Maral's progress were not long in arriving. First came shouts, then cries, and then, inevitably, screams. Some of the screams were cut off before they could finish, others tapered and modulated, renewing with fresh urgency at some unseen impetus. Javani wasn't sure if merely hearing carnage was worse than witnessing it first-hand, given the fecund playground that was her imagination, but then her eyes alighted on the festering remains of Ferenz and Berant and her stomach pressed once more at the back of her throat. Sounds she could take. Maybe all the screaming meant people were running away. It was probably worse if the screaming stopped, as that would mean—

The screaming stopped.

Javani waited in anxious silence, still nowhere near acclimatised to the noxious air of the animal pens and the putrid reek of Berant's exposed bowels. Then came a sphincter-clenching moment when she thought one of the two ex-slavers had moved, but it was, reassuringly, only the passage of their new coating of flies.

She retched, her stomach empty, then a shadow filled the doorway.

'You came back.' Javani held up a hand against the light, but was glad to be seeing Maral in little more than silhouette against the day outside. The silhouette was dripping.

'I thought you might have got yourself out by now.'

Javani shook her head. 'Too busy . . . throwing up.' She gestured towards the other gate with a weak hand. 'Key?'

Maral walked back into the pens and thumped down a set of saddlebags, well away from the corpse pile, along with a bundled saddle blanket. 'I was looking for my horse.'

'Any . . . luck?'

'Gone, along with most of the camp. Mules remain.'

'Hooray.'

'But I found my saddlebags.' She crouched down and rummaged in the blanket bundle, pulling out a thin and evidently very sharp knife, which she stowed in a sheath at her side. A few other bits and bobs went into pouches and pockets, then she stood, the saddlebags over one shoulder, and walked back to the corpses. Maral stared at them for a moment, face taut, eyes inscrutable. Javani realised she was looking at the necklace, which twinkled from its resting place on Ferenz's chest.

'Go on,' Javani called, 'take it. It's not like he needs it any more.' It was doubtful he could keep it on, for a start.

The Mawn stared a moment longer, then shook her head. 'It is not for me.'

'Why's that? It's not like he deserved it – he probably stole it from someone they took, or at best bought it with slave-coin.'

Maral shook her head again, once, then reached a hand into the saddlebag at her chest and felt for something. Javani caught a shimmer of material between her fingers, then the Mawn pulled her hand away, her expression undeniably guilty.

'What was that?'

'Nothing.'

'Is this another bit of nonsense from the man who killed your clan? What did he tell you? That Mawn aren't allowed jewellery?'

'No. It's not that.'

'What is it then?' Javani sucked in a breath in preparation to berate the woman the other side of the gate and received a fresh lungful of stinking corpse-air. She broke off to gag. 'And pass me . . . the fucking key . . .' she croaked at length.

Maral was staring at her, still unmoved from her station beside the bodies, and apparently unbothered by both their appearance and stench. 'What you said about my people . . . Was that true? Were you manipulating me?'

'What? Gods, no.' Javani wafted a hand before her face in a futile attempt at clearing the air. 'I mean, Ree told me some pretty horrific stories, but she'd be the first to admit that the truth is often somewhere in between.'

'What do you mean?'

'She once called the Mawn "those who fought back", and I guess some of that fighting back might have involved the odd atrocity . . . Doesn't mean your people are, like, inherent murder bastards. If that's what you're worried about.'

'I am not.'

'I mean, it does sound to me like Beralas murdered your clan, then kidnapped you and brought you home as a sort of novelty pet, then raised you as his own private assassin while telling you over and over that your people are despised subhumans capable of nothing but murderous savagery, and for some reason aren't allowed jewellery. But, you know, what would I know. I'm just a breathtaking horse archer trapped in a stinking animal pen with a bunch of festering corpses a few feet away, and I just want to get out, so can I PLEASE have the key?'

She already saw she was wasting her breath. The Mawn was lost in her own world, deaf to her words. Javani considered throwing something, but there was precious little in the pen she wanted to touch, let along pick up and hurl. She was sore, tired and – despite the press of her gorge and the vile smell – very, very hungry. She wanted to go home. She wanted to see Ree, now her great wave of terror had passed, if only to tell her mother that despite her castigations, Javani had done everything right. It wasn't her fault things had gone sideways – who could have predicted this, after all?

'Maral? The key?'

Now the Mawn looked up. 'Pretty things are for pretty people,' she said, and her intonation was not her own – this was something she'd been told, and from the sound of it, more than once.

'Horseshit. Everyone's allowed pretty things.' Heat rose in Javani's cheeks, and she leaned forward at the gate, fingers wrapping the bars. 'Did he tell you you're not pretty? I mean, not right now you're not, sure, you're coated in guts, which is going to be a bastard to accessorise, but I bet you scrub up perfectly, uh . . . I mean, even if you're not beautiful, nor are most people, right? Otherwise nobody would write all that poetry or those godsawful songs, you know, if it was commonplace.' She tried to picture the Mawn without her coating of gore, as she'd first seen her in the gloaming of the farmhouse. 'You know what? You're fine, you're nondescript, which I imagine is ideal in your line of work. But you're not ugly, you're not disgusting, and you're worthy of nice things!'

The Mawn's bloodied face was unconvinced. Some of the blood had dried enough to flake away as she curled her lip. 'I could never be beautiful.'

'That's just a . . . *weird* thing to say.' Javani was getting light-headed from all the shallow breathing. 'You're a bath and a haircut from unremarkable, then it's plain sailing from there.' She leaned her head against the bars. 'Now will you please let me out? It's time we left.'

'We?'

'You gave your word, remember? You're coming back with me. To make yourself useful, then go on your merry way. Maybe Ree will even let you use the bath while you're with us. Gods know you need to clean the worst of that off before we get underway, or you'll bring an army of flies along for the ride. Is there a trough or anything out there?'

'I am not coming with you.'

'The fuck? You very much are.'

The Mawn shook her head. She was still beside the corpses, which seemed to have somehow melded together in a seeping mass. Javani tried to keep her focus on Maral.

'You gave your word!'

Maral couldn't meet her glare. 'And what do you think my word is worth?'

'Well, what do you want it to be worth? You get to choose, dickhead. And you can start by getting me out of this shit-plastered charnel house!'

'I am sorry.' Saddlebags over her shoulder, the Mawn turned towards the door. 'About your mother, too.'

'What about my— Come back here, you f—'

Maral paused, then bent to scoop up the rope from Berant's ruin. She sliced through the loop that wrapped him with her narrow blade, then tossed the blood-sodden remainder towards the gate where Javani stood.

'Don't follow me.'

'Wait! Come back! Come back you miserable, cheating, lying . . . Aaaah shit.'

Javani stared down at the spool of dank rope by her feet. The key still hung from the gate next door. She could probably snare it first time, if she really concentrated.

EIGHTEEN

An hour and a half later, Javani stumbled into daylight and sucked in a huge gulp of clean air. She still felt sick and weak and tired and hungry, but the feeling of the sun on her face, a brilliant red through her gleefully closed eyelids, warmed more than her skin. It warmed her soul.

'Aye, fucken hells, *there* she is!'

Javani opened her eyes. The woman she was fairly sure was the Commodore was striding towards her across a patch of open ground, flushed and sweaty in her riding clothes, her great mound of hair darkened in streaks, plastered to the sides of her face and neck. 'All this your doing was it, you wee slayer?'

Javani looked past the approaching Commodore to take in the scene beyond. The old farm where the slavers had made their camp sat in a rocky elbow, low mudbrick buildings of varying shapes and decrepitude spreading off to either side towards picket walls and a well at its centre, surrounded by a couple of open pens and a corral, their timbers bleached and crumbling. No animals were in sight, bar carrion birds and a drone of buzzing insects which Javani realised she had not, in fact, left behind her.

Corpses were everywhere. She tried to count them: three, four, five, five and a half . . . but there were too many, the sun was too bright and hot, her mouth too dry, her knees going. The Commodore caught her as she toppled, propping her under the elbows and steering her into the shade of the overhanging rock. 'Easy there, young lady, looks like you've had quite the day so far, eh? Have a wee drinkie and catch your breath for a mo.' The Commodore passed her a canteen, then leaned up beside her with amicular proximity. 'Ancestors' danglies, you led us a merry chase. Aye, don't fret, just glad you weren't nestled amongst the dead and dying here, at least. Saved us lugging your carcass back.'

Javani drank, resting her head against the cool red rock, letting the water splash away the foul taste in her mouth, restore her parched throat and lips.

The Commodore wafted a hand over her face. 'Far be it from me to be passing comments concerning the aromas of my fellow travellers, but you have a certain ripeness to your presence that will demand attention before any onward travel may occur.'

'What?'

'You smell like a demon's abattoir. In there long, were you?'

'Yeah.'

'And all this is . . . your work? Or is there someone here we should be making ourselves acquainted with? Perhaps your quarry slash perpetrator?'

Javani reluctantly focused her eyes and looked out over the scene. It didn't seem right to call it a battlefield. That would have implied there had been a battle. Most of the dead still had their weapons sheathed, or stuffed in belts, or barely in hand. All men. All slavers. Maral had systematically murdered every man left in the camp. Despite the heat of the day, Javani shuddered, the canteen rattling in her hand. The Mawn was frightening. She was lethal. How had Javani ever thought she could bring her in alone? She felt cold and sick, and she knew it was not just hunger.

'Not me.' Javani's voice came out weak. Her teeth had started chattering and her head was swimming. 'Anyone else here? In the camp?'

The Commodore took in a long breath through her nose as she shook her head, loose strands of coppery hair flying. 'Looks like a body of them moved out some time earlier today, some mounted, most on foot. Slavers, eh? Took off heading north.'

'One of them . . .' Javani's teeth were really chattering now, '. . . said something about . . . needing to get to Kilale.'

'Oh aye? Well, they've a journey ahead of them, especially at a walk. Anyone you're looking to catch up with?' The Commodore mimed energetic stabbing. 'Could come back and ride them down in a few weeks, no bother.'

The chattering subsided. 'Was that it? Any other tracks?'

'Maybe one other set heading back west, you'd have to ask your pal Sarian.'

'Yeah?' Javani took another swig. 'We'll need to get on that trail right away. Who else is with you?'

The Commodore motioned to a pair of figures Javani had failed to notice, sweeping the derelict buildings on the old farm's far side. 'Friend Sarian has been scouting for us, as aforementioned – you can thank him for picking up your trail so smartly – and those other two work for me: Teg and Stefanna, not my best between us, but I felt I should be contributing some squad-mates, you know, what with . . .'

'What with what?' Javani swallowed again. 'What with what?' She looked around the ravaged farm, brows pinched, the realisation hitting her all at once. 'Where's Ree?'

'Aye, well, couldn't make it. We'll need to be getting back to her, as opposed to likewise.'

'What? Why? Too lazy to come all this way after me? Gods, the fucking nerve—'

'I think it would be in everyone's best interests if we made prompt progress, eh? Once you've had a wee scrub, of course.'

'Ugh, *fine*. But if she couldn't be bothered to—'

'Young lady, your mother is . . . unwell.'

'Unwell? What do you mean, unwell? Unwell how?'

'She was not up to travelling out with us, that's all I know. Left somewhat low by that tussle you interrupted, it seems.'

'What? Horseshit, she barely winged her. No, this is a gambit, a manoeuvre – she just wants me to come running back. Well, not fucking yet. Come on, let's get moving.'

'Aye, will you just— Will you— Yon mount is spoken for, young lady. Yours is that one over there. Grandfather's danglers, you're keen as wossname, eh? And twice as tart.'

Javani shuffled the saddle blanket on her nominated pony with a critical eye, then set about hauling herself onto its back. She was very, very tired, fatigue and hunger hanging off her like anchor-weights, but a fire of impatience burned beneath her ribcage, lending her movements a fierce urgency. 'What are you all waiting around for? We need to get on the trail!'

'Astonished as you may be to hear it, I am well aware of this. Nevertheless, our departure shall be orderly and meticulous, given what has happened to who in this location.'

'What's that supposed to mean?'

'Would you care to shed any more light on the perpetrator of our miniature massacre? The chosen vocation of its victims notwithstanding, this is the work of one person, yes? The same person who came after your mam? Some information pertinent might be well received on our return.'

Javani's fists clenched around the reins. 'Oh, I can do better than that. We're bringing her back with us.' Her gaze settled on where Sarian and the Commodore's riders were stacking the slavers' bodies, and suddenly the doubt was back. How could a person capable of systematically murdering half a dozen armed and armoured slave-takers have struggled to do more than nick Ree's arm? How had she allowed Javani to come so close to capturing her in the hours that had followed?

I am sorry. About your mother, too.

What in hells was going on with that girl?

She'd find out soon enough.

'Let's go. She's got a head-start, but if we ride hard, her sign should be—'

'Young lady—'

'Will you stop fucking calling me that?'

The Commodore's eyebrows rode a fair way up her freckled brow. 'Lacking as we are a full and formal introduction, I will, in the interests of expedience, skip ahead to using your given name, and you in turn may address me as "Madam Commodore" or simply "Boss."'

'I'll call you "obstructive dickhead"—'

'—And perhaps we'll all get along with minimal head-knocks, eh? Now let's hop along to said matter salient: just where in the name of my sweaty, dead ancestors do you think you're off to, you wee pisswipe?'

Javani stared, open-mouthed, reins still tight in her fists. 'After Maral! To catch the Guild's assassin, bring her to justice, make her spill her guts.' For a moment the image of Berant's guts slopping over the animal pen floor filled her mind, and she shuddered, fighting to clear it. 'She can't have got far, there were only mules left after the rest of the slavers moved out. We've got to catch her!'

The Commodore leant heavily on her pony's saddle, looking up at Javani with a mixture of bafflement and disdain. 'Far be it from me to tell others their business, especially those so recently escaped from what looks to have been a pretty dicey predicament, but it might be a step along the path sensible to take a more holistic approach to consideration at this time, if you follow.'

Javani did not. She shook her head, brows pinched, lips pursed.

'Matters stand at suboptimal, young la— Javani. Your mam is unwell, that much I know, but her precise state as we yap is unknown. It's possible that a quick trip to check in on her might offset a potential lifetime of regret and self-recrimination, but I am but a simple daughter of Clyden, and while blessed with both bounteous ancestral wisdom and a hard-nosed sense for the cut and thrust of commercial warfare, I cannot make prognostications regarding the inevitability of your eventual spiral into self-loathing and no doubt pitiful end.'

'Are you . . . threatening me?'

'I am merely suggesting that sometimes – *sometimes* – you might want to think about other people for a change.'

'What's *that* supposed to mean?'

'Girlie, if the meaning of that is lost to you, I pity your education. Not everyone can be blessed with a schooling as rich and purposeful as my own, of course, but, well . . . Put it this way: we are returning.'

'But we can't go back yet. I *won't* go back to her empty-han . . .'

'Won't go back to her what?'

'Nothing.'

'Aye, right. Might be time to pull your head out of your arse, eh? For starters, it'll do wonders for your diction.'

Stinking and ill-tempered as the mule was, it knew it was outmatched. Its seething rider travelled beneath a mantle of flies, and occasionally still dripped. Whenever the mule was tempted to behave much as mules are wont to do, the rider's glowering intensity curbed the urge. Had the mule been observed from distance by a student of its ilk, it would likely have been recorded as exceptionally well-behaved, a paragon of the species. Had it been observed up close, the flickering whites of its eyes and trembling step might have given the game away.

It was not observed, up close or otherwise.

Maral rode, and Maral brooded.

'I cannot believe you are making me let that snake get away!'

The sun was already dipping, the day's heat waning at last. Filthy smoke rose in columns on the horizon at their back as the ruin of the slaver camp burned. Javani was slumped in her saddle, powered at this stage by little more than hardtack and simmering rage.

'I am making you do nothing in particular.' The Commodore's manner remained exasperatingly mild, which was doing nothing to improve Javani's mood. 'And far be it from me to remind you that the last time you went in pursuit of said reptile you ended up captured and awaiting death at the hands of some of the least endearing types to stalk the vastness of the expanse.'

'I escaped!'

'Aye, and how was that accomplished, again?'

'Fuck's sake.'

'Your vocabulary continues to impress. When is it you turn fourteen, again?'

'Why are you being such a dick to me? If you're one of Ree's friends, you should be trying to ingratiate yourself, shouldn't you? Gods, Manatas has been falling over himself to be nice to me.'

'Aye, right, mayhap that's where our confusion lies. I am not a friend of your mother's, Javani. I rode with her, long ago, and we got on much of the time. But I owe her nothing more than diligence, which is a thrice-damned sight less than your good self.'

'Oh by the gods, I am so sick of everyone telling me I should be grateful for a mother who ignores me, berates me, and wants to be rid of me! Is it so hard to understand why I might not be rushing back into her arms?'

'Your concern for her well-being fair moistens the armpit.'

'Well. Yeah. She's been a dick to me as well, though.' Javani hunched her shoulders, ignoring the thousand aches that roamed her body. 'I don't want her to get hurt, I just . . . I just don't want to be around her any more.' She shook her head. 'She's probably fine. It was a tiny scratch, I saw it. After the big argument with that tall woman. Was that really the Swan?'

'Exalted Matil herself, Keeper of Arowan and its splendid environs.'

'Shit. Ree was really arguing with the Swan. Like, to her face.'

'The fancy cloak not tip you off? Or the missing arm?'

Javani shrugged. The movement was harder than it should have been. 'They knew each other? Before?'

'Aye, you could say so. Long, long before. They had some run-ins over the years, the last of them just before the siege.'

Javani perked up, if only a touch. 'The Siege of Arowan? What happened? Ree's mentioned it so many times, in so many words, but she never actually tells me what actually happened!'

'Aye, right, weeell . . .' The Commodore leaned back in the saddle with the practised ease of a seasoned anecdotalist. 'A year or two before you were born, there came to be something of a ruction in the power structures of Vistirlar, that kingdom to the south of Arowan that you lot call "the Sink". Bit of a disagreement between church, monarchy, and everyone else over who should be in charge, and, well, not to put too fine a point on it, harsh words were exchanged, blood was spilled, and it wasn't long before a mighty army was sweeping the nation, converting those inclined towards disagreement into smouldering ash heaps. A small but impeccable band of said disagreers made it as far as the fair city on the gorge – yes, Arowan – only to find said big old army of bastards were hard on their heels.'

'That was what the siege was about? Wait, was Ree one of the disagreers?'

'Aye, well, you know your mam – naturally inclined towards disagreement, wouldn't you say? Anyway, after a brief encounter with Exalted Matil, she buggered off before the siege began, and I'm guessing that was the last time she came anywhere near the place.'

'But . . . but how did she know the Swan before that? It sounded like, you know, they *really* knew each other. Were they friends?'

'Ah, that's a story she'd best tell you herself – I'm not one for exposing others' intimates. I'll tell you one thing, though: they were not friends.'

'She'd better be all right, then,' Javani muttered. 'She owes me one good story. Although not too well,' she went on, 'as this whole ride feels enough of a waste of time as it is. I bet Ree's fine, all hale and hearty and sour and bitter. I had her, you know. Maral – the assassin. The first time. Tracked her, isolated her, brought her down – had her all trussed up when those slavers arrived. It's not too late, we've gone so slowly we could just turn the horses around, it's not like Ree will even want to see me—'

'Ancestors' tits, you're just like her, aren't you? It's like riding with a wee fairground version, gabbing away.'

'What? How?'

'You don't listen because you think you're already right. Doesn't matter what anyone says, no matter how convincing the argument, you just talk yourself right back round to your rightness.'

'I do not!'

'Oh aye? And what have you been pissing in my ear about for the duration of our travels so far?'

'That's different! You said yourself we don't know if she's really unwell, and you were right, I was planning on travelling my own path. She doesn't want to see me again, I'm just . . . in her way.'

The Commodore was quiet for a moment, swaying with her pony's steady gait, drifting from side to side in the saddle, her hair always half a sway behind. 'Do you understand,' the Commodore said quietly, her voice barely audible over the sound of hoofs and tack, 'quite how many of those closest to her your mother has seen die over the years?'

'Uh, well, I know—'

'Can you imagine,' the Commodore went on, in a stronger voice, right over Javani, 'why a life like hers might make her a little twitchy around the welfare of her only child, who displays a staggering streak of recklessness and will not, under any circumstances, hear the word "no"?'

'That isn't fair, I—'

'You are mistaking love for punishment! For the love of all that is holy, will you stop fighting with your mam over every wretched thing and talk to her as an equal?'

Javani threw up her hands, reins loose. 'I've been trying! Did talking to her as an equal ever work for you?'

'This isn't about what may or may not have been a fucken disaster for me.' The Commodore softened her voice again. 'But she loves you, girlie, and she wants you safe, and your mam being your mam, she is fucken dreadful at showing it.'

'Fine. I'll talk to her again, I guess. One more time.'

NINETEEN

Their path cut north, away from the city and its sprawling outskirts, and Javani stirred from her saddle-trance.

'We're not going back to Aki's Rest?'

'Matters have overtaken us somewhat. The part where the Guild sent someone to kill your mam in the middle of a secret meeting somewhat robbed it of its mystical allure. Well, that and the fracas in the downstairs. We'll be convening outside the township, in the interests of prudence.'

Prudence. That made Javani think of Ree, and the supervision of her childhood. She couldn't say exactly when the feeling of being watched over in her youth had become claustrophobic – less care than constriction – but by the time they'd reached Kazeraz in mining country, Javani was already firmly of the opinion that she was old enough and tough enough to embark on her adventures without the need for constant surveillance, which in turn, of course, had only made Ree's lectures on the necessity of prudence all the more frequent, and, inevitably, pointed. After a while, Javani had simply stopped listening, the words so familiar as to be meaningless. They washed over her while she thought of other things, considered her gambits, plotted small insurrections.

She'd never really left that mode. Even when the hunters came to Kazeraz, and Javani learned that Ree had been far from prudent herself in the years before; even when they'd fled west into the Ashadi mountains and stumbled across the village of Ar Ramas and its mercenary problem . . . Prudence had taken on a new significance, but in spite of the real and obvious dangers that appeared to dog them at every turn, Javani's faith in her own abilities, her growth in stature in all senses . . . once more, the urgency of Ree's admonitions had dulled.

Chasing after the Mawn had been no different. Javani had known she could track her and capture her, and she'd done just that, despite Ree's barking at her departure. And if it hadn't been for those slavers turning up when they did—

You never think about what might go wrong.

You might want to think about other people for a change.

That had stung. Her immediate reaction was denial. She thought of other people all the time – she was only pursuing the Mawn for the benefit of the wider rebellion, of course. Of course. And she'd planned for a mishap, left a trail of her own wide and obvious enough to ensure that those who followed would track her straight to wherever she'd cornered her quarry. Only they hadn't turned up in time, and the slavers had. That was hardly her fault, was it?

The silence on the ride back towards Arowan's outskirts was oppressive, heavy as the thick air that surrounded them. They were due a thunderstorm, the shrill chorus of insects in the fields around them rising with the pressure. The silent hours left her with too much time to think, to ponder, to dwell. Why had she gone after the Mawn, after all? Why had she believed herself capable of apprehending a professional assassin on her own?

Because Ree had forbidden it, and Javani wouldn't take no for answer. It had been a *fuck you* to her mother, a *stick your prudence up your arse*. She'd been going to prove Ree wrong, once and for all – Javani was a baby no more, and not only could she contribute, she could tip the scales. Prove her wrong for shoving her away, keeping her out of things, treating her like an embarrassment, a millstone. I exist, she'd wanted to shout. I exist, and you can't ignore me. I only exist because of you, I'm your fault, and I'm . . . I'm better than you!

Except . . .

Except.

Maral could very easily have killed her. That was inescapable now. It had taken all of a few moments of cogitation to realise that if

Maral hadn't seemed so . . . amused . . . by her attempts at capture, she'd have cut Javani open as she had the man in the pens and left her to die with her guts around her neck, or something else equally horrible. She'd been furious when she'd worked over Berant, simmering with cold rage when she'd marched out into the camp and butchered the rest, but when she'd tussled with Javani, she'd been . . . smiling.

Javani shook her head. This wasn't about the Mawn, not personally, but what she'd represented. Ree had ordered Javani not to pursue, and Javani had known better.

You don't listen because you think you're already right.

Maral could have killed her. The slavers could have done likewise, or had the timing been different, she'd have been herded off with the rest of the unfortunates across the plains towards Kilale Port. Why Kilale Port? she wondered, suddenly struck by the notion. Slavery was outlawed across the protectorate, but the Guild turned a blind eye where they chose to in the north-western reaches. Kilale was on the east coast, a long way north, on the very fringes of mining country. What kind of market was there for flesh up there?

She shook her head again, eyes clenched. She was too tired to keep her thoughts straight. She'd been on the edge of something then, before she'd drifted, some kind of conclusion. It was still in there, at the edge of her mental reach.

Ree had told her not to go, to be prudent. Javani had gone. And now she was coming back. Empty-handed. It was Ree who was injured, not her, bar a few bruises. But maybe, just maybe . . .

You are mistaking love for punishment.

Maybe she should have stayed.

'You still with us, Slayer? We'll be rendezvousing yonder, at the wee canyon. Might want to, you know, gird yourself.'

'Hm? What do you mean?'

'Seeing as we're somewhat incognisant, vis-à-vis your mam's health, perhaps consider it a notion of merit to prepare yourself for the darkest of potential outcomes, and we can keep our parts crossed for a pleasant surprise, eh?'

'Yeah, fine. I'm prepared.'

They rode into the canyon.
She was not prepared.

It was seeing Anashe that did it, before Javani even saw the tilted cart and its occupant. It was the look on Anashe's face when she saw Javani riding up, the way her normally stoic, expressionless features crumpled, the compassion and heartache in her shining eyes. It hit her like a fist to the gut, almost doubling her over in the saddle, because in that moment she knew that her mother was dead.

Every hair on her body stood on end, a terrible cold spreading outwards through her, making her shake and shiver. Her hands trembled, the reins numb in her hands, and she couldn't think how to get herself down from the saddle to the ground. She couldn't ask for help, couldn't form words, her lips beyond control, her tongue too big for her mouth.

Then the White Spear was beside her, leading her pony, offering a giant hand, and Javani let herself fall into the woman's arms. She wasn't yet able to cry, able to do more than lean against the strapping Horvaun, who was oddly soft without her armour, the fibres of her coat rubbing Javani's cheek. Distantly, she heard the Commodore dismount as Sarian and her agents rode in behind them, heard the Clyde swagger towards where Anashe stood looking bereft.

'Aye, right, what's the gas? How bad?'

Anashe took a long, sharp breath. 'She is alive. But I cannot say for how much longer. She is fighting.'

'Right. Fuck.'

Javani pushed herself back from the accommodating bosom of the White Spear. Words were no longer an impossibility. 'She's still alive?'

'Aye, not so sure about the "still" in there, young lady.'

Anashe held her gaze, her eyes brimming with sympathy. 'Ree is gravely ill. Whatever was on the blade has worked its way to her heart. She may . . . she may not wake again.'

'What? It was poisoned?'

'Aye, well, on the matter technical, it's poison for something ingested, whereas what we're talking here is v—'

'*But she's still alive?*'

A note of puzzlement marred the benevolence of Anashe's gaze. 'Yes. For now.'

'I want to see her.'

'I must warn you, her state is—'

'She's in the cart, isn't she?'

'Yes.'

Javani strode, boots light across the ground, giddy with fatigue and emotional countercurrents. The cart was two-wheeled and tilted on its axle, traces empty, parked beneath the shade of the looming red-rock wall and the spreading branches of a silvered olive tree.

The figure in the cart-bed lay piled on pallets and cushions, strapped beneath taut sheets darkened with sweat. Javani stared, mouth dry, at the ruin of her mother, the cadaver-to-be of the woman who'd raised her, her emotions swirling like rags in a gale, the flare of guilty relief fading like dusk, while beneath her yawned a void of terror and uncertainty. Her jaw was trembling, her fingers still numb, and her chest was tight, too tight. Tears pressed unbearably at her eyes.

No.

She clenched her fists, stilling their quiver, forcing feeling back into her fingertips.

No. She would not be overwhelmed. She refused.

How dare Ree make her feel like this.

'Look what . . . look what you did to yourself,' she whispered. 'I could have been in the room with you. If you hadn't . . . if you hadn't *got* at me like that. I'd have been there. We could have fought her off together, properly. I almost had her by myself. Then I was ordered back again before I could catch her a second time, so we can't even . . .'

Javani's cheeks sizzled, her fingernails digging into her palms, stomach locked tight. She cast a look back over her shoulder to where the rest of the group gathered in the canyon's shade, their faces drawn, eyes hollow with concern. At least nobody was listening.

Ree shifted on the cart, let out a small moan. Her skin shone with sweat, the lines in her face taut and deep. Somehow, lying down like this, she seemed so much smaller. It infuriated Javani.

The crunch of Anashe's footsteps on the scree of the canyon floor put a lid on her emotions, if only temporarily.

'It was not safe to remain at Aki's Rest,' Anashe said at her shoulder, seemingly for want of something. Javani knew as much already, and tried not to snap.

'How do we heal her? Is there an antidote?'

'We do not know what was on the blade. We cannot take the risk that any treatment makes it worse.'

The rage bubbling inside Javani pressed against the back of her teeth. 'If I'd been *allowed* to go after that Mawn again, we could have made her tell us.' She took a long and shuddering breath. 'What can we do, then?'

Anashe's voice was weighted with exasperating pity. 'She may have to fight it off herself. Your mother is tough. She can do it.'

'Yeah. Too tough by half.'

A whistle sounded from overhead, then a rain of loose scree indicated Anri's imminent arrival, sliding down one of the shallower slopes towards them.

'Visitors,' he called as he reached the dusty floor. 'Looks like some familiar faces.'

'What? Who?'

Anri ignored Javani, addressing Anashe with the tip of his bow. 'Your drummer pal's with them, she is. Leading them up the trail, no less.'

'What, Sefi?'

Anri's expression darkened. 'She supposed to know where we are?'

'I told her only that—'

'Oh, cracking approach to secrecy, that is. Who else did you share our confidential location with? Anyone who might bring me up a pie?'

Javani put out a hand. Her anger was gone, and in its place was nothing. She felt hollow, numb, her fingers barely her own as they rested on Anri's arm.

'Anri, enough. Who's coming?'

'The good captain, isn't it. Him and the big lad, and a bunch of horses.'

Javani's brows flexed in confusion. 'What are they doing here? They're supposed to be with the main body . . . What in hells is going on?'

He shrugged with his mouth, silvered bristles flexing. 'Dunno, do I. Whatever it is, though, not likely to be good, is it?'

Anashe pulled herself up straight, and turned towards the canyon entrance. 'I will meet Sefi. I'm sure she has good reasons.' She gave Anri a pointed look as she set off.

'Ask her where my pie is, won't you,' he called after her.

'Anri.' Javani's hand was still on his arm.

He looked down at her at last. 'You're back then.'

'Yeah. Almost had caught the . . .' She gestured to the cart. 'Perpetrator.'

'Almost, eh? Well, that's almost useful then, isn't it.' When she didn't reply, his tone softened a touch. 'Sorry about your mam, like.'

'Yeah. Thanks.'

'Least she's not going to be feeding me my sack for letting you run off any time soon, eh?'

'*Anri—*'

'You'll be wanting to give her broth, mostly. Wash her every day, especially when she's sweating like this, and keep her moving around. Don't want bedsores, do we. She's moving herself at the moment, but she'll weaken, especially if she's not looked after.' He caught Javani's look. 'What? Had some experience of minding the immobile, haven't I.'

'I guess you . . . yeah. Thanks, Anri.'

'Right, off you piss, then. I'm back up to my perch.'

He scrabbled away. Javani gave Ree another long, ambivalent look. She couldn't shake the anger, not all of it, but beneath it was something else, something scared and shameful, and she was not ready to delve into it yet. She shook her shoulders, clenched and unclenched her fists and let out a sharp breath through her nose. Was Manatas really on his way up? She looked back at her mother. Gods, what was she going to tell him? The man worshipped Ree in his every act; this could break him. That and the fact that the fate of the rebellion and the fight against the Guild now likely rode on his shoulders. She did not envy him that.

She took another long breath and started walking back towards the horses. She needed to break the news, right away, then she could go back to working out her own feelings on the matter. Best to be direct, no sugar-coating it. *Captain, Ree is dying.* No, too much at once – and hopefully wrong. *Captain, Ree has been poisoned.* Too many immediate questions. Perhaps just set the mood, get him prepared: *Captain, something terrible has happened.* Then she could go into detail.

She rehearsed it in her head as she walked, all at once feeling the effects of her overnight trek, battles, confinement and ride. She needed to sleep. She needed to know Ree would be all right, then she could sleep. Ree had to be all right. She'd fight it. She'd fight anything. And then Javani could tell her what a fucking idiot she'd been.

Something terrible has happened.

Something terrible has happened.

Hoof-beats and a whinny raised her gaze to the canyon-mouth. There was Manatas, looking every bit as filthy and exhausted as Javani felt herself. He slid from his mount and looked around, his eyes locking straight onto Javani, then approached her with swift bandy-legged strides.

This is it. Be direct. Don't make it worse than it needs to be.

As he reached her, he put his hands on her shoulders and met her gaze with agony in his eyes.

'Javani,' he breathed, 'where is Ree? Something terrible has happened.'

TWENTY

It was well into the evening before each had the full story, and Javani was struggling to stay awake, hunched as she was beneath a blanket close to the fire. Behind her, lost in the dancing shadows, Tauras tended to the unconscious Ree, mopping her brow, soothing her contortions. Javani was long past being disconcerted by the hulking mercenary's tenderness, and even the notion of Ree as an invalid had become normal. No, not normal, just . . . no longer shocking. No longer wrong.

Manatas sat close by, and to Javani's tired eyes the man was struggling to keep himself together. It was only the urgency of their collective discussion that kept him there. She watched him for a moment, deaf to his words, seeing anew the strain of the ride, of the news, of everything. He looked older than she remembered, the silver in his stubble gleaming in the firelight, the swathes of hair at his temples glowing likewise. He looked as tired as she felt, but she'd at least had a little longer to digest what had happened.

'It was coordinated, then,' said Anashe. Considering the specialist had had no formal role in the rebellion until Ree and Javani's descent upon her place of business, she'd acquired a rapid grasp of the situation. 'The attempt on Ree, and the attack on the camp, within a day of each other.'

Manatas sighed and ran one hand through his hair, sending up a drift of trail-dust, shining in the firelight. 'The evidence of our united telling would appear to lend itself squarely to that interpretation. In truth, had we not already been preparing to move out, it's possible our entire force could have been extinguished. Those that came at us were not looking to negotiate.'

For a moment, Javani felt a sliver of warmth, a comforting thrill that it had been her gambit on the *Illustrious Den* that had triggered Ree's overreaction, and the subsequent preparations to move. Then she remembered her feeling beneath the rock tower when she'd shot the three pursuers. That feeling of being watched. What if Ree had been right? What if she was the one who'd led the Guild right back to their camp?

She swallowed. What if she was the one who'd led Maral straight to Ree?

'Straighten this for me, bonny lad, for I am but a simple daughter of Clyde.' The Commodore stirred the fire with a long stick. She'd regularly offered swigs from something in a flask that smelled of burning to those around the fire, and nobody had yet taken her up on the offer. 'The Guild came at your encampment in numbers, but you were already half fled?'

He nodded. 'The camp was already struck, the bulk of our force in train. When the attack came, we scattered as planned, and our overall losses were few.'

'That why you pitched up here with so many horses between you?'

'Four to each rider.' The captain met Javani's eye for a moment. 'Plus spares. We planned ahead.'

'Aye, right, all's well and good with the rapid dissemination in the face of incipient violence, sure. But what's the state of your fighting forces and your raiding parties now? Lines of communication and whatnot?'

Manatas sighed again. He seemed to be doing a lot of sighing. 'We have our protocols, of course.'

'Of course.'

'But the truth is, I am . . . unfamiliar with many of the precise details of implementation.'

Javani stirred. 'Wait, what are you saying?'

He didn't look up, his gaze lost in the flames. 'That our forces have scattered and gone to ground, and I do not know how to find them.'

'Who does?'

He lifted his gaze a fraction, just enough to look over her shoulder. In the darkness, where Ree lay, sweating and moaning and possibly gasping her last.

'Nine fucking hells,' Javani growled. 'Did she write it all down anywhere?'

He frowned. 'That would not have been, uh, prudent.'

'It's all in her head? That head over there?'

'Not everything, of that I am sure. We brought with us what records we could, but when the attack came, there was little warning. You understand this, Javani.'

'Yeah. Sure.' She stifled a yawn. 'So what do we do?'

His gaze dropped again. 'In circumstances such as these, I cannot rightly say. We had made precautions, contingencies, but they were, uh, somewhat ill-defined.'

Javani cast a look back over her shoulder. 'In her head again?'

'Indeed.'

The Commodore shifted on the bleached trunk she sat on, took a swig from her flask, tried to burp, produced nothing, and tutted. 'Aye, well, bollocks. This here assailant, the one you chased hither and yon, Slayer. How long was she in the chamber with your mam? How much of the audience with she-who-should-not-be-named did she hear?'

'I don't know. She can't have been there long – she'd have gone for the Swan otherwise, right?' Javani yawned again, and this one got through. Her head was getting really heavy. 'I think she heard me and Ree arguing.'

'Oh aye? How so?'

'Something she said. She was weird. Mawn, but raised in captivity. Basically a pet of Chairman Beralas.'

'Careful now, that's an ugly thing to say about a person, especially someone of plains history. Even if they are a nasty wee stabber.'

'What if it's true, though? I guarantee you, he murdered her clan and took her home as a prize, then raised her to be his in-house killer. Playing up a bunch of slanted Mawn mythology.'

'If you say so.'

'Anyway, she seemed almost apologetic about it. But I still couldn't convince her to come back with me.'

Anashe snorted. Sefi was asleep on the ground somewhere behind her, wrapped in all their blankets, producing the occasional snuffling snore. 'Why in the name of the Goddess would you want to bring her back with you? To finish the rest of us off?'

'No!' Javani's cheeks were hot again. 'To face justice. To—' She almost said 'spill her guts' again, but the image of Berant came rushing out of memory, and she shut her eyes tight. '—tell us everything she knew.'

Manatas tilted his head. 'You thought this a possibility? The tame killer of our enemy would turn on him and reveal his confidences?'

Javani swallowed, her shoulders rising. She was not enjoying the attention of the entire campfire. 'I can be persuasive. You know me.'

Manatas nodded. Of all of them, he did not seem sceptical. 'I do indeed.'

Silence descended, but for the crackle of tinder-dry wood and the hoots and screeches of the wild night. Javani longed to lie back and let her body sink to the earth, to stare up at the stars that swirled above in their brilliant billions, and let sleep claim her. She would sleep for days, and when she woke, Ree would be better. She would get better. She would.

A choked sob snapped her out of it.

'Captain Manatas?' She reached out a gentle hand and placed it on his shoulder. His fist was crammed against his mouth, tears running free down his cheeks, golden tracks in the firelight. 'Are you all right?'

'Forgive me,' he croaked, his words halting, his breath shudders. 'I should not burden you all, when there is so much else to do. It will pass.' The shake of his shoulders began to subside beneath her hand, but tears still flowed. He wiped at his eyes and blew his nose with a handkerchief that might once have been white. 'I have faced the like of this before, and I will not lose hope, I will not flounder, nor expect it of others. She would want us to proceed, to progress.'

'Aye, well, that's grand and all, but at what, precisely?'

Javani felt her heart sinking down through her ribs and into her gut, her rage at her mother now cooled, ossified, in stone. Nobody knows what to do, she realised. Ree's been ordering everyone around for so long that now she's unconscious, they're just milling. See what you did to them, Ree? she carped in her head. You never delegated, never shared anything, and now everything's going to fall apart. There's no rebellion without you. Manatas can barely hold himself together, let alone anyone or anything else. *How could you let this happen?*

'Anyone?' the Commodore went on, after an uncomfortable pause. 'I mean, while I'm sure we have no shortage of scintillating stratagems between us, whatever our General hashed out with she-who-must-not-be-named, neither one is currently in a position to enlighten us, and I very much doubt the latter would appreciate being approached for clarification. And while I was on hand to ensure said meeting was an eventual triumph – subsequent assassination attempts notwithstanding – I was not privy to the meat of their conclusions. Only two people know what they agreed, and neither's talking to us any time soon.'

Javani's inner monologue came to a crunching halt, and she sat up, momentarily banishing somnolence. 'Wait. Wait, that's not true.'

'Oh aye, reckon we'll be getting some chat from our principals in the nearsome?'

Javani shook her head, her mouth set in something that was not a smile of triumph, but nor was it entirely without satisfaction.

'I know what they said.'

Manatas was watching her closely, the lines in his face cast black by the firelight. Anashe sat back, reserved, uncertain, while the Commodore regarded her with open scepticism. 'Aye, right, you heard all these machinations through the keyhole, did you?'

'I'm telling you, that's what they agreed.'

Manatas's eyes were little more than dark lines in the half-light. 'If it please you, kindly indulge me with a retelling, for in my state of enervation I fear there lurk niceties that escape me.'

Javani sighed and shifted. Her fatigue had receded in the face of a burst of nervous energy, but she knew it would not last. She wished Anri was at the fire to back her up, instead of up on the ridge. Then she considered what he'd likely contribute, and decided perhaps that she'd been spared after all. 'The Guild needs to renew its charter, right? The thing that gives its badge-toting bastards the right to bollocks around making everyone else miserable. The original fifteen years is up, or whatever it was, so they're looking to get it renewed. That gets voted on by the windbags in the Arowani senate, then it gets stamped into law, with the Great Seal of Arowan.'

'And it's aforesaid seal that they have in their possession?'

'It is. And we're going to steal it. Publicly.'

Anashe had leaned a fraction forward, the sharp angles of her body inclined by a few degrees. 'In my experience, when retrieving items of value from those who should not have them, it is considered good practice to draw minimal attention to the act.'

Javani waved a hand, her head shaking in echo. 'No, see, that's the whole point. We don't need the seal, we just need everyone else to know they don't have it. Without the seal, they can't complete the renewal of their charter, and when the old one expires it's open season on their operations. Anyone can mine, anyone can trade, the townships won't have to kick back to them, all the good stuff.'

Manatas rasped a hand over his chin. 'How confident would you describe your apprehension of the legal particulars to be, in this instance?'

The Commodore puffed out her cheeks. 'Aye, say one thing for Slayer here, she's not wrong on this. No seal, no charter; no charter, friend Guild and all who sail in her begin to look mighty precarious. No shortage of those with ironware to grind in their direction, after all, and a lot of folk up and down that particular food chain are going to start looking lateral come the expiration of the old aegis.'

Manatas glanced at Javani. 'What did she say?'

'Now you know what it's like,' Javani replied tartly. Then she felt guilty, with her mother fighting for life but a few strides away. Then she felt angry for feeling guilty, her fists clenching around the blanket's edge.

Manatas must have caught the canter of emotions across her expression. 'Javani,' he said, kindness and pain in his eyes. For a moment she'd forgotten that he, too, cared for Ree; if anything, right now, he cared more about Ree's state than she did. She chided herself for her callous thought, but part of her secretly held it was right. 'It has been a long day. Perhaps we will be better able to discuss these matters after a restful night?'

'I'm not sure I can sleep at the moment,' she replied honestly. The exhaustion was at bay for now, even if her emotional regulation was at a low ebb, and she had more to say. 'I need to know you're all with me on this.'

Anashe's chin lifted. 'On what?'

'On stealing the Great Seal from the Guild. Soon.'

The Commodore took another swig from her flask. 'Now, don't get the wrong end of my wossname on this, I'm all in favour of depriving the diggers of their ornaments and perquisites ... but, you know, in terms practical, how does one go about lifting an item one has never seen, has no location for, and no information about in general? I mean, what if they're keeping it in a vault under a fortress somewhere, surrounded by a thousand Goldhelms and, you know, a fucken dragon or somesuch?' She burped, looked surprised, then pleased. ''Scuse me.'

Javani was shaking her head again, memories of Ree's meeting with the Swan rushing back. *They move it around. It travels with their functionaries. We've never been able to pin it down. But they'll have to bring it into the open for the renewal.* 'It travels around with their parchment-pushers, their auditors and notaries ... but they're going to want it present for the big renewal, which means it's going to be moving towards wherever they're planning to hold their grand renewal party.'

Anashe was another couple of degrees further forward. 'Where will that be? Arowan?'

The Commodore threw up a hand, her head shaking, the mountain of hair waving like a briar in a squall. 'Aye, no chance, too crowded for pomp and very much on the doorstep of their political foes, which might be considered a touch indelicate, even for the diggers.'

Manatas had something like hope in his eyes, but it was a cautious, fragile thing. 'Where, then? At one of their estates, one of the grander Guildhouses somewhere?'

The Commodore scratched at her head, although it was too dark to see if anything drifted out of it. 'Aye, right, could be, I guess, but I feel it lacks what they call in Tenailen a certain "I don't know what".' She sniffed, noisily, pulled her mouth to one side in contemplation. 'What we could really use is a set of travel itineraries, see where the bastards are heading at the end of the month.'

Revelation struck Javani like a gong. 'Anri . . . Anri!' She whistled, badly. 'Captain, can you whistle for Anri for me?'

He gave her a studied look, then nodded, put two fingers to his mouth and issued a fearsome note. Anri arrived shortly afterwards in an ill-tempered cloud of rock dust.

'Lonely, are you? You'd better have something to eat down here, all that racket fair gave my guts a shock, could be all sorts in my stockings by now.'

Javani sailed past it, near delirious with excitement and fatigue. 'Anri, that ledger we took from the boat. Do you still have it?'

His eyes narrowed, gummy mouth sucked tight. 'Whyyy?'

'Schedules and rotas,' Javani intoned. 'Just bureaucrats and functionaries sashaying between outposts.'

'Come again?'

'That's what's in the ledger. That's what Ree said was in the ledger.' She jabbed a wild finger in the direction of her unconscious mother. 'We know their travel plans for the next month. More. We know where they're all going.'

'And that's important now then, is it?'

'Have you got the bastard or not?'

He snorted. 'Course I have. No need to tangle your underparts.' He paused, one hand to his satchel. 'And this is important because . . . ?'

'Anri!'

He produced the ledger. 'One of these days, pest, you and me are going to have a falling out.'

She was already deaf to him, thumbing through pages, trying to make sense of what was written within, squinting in the flickering light of the fire. 'Let's see . . . The last place we know it appeared for certain was here . . . since then, it could have crossed paths with any of . . . these *five* people, hmm, currently spread across the expanse . . .' The entries got thinner towards the end, but one symbol appeared with emphatic consistency, and she almost shrieked when she found an entry that referenced it.

'They're going . . . they're all going via . . .' She looked up at the faces surrounding her, glowing in the firelight, expectant, hopeful, trepidatious, or in Anri's case, belligerent with confusion.

'. . . the Iron Road.'

'Fuck's that, then?' said Anri.

Anashe was almost folded forwards. 'I have heard of this Iron Road. Something new, in the north?'

'Aye, right,' added the Commodore, tossing her head. Her flask appeared to be empty, an evidently unsatisfactory state of affairs. 'There's been talk of big building across the plains, grand diversion of funds which meant a greater squeeze elsewhere.'

'It's a road, then, is it?' Anri did not sound impressed. 'Sparse on the ground, them.'

'It's . . .' Javani racked her brain, trawling her memory for the snatches of conversation she'd overheard. 'They're going to use it to move ore and stuff, straight from the mines, across the plains to a port. To sell it to someone. The Swan seemed pretty furious about that part.'

'So it's a road . . . for iron ore . . . is it? A road for iron.'

'Yeah, right. That's what it is.' Javani scratched at her head. It didn't seem so momentous said out loud.

'Which port, then?'

'Huh?'

'Which port does it go to? Starts in the mountains, goes all the way to the port, you said. But which port? There's a bunch of them up there, there is.'

'Oh.' She swallowed, leafing back through the journal. 'It doesn't say exactly, but I reckon if we—'

'Kilale.' The Commodore was still trying to shake the last of the drops from her flask. 'That's where the road ends, so goes the word. If you're inclined to listen to the grander end of the whispers, they've turned that place from a fishing village to a teeming metropolis in the space of a couple of years, although by my reckoning that's a load of old goat cock.'

'Kilale?' Javani blinked. 'That's where the slavers were trying to get to. And in a hurry.'

Manatas was watching her, his gaze intent. 'You believe these details to be connected?'

'I don't know. But it feels like they should be.'

The Commodore hiccuped. 'Aye, well, 'scuse me, stands to reason if the diggers have spent a god's fortune tarting up Kilale to some semblance of international splendour, they might be planning on holding their grand recertification amongst the trappings of their glory, eh?'

'You think they're all going to meet at Kilale? With the slavers?'

'Aye, no, I don't reckon our friends the Brotherhood will be guests of honour at the grand shindig or whatnot, but if there's a spirited opportunity for commerce with traders from far shores, stands to reason that others might have caught a whisper, and be planning some grand trades of their own.'

'The people buying the ore will also buy slaves?'

The Commodore shrugged. 'Aye, maybe, who's to say, eh? Come for the rocks, get a two-for-one on a brutalised human or two.' She turned and spat into the darkness. 'Point is, if you know where everyone is going, when they're getting there, and the route they're travelling . . .' She waggled her eyebrows.

'We can intercept them,' Javani breathed.

'Bang on, three silvers for Slayer. As a reward, you can get me another drink.'

'Piss off, get your own drink.'

The Commodore affected a look of great hurt. 'After I broke the back of these ruminations and laid out the course, all by my lonesome? What thanks is that, I ask?'

Javani ignored her. Anri chuckled twice, then turned. 'Can I go now? No bugger's watching the road at the moment, and I left the remains of my dinner up there. Sort all this out by yourselves, won't you, eh?'

Javani waved him away. Anashe was watching her, brows low, mouth narrow and tight.

'Anashe, you don't look convinced about the plan.'

The specialist shifted, unfolding and refolding her limbs. Behind her, Sefi snored on. 'I am,' she said slowly, 'unclear as to what might be called a plan.'

Javani frowned. 'Weren't you listening? We know they'll be moving the Great Seal down this iron road in advance of the big ceremony at Kilale Port. So we head north, set up to watch the road, and swoop on the next Guild type who comes past. The notaries only have a couple of guards each, we can take them as we are.'

Anashe's brows lowered further, deep lines shining from her forehead in the firelight. 'This is what I mean. What you have described is not a plan. It is barely even a notion. Even my brother would have hesitated to call it a plan.'

'That's a low blow.'

Her expression softened a mite. 'I apologise. But you must see that what you are describing is no kind of operation.'

Manatas coughed beside her, rubbed a hand through his hair. 'Pained as I am to seem to be doubling up in counter to your hypothesis, I too am laboured by concern. We know nothing of this road or who travels on it, the timing is uncertain, and the precise carrier of the object we seek is likewise uncertain.' He shook his head with a sigh. 'I am sorry, Javani, but I fear without your mother to act in her executive capacity, we are once again facing—'

Javani's cheeks were burning, her pulse thudding in her ears. The rage flared suddenly, and she could not, would not contain it. 'Get your heads out of your arses, will you? We don't need her! She's been bossing you all around for so long you've forgotten how to think for yourselves. So we don't know enough to make something that's an official plan yet. So what? Let's . . . let's . . . let's find out what we need. Let's mount up, ride north and east, sniff out what we need to know. If this road is as big a thing as everyone seems to think, it should be easy to find someone who knows where it goes. We can work the rest out from there.'

Manatas looked stunned, Anashe wide-eyed and wide-nostriled. 'Uh, Javani,' Manatas began, 'your mother is in no fit state to cross the plains at speed.'

'Then we leave her the fuck behind,' Javani hissed. 'It's what she'd do. Don't look at me like that, you know I'm right. What would she want, eh? If we could ask her, what would she want? Would she want us all cooing around her sickbed, mewling and weeping, or would she want us riding across the plains and putting the Guild in the earth? Well?'

She stood, shaking out her blanket. 'You know I'm right. And

I'm going to bed. We leave in the morning. If she wakes, she can come too.'

Javani turned her back to the fire and lay down in the blanket, and waited to hear their retorts. There came only silence.

Darkness surrounds her, and there is poison in her body. She cannot wake, she cannot speak, she can do little but lie, and sweat, and, little by little, die. Her thoughts are scattered and vague, shot through with panic and urgency.

She dreams, and with the dreams come memories. Her body has known poison before. Her veins have coursed with it, and she has lain at the brink of death and looked over the edge. She remembers now. She remembers the feeling, the agony, the terror, the sorrow . . . but above it all, the relief.

Rai has lived barely seventeen years, and she is dying. In years to come, she will forget her precise age at this moment, will allow time to fudge memory and spans to distort. She will tell herself she was younger, that she endured for longer, that she suffered for years, and almost from infancy. In truth, the duration was unimportant; whether years, months or days; what she has endured has left her forever changed.

She knows she was not the first, but the relief that lifts her head upon the sweat-black pillow is born from the knowledge that she will be the last.

She knows this from her snatches of wakefulness; from the bells that toll distantly through the thick, yellow stone of the upper palace, from the mourning white of those who attend her, the changed hangings in the plain little room in which she lies. The palace is in a hush, murmured conversations and downcast eyes, and even at the edge of delirium she understands why, that she has succeeded.

She knows that down the marbled hallway, through the great double doors at the end, a man is dead, and she has killed him. She knows that the new life is gone from within her, and in time she will believe nothing will ever come in its place. She had expected to take three lives, but somehow she clings on, and with that awareness comes certainty. She knows she's stronger than he was, and Rai has chosen to live.

She has begun to imagine a life without fear. Live or die, the victory is hers, but victory is no longer enough. Now she thinks of escape. Escape, freedom and rage: rage at the man who kept her caged and cowed, for whom she was but ornamentation and poseable meat; rage at the Exalted mother who enabled and indulged him, the vile sister who saw exactly what he was and still did nothing; rage at the city, for elevating and preserving such putrescence at its heart; and rage at her parents, whose schemes and designs saw her hawked and sold, dangled like bait, traded as market goods. She never heard what they got from the deal – she has seen and heard nothing from her family in months, and now she has no wish to. What is there to say, after all?

The dream shifts, scatters and reforms, and with it, the trail of memory. She rises from the bed, takes up the sword, strides from the city. The sword: the only gift of his she retains, aside from the scar. He'd not kept the smirk from his face at its presentation, no matter his original intention. A sword. A sword of beauty, of refinement, of artistry, but a sword nonetheless. She knew it was meant as an insult, as a cruel joke, despite its extraordinary value. But she didn't care. She was captivated by it. So light, so balanced, so very, very sharp. She dreamed of killing him with it. But in the end, she was far more elegant, and far more comprehensive.

She is astonished to meet no punishment for her extraordinary crime, beyond what she has already suffered. She is afforded a chance to slip away, to fade into myth, because the throne of Arowan is unwilling to risk the embarrassment of inquiry. She takes little with her, bar the sword, and the scar, its crude stitching always an afterthought. Already her hair is white at the root.

She turns her back on the rotten city and all within it, and vows she will never return. Her future is her own; he can't hold her back any more. No one can.

Rai has survived barely seventeen years, but now she is going to live.

TWENTY-ONE

Breakfast was an uncomfortable affair. Javani was almost surprised that the others were up with her at dawn, sitting around the rekindled fire in the same blanket of silence that had covered the night. Occasionally someone exchanged a muttered word or a request for something, but in general the tattered members of their camp kept their heads down and got on with all the tasks that needed doing, preparing – without ever announcing or acknowledging it – to depart.

Manatas had care of Ree while Tauras ate, which was an undertaking in its own right. Javani had not yet approached her mother, had not checked on her. She told herself that if there was something to know, a change in her condition one way or another, Manatas would say. He'd no doubt do more than that, and surely with no shortage of verbal padding . . .

That was uncharitable of her, she knew. But her anxiety remained, the edge to the air that she'd put in place so thick she could almost taste it. Her sleep had been wretched, her dreams ragged and vexed. She hadn't seriously expected Ree would be up and about come the morning, and all unpleasant decisions whisked neatly from before her, but she was nonetheless piqued that nothing appeared to be different. Not enough to wander over to the cart and find out for herself of course, but enough to render her meal bitter in her mouth.

Sooner or later, everything would be ready, and she'd have to tell them to leave Ree behind. Javani stood at the camp's edge, her sightless gaze on the makeshift corral. Without realising it, she'd removed the blue stone from her shirt, was rubbing it with a gentle thumb. She wasn't sure she could do it. She wasn't sure anyone would come with her if she did. But she had to do it, didn't she? It would be what Ree would want, after all. Hells, she'd probably be proud.

The thought stung her beneath her ribcage, and she rubbed a quick palm across one eye.

'Javani?'

'I wasn't crying!'

Anashe was beside her, soft-stepped. 'I thought . . .' She peered forward, watching the budding daylight dance across the stone's surfaces in Javani's grip. 'Is that, by chance, the same stone that my brother lost . . . ?'

'The one I gave him to lose, you mean? Ree's greatest treasure. Yeah. I tracked it.'

'Oh?'

'Sure did.' She turned the stone in the light, watching reflections shift and shimmer. 'Jewel like this leaves a trail, as you can imagine.'

'I can.'

'The rider that made off with it pawned it at the first opportunity, then it passed through the hands of a number of gambling types with more coin to burn than brains to maybe consider not wagering it the next time things got tight.' She sniffed. 'Took me a lot of time, effort and investment, but eventually I traced it to a Guild official who had a fondness for the tables at the *Illustrious Den*. So I *retrieved* it.'

Anashe offered a tight smile. 'I did hear something about a fire aboard.'

'Yeah, well, omelettes and eggs and all that. Shouldn't fill your lacquered wooden boat with flaming chandeliers if you don't want the occasional conflagration.'

Anashe let the moment sit, then asked with a casual tone, 'And now?'

Javani tucked the stone back into her jacket. She wouldn't look to where Manatas sat, where Ree lay in the cart. 'I'll hold onto it a while longer, I guess.'

Anashe's eyes were steady, her posture upright, but Javani couldn't shake the feeling the other woman was uneasy. 'What?' she snapped, again with greater force than she'd intended. Her sleep had been bad, there was no escaping it.

'Javani.' Anashe swallowed. 'Little one.' She tried to look maternal, and it did not suit her. 'While I know you have not cried, perhaps . . . perhaps you would feel better if you did?'

'What?'

'When I lost Aki, I was racked with tears for many hours in the days and weeks that followed, but there was . . . catharsis . . . in such surrender to one's emotions.'

Javani sniffed again, hard. 'She's not dead.'

'I know this, I did not mean—'

'But that's the fucking point, isn't it? Not dead, but not alive. Gone, but not gone. Still here, still *ruining* everything even from her deathbed. How do you mourn someone who hasn't died? How am I supposed to know what to feel?'

'Little one, I only meant that—'

'We need to leave. Are you coming? You can go back to your happy life if you want, singing with your friends in your little club while the rest of us slog our guts out fighting the fucking diggers, just as we have for the last two years. Carry on, don't let us hold you up.'

Anashe's cheeks were sharp lines, her mouth drawn tight, but she didn't reply, and Javani felt a tide of shame creeping up from her gut. She fought it back down. 'We've wasted enough time. Thanks for coming this far.'

She turned and strode away, her cheeks burning, a hot feeling in her chest that pushed at the base of her throat. Tears were there, lurking at the corners, the dam ready to burst. She marched to the corral where ponies milled, looking for hers, focusing only on what she'd need to pack for the trip north.

'Easier to be angry than sad, isn't it.'

She almost jumped sideways. Anri was somehow there, chewing something charred he'd taken from the cookfire. 'What?'

'Someone said that to me once, they did. Right after Tanith went. For good, I mean. Remember that, do you?'

Javani focused on her tack as her pony bent a head round to nuzzle her. 'I don't know what you mean.'

'Pigshit, you were so chuffed with yourself for that I worried you'd pop. No way you've let that slip your feral little mind.'

She threaded a buckle at the third attempt, her fingers insubordinate. 'All right! I remember. I said it to you.'

'Aye, you did. And look at you now, its living embodiment. Chubby little fists all screwed up, face like a slapped arse.'

'Excuse me?'

'Cross little thing, aren't you? On account of not wanting to be sad. Which, as I led with, I understand, eh?' He patted his grimy chest with a black-fingered hand.

The next buckle was proving singularly insolent. 'Do you want something, Anri?'

He sniffed, wiped his nose on his sleeve and made an impressed face at the streak it left. 'Nope.'

'What?'

'Don't want anything.'

Javani paused, blinking, her fingers still wrapped in straps. Her anger had fizzled, and she felt unmoored, light-headed and lurching. 'Then . . . then why are you . . . what—'

'I'm just, you know, saying, I am. That I get it. Been there, I have.' He tilted his head, looked almost sympathetic. 'Gone, but not gone.'

'You heard that?'

He shrugged. 'Little voice carries when you're upset, doesn't it. Got that penetrating pitch, like a buzzard.'

'It does not.' She was wobbling, her legs unsteady, only her hands on the pony keeping her balanced. Her throat was tight, her words thick. 'Anri?'

'Yes, pest?'

'Can I have a hug?'

He managed to wipe the horrified shock from his face with impressive speed. 'If you must.'

She fell away from the pony, wrapped her arms around him, buried her face in his stinking leathers. For once, his odour barely troubled her. She didn't cry, though, just held herself there, her face on his chest, his hand gently patting her back as if she needed burping.

'There, there, I suppose.'

'How long will she be like this, Anri?' Javani spoke from his shoulder. 'Is she going to get better?'

'Can't tell you, and can't tell you.'

She looked up, blinking away the few tears that had formed. 'How did you cope? When it happened to Tanith?'

He pulled a face. 'You saw me. Didn't, did I? Just . . . carried on.'

She stepped back from him, took a breath and gathered herself. 'Right. Then we carry on.' She took another long breath, trying to keep it from shuddering. 'Time to see who's coming with me.'

Javani scratched at her head. 'Are you serious?'

Manatas was on the cart bench, ponies hitched in front and Tauras packing carefully around what lay in the rear. 'While our pace may be somewhat short of that set by those in the lead, we shall nevertheless be engaged in northward transit with all the alacrity that can be mustered, while the needs of our passenger remain paramount.'

'But . . . surely she's in no state to travel?'

'While it would be erroneous to claim her condition is improved since yesterday, she has not worsened, and what care we can provide within the confines of this gulch will be little different from that on the hoof. This is not an area for recuperation.'

'I . . . guess.'

The captain leaned forward, and his eyes were dark and serious. He kept his voice low enough that Tauras wouldn't hear. 'Javani, there is another reason we should be moved from this place. We are not yet certain how our adversaries came to know our precise movements and intentions, and there is every chance that should we dally, they will come in numbers to finish their task. Taking ourselves, all of ourselves, away from this place at whatever pace we can marshal is prudence if nothing else, and I like to think that our general would approve of such. Would you agree?'

Javani's eyes flicked past him to the rear of the cart before she could stop herself, and she forced them back. 'Yeah, maybe.'

'By all means, take your outriders and make all haste. Tauras and I will travel as we can, and we will mind her for as long as she needs it.' He reached down to squeeze her shoulder. 'She will endure, this I know. She is tougher than the gods.'

'And twice as vindictive,' Javani mumbled, staring at her boots.

'Do not wait for us. We will catch you up, and we will do so in health.'

'Sure. Right.'

He sat back, then raised one hand. 'And before I forget again, we collected the last of the messages before we abandoned camp. There was one for you amongst them.'

'A letter? For me?' She took it and inspected the markings on the outer casing. 'About thrice-damned time.'

Calls at the neck of the canyon drew their attention. 'Well I'm a buggered bunny,' called the Commodore from her perch beside the fire. 'We've another taker for the suicide voyage.'

Anashe was in the middle of a triumvirate as Javani reached her, Sefi on one side, the vast form of the White Spear on the other, casting them all in shadow. The White Spear was dressed in travelling clothes and carrying a lot of gear (although part of Javani was disappointed she had not found a way to reclaim her great suit of armour).

'But who will mind the club?' Anashe was asking. 'You said yourself, we must remain diligent on our expenditure—'

'Sefi.' The Horvaun nodded towards Anashe's friend. 'Yes?'

Sefi nodded. 'I will keep things clean for you, Nashi. And not let anyone behind the bar who shouldn't be there.'

Javani stepped close enough for them to notice her. 'What's going on?'

Anashe turned slowly, her chin lifted, features an impassive mask. 'If it is not too much of an inconvenience, I will be accompanying you north.'

'You're coming?'

'If you will allow someone who has lived a life of comfort for two years to besmirch your expedition.'

Javani stared at the floor. 'Anashe, I'm really sorry about what I said. I didn't mean—'

'Good.' She put a gentle hand beneath Javani's chin and lifted her back into her eyeline. 'Just because you did not see us, it does not mean we were doing nothing.'

'I – I know, I should have—'

'Still, I am looking forward to playing a more active role in proceedings.'

'Yes,' rumbled the White Spear. 'It is time to remove the stain of the Guild.'

'Aye, fucken hells,' sighed the Commodore from behind Javani. 'Are you going to expect me to tag along with this grand transit and all?'

Javani turned. 'It's not a suicide voyage. We know where we're going, we know what we're looking for, and we know when it'll be coming through. The retrieval will be the easy bit.'

'Oh aye? Fuck's sake. Can't very well let the bunch of you wander off without adult supervision, can I? You'll be riddled with dysentery within the day, or you'll eat some risky fungus or something. And then what would I say to your mam?'

Javani nodded to the cart. 'She's coming too.'

'Ancestors' gleaming bell, this is making less and less sense with every utterance.'

Javani frowned. 'Captain Manatas made some good points . . .'

'Aye, fuck, fine. Let's get on with it, then. I'm old enough to be counting my days now, and I'd rather not waste any more of this one yapping around when we've got the plains to cross.'

The White Spear gave her a firm nod. 'Welcome aboard, Commodore.'

'I don't know what you're so fucken pleased about, you're the oldest one here. Probably rot away before we even get halfway.'

'I hear you were an accomplished warrior in your day, Commodore.'

'My day? Tell you what, pal, my day has daylight to burn yet, and my accomplishments require little in the way of burnishment. Did anyone bring a hammer? Something with a bit of heft? No, no, it's fine, I've got a few somewhere. And you know exactly where we're going, do you, Slayer? All the way to this road for iron?'

'I do.' Javani took a deep breath. Everyone seemed to be taller than her, with the exception of the Commodore, but her hair made her exact height hard to gauge. 'We go north, and east, and north again, until we reach the mountains. Then we'll see it, leading down across the plains to Kilale Port. Mount up, rebels. The Iron Road is waiting!'

Within ten minutes the canyon was empty, with no sign of its previous occupants but a buried fire-pit and a lot of tracks. Overhead, a hawk circled, riding thermals in the morning air and winding ever north.

TWENTY-TWO

The parade ground baked beneath the punishing sun, its sandy floor glowing white with heat. The men – and they were all men, Beralas insisted on it – who marched and drilled in formation dripped with sweat, faces dark, fallen beads glossy against the sheen of their burnished plates. They shifted in time, spears hefted, helms sharp, grinding and stamping and shouting as one. Fluid. Precise. Magnificent.

Maral hated them. She hated them collectively, these absurd peacocks, these gleaming glass hammers. Their synchronised prancing would be less than fuck-all use out in the wild, and their dress plate was so heavy and baroque as to be unwearable on horseback. She could appreciate the artistry but the subversion of its purpose was not something she could overlook.

She hated them individually, too. All this 'training' of theirs, wasted on meaningless presentation, on some twisted facsimile of arms. She was in no doubt that should the mood take her – which seemed ever more likely these days – she could systematically dispatch each and every man in the square, one by one or in groups, and not one of them would land a blow. Each of them had chosen, had applied, had undergone selection to serve in Beralas's Invincible Goldhelms, as he insisted on calling his private guard – never mind that the original Invincible Goldhelms of General Diin's day had been volatile social climbers who definitely murdered and probably ate the one person they were supposed to protect. Each of these sweating, grunting, pointless men had elected to spend their days twirling heavy, ornate, pointless spears under the pitiless sun beneath their patron's distracted, benevolent gaze. No tracking, no learning the plains and the cuts, no finding the secret trails and the lost water holes. These men could not hunt. These men could not fight. All they could do was perform. At least none of them had fainted today. Yet.

'You all right, sis? Look like you're chewing a hornet.'

Kuzari was leaning against the next shining column along, one tattered boot poking into the scorching line of sunlight, contemplating a large, sticky pastry he'd no doubt lifted from the kitchen on his way past. He went to bite into it, then proffered it to her with a smile. 'Want some? Might lift your mood.'

'No. Thanks, Zari.'

He took an enormous bite, flakes of pastry drifting down his front like mountain snow, then, still chewing, resumed his interrogation. 'What's up? You've been ever so dark these last few days. I thought everything had gone well out there?'

Things had not Gone Well out there. Things had gone Very Badly Indeed, and soon the Chairman would arrive to demand her explanations, and quite possibly order her own resolution. But somehow her mind kept drifting. One hand was in her pocket, twisting the scrap of silk so tight it warped. In the other hung volume forty-one of *The Histories*. She could not find any subsequent, nor any detailed mention of the Mawn. Out in the courtyard, the men swung and barked and stomped, each with the same intense look of concentration as a toddler soiling its breeches.

'Do you remember much of your mother, Zari?'

'Hmm?' He puffed crumbs, wiped vaguely at his mouth. His jacket was sublime, richly patterned and tapered at the waist, artfully speckled with his breakfast. 'No, not really. Died before I was born, didn't she?'

Maral wasn't sure if that was a joke.

'That what this is? Missing your dead family?' He didn't sound cruel as he said it; it was just his way. 'Bit late for that now, isn't it?'

'Not that. Just . . . just thinking about . . . the early days. When we first arrived.'

He shrugged, popping the last of the pastry into his mouth and smearing grease down his lapel with his fingers. 'Why bother? It's not like we can remember much, and we're both lucky Beralas took us in.'

'Yeah. Yeah . . .'

'Wasn't all bad, was it? Plenty of food, lessons with the girls—' Maral had joined the tutoring of the daughters behind a screen; Kuzari had lounged by the window, pulling the wings off whatever passed, '—and of course . . .' From nowhere, a knife flashed in his grip, for a moment searing as it danced into the sunlight at his shoulder. 'We learned to fuck stuff up.'

The knife vanished, and he wiped his hand down his front one more time. The velvet of his jacket shone in streaks. 'I know you had a head-start and all, but I'm big enough to admit it: it's the one thing you were best at.'

'Yeah. I was.'

'Of course now I like to think of us as equal up-fuckers,' he declared, his eyes and smile slightly too wide. 'Nature and nurture, eh?' He giggled.

Maral lingered in the shadows. 'Zari?'

'Yeah?'

'What would you be, if you could be anything?'

The question gave him only a second's pause. 'Anything. I'm going to get another pastry. Want one?'

Maral shook her head. As his footsteps died away, all she could think about were those lessons – true training, hand, blade, bow and anything that could inflict bodily damage – delivered by hard-faced veterans of the conflicts, scarred and bitten folk with thousand-yard stares and dwindling prospects. Beralas had swept them up wholesale after the collapse, and for ten years Maral and Kuzari had enjoyed (if that was the word for it) the toughest, most demanding, most lethal tuition available short of taking up professional soldiery at the outbreak of yet another war, and not immediately dying.

And she had been grateful. She had. Beralas had cared for her when she'd had no one else, taken her in, treated her as his own.

Almost.

But . . . all that training. She didn't remember ever being asked if she wanted to learn to tear out a man's throat with a hoof pick. It was assumed that she did.

Natural aptitude, they'd said. She was Mawn, after all. A born killer. A beast of the plains.

At five years old.

She was certainly a killer now, of that she had no doubt. A very good one. But whose choice had that been?

With a rippling thump the glass hammers on the parade ground threw themselves into their final pose and held it, steaming sweat into the punishing sky. As the echoes of their flourish died away, it was finally quiet, finally peaceful, the background noise fallen away enough to hear Gurbun yawning with maximum force and minimum tact. At least this time he hadn't farted. The man delighted in the volume and pugnacity of his emissions, and woe betide any junior stewards who caught his eye after a particularly effervescent dinner. It was rumoured he'd once trapped an apprentice vizier with one of the vile expulsions beneath an upturned silver tureen, and choked the man to death. Maral wasn't sure she believed it, if only because the logistics of the act bothered her. She'd killed people with a lot of things, but never flatulence, and she was happy to keep it that way.

Footsteps, echoing around the colonnade, and the presentation was over at last. The gleaming horde were dismissed with a shout, and dispersed in a crunching stampede through a darkened hallway, the thunder of their passage faded before their patron and his retinue rounded the statues at the corner and into Maral's view.

'. . . impressive, Chairman,' the narrow woman with the scarred lip was saying – Ziba Rahdat, the intercessor. She walked at Beralas's elbow, a respectful half-pace behind, which also reduced the amount of dodging necessary to avoid being clipped by one of his expansive gestures. 'They drill like that every day?'

'Twice daily,' Beralas replied with a prideful smile. 'And more in winter. It's so important to keep them sharp. As General Diin so famously said, "Rusted is the blade never sharpened."'

Maral wrinkled her nose. General Diin did not say that. The historian Ilay of Whitestone had written something vaguely similar, but the context was completely different. It was probably a while since Beralas had read the *Histories*, though. Probably.

'It must be reassuring to know you have troops of such high calibre to call upon, should the need arise,' Rahdat replied. Either she was as unfamiliar with the ramblings of General Diin as Beralas, or she had chosen to let it slide. Maral found herself uncharacteristically irked at the woman.

'Far more reassuring is your news from the plains,' Beralas beamed. 'Very well done, Ziba. I knew we were right to put you in charge.'

'Said it, didn't I?' came Gurbun's voice from behind them, his lumbering bulk obscured by the fine trail of his brother's robes. 'Said those gutless toads were taking the piss, didn't I?'

'Yes, yes, you did,' Beralas waved over his shoulder. 'Well done, you.'

'We should off the rest of them. We don't need *guildmasters*. They need us, and too many of them have forgotten it. They've had their hands in our pockets too long.'

Beralas's smile thinned. 'Can't really off the lot, Gurbun. At some point we do need someone to take care of the local administration. That's rather the point of local guildmasters, after all.'

Gurbun snorted. 'Won't matter soon, anyway.'

Beralas's smile re-thickened. 'Indeed. Now, tell me, Ziba, what's left to resolve?'

They paused in a shaft of brilliant light, half-turned away from where Maral lurked in shadow.

'The pirates are scattered, but not eliminated.' Rahdat's mouth pursed, her scars twisting. 'They are slippery, but with time, we can hunt them, or at least drive them back into the plains so far they pose limited risk.'

Gurbun barked again. 'What? Said to burn them to ash, didn't we?'

Rahdat nodded with a precisely calculated level of deference. 'They are skilled at irregular warfare and very well prepared. They outwitted and humbled the Guild's most experienced troops – excluding your Goldhelms, of course, Chairman – for the better part of two years. I regret that we have not been able to exterminate them, but I am confident that – with your continued dispensation, Chairman – we will continue to make progress towards this end.'

'Indeed,' Beralas repeated heartily, 'and we must be patient,

Gurbun, really. "Patience is its own reward" – know who said that? No? It was the philosopher Amberlo.'

It wasn't.

'Ziba, I'm happy for you to continue, delighted even, but reassure me that matters in the north are in hand. This man of yours, the one you left in charge, he's up to the task?'

'I believe he is, Chairman. Guvuli has done sterling work for the Guild since I engaged him in Kazeraz. He may not be, strictly speaking, one of us, but he understands the miners and the working types, speaks their language. We've done well to settle things down in the north, and it's largely thanks to his efforts.'

Beralas snorted. 'Never one inclined to modesty, were you, Ziba?'

'There is no shame in imparting the true measure of achievement.'

'Oh, I know that one, was it Sincoq?'

Maral knew that it wasn't, but at least this time Rahdat said, 'No. It was me.'

'Very good, Ziba. Very good. So this man, Guluvi . . .'

'Guvuli.'

'Do you trust him?'

Rahdat laughed, or at least her pinched, teak-skinned face convulsed and a puff of air emerged. 'Gods, no. The man's a weasel. But as long as we're keeping him in the manner to which he is accustomed, he's our weasel. And once matters in the south are resolved, well . . .' She brushed invisible dust from her sleeve. 'He will be surplus to requirements.'

Gurbun snorted a laugh. 'We'll off him and all, the fathead!'

The lines beneath Rahdat's eyes grew fractionally tighter. Beralas only smiled. 'Indeed.' He turned back to Rahdat. 'Then, as dear old Dad loved to say, carry on. And in the meantime—'

Kuzari emerged from the passageway beside them, a pastry in each hand and another in his mouth. Beralas's smile broadened. 'Kuzari! I was about to send a runner. Is Maral with you?'

Mouth full of pastry, Kuzari could only turn to the pillars where Maral stood, cloaked in shade, his noble brow furrowed in confusion.

Feeling suddenly ashamed, Maral stepped into the light, her eyes on Beralas. She saw it flash across his features as he registered her, that rictus of shock, of distaste, of . . . could the infant have been right? Was it fear?

Whatever the emotion, Beralas covered it instantly, his smile barely dipping. 'Maral, my girl,' he called, one hand extended, sleeve shimmering in the sunlight. 'Come and meet Ziba. You and she will have much to discuss before your departure.'

'My departure?' Her voice sounded so rough to her ears compared with his rich, booming speech. 'But what of my failure? Their General may still live.'

'Nonsense, my dear. All goes according to plan, and the Guild has need of you, once more. And this time could be the most vital time of all.'

TWENTY-THREE

Javani blew sweaty hair from her eyes. 'Up here.'

'Up there?' Anri craned his head back, taking in the towering pillar of red rock. It glowed in the sunlight, deep slashes of shadow in the ridges along its flank. 'All of us need to go up by there, do we?'

Anashe was already beginning her climb, her skin sheened but movements fluid. 'You didn't have to come with us. You could have stayed behind.'

'Not up to me, was it,' he grumbled, and shifted the bow on his shoulder. 'Need someone along with a head for thinking, you do.'

Anashe paused, arms and legs extended, a static spider on the sloping rock. 'And what is that supposed to mean?'

'Nothing, nothing.' Anri put a reluctant hand on the narrow stone shelf in front of him. 'I'll cover the rear, shall I? Make sure we're not, you know, ambushed in the hinterland.'

'Will you get a move on?' Javani called down. 'The sooner we're up, the sooner we'll get a look at our target.'

Anri still had both feet at ground level. 'And you're sure about these directions, are you? Trust that little fella with the squint to point us at this road for iron?'

'He was as sick of the Guild as we are,' Javani snapped. 'He said we'd see the start of the road from up here.' And he'd wished them more luck than she was comfortable receiving.

'Do roads even have starts?' Anri muttered, finally putting one boot on the rock. 'Don't all roads just carry on from somewhere to somewhere else? Not like they're rivers, is it? Don't just spring out of the bloody ground in high places.'

'Of course they have starts,' Anashe replied with airy confidence as she climbed. 'The Gonamin road in Banasahr starts in Banasahr, and goes to Gonamin.'

'Oh aye? What if you're already in Gonamin, eh? Where's it start then?'

Anashe pulled herself another head higher. 'That is merely a question of perspective.'

'And you're telling me that road just ends in a wall at each end, are you? Just a big fuck-off dead end, hard stop. No chance they wander on under new names, to new places?'

'Then if they have different names, they are different roads.'

'Bet that makes all the difference to the fella walking on them, it does. We'll get to the top of this great tower of gravel and see a line in the dirt, that's all. Start of a road my arse.'

'Anri,' Javani called down, 'get a move on.'

'Your friend appears to enjoy complaining.' Anashe was passing her now, her breath steady, her face shining.

'Course I do,' came the ever-more-distant mutter from below. 'Costs nothing and spreads cheer. Should all complain as much as possible.'

'Anri!'

'Kypeth's hog, pest, fine. I'll be there now.'

'You took your time.'

'Being careful, wasn't I? Feel you could learn a thing or two about caution, eh, pest?'

'Shut your hole, old man.' Javani shuffled aside to make space for him. 'On the other side of that ridge should be a good view of the foothills, and if Old Squinty is to be believed, we'll see the road crossing from west to east.'

'Or east to west.'

'Yes, very good. He said there's a loading station at the top of the road, then it follows the slope down. And we can't miss it.'

'Not seen a road before, I haven't. Will I know what to look for?'

Anashe cleared her throat. 'Shall we proceed? I suggest we keep low on the ridge, in case we are close enough to be spotted.'

'Good thing she's here, isn't it. We'd never have thought of that ourselves, struck dumb as we are by congenital idiocy.'

'If someone wishes to be struck,' Anashe replied sharply, 'he is travelling the right path.'

'Greatest pity, but *someone* is unfamiliar with paths, too, so likely to fall by the wayside before reaching his destination.'

'Nine blistered hells, will you two pipe down? It's too hot for this nonsense. Let's just get up to the ridge, mark off the passage of the road while it's daylight, and get out of here, shall we? Is that too much to ask?'

Anashe was smiling with her eyes. 'You sounded like her, then.'

'Aye, you did. A bit.' Anri scratched at his bristles. 'She'd probably have called us dickheads though.'

'That can be arranged,' Javani growled. 'But can we get this bit done? Just a few possible ambush sites we can scout later, that's all we need. That's not so much to ask, is it? Then we can get back before sundown and see what kind of camp the others have set. Anashe, do you have your spyglass?'

'Of course, little one. I would be a fool to have forgotten something so vital.'

'Oh, that's a dig at me, is it? Look here, I can't be expected to pack everything for everyone else, can I—'

'Anri, *by the gods*! Can we get on with it? We don't want to be stuck out here come nightfall.'

'Don't see why I was expected to bring everything, it's not like I'm the only one with a bag with straps. "Oh, Anri, could you pop that in your bag," and "Oh, Anri, would you mind sticking that in, too," and before you know it I'm lugging half a camp on my back, but you forget *one thing*—'

'Anri, I swear to all the gods I will throw you from this mountain . . .'

'Take my bag with me, won't I. You'll have to scrape it from my flattened corpse.'

Javani rubbed her eyes, pressed the heels of her hands against them. Was this why her mother was so terse and ill-tempered the whole time? Why was it so hard to get people to do the things they needed to do, that they wanted to do? Why were people so difficult?

'Anri,' Anashe said softly, 'the charcoal pens, please.'

'Oh, go on, then.' He passed them across, to Javani's exasperated disbelief.

'Right. Fine. Good.' She took a long, hot breath. Afternoon was fading, but it was still far, far too hot to be out in the direct glare of the sun. 'Let's keep low, mark up the map and see if we can spot some places to ambush our glossy digging friends. A long old road winding through the mountains, there should be a bunch of good options.'

Anashe cracked half a smile. 'I have some experience with mountain ambush. It will be nice to be on the other side of things for once.'

Javani took another breath, held it, felt the slowing of her heart. 'Right. Here we go.'

As one, they shuffled forward against the rough red stone, sliding to the lip of the ridge. The vista opened before them, the hard crags of the mountains to their left, a wall of ruby teeth, then lower undulations, the mesa, and in shimmering distance to their right, lost in haze: the plains, the coast, and, somewhere, Kilale Port.

And running across it like a black spear, was something else entirely.

'What the fuck,' breathed Javani, 'is that?'

'A road, you said.' Anri sounded almost delirious, his eyes wide and wild. 'A road for iron. That's no fucking road! That's . . . that's . . . I don't even know what that is!'

Anashe was equally mesmerised. 'They have carved the earth itself. They have plumbed Usdohr's domain.'

Javani nudged her with an elbow. 'Can I have the spyglass?'

Anashe passed it without a word, her attention still fixed on the vista before them. Javani took it cautiously, aware that the lensed tube belonged to the White Spear, and was one of her few remaining treasures. A mishap out here might lead to an uncomfortable discussion, and possibly the rearranging of parts of her skeleton.

'Right, right. So.' She peered through the cloudy lens, her vision a refractive sparkle. Twisting the tube helped a little. 'The road . . . by the gods, the road is *made* of iron. It's literal.'

'How do you make a road of iron?' Anri grunted.

'And why?' Anashe breathed. 'For what purpose have they wrought such monstrosity on the landscape? They have progressed from blasting holes for their mines to remaking the very earth itself.'

'It's, you know, tracks. Rails. Like they have in the mines for running the carts to and fro. You know?' She scanned one way, then the other. 'It's just a bigger version of what they have in the big digs.'

Anashe was up on her elbows, brow crinkled like a ploughed field. 'That does not answer my question. For what purpose have they done this? The labour, the materials, the . . . the damage. To push a cart of ore from here to the coast will still take days.'

Javani squinted through the spyglass. 'There are . . . ropes, chains, pulleys. Within and alongside the tracks. Running between little towers, evenly spaced. It's all . . . moving.' She scanned along the tracks, up the slope into the mountains, through the cuttings, over the embankments, then back to her right, following the path of the bowing, swaying cables and ropes.

'Nine hells!'

Anri was uncomfortably close, reaching for the spyglass. 'What, what is it?'

Anashe was faster. 'May I?' She plucked it from Javani's unresisting hand. Javani hardly needed it anyway, now she knew what to look for.

'By the Goddess . . .' Anashe breathed, the spyglass pressed to her eye.

Anri huffed and shuffled. 'What? Going to tell me what's going on, or what? I'll just sit here and guess, shall I? Make that the body of my report. "Oh, a right sight it was, the road of iron, made, as it was, entirely of fucking cheese, and surrounded by little goblins in tall hats who—"'

'Ugh, see for yourself if you must,' Anashe growled, 'just cease this infernal prattling.' She proffered the spyglass, then whipped it back as he reached. 'When did you last wash your hands?'

'What? I'm clean!'

Anashe narrowed her eyes. 'Are you?'

'Bathe regularly, I do.'

Anashe turned to Javani. 'Does he?'

'Yep.' Javani nodded, and Anashe passed the spyglass, with evident reluctance. 'Twice a year, whether he needs it or not,' Javani finished.

'Rubbish,' Anri muttered, setting the spyglass against his good eye. 'As if I'd waste water on two— Kypeth's runny arse!'

'Yep,' Javani replied.

'Mine carts, you said!'

'I said it was *like* the tracks they push mine carts on.'

'It's like a mine cart ate all the other mine carts, or, or, or triggered some fairy curse or something. Why is it so massive?'

Anashe stretched out her neck, head tilting from side to side. 'The lenses make the judgement of scale a challenge, but the monstrosity's purpose seems clear.'

'Oh aye? Care to enlighten us on the purpose of this . . . thing? Why is there something that looks like a chain of cabins on wheels wandering across the landscape beneath our clear blue sky?'

Javani nudged him. 'It's for moving things. It's like, like a giant version of that wagon Ree and I rode out of Kazeraz. That was an old ore transport. This is the same, just, you know, bigger. And with others attached behind it.'

Anashe pointed. 'See how the wagons to the rear of the chain are empty? But a few contain timber . . . Are they still constructing, or is this some measure of material or payment for those in the hills?'

Anri looked unconvinced, the spyglass glued to his good eye. 'How are they even pulling it? It's all rolling uphill, no horses, no oxen, nothing. Bunch of fellas inside turning a crank, is it? This where all your slave pals end up?'

'No, I don't think so.' Javani gazed across the sloping landscape towards the contraption now crawling along the Iron Road, inexorably uphill, then beyond it. 'Two sets of tracks.'

'You what?'

'There are two sets of tracks. I think . . . I think there's two of them. Two of the . . . wagon-trains-on-rails. They're roped together at each end, like a great pulley.'

'How does that work?'

Anashe laughed, and not in a kind way. 'One goes up, one goes down.'

'Then what?' Anri removed his eye from the spyglass, cheeks flushed. 'How comes you both seem to have the measure of this nonsense, having never laid eyes on it before? Been doing some secret reading, have you?'

'Well, yeah,' Javani replied, 'but not about this.' She waved a hand. 'It's like the hoist, up to the stores in the Grandfathers, back in Ar Ramas. You can still pull heavy things up with not a lot of effort if something just as heavy is travelling in the other direction.'

'There's two of these fuckers, is there?'

'That's my guess. They fill the first full of ore and other *heavy* mining stuff, give it a push and off it goes down the mountain and across the plains, all the time pulling the other one up in its place.'

Anashe was nodding. 'As long as some level of slope remained, a gradient that kept up the momentum, it should be possible to force the other up into the mountains with minimal mechanical assistance. Perhaps a set of wind drivers, or even a few of those people you mentioned turning a wheel, here and there.'

Javani coloured at the reminder of the slavers. It had taken her some time to realise just how much danger she'd been in, how dependent she'd been on others to rescue and reassure her, but she'd entirely failed to hunt the slavers down afterwards and free their captives, or go after Maral for that matter. The woman who'd poisoned Ree and left her fighting for life. The woman who'd seemed every bit as lost as Javani.

Where was Maral? Was she still following them? Was she watching them now? Javani fought the urge to spin around, scan the hillside behind them.

'It is likely to carry people, as well as cargo,' Anashe mused. 'It is possible that these even tracks offer a more comfortable ride across the plains than a coach on the road.' She sucked her teeth. 'It would account for the functionaries you described completing their voyage to Kilale Port.'

'Well, consider me educated, why don't you,' Anri growled. 'Perhaps I'll trade in my bow and seek a life of perpetual enlightenment in the field of applied mathematics now, eh? Oh, just one small thing, almost slipped my mind, it did, namely: how the fuck do we ambush and rob a moving citadel that's up on raised fucking tracks?'

There was nothing but silence at the top of the red rock for a while, no sound but the distant shriek of buzzards and the occasional kestrel, and the irrepressible hum of legion insects.

'Um—' Javani began.

'We could—' Anashe said simultaneously.

'Doomed, we are,' Anri muttered. 'Double-doomed and nose-fucked.'

'We are not,' Javani retorted. 'We just need to, to, just, get a bit closer and see what we're up against.'

Anashe put a hand on her arm. 'Not today, little one. See the dust around it?' She pointed.

Javani squinted, then grabbed the spyglass back from Anri. 'Riders. An escort?'

'Presumably. They may be there to monitor its function – it seems from its light load that its operators do not yet have total faith it will not break apart from the stresses upon it. Perhaps we are still in a testing phase.'

'Yeah, maybe. Or they're holding back for a special occasion. Like . . . like the renewal. They're going to tie it all in together, aren't they? The renewal of the Guild's charter, the grand opening of the Iron Road, and whatever in the sight of the gods is going on down in the port.' She whistled. 'That is going to be a busy day.'

'Now all we've got to do is think of a way to fuck it up for them,' muttered Anri. 'Come on, pest, let's get off this rock.'

Javani was the last to descend, taking one last look at the giant train of heavy wagons rattling and shuddering up the slope of the mountain on the road of iron. It didn't look any more comfortable than a coach, but maybe its scale absorbed some of the shaking. Maybe.

As she began her climb down, the sun's decline already drenching the red rock in shadow, it was hard to shake the feeling she was being watched.

TWENTY-FOUR

The captain blinked several times, then rubbed his fingers over his eyes. He looked tired. Javani knew he spent most of his waking hours watching over Ree, but she didn't like to think about it.

'Describe it to us again, if it please you, Javani.'

'It pleases me not but I'll do it anyway,' she sighed. The others around their temporary camp shared the captain's exhausted agitation, and Javani was already tired of it, tired of their anxieties, their worries and pessimism. It was late, she'd had a long day climbing up and down rock pillars and riding hard, and she just wanted them to accept what she was telling them and let her go to bed. Once more she thought of Ree, and her visible, tangible impatience with people who couldn't keep up with her, physically or intellectually. *Am I just like her? Or was she like that because she'd spent half her life being held back? Being held back by me?*

'Please, Javani.' Manatas sounded wrung out, the lower half of his face thick with silver stubble.

'Oh fine,' Javani sighed again. 'Listen very carefully, all of you, I'm not doing this again.'

'Right you are, Javani,' came Tauras's voice from beside the cook-fire, and she felt bad. He was doing more of the cooking now, which he seemed to relish, although the White Spear kept a close eye on his culinary explorations.

'So the old road for iron,' the Commodore interjected, her voice already cheeky with booze, 'turns out to be a road *of* iron, eh? Bit of iron-y there, eh, folks? No? Ah, sod the lot of you.'

'It's not actually all iron,' Javani snapped, distantly appalled at her own peevishness. 'We checked through the spyglass, the tracks and rails are wood but there's a thin layer of iron over the top . . . to protect them, I guess.'

'Still counts,' the Commodore muttered, then hiccuped.

'You said it's like a wagon train?' Manatas was leaning forward, a yearning for comprehension in his red-rimmed eyes.

'Yeah, sort of.' Javani waved a hand. 'But that doesn't really, you know.'

'Do it justice,' Anashe supplied.

'It's like a train of massive armoured cargo wagons, linked together. Although what we saw may be an early version – the whispers we heard mentioned some kind of moving fortress, and we saw nothing like that.'

'And it travels on those rails? Not direct upon the earth? Why?'

Javani exchanged a look with Anashe. 'I guess so they don't need to worry about steering?'

'Not just that, is it, Javani?' Tauras piped up from his cooking, his attention still on the smoking foodstuffs before him. 'Slotting the wheels in the tracks makes for lower friction between the surfaces, and allows the weight of the wagons and cargo to spread over a long distance without grinding great grooves into the earth, as they'd do on a normal road. And if the path of the vehicles is set, the engineers can devote their energies to making the track as smooth as possible, so the wagons can travel faster than they would over open ground without risking their cargo or their axles. I imagine.' He looked up, earnest and diligent, and met a ring of wide eyes and open mouths.

'Tauras,' Javani said slowly, 'are you an expert on the Iron Road?'

'Me, Javani?' He shook his head, his smile fading. 'No, Javani. I just thought it made sense. I think about, you know, the weight of things.'

'Oh, it does. It, er, does.' Javani met Manatas's eye, and the captain merely lifted his palms in incredulous surprise.

'You think so?' Tauras now looked worried.

A shape loomed over him, hellish in the firelight. 'Boy, you are burning dinner.'

'Right you are, Mistress Whitespear.' Tauras returned his attention to the cooking.

Manatas sucked air through his teeth. 'Then it concerns weight and speed. They have armoured this abomination, to protect their shipments in transit over the length of the trail, and can carry far more than a set of wagons overland, in far shorter time, both downhill and up.' He whistled. 'It is some feat those diggers have accomplished.'

'Aye, right, I bet they had help though,' the Commodore chimed in. 'Old Swanny mentioned something about the Iokara, and she knows a thing or two about them, and they know a thing or two – hic – 'scuse me, about engineering. I could tell you some stories, oh aye.'

Javani cleared her throat. 'Who are the Iokara?'

'Ancestors' breakfasts, what's that mother of yours been teaching you?'

'I feel like I get asked this a lot.'

'Aye, well, friend Iokara is known by many names – down in the Sink they call them Norts, whereas up in the protectorate we are a mite more *refained*.' She wiggled her fingers, then burped. 'But, well, basically, they're a bunch of bastards from over the Borabod. Keep themselves to themselves, by and large, don't care much for outsiders as they've got a pre-tty high opinion of their own constructions and capabilities. And, you know, don't tell anyone, but they're the reason there's quite so much blasting powder in these parts.'

'They trade it?'

'Aye, no, one of their wee alchemists got loose and fessed up the recipe around the time of the Siege of Arowan, and it's been all booms and bugger-ups since.'

'Wait, they're the reason the Guild came to have blasting powder and become so powerful? They're responsible for this whole mess?'

The Commodore didn't answer for a moment, her eyes darting, words half-formed on her lips. 'Um . . . yes.'

'That was a long pause.'

'Aye, I was, uh, checking a few things. Mentally.'

'Why are the Iokara helping the Guild with their Iron Road?'

Anashe had one finger resting on her chin. 'Because they stand to gain from it. Not just in payment, but Kilale Port is the logical destination for a shipping route to Serasthana.' She inclined her head to Javani. 'The name of their nation.' She raised her voice again. 'The Guild are intending to trade directly with the Iokara. Ore, stones and who knows what else, direct from the mountains to the port, and from the port to their ships and across the sea.'

'This is what the Swan was worried about,' Javani breathed. 'This is what she told Ree. The diggers are going to cut out the whole of the Serican state and take everything for themselves.' Her mouth was dry. 'Their wealth will make them unstoppable, they can buy up the entire expanse and everyone in it!' Another thought occurred, a sharp and sickly one. 'The Iokara . . . would they be interested in . . . slaves?'

'Oh aye,' the Commodore sighed. 'Huge fans of indentured labour and its derivations, they are.'

'Shit. That's why the slavers were desperate to get to Kilale. They want to sell those people to the Iokara, along with everything dug out of the mountains. Gods!'

'This Iron Road,' Manatas said, brows lowered, 'this wagon train on rails. It carries people – passengers?'

Anashe's nostrils were flared. 'We must assume so, not least the guards and operators. We saw riders in its orbit, as scouts perhaps, or tasked with ensuring the path is clear, and there is the matter of the itinerary Javani discovered.'

'Then we are to believe that these functionaries, these bearers of the Great Seal that are the target of all our endeavours, are likely aboard this monster of iron? That they may cross the plain in the belly of a rolling fortress, watched over by guards, flanked by outriders?'

Javani realised he was looking at her. 'Uh, yeah. I guess. The ledger said they'd be travelling the Iron Road to Kilale.'

Manatas dropped his head, ran his hands through his ever greyer mop of hair. 'Then we must find a new plan.'

'What?'

He looked up, hands linked behind his neck. 'We cannot ambush this device, this rolling citadel, as it travels across elevated tracks over miles of open ground. We cannot flag down and rob those who may or may not carry the seal. They will roll over us and grind us to paste, assuming we are not perforated from the safety of its redoubts. They will not even slow.'

Anashe released a long breath. 'I fear the captain is correct. From what we have seen, to reach this thing, to attempt to gain ingress in the hope of retrieving the seal . . . it cannot be done. We must consider alternative strategies.'

Javani felt stung, a sharp feeling at the base of her ribcage. 'What?' she said quietly, searching Anashe's eyes, then the captain's, for a sign of hope. There was nothing. 'Commodore, you don't think—'

'Aye, right, well, to put it into words, that is, yes. Indeed. It's a mighty tall order, that's all.'

'But we can do it, right?'

'Aye, well, no.'

'Whitespear? Tauras?' They were no less hesitant, and the Commodore's riders, Teg and Stefanna, wouldn't even look up from their game of stones. She wished, once more, that Anri was not on watch. At least there'd be someone to back her up. But then of course, that was no guarantee. In fact, more often than not, he did the complete opposite of what she wanted. When it came down to it, the only person who did what she wanted was her.

Javani fought down the sick feeling in her stomach and clenched her fists.

'No. Bullshit and bollocks. No.'

Manatas raised an eyebrow. 'No? To what?'

'No to no.'

'Aye, right, all very well to say there, Slayer, but the facts material remain unchanged. And much as it pains me, without the scheming of your lamented mam, I'm not seeing much possibility of progression on this one.'

Manatas nodded, turning a mug in his hands. 'The Commodore has, as the saying goes, put her finger on the nub.'

''S just how I'm sitting, honest.'

'*By which I mean* that without our General, your mother, we are shorn of command, we are shorn of strategic analysis, we are dissolute and adrift. And while you have achieved so much for your age, for your relative inexperience . . . you have driven us here, taken us this close . . . but it is asking too much of you to fulfil for us the same role that your mother performed.'

Around the fire, the others nodded and murmured their cowardly assent.

Javani could feel her jaw muscles flexing, her teeth clamping rigid. 'No.'

'Excuse me?'

'To all of this! To this mewling defeatism! So Ree is lost to us, so what? You all had lives before you knew her, and in some cases lives since. You did perfectly well without her, didn't you?'

'Aye, well, if we're being *technical* on this one—'

'Shut up! Shut up and listen! How many battles did Ree fight, since the rebellion started? How many raids did she go on, how many duels did she fight?'

Manatas coughed. 'Well, uh, none, but that was not in principle the—'

Javani lanced a finger at him, and he flinched back. 'Exactly, she's the brains in the back room, right? The planner, the strategist, masterminding the raids. Remind me, how many did she plan? Did she tell you what to do at every turn?'

'She did not.' Manatas ducked his head and dusted one knee with the palm of his hand. 'The precise operational specifics, and their subsequent execution, were the preserve of the raiders themselves.'

'But she told you what to raid and when?'

He sucked his top lip against his teeth, flashed a mirthless smile in the firelight. 'You know that she did not.'

Javani nodded, her own jaw set in grim satisfaction. 'Indeed I do, captain. But it feels like you all need a reminder, doesn't it?' She stood tall, looking over them, one by one. 'Ree let you do what you do best. She gave you purpose and direction, that's all. But the rest of you were the ones who got on with it.'

'Aye, right, but those of us who were minding our own particulars well to the south for the duration of said rebellion—'

'Have some catching up to do,' Javani growled. She did not look at Anashe.

'Righto, fair enough.'

Javani took another step forward, the fire hot on her skin, her legs immediately sweating. 'Listen. There is a way to do this. How many caravans have you taken on the hoof, captain? This will be no different.'

'Uh, in fairness, I feel—'

'The Guild are *not* super-human. They're just people, dolts who got a bit of coin and a bit of luck and spun it for all it was worth. Just people. Fallible, greedy, complacent people. They are *not* cleverer than us. They are not better than us. They just think they are.'

'Let's disabuse them of that. They will not see us coming.'

Anri found her as she was shaking out her bedroll.

'Talked them round then, did you?'

'Maybe.' She gave it another swish, just in case something had crawled onto it since the last one. 'Wasn't exactly a full-throated endorsement of my ambitions.'

Anri examined his blackened fingernails. 'Better than nothing.'

'Well, yeah, obviously. Thanks for all your support, by the way. Really made the difference.'

He puffed out his bristly cheeks. 'Want the camp watched or not? Don't need to remind you of what happened to our comrades to the west, do I?'

'No, no, fine.' She remembered the feeling she'd had as she descended. 'Definitely keep watch, very, very vigilantly. You never know who might be out there.' She gave the bedroll one final waft then set about draping it out on what passed for smoothed earth. She'd spent what felt like an age picking out all the sharp stones and spiky growths, flattening the ground with hand and boot in an attempt to produce something that while a long way from comfortable was nonetheless not in the same league as trying to bed down on the back of a porcupine. Yet every time, within moments of lying down, a previously unknown blade of rock or wandering briar would make itself immediately, sharply felt. She was sure someone had to be sneaking them under her, and she was beginning to suspect Anri.

'Did you eat?'

'Big lad did the cooking again, did he?'

'He's getting better!'

'I'll stick to rations.' He retrieved something from his satchel and began chewing in the gloom. 'What's the plan, then? Assaulting the buggers at dawn, are we?'

She almost smiled. 'No. Not yet. Before we can decide on anything, we need to know a lot more about what we're up against, and how it operates. And we don't have long . . .'

TWENTY-FIVE

Javani trailed the Commodore, and Manatas trailed Javani. 'I remain . . . far short of convinced . . . as to the wisdom . . . of this action,' came the captain's breathy croak from over her shoulder as they crouched against a natural cleft in the rock. The sun was still low, and much of their climb since they'd left the horses had been in chill darkness, but now Javani's pulse was thudding like a marching drum and sweat had glued her shirt to her back.

'We need to know what we're up against, right?' she shot back, trying to keep her voice low. The sounds of the outpost were loud around them now; another turn or two, another climb, and it should be in sight. 'So we need to get closer. Feel free to head back if you're scared.'

He flashed a tight grimace of unamusement. 'It is not for myself I am concerned.'

'Oh. Commodore, are you worried?'

'Me, worried? Pah. Been in tighter corners than this with both hands locked in my undercrackers. This is no bother.'

Javani and Manatas exchanged a look of mutual confusion, before reassuring themselves that the Commodore had been speaking metaphorically. Probably.

'Commodore's not worried. I'm not worried. Let's go.'

'As you wish,' the captain sighed, and they resumed their climb.

The sky was deepening blue as they crested what the Commodore assured them was the final ridge – it apparently being necessary to take 'the long way round' – dawn's golden wash already a memory, and the day's heat rising with the fearsome sun. The three infiltrators tucked themselves in the shadow of a sand-scoured boulder and peered down at their quarry.

'They've been busy little buggers, eh?' muttered the Commodore.

The Guild had indeed been busy little buggers. The mountain outpost, which had, on Ree's original charts, been marked only in the most minor terms, was enormous. It had expanded twice past its walls, and new roads snaked from north, south and west to its freshly carved gateways. Those roads teemed with traffic, even at the early hour, much of it mine-based. Beyond the walls sprawled a giant market, undulating with the irregular terrain and rocky shelves, covered stalls and hangings sliced into neighbourhoods by terracing and informal pathways through the press.

The outpost's east was dominated by the works yard and the terminus, as the Commodore had called it: the great mechanism that connected the twinned tracks of the Iron Road, the precise workings hidden within a great blocky edifice of yellow stone. Track stretched away from it, initially banked and flattened with raised wooden platforms either side, dotted with cranes and funnels, then cresting the edge of the outpost's rocky plateau and sweeping from sight, ramped down towards the plains and the distant coast. High walls blocked their view of exactly what lurked at the tracks' start, but their outward path was stark.

Guards were everywhere. They weren't hard to spot: their burnished breastplates gleamed in the sunlight, and they lurked, loomed and preened from every gateway, tower and wall, and were inescapably prominent in the access points to the terminus. There seemed to be so many of them, standing around or in loose patrols swaggering through the inner walls, inspecting the arriving shipments or menacing merchants, that Javani wondered how the Guild could afford to have so many people on its payroll who just hung around.

'Is it conceivable,' Manatas murmured from beside her, 'that we have learned enough of this place and may now retire?'

The Commodore scoffed. 'Thought you were a military man? The whole "captain" nonsense some kind of affectation?'

Manatas pursed his lips. 'I was a chapter captain for a free company for a time, it's true.'

'Oh aye, bet you were cracking. "Is that enough fighting, can we go home now?" Actually, now you mention it, that is approaching standard practice for the exemplars of freelance soldiery, so perhaps you were a champ after all.'

Manatas's brows were lowered and pinched. 'Was there, by chance, a point to this?' He sounded almost hurt.

'Aye, right, point, aye. What we're getting from up here's what you might call the broad strokes. What we'll be needing next is the, uh, other bits. The vinegar strokes, mebbe.' She chuckled, but Javani didn't get it. 'So, aye, we'll need to be getting inside for that.'

'Inside? Have you taken leave of what I presumed pass for your senses, woman? There is more force on show at this location than the rest of the mountains combined. We cannot possibly infiltrate and remain undetected!'

The Commodore raised one eyebrow, shook her head in a disappointed manner. 'See, this is the trouble with company types. No subtlety, no nuance. No, uh, *panatch*.'

'While you may have the right of the matter in the general sense, I fail to see how I am wide of the mark in this instance. You are aware of some way to remain undiscovered?'

'Ha, course not. The intent is to be firmly discovered, but there to be no shame in it.'

'You are insane.'

'I am charming. There's a narrow distinction.'

Javani had reached her limit. 'Will you two stop talking over me, please? Commodore, are you saying we're going to walk right in there?'

'Aha, fucken hells, no.'

'Right. Good. That's what I thought.'

'*I* am.'

Javani stared into the wide, round, pale eyes of the Commodore. 'You *are* insane.'

Manatas was rubbing one side of his head. 'You are, in the kindest possible sense, an outlander here, and peculiar with it, and liable to attract greater scrutiny than any of our party. How do you expect to—'

The Commodore stood, brushed herself down, then tied back her mountain of hair. 'You see, the thing about being a foreign weirdo,' she said, then stuck two fingers in her mouth, rubbed them in dirt and proceeded to draw a pattern of muddy streaks on her face, 'is that foreign weirdos turn up everywhere, and, by definition, nobody knows what to make of them. 'S just a question of perspective.'

She wiped her hand on the front of her trousers, then pointed to Javani. 'You, keep an eye on him.' The menacing finger swung to Manatas. 'You, keep an eye on her.' She turned and began scrambling down the slope in the direction of the new south road. 'See yous buggers presently,' came wafting in her wake.

Javani and Manatas were alone on the ridge.

'Well,' said Manatas.

'Well,' Javani replied.

Somewhere, an eagle cried.

'See her?'

'That I do not . . . wait, there she is. That is an . . . unusual walk.'

'Pass me the spyglass, let me see. Whoa, no kidding.'

'Is . . . uh, is this a customary mode of perambulation for her?'

'Couldn't tell you, captain. I only met the woman the other day. The night Ree . . . you know.'

'Ah. I see. What is she doing now?'

'Lost her again, hang on . . . She's in the market. She seems to be . . . talking to stallholders.'

'That seems reassuringly quotidian.'

'It's what?'

'Normal. Given her approach, appearance, and, well, general demeanour.'

'Don't get your hopes up, she's, uh, trying some of the merchandise?'

'By which, of course, you mean sampling some of the sweetmeats, or perhaps weighing the purchase of a new hat by assessing its most fetching angle?'

'Kind of the other way around.'

'She's wearing food and eating clothes?'

'It's hard to say at this range, but, yeah, I can't rule it out.'

'Grace of the gods save us.'

'Shit. Here come the guards.'

'What kind of . . . Her "plan", such as it was, bore only the slightest connection with reality—'

'Oh.'

'What?'

'She's lost them.'

'What?'

'She's lost the guards. I'm not sure how, but they're looking for her all round the market, and she's . . . nine hells, how did she do that?'

'What now?'

'She's inside the . . . She must have drawn them away, and now she's inside the walls.'

'Is she still . . . ?'

'Yeah, still walking like she's been kicked in the head by a horse.'

'Mercy of the gods.'

'Still, between her and the inner walls, there's a whole bunch of . . . Gods, she's heading right for a patrol!'

'This course contradicts every operational tenet I have known. Does she expect us to mount a rescue? Are we to—'

'Oh, by the gods . . .'

'What *now*?'

'She's making them laugh. They're . . . they're in fits.'

'What? How?'

'Some kind of . . . Clydish wit, I guess?'

'That there should be such a concept astounds me. What are they doing now?'

'They've . . . they've gone into . . . I think it's an alehouse.'

'The guards? Where is the Commodore?'

'Oh, she was leading the charge.'

'Was it distraction? Has she emerged?'

'Nope. I guess not. Must be thirsty after all that . . . capering.'

'Now what do we do?'

'I guess . . . I guess we wait.'

'Well.'

'Well.'

TWENTY-SIX

The silence soon became oppressive, the drone of insects loud in Javani's ears, the clamour and shouts of the outpost drifting on the feeble breeze. The sun climbed, and the air shimmered with heat. Even in shadow, Javani felt she was being slowly cooked.

'I do not wish to pry,' the captain said, unprompted. He wasn't looking at her, the borrowed, murky spyglass pressed to his eye, watching, presumably, for signs of an orange-haired stranger being strung from the walls.

'Huh?'

'That is, I have no wish to impose discomfort.'

'Unless you can install a feather mattress on this ridge, captain, I think that ship has sailed.'

He smiled, winced, released a puff of air that was halfway between a sigh and a laugh. 'You are so like her,' he murmured, so softly Javani was sure she had not been meant to hear.

Her voice took an edge. 'Was there something you wanted to ask?'

'As I said, I do not mean to—'

'Pry, yeah. Go on, then. Un-pry.'

He took a long, slow breath, the spyglass relaxed in his grip, his gaze now somewhere off on the red rock horizon. 'I am . . . I am impressed, Javani, at the energy, the tenacity you have displayed, with which you have moved us forward. It is . . . testament to your capabilities.'

Javani waited. 'But?'

'I have . . . to call it a worry is too strong, perhaps not even a concern, but something akin to a notion with which I am a little uncomfortable . . . That we, collectively, are placing too great a burden upon you, and in time all will suffer for it.'

'What do you mean?'

'We must not hurt you by asking too much.'

'Hurt me? I'm here because I want to be, because I choose to be! No one is asking anything of me, I'm the one telling you all!'

'. . . And that is why I am concerned.'

'You said it wasn't a concern.'

'It has blossomed.'

Javani's tone was the warning growl of a mastiff. 'Are you saying I don't know what I'm doing?'

To his credit, he took his time preparing an answer. 'People of your age are not, historically, the best makers of decisions.'

'And what age is that?'

'The murky landscape between childhood and a truly adult existence, I suppose.'

'I'm an adult already! I'm fifteen.'

'And a half, I believe.'

'Damned straight.'

He rested the spyglass on the warming rock and turned himself to look at her, resting on one elbow. 'There are schools of thought on the true demarcation of becoming full grown, and they range anywhere from sixteen to thirty-five years of age. But I am not talking about numbers, Javani. I am only . . . I do not wish to see you come to harm.'

'I know what I'm doing.' She hated how childish she sounded when she said it.

'I believe that you do. But there is doing . . . and not doing.'

Javani blinked sweat from her eyelashes. 'I don't follow.'

He sighed and shuffled against the rock, wincing as something in his shoulder produced an alarming crunching noise. 'I am too old to be lying on mountains and watching things again,' he muttered.

'Captain?'

'I am sorry. I meant only to, at least in the hope of so doing, impart a degree of advice, I suppose.' He rubbed at one eyebrow. 'I must stress again, that I have the greatest faith in you, Javani. You are exceptional, and . . . we are all proud.'

'Thanks. I guess.'

'And I know that you are more than capable of achieving what you have set out to do. My advice comes only from a place of . . . what might be termed "wistful melancholy".'

'Wistful melancholy.'

He rubbed at the eyebrow again, dragged his hand over his face. The bristles of his silver stubble rasped. 'All I wish is for you to be spared the mistakes of my own youth.'

'Oh. Isn't that what all advice is, though? "Don't do that, I did it and now I've only got one leg"?'

'Perhaps you are right, although it is not the leg that my misapprehensions cost me.'

'Well, why don't you tell me what you did wrong, and I'll promise not to do that, and then we can all get on with things?'

His smile was bleak, a sadness in his eyes. 'You make it sound so simple. Perhaps it is.'

'We won't know until we try.'

'Very well.' He flopped back onto his stomach, as if he couldn't look at her while he spoke. 'My life, taken in sum, has been a litany of failures.'

Javani waited to see where this was going. It was not what she'd expected.

'I have failed, more than I have succeeded, in gods know near every endeavour I have undertaken since I was old enough to walk my own path. But that is my burden, and I will make my peace in time, or will not. That which pains me, and which I am minded enough to express in your direction, is that the primary victims of my failures, those who suffered most, were those other than myself.'

'You fucked up, but other people got hurt?'

'Succinctly put. But I was blind to so much of that hurt, and the degree of my part in it. The mind can do remarkable things to swerve culpability, to deny guilt's gnaw. But in time I reached an age, and I could not tell you which but that it was somewhat greater than thirty-five, where I could look back upon the trail of ruin that was my life lived, where I could mark the char of my passing upon those

I had encountered, and see in day's clear light that it was my action, or inaction, that lay at the heart of so much grief.'

'Do you mean—'

'I failed them all, one after another. I failed the family of my birth, after they raised, clothed and fed me, I struck out into the world and never looked back, repaid them nothing. Their surviving, healthy son, who cut them loose to wither and starve.'

'Did they actually—'

'My chosen family, the wife I took with such promises and intent, the children who lived . . . I abandoned them for a life on the trail, in pursuit of profit and adventure. The meagre coin I sent could never repair the damage of my absence, and they were right to spurn me.'

'Riiight . . . I get the impression there's a lot more to come, but you learned your lesson, right? That's the advice?'

He took a long, juddering breath, and when he spoke again, his voice was soft and mournful. 'I wish I could concur. But I remain condemned to repeat this pattern of murderous failure; and now I am cursed with the knowledge of what has happened, what continues to happen. If I had listened to Kediras, she might yet live. If I had trusted Arkadas, he likewise. And now, your mother . . .'

He put his hands over his face, and Javani was shocked to see tears tracking down the stubble of his jaw.

She tried to make her voice as soft as his. 'I'm . . . I'm not sure I know what you're advising me.'

He smiled without mirth, his hands dropping, leaving red-rimmed eyes that in Javani's estimation had seen far too much for one lifetime. Not that she could really tell, but there was something about the lines around them, the slump of the surrounding skin, the darkened hollows beneath . . . She didn't want to end up like that. She resolved to sleep more, when she was old.

'I suppose,' he said, his voice resigned but not entirely without humour, 'that all advice is doomed by difference. The wisdom we wish to impart is only to our younger selves, and the world has moved on in a way that can never be repeated. One cannot cross the same river twice.'

'That's bollocks.'

'Excuse me?'

'I've crossed the same river twice. Multiple times. You've been with me on some of them. We crossed the Ouris twice just last week, even if it's just a dry creek this time of year.'

'That's – that's not the meaning of the saying.'

'Well, it's a stupid saying.'

He tilted his hat back and mopped at his brow with a neat handkerchief. 'The essence of the aphorism is that one cannot repeat aspects of one's life, in the same way that the water of a river—'

'I get it! It's still stupid though. And I'm no closer to understanding what it is you want from me!'

His hollowed eyes flared with concern. 'Please, do not exercise yourself. I meant not to inflame. I worry only that—'

'Oh, it's a worry now, is it? Upgraded again?'

He took a steady breath through his nose and adjusted his hat again. 'Javani, you do not need to throw yourself so wholeheartedly into this venture.'

'Do I not? You lot were doing a bang-up job before I gave you a shunt, weren't you?'

One of his palms was up, calloused and dusty. 'And you had the right of it, I see it now. But I wish only for you to countenance the potential of other avenues for your attentions and efforts.'

'Meaning what, exactly?' The warning growl had returned to her voice; she suspected she knew exactly where this was going.

His hand was still lifted. 'It has not,' he said quietly, his voice barely louder than the moan of the wind through the rocky cut, the cries of birds and the distant shouts of some frustrated guards, still turning the market upside down in pursuit of a deranged foreigner, 'escaped my notice that you have not spent much time with your mother.'

Javani's cheeks were hot. 'I don't want to talk about it.'

'You do not ask after her, you do not come to see her, you do not tend to her.' It wasn't accusatory, merely dispassionate statements, and that made it all the worse.

'I said I don't want to talk about it!'

'Javani, I am not asking you to take over her care. I am prepared to take that burden, such as it is, and Tauras and Mistress Whitespear have done more than enough to assist. That is my choice, and I make it gladly.'

'Then why are we—'

'But this distance between you, this . . . absence . . . It pained me when both of you were upright and at each other's throats, but I confess I do not understand why, in our current situation, matters have deteriorated, not ameliorated. I seek only to understand, Javani, and urge you not to let your pain and whatever else ails you cause you regret in the years to come.'

Javani wrapped her hands around her knees, top teeth pulling at her bottom lip. She knew she was scowling, she could not help it. 'What do you want from me? You want me to come and, what, sing her songs or something? What am I going to regret otherwise?'

He held her surly gaze, eyes steady, until she broke away. 'I could not say,' he said, without rebuke, 'but I believe if you were to stop by, on occasion, and speak to her, it might yet help.'

'What? What's the point? She's unconscious, and she's probably dying, and it's just a matter of time, right? If she was going to get better, she'd have woken up by now, and she hasn't, so she won't.' The words were coming in a hot rush, her throat closing, voice thick. 'It's just like Anri's wife, she'll be less and less there until one day she's just gone, but it won't make a lick of difference because she'll have been dead to us since the beginning.' She broke off, eyes stinging, cheeks hot, her breath hitching.

'I do not believe that.'

'You think she'll wake up? Seriously?' She couldn't measure the sincerity of his words, or of her own – she'd meant to sound sarcastic, but it came out hopeful.

'I believe she will. She is not gone from us, Javani. She fights on. She can drink, and consume broth, she can shift and turn, she moves herself without assistance. But she is weak, and she is fighting, and it is a battle that is taking everything she has. And I believe it is one she will win.' He tried to smile, the deep lines in his weathered face cracking like bark. 'And we can help her.'

'By talking to her?'

'Who knows how what we hear in our sleep permeates our dreams?'

Javani swallowed, her voice small. 'You think she's dreaming?'

The rock shelf beside them erupted in a fountain of dust and orange hair, then the mud-flaked face of the Commodore appeared over it.

'All right, fuckers? Kept busy, did you?' One patched elbow came over the side, and she blew a drifting wedge of hair from in front of her face. 'Going to give me a fucken hand here or what?'

Javani scrambled up. 'Right, yeah, of course.'

Manatas was right behind her. 'How did it go? We, uh, lost track of you, somewhat.'

'Oh aye, grand,' came the reply. 'I'll fill yous in on the soupy nuts downslope, though, as we likely shouldn't hang about here.' She cast a look back towards the outpost. 'It's not going to be much longer before that big fella realises I didn't pay for quite as many drinks as I may have implied.'

She waggled her eyebrows, then somewhere in the outpost a bell began to ring with a furious urgency. On a billowing cloud of booze, the Commodore crested the rock, cackling. 'Aye, right, off we fuck, pronto!'

They went.

Rai dreams, and remembers, surfs memory like a tide. A torrent of images, of experiences, of sights and sounds and visceral encounters. South she travels, ever south, away from the gorge and across the Sink to the blighted lands. Vistirlar! The language and dialects come easily, along with everything else; she is sharp and stunning and bears the richness of her education as another weapon. She'll keep an accent no matter her years in the south, but its strength will depend solely on her mood.

Vistirlar's state amazes her, the laughably described Free Cities, the quarrelling provinces, the insidious church; she knows the land, knows the politics, remembers everything she learned and learns in turn with ravening hunger. Her parents insisted on the finest teaching their scrabbled funds could buy, in the hope she would ascend from their lowly position in the social ranks. Well, they certainly got their wish.

Her mother was a musician, a harpist, and her father a minor functionary in Arowan's baroque bureaucracy. They were no one of note or importance, secondary or tertiary in the rooms they inhabited at every turn. Rai was their fourth child, the third survivor, and she was marked by her beauty from the day she was born. Her parents made no secret of their astonishment at the breathtaking girl in their midst, this confluence of favourable genetic outcomes. To the growing ire of her siblings, Rai was on an elevated path from birth.

When she thinks of it now, the fury at her parents returns. Their feckless venality, plotting from her infancy to trade her for their own advancement. They ploughed what wealth they had into tutoring for her, spent coin and all their meagre influence to train and dress her for the upper city. Her mother took extra work, played at the private residences of the great and good, to afford the silk they needed for her formal dress. Her father sold heirlooms, worked late into the night in the lower chamber offices, to ensure she'd get the same dance tuition as the daughters of upper Arowan. They had one goal, and one goal only: to get her into the hall of dance. To be seen.

And it worked. Not knowing otherwise, Rai delighted in dance, in learning, in putting herself before her siblings. She was a child – what else was she expected to do? The golden offspring, the chosen one, first to eat, first to learn. She excelled. She threw herself into everything before her, marvelled in instruction, danced with gods-given grace. She sailed through the examinations that left the scions of the great families sweating and stumped. She travelled the path her parents laid out for her, and she picked up speed. At the end of it, he waited.

But it's Merenghi's stink that draws her, anchors her to the moment. Cold a city, and wretched, the grey stone pitted and motley with guano, the mud hard and cracked beneath her boot. Beneath the other: a man's head. Occasionally he struggles, and she presses down with her heel.

Zaven is there, opposite her, lounging, pouting with delight at the scene in the alleyway. Zaven the fence, the contact, Zaven who works for those who do not wish to be seen. Rai has found what work she can on her journey south, and has followed her talents. Her golden path has led her here, and she has excelled.

Zaven collects the take with only a raised eyebrow and a smirk, then pauses, his fingers light on hers. She envies the streaks of colour in his hair. 'How old are you?' he says, the challenge clear in his eyes. She knows he's dangerous, but not to her. She's been reading people for so long it happens without the slightest thought.

'Old enough to cut my own path.'

'Varolo is impressed. He's taken an interest in you and your crew.'

'There's no crew.' The head beneath her boot struggles again, gag-muffled, and she kicks downwards, quelling it. 'Only me.'

Zaven's smirk expands. 'Clearly, you're not sentimental. I thought you two were something of an item.'

'We had a mutually beneficial arrangement.' She feels nothing as she says it, doesn't even look at the man beneath her boot. As with those before him, she's learned all she can from him now, and his creeping desperation made him stupid. 'For a time.'

'And are you interested in more . . . sensitive work?'

Rai is hungry, so hungry. She is ready to make her mark.

'Try and stop me.'

TWENTY-SEVEN

The crew, such as they were, were gathered around a low plinth of weather-cracked, sand-coloured rock, where the Commodore had assembled . . . something.

'Aye, right, shuffle up now, I've tried to do everything to scale but 'tween us I've had shite-all but shite to work with, so some of the measures are more, what you might call "indicative".'

Anashe exchanged a look with Javani. 'Do you know what she is talking about?'

'Well, maybe. Sort of.'

They shuffled closer. It was not yet dark, the arroyo where they'd made camp still sun-warmed, bathed in ruddy western light. Teg and Stefanna were absent, out 'on patrol', whatever that meant; the Commodore's taciturn riders mostly kept their distance from the rest of the group, and seemed to be present on sufferance. Javani assumed that they owed the Commodore money. Sarian was on watch, and Tauras was once again at the cookfire in the background, on double-duty with minding Ree in the shelter they'd made for her from the surviving yurts. Javani had not yet investigated it since their return to the camp, but she knew it wouldn't be long. She couldn't take the looks from Manatas much longer.

'Right, my wee terrors, feast your eyes on . . . Gonaraz!'

'Fuck's that?' came Anri's voice from the far side of the White Spear. Javani was glad he was present, for once, despite his sour mood; it would save time on explaining things again later.

'The name of the mining outpost, dickhead,' she called over. 'Where the Iron Road begins.'

'Or ends,' the Commodore added with a manic grin. She'd not yet cleaned herself up since they'd returned to the camp, and the flaked mud on her face combined with the lingering reek of booze made her a challenge to stay near. 'According to, y'know, perspective. Anyway, eyes feasted, right?'

Javani looked down at the top of the wide table of rock. True to her word, the Commodore had constructed some kind of miniature edifice, and she had done it primarily with pony dung.

Anashe waved a hand in front of her face. 'This seems extreme, even for you.'

'What are you talking about? We're hardly overflowing with modelling materials, and it's good and dried.' The Commodore reached out and gave what Javani presumed was a chunk of the outpost's outer wall a squeeze. It oozed. 'Mostly.'

Anashe's mouth was a downturned crescent. 'You are banished from the sleeping area until the smell is gone.'

'Oh, come on, that's hardly fair. That could take weeks. I'll get you a wee peg for your nose in the meantime.'

Manatas cleared his throat. 'I believe we had some important information to impart?'

'Aye, right, if people could stop obsessing over minor things like aroma . . .'

'You smell like a corpse pit,' the White Spear rumbled. 'In summer. After a dysenteric plague.'

'Hush your moaning, you'll get used to it. Anyway, right, where were we?' The Commodore went to brush hair from her face with her hand, then thought better of it. 'So the Slayer and Captain Moodyguts—'

'Manatas.'

'—and my good self went on a wee jaunt up to Gonaraz, and I took a bit of a look-see around the place to fill in our understanding collective, you see. And quite the things I learned!'

'This going to take much longer, is it?' Anri muttered. 'There's a decomposing fox carcass up on the ridge, might go back to watching it dissolve.'

'Fucken hells, man, you should all be on tenterhooks for this! What's wrong with you?'

The captain cleared his throat again, some kind of conversational prelude to announce that, while he would never dream of interrupting or speaking out of turn, if nobody had anything else to say then he might, perchance, venture an opinion of his own. 'Might we, perhaps, advance towards the impartation of meaningful intelligence?'

'Aye, right!' The Commodore clapped her hands together, and something definitely splattered. 'So you're all asking yourselves, what's the word in Gonaraz? What's the impact of this here road of iron, this pathway across the plains. What does it mean for the divers and strivers who make up the local populace, and, most of all . . . what does it mean for our little scheme, eh? Well, and this is the big one, folks, I can tell you, without further ado, that—'

'It's not finished,' Javani broke in.

'Hoy, I was getting to that!'

'You were taking too long.'

'Aye, fair.'

Javani took a step around the stinky plinth to face the others. 'The Iron Road isn't yet complete, not at the far end.'

The White Spear leaned forward, giving the dung-sculpture an increased level of scrutiny. 'It does not reach Kilale Port?'

'Not yet.' Javani pointed down at the plinth, where two lines of dung balls stretched away from the mass by the Commodore and out across the rocky surface. 'It stops outside, a place called, um, the Old Oak, or something. A few miles from the port itself.'

Anashe still wore a curdled expression, but it was tempered with interest. 'What use is a set of tracks that does not reach its destination?'

'Aye, good question, one for those blessed with a mightier intellect than our own, no doubt.' The Commodore gave a lopsided grin to indicate just how ludicrous she considered the notion. 'According to some ever-so-loquacious fellows I got chatting, they've been ferrying goods by cart and canal, running a temporary set of gears and wheels while they finish the final section of the tracks. And they're almost there.'

Javani lifted her gaze to the group. 'Ask me when they're planning to link it up.'

Anashe pursed her lips in wry amusement, while the White Spear nodded, her face impassive. Anri looked from one to the other, then huffed. 'Well, when, then? All know something I don't, do you?'

'They intend to unite matters on the day of the charter renewal, I take it.' Anashe didn't even make it a question.

Javani felt a weird tingle of excitement, an urge to hop from foot to foot and clench her fingers into her palms. 'Exactly. The diggers want a grand opening – an, uh, investiture – to go with their charter renewal. And they're shutting down the road for the period beforehand to connect the new track. Which means nothing will be travelling down it in the days beforehand.'

Anashe had one long finger against her chin. 'Meaning, if our friends the functionaries, the potential carriers of the seal, have not yet reached Gonaraz . . .'

'They won't be able to take the Iron Road until the day of the renewal itself,' Javani finished, feeling a flush of something that wasn't triumph, but had a strong whiff of vindication.

'They will be confined to the outpost, awaiting their transit,' Anashe mused. 'And the seal will be with them.'

'Are yous lot going to let me announce anything?' the Commodore grumbled. 'Spent ages on my poo houses, I did. They've got little people in them, look.' She flicked disconsolately at some musty fragments.

Javani offered her a tight smile. 'You take too long. Why don't you point along for the next bit.'

'Oh, aye, fine, fuck's sake.'

'Right.' Javani turned to the others, her hands extended as if holding an invisible box. 'There's loads more to find out, of course – timings and storage and these new wheeled containers for passengers—'

'These what?' asked Anashe, one eyebrow a sharp and inverted V.

'But we have a window here, a definite period to act. As of now, the Iron Road is closed, and it won't reopen until the day of the renewal. That means the seal must be aboard it on that morning. And that's our chance to make off with it.'

Anashe was tapping her finger against her chin. 'If the potential carriers of the item are departing early on the day, they will likely be lodging the night before. If we can locate their sleeping place, and their belongings within it . . .'

Javani shook her head. 'Thought of that. But it's at least three of them, likely all staying separately in official lodgings inside the inner walls, and their luggage will have more guards around it than ever.'

Beside her, the Commodore indicated some mounded dung with a flourish. 'Aye, right, place is crawling with shiny-boy patrols at the best of times, the night before a grand jamboree we'll be up to our wossnames in the wee bastards.'

Manatas nodded. 'The need to locate and investigate multiple targets lends an excess of risk to an endeavour that is already somewhat elevated in that department. Should any one of us be apprehended or trigger a more general alarm, our chance would be lost, if not worse.'

'And why bother?' Javani spread her hands. 'We know where the seal will be on the morning. They'll all be aboard the people-carts, their luggage and effects with them.'

The Commodore whipped her unclean finger to another area of the manure model. 'My pals down in the alehouse let slip that cargo gets loaded in the yards here, one either side, while those folk deranged enough to travel on the manic mine cart down the mountain climb aboard in this middle section.' Javani had to admit, when you squinted, the detail was there, right down to a row of what she hoped were pebbles glowing red in the late sun. 'And there's a wee promontory in the rockside over yonder that'll give us a spanking view of proceedings as they go. Note well, chums, that at each end of the wagon-string are two big old steel-plated bastards, archer turrets on wheels, from the sound of it.'

'And how do we use this knowledge?' The White Spear's expression hadn't changed throughout, indicating neither intrigue nor scepticism. 'If there are many guards within the walls, there will be many guards in these yards. You suggest there will be more guards in these moving towers at each end. How is this good news? There is a limit to the number of skulls that can be cracked without cost.'

Here the Commodore started to giggle, and Javani wondered just how much she'd had to drink in the alehouse in pursuit of intelligence. 'Aye, right, that's just the badger, isn't it?'

The White Spear did not respond, but one eyebrow lifted a fraction.

'All the guards are inside the walls, then they're up in their wee towers on the end, er, wagons.'

'We need a better name for those,' Javani muttered.

'Aye, so, morning of, all the great and good who are making the grand downhill wobble their way on *here*, while the cargo is loaded *here*, and, we believe, *luggage and other accoutrements* heaved on *here*. Word is, the process of getting underway is long and tedious, and must be done to a strict timetable as they have to coordinate with what's happening at the other end.'

'How'd they do it, then?' Anri demanded. 'How do they coordinate all the big wheels and what have you. It's miles and miles, up and down mountains, and all.'

Javani looked at Manatas, who looked at the Commodore, who shrugged.

'We don't know. The important thing, though, is that when it starts, it starts very, very slowly.'

The Commodore hiccuped, then gestured vaguely to where her narrow dung-trail crossed the lip of the rock plinth and disappeared over the side. 'Picks up a fair bit of speed on the way down, course. But these early parts, there's counterweights and whatnot, levers and things. For, uh, safety.'

Anashe pursed her lips. 'Who would have expected the Guild to put the safety of their workers in such pride of place?'

'Oh, aye, no, I think it's more concern for the fucker slipping off its tracks and spilling something if it gets away too sharpish. Sounds like our pal I Ron Roady has already mangled a bunch of folks who got too close at the wrong moment, so you can rest assured that the diggers remain unreconstructed bastards on that score.'

'How reassuring.'

The White Spear leaned forward a fraction, her massive shadow lengthening as she studied the faecal facsimile of the outpost. 'Then you propose to act early?'

Javani nodded. It was basically her plan, when it came down to it, once they'd got all the information out of the Commodore on their way back down from the scouting. If anything, Manatas and the Commodore had tried to talk her out of it, but the fact was there weren't many better options. 'Yeah. Between leaving the walls and the start of the initial descent.'

Anri snorted. 'And how's that, then? Going to climb aboard and ride it down the plains, are we?'

Javani stared back.

'Yep.'

Anri scratched at his beard, his scalp, his neck, and many other parts besides, then gave his head a vigorous shake. 'Sorry, pest, think I must have had gunge in my earhole then, because it sounded like you said you intend to board this rolling wagon-snake and ride along, which can't be right. Even if you are still a bloody infant, you can't be that demented.'

She held his gaze, not backing down. 'You heard the Commodore. The outpost is too well-guarded for us to sneak in and rummage around. But once everything is loaded, the . . . What are we calling it? The thing that travels along the Iron Road. I'm not calling it a wagon-snake.'

Manatas rubbed one hand against his chin. 'It does resemble a wagon-train, albeit with stark and unsettling changes.'

'Ugh, fine. For the sake of expediency, we'll call it a wagon-train. Anyway,' she turned back to Anri, 'once everything is loaded, the wagon-train sets off, very slowly, along a predetermined path, and leaves the walls and the guards behind. Now, if someone were to be lying in wait, say, around . . . around *there*, they could hop aboard the thing when it's at barely walking pace, still in the shade of the cut in the rocks and before we hit open country.'

'Fellas on the towers are all focused on what's ahead and what's behind,' the Commodore supplied, looking pleased that her excremental exhibition was being studied at last. 'Not so much the soggy middle.'

'We can spend a bit of time working out the where and the how,' Javani continued, 'but we should be able to get at least a couple of people on board before it gets anywhere. Then it's just a matter of moving from the cargo section up to where the luggage is kept, collecting the seal, and making our escape.'

Anri's chin lifted as he steepled his fingers. 'Ah, yes, wondering about that part, I was. Pray tell, pest, presuming the search of said snake-train has taken a while and some speed has been collected in the downward sections, how exactly are you planning to get off the fucker?'

Now Javani's composure ebbed. 'We're still working on that bit.'

'Kypeth's hairy arsecrack!'

'It can't be that hard! It never gets much faster than a cantering horse, right, Commodore?'

'Aye, 's'right – even on the downslopy parts, the whole shebang's still cabled up to the other wagon-snake—'

'*Train*,' Javani averred.

'Aye, right, train . . . So whichever one is at the top, starting in Gonaraz, that's got all the, wossname . . . *potential* energy. And as it starts to move, said *potential* energy is converted to *kinetic* energy, but 'cos of the cables, it's also connected to the one at the bottom, so via what you might call a prolonged pulley system, said energy is shared between them, meaning the force is split and a large portion is spent on getting the one at the bottom moving up the slope. So even on the very downhilly bits, there's still an effective braking action provided by the chappie coming the other way. See?'

Anri gave her a very cold stare. 'Making fun of me, are you?'

'What? Course not.'

'Think I don't know what kinetic energy is?'

'Ah, well, not everyone's had the benefit of an education, see—'

Anri turned the glare back on Javani. 'And you're banking our survival on this bollocks, are you?'

'I mean . . . maybe? I was thinking that, you know, as one goes down, the other comes up, so they pass at the halfway point, right? So we could, maybe, hop . . . from one . . . to the other?'

Anri barked a bitter laugh at that. 'Might not be as educated as some around here—'

'Hoy, it's not like I *hattended* an *Hacademy*!'

'—but even given a rudimentary understanding of the natural world, my instincts tell me that the halfway point is where the snake-trains will be travelling at their fastest!' He looked to the others. 'Right, aren't I? Come on.'

The White Spear shrugged with only her mouth. 'Perhaps.'

Anashe flexed her mouth and flared her nostrils. 'I would not like to say.'

Anri shook his head. 'No faster than a cantering horse. So that's one cantering horse going one way, one going the other, and you're thinking of leaping between them, are you, pest? How the fuck am I supposed to keep you safe if you're playing silly buggers like that?'

Javani started, her brows lowered in surprise. 'Who said anything about . . .Why are you keeping me safe, all of a sudden?'

He took a sharp breath through his nose, chin lifted, then nodded towards Ree's shelter. 'Told me to, she did,' he muttered. 'Shit job I've been doing so far.'

'What? No, that's not . . . What are you . . .' Javani pressed her fingers to her eyes. Things had taken a turn into an unexpected and unwelcome area. 'We're not here to talk about that.'

'Aye, right, I think we've covered the essence though, eh? Unless anyone wants another tour around the masterpiece?'

Manatas was at her side, perhaps intending to be reassuring, but instead all Javani felt was crowded and scrutinised. 'We have maybe a week,' the captain said, 'to discern the missing information we require, make preparations and decide on the manner of the escape.'

'And who,' Anashe said, arms folded.

'Excuse me?'

'We must decide who will be boarding the wagon-train in search of the item, and who will be in support.' She put up a hand when Javani began to gabble. 'This is not for now, but should be considered without haste or fervour.' Her gaze shifted towards Ree's shelter. 'And there is the question of who will be caring for our general, and whether she should be here at all.'

Javani's stomach lurched. She did not want this conversation now, she wanted only to focus on the plan, on what was to come, on a bold sense of the possible. Ree was not possible. Ree was misery and despair.

Manatas gave a heavy sigh. 'We could not have left her, of that I am in no doubt. But perhaps there may yet be a safer—'

'No!' Javani barked. 'We're not discussing this now, remember?'

She worked to get the pitch of her voice back under control. 'We can settle everything when we prepare.'

'Aye, right, roles and responsibilities, all part of proper planning, and proper planning prevents piss-poor performance, I always say.'

'Uh, thanks, Commodore. I guess.'

They began to disperse. It was too much to think about all at once, and from the smells wafting up the arroyo from Tauras's cookfire, dinner was ready, and he was improving.

'Actually, on that matter,' said the Commodore as she fell in step beside Javani, 'I had a wee question.'

'You're going to wash your hands before you eat, right?'

'What, scared of a little cholera, are you? I'm telling you, dysentery is cleansing. Ah, don't give me that look . . . Fine, I'll give them a wee splash.'

'A question, you said?'

'Oh, aye. When it comes to the assignment of roles . . . I've been meaning to ask, are there . . . many wolves, out on those plains?'

'Uh, maybe? Some? Jackals and foxes and various kinds of wild dog, I guess. Why?'

'Oh, no reason. No reason at all.' Then, under her breath, 'Bitey wee gobshites, just you try it.'

TWENTY-EIGHT

'One thing remains unclear to me.' Anashe had been chewing slowly, the last to finish, and the expectant looks she got from those around the fire were edged with no small amount of impatience; Manatas had decreed it poor manners to begin the clearing of dinner before all seated had finished, and for some reason everyone seemed to go along with it. Javani was both baffled and, on another level, quietly proud, but her impatience was no less diluted along with it. 'The role of the Iokara,' Anashe went on, at last. 'They have been content to lend their engineering expertise to this debased construction, this scar of man across the Goddess's lands . . . Are they present, still? Do they linger, as supervisors, guards, ambassadors? Do we risk . . . a diplomatic predicament?'

'Aye, right, well.' The Commodore had officially finished eating, but was now in full sweep-up mode, plucking unfinished morsels from the platters of her neighbours. 'Heard a bit about that on my jaunt. Sounds like they took care of the bulk of it without much sharing of the secret knowledge, then fucked off leaving only a few instructions on jamming the last few bits together.' She sniffed and rubbed her nose, hard. 'Always were a jealous lot when it came to sharing their toys.'

Anashe pursed her lips, one thumb to her chin, her remaining dinner increasingly at risk of the Commodore's predation. 'And their motive in the engagement – do we understand it? To undertake such work for an outfit like the Guild, at such cost . . .'

'Ah, well, indeedy.' The Commodore leaned ever closer, her eyes squarely on the last of Anashe's dinner. 'You see, friend Nort has no moral centre. It'll be pure calculation on their part.'

This stirred something in Javani's memory, something Ree had once said. 'Nations don't have morals,' she blurted, 'only interests.'

'Aye, right. Irrespective of the character of your individual Norty – or lack thereof, is what I'm saying – they'll have looked at this and seen opportunity. Cut-price ore and gemstones, local power and influence within our borders, access to favourable trade across the expanse, care of their new clients . . . what's a little up-front investment to get the Guild on their hook for all time?'

'Don't forget the slaves,' Javani growled.

'Well, I was kind of counting that one under "favourable trade", but I grant you it's worth its own category of villainy, aye. Like I said: bunch of bastards.'

'The Iokara or the Guild?'

'Aye, that's the one.' The Commodore swiped the last of Anashe's dinner from her platter and stuffed it into her mouth. 'Looks like you're all finished, eh?' she said, through chews.

Anashe looked down in surprise, then her mouth became a thin line. 'So it appears.' She looked up, brows still drawn. 'Then we are confident we will not be surprised by any implacable foes in war masks?'

'Well, never say never, I always say,' the Commodore mumbled, her mouth full.

'This has not been a reassuring conversation.'

Javani sighed and stood. 'I guess at the moment they're in short supply. Tauras, do you want a hand clearing up?'

She was not, if she was honest, particularly inclined to help with menial tasks, especially when it involved cleaning and scrubbing down irons or facing the Commodore's leavings (Anri's were bad enough, but he ate by himself on the ridge by habit, and however much Javani wished he'd join in a little more, she was in no hurry to create more work for herself). If anything, Javani had spent her lifetime perfecting a certain skill in chore-dodging, not so much work-shy as work-reclusive. This was no mean feat with Ree as your parental supervisor, and she was, in a perverse way, quite proud of her abilities.

But if she was helping Tauras, then she couldn't possibly be expected to be doing anything else, like meeting the captain's meaningful look and joining him in the next shift of Ree-watching in the shelter. Not long, he'd assured her; you don't need to spend the whole watch. Just come inside, speak to her, hold her hand. Let her know you're there.

Javani swallowed. But she wasn't there, was she?

'Yes, Javani. Thank you, Javani.' Tauras was still enormous up close; she knew she'd grown in the last two years, and quite a lot – the premature termination of all her old sets of trousers had been a giveaway there – and she was proud of finally getting somewhere after a bit of a slow start, but Tauras had been massive when she met him, and he seemed no smaller now. The same could not be said of any of the other grown-ups, some of whom Javani now met eye to eye (she immediately discounted Ree from that consideration), with the exception of the White Spear. Javani had remembered the Horvaun mercenary as blotting out the sun when she'd encountered her nearly three years before, and even without her vast black armour the woman towered over them all. She was somehow bigger than Tauras, despite his muscular bulk, and the two of them made for quite the pair as she joined them at the slop-station, a pair of giants with her their stunted child.

'Not like that,' the White Spear growled at Tauras, one great pale hand over his. 'With the grain, or you will scar the metal.'

'Righto, Mistress Whitespear.' He altered his movement immediately. Tauras took instruction without question or challenge, and performed to the letter. It boggled Javani's mind.

'Good work, boy.'

'Thank you, Mistress Whitespear.'

Javani tried to join in, but she felt like she might be crushed between the pair of them. She hovered at the edge of their combined orbit.

'You don't mind clearing up, Tauras? You did the cooking, after all.'

'Cleaning up is part of cooking, Javani, and I am happy to do both. I am improving, you see. Practice makes progress.'

'Yeah, you're . . . definitely getting better.' Some of the evening's meal had been almost tasty.

'If I keep doing it, I'll keep getting better, Javani.'

'How much better do you want to get?' She felt a pang of guilt; it seemed wrong to take advantage of his nature and his ambition to make everyone else's lives easier. But then, if he was really happy to do the work, was it so bad? 'Does cooking make you happy?'

'Yes, Javani, very happy. I like making food for my friends. I want to keep doing it, so they like the food I make more. Practice makes—'

'Progress, yeah.'

'One day, the captain says we'll go back to the Lake House, and I'll cook for everyone then. By the lake. I'll make the breaded fish that Lieutenant Arkadas likes. The captain says he'll show me how. And we'll all eat by the lake.'

'And that would make you happy?'

He turned to face her, and the earnest passion in his gaze was utterly disorientating. 'Yes, Javani. We'll all be happy. That's what the Lake House is.'

'Boy, you are not concentrating. This will take longer, and you may make mistakes. Where I grew, boys were bone-whipped for such errors.'

'Yes, Mistress Whitespear.'

Javani wiped idly at a platter beside Tauras, and muttered, 'Gods, it's like she's your ma, eh? I mean, she almost could be. If you were Horvaun.' Javani remembered the White Spear mentioning, in passing on one of the many occasions they'd been under murderous threat, that she'd had children of her own, down south, long ago, but she hadn't seemed particularly wistful on the subject; she'd given the impression that it was, on some level, a duty to her clan, which she'd gladly fulfilled, but now it was performed and she had moved on, she had no further interest or connection to anyone involved. There had not been a chance to dwell on her words at the time, but now Javani thought back, she was convinced she saw something in the White Spear's stern gaze when she barked at Tauras. She wasn't yet sure what it was, but it was . . . something.

'Oh no, Javani, I did have a ma, and it wasn't Mistress Whitespear.'

'Oh, right, yeah, of course. I only meant—'

'I didn't know her long, because she died birthing me, so I know it wasn't Mistress Whitespear, as she is still alive.'

'Oh, uh, gods, Tauras, I didn't mean—'

'I was too big, you see.' His hand slowed on the pan, just for a moment. 'Even then. I was always too big, Javani.'

'Uh . . .'

'Then growing up, I was big, which was good, but I always ate too much. That's what my granda said. It got so they couldn't feed me. So I had to go. But I was big enough to join the regulars, even if I wasn't old enough really, and they had rations from the store. But there was fighting. I was too big.' He looked down at the blackened pan, seeing through it and into the red earth below. 'People always wanted to fight me, even though I was big.'

'I guess, uh, some people are like that.'

He recommenced his scrubbing, cheer returned to his voice. 'But then I met Captain Manatas, and Captain Kediras, and Lieutenant Arkadas – not all at once, but once I'd met them all, we stayed together. As long as we could, anyway. And one day I'll cook for us all.'

Javani knew that Kediras and Arkadas were dead. She was fairly sure that Tauras knew that too, but seeking to remind him at this point just seemed mean. 'Yeah. I'll look forward to that.'

'So I know Mistress Whitespear isn't my ma,' he said with a smile. 'I had a ma. Then I didn't any more.'

She met his smile with a wobbly effort of her own. 'Yeah, I . . . kind of didn't have a ma, then did . . . and now . . . now I couldn't say.' Her gaze drifted back across the camp, towards the dark of the shelter. Manatas was outside it, pointedly not looking in her direction.

'I've, uh, got to go. Sorry, Tauras.'

'That's all right, Javani. You'll be better next time. Practice makes progress.'

'You are under no obligation to linger, you understand. Merely a passing visit, the sound of your voice, I'm sure—'

'Yeah, I get it, captain.'

'I have . . . I have prepared her for you, as best I was able.'

'What? What do you mean?'

The captain's eyes were dark and glossy pools in the gloom of the awning. A dim lantern burned somewhere within the shelter, its quivering light twin sparkles in his gaze. 'I am cognisant that it has been . . . some time . . . since you last saw your mother up close. I did not want you to be, uh, unsettled by her appearance.'

She was ready to deny it, ready to snap at him, but he was hardly wrong. She was sweating, despite the cooling of the day's fierce heat, and her stomach was knotted and tight. When he stepped deeper into the shelter, she remained, lingering by the awning, the bright slash of evening rose.

'Javani?'

'Why do you do it?'

'Why do I do what?'

'Why do you stay? Here. With her. Why are you looking after her like this, when . . . when she's been nothing but cruel to you for the last two years?'

He paused, then walked slowly back to her in his swinging, sauntering way. 'Leaving aside that inaccurate assessment, why do you think?' He regarded her with kindly eyes, red-rimmed and hollowed as they were, his head tilted. 'Why does any of us stay?'

She couldn't hold his gaze. 'I dunno,' she muttered to the floor.

To her relief, he didn't force an answer from her. 'Because we care, Javani. About the mission, of course, about the hobbling of the Guild and the restoration of some measure of equanimity to the expanse, but because we care about your mother, too.'

The dusty earth kept her eyeline, well-trodden and cracked. 'But you could leave. You could pack up and ride off, you don't owe her. You've only known her a couple of years, and she's been fucking horrible to you for most of that time.'

'She has not.'

'She has! She's taken you for granted, treated you like utter shit, bossed you around and belittled you, never listened to your ideas, never let you do—'

'Javani.' His voice was quiet, but she let him stop her. She was still staring groundwards, her cheeks flushed, her shirt stuck to her back. He put a tentative hand on her shoulder, and she didn't shy away. But she wanted to.

'I am not going to leave her, Javani. I love your mother, and I am more than willing to make whatever sacrifices are required to see that she has the best chance of fighting off this scourge. I am grateful for the support of those around us – Anri's contribution has been of particular note, I must credit – but the one thing I will not do is flee. I will not . . . fail her. You can ask the same of any of us here, of why we have hitched ourselves to this madcap endeavour, why we are hitched still. I cannot speak for the others, but that they are still here in this camp with you after all that has befallen us on both the personal and professional strata suggests that their answers will not differ vastly from my own.'

He gave her shoulder a hesitant squeeze. 'It is not a failing to care for someone, Javani, nor to let somebody care for you.'

She refused to look up, and after a moment he removed his hand and made to step away. She wasn't ready. She needed to delay him.

'What's the Lake House?'

He paused, one foot tilted away. 'You heard about that?'

'Tauras.' She swallowed. She could look up now, meet his gaze, but the churning feeling in her abdomen was unchanged. 'He said it was . . . happiness. In so many words.'

Manatas rubbed a hand down his cheek with a soft rasp, and cracked a tired smile. 'It's just a place we went a few times, between tours and contracts. As the name implies, it sits on a lake, just off the trade route to Pasaj at the elbow of the mountains. The weather remains clement, even over winter, and the food is plentiful, if not of the highest standard. Why did he mention it?'

'He wants to go back, uh, I think. And cook for everyone.'

His smile flexed, momentarily wider, then frozen in sadness. 'That . . . that would have been a fine thing.' He took a long breath through his nose and pressed his palms together. 'Are you ready?'

Javani didn't answer as he crossed the shelter to the darkened bundle beyond. As if sensing his presence, the bundle shifted and whimpered as if hurt or afraid. A single hand dropped into view from the mass of blankets, the palm pale in the lantern's weak light. Javani stared at it. Small. Thin. Wasted.

'I . . . I can't.'

'What's that? You can take—'

'I can't do it. Not now.'

'Wait— Javani!'
She bolted into the evening.

Javani came to a halt on the ridge, breathing hard, hands on her knees, sweat dripping from her brow and splashing in dark clumps in the sandy earth between her boots. Evening had fallen, the sun no more than a daub of ruby at the western horizon, shot through with purples and golds, the peaks below cast lilac in the fading light. To the east, the paling sky plunged into indigo, bejewelled with the first sharp twinkle of stars. The air was cool and still, and around her the land had fallen quiet but for the muffled chirp of insects and the distant cry of a drifting hawk. She took several deep breaths, trying to still herself to match the landscape, to calm her heart and lungs. The pounding thud in her ears receded, the ragged gasps of her breathing finally subsiding. She stood back up, wiping slick salt from her forehead.

'Fancied a walk, did we?' said the briar of black gorse beside her. 'Nice evening for it, I suppose.'

Javani shrieked and leapt sideways.

'No need for that.' Anri's head emerged from the bush, affecting a convincing look of hurt. 'Just minding my own business, I was, keeping out of the way.'

He stood up, walked around the bush, then sat heavily and showily down, looking out over the mesa to the north-east. Somewhere, through the crepuscular haze, the Iron Road lay waiting, ready to fulfil its nefarious purpose. 'Happy now? Nice and obvious, am I? Honestly, can't just leave a man in peace.'

Emotion surged through her, a sudden swell that rose from her gut and closed her throat with a sob. She collapsed to her knees in the rough grass, face in her hands, fighting back tears, blotched and snotty, furious with herself for breaking down.

Anri cleared his throat. 'Uh. You, uh, all right or what, pest?'

'I'm fine,' she croaked through her grimy fingers.

'Righto, good good.' He sounded awkward and wrong. Good humour did not suit Anri, a man as sour as a gooseberry that had lost a bet, and nor did placation. 'Leave you be then, shall I?' He set about standing up again, and she realised she didn't want him to go.

'Anri, why are you here?'

'Said I was going, didn't I? Kypeth's dancing ringpiece, give a man a minute.'

'No, no.' She wiped at her eyes with fingers and palm, vowing that whatever that moment had been, it was done. 'Why are you still with us, here in the camp? Against the Guild?'

He hovered, uncertain, shifted the bow on his shoulder. 'How do you mean?'

Javani flopped back against the earth, settling on a patch of less spiky wildgrass. Her sweat was drying, leaving her feeling a sudden chill and rimed with salt. She shuffled her jacket around her shoulders and patted the earth beside her. 'Have a seat.'

'This going to be a Meaningful Chat, is it? Happens I've just remembered—'

'Sit.'

He sat.

'Why are you with us, Anri?'

'Why are you asking?'

She thought of Manatas, and felt a hot flush of guilt. Surely Anri wasn't here for the love of Ree.

'I'm . . . curious.'

'Oh. Well, as long as it's a good reason, then.' He pulled up his knees and rested his wrists upon them, thumbs crossed, his bow balanced alongside. 'Ordered to, I was, wasn't I? Don't let that girl out of your sight, or some such, or you're swallowing scrotum. Almost managed it too, I have, given you're a slippery little bugger.'

She let the wind ruffle the grass around them, rustling and swishing. 'And?'

'Eh?'

'Come on, Anri, you never do what you're told as a matter of personal pride. That can't be the real reason you're still here.'

He sniffed and looked away, bristly jaw working, then scratched at his cheek and turned back. 'Serious then, are you? Getting all, whatyoucallit, earnest, are we now?'

Javani matched his sniff. Her chest still felt hot, her nose stuffy, and she was conscious that the wrong emotional step might tip her into renewed sobs. 'Please,' she said quietly.

He looked down, then away again, his discomfort radiating. Anri was not one to bare his soul at the best of times, she knew, but right now her urge to interrogate his motives outweighed her concern for his ease. 'Well, I suppose I'm not completely against the objectives of this here undertaking. Overthrows and that.'

'You're here for the mission.' She didn't make it a question, and the silence between them grew.

He shifted, shuffling against the grass, then rubbed his knuckles briskly against his whiskers. 'Nowhere else to be, is there?' he muttered at last. 'Not for me. All out of companions otherwise, aren't I?' He gestured towards what Javani was fairly sure was the south-west. 'Left my young life behind to go with Tanith into the mountains, then left my old life there to come with you lot.' He stared down at the snarled growth between his boots. 'Not that there was much to leave in the end, mind you.'

He raised his head back up to look over the purpling plains beneath them. 'So, happy now, pest? Got me to admit I've got no friends and no family. Made yourself feel better?'

She couldn't help smiling, a tight and close-lipped thing, but irrepressible nonetheless. 'You've got friends, Anri. You're among them now. But . . . I don't know, maybe you could come down and join in a bit? At mealtimes and things. How are people going to get to know you if you just grab your dinner and bugger off back up the hill?'

He made a face. 'Not much of a person for people, me. Not really a, uh, friend-maker.'

She nudged his shoulder. 'That's only because of your dreadful personality.'

'Hoy!'

'But you can work on that! You're never too old to learn new things.'

'How old do you think I am, pest?'

'Don't know, don't care. You're out of your shell a bit already – when I first met you, you were a taciturn, obnoxious sod, and look at you now! A garrulous, obnoxious sod.'

'Bordering on whimsical, I am.'

'Remember, it's, uh, not a failing to care about other people, or let them care about you. Come and spend some time with the others, get to know them, and maybe – just maybe – put a bit of effort into not being a dick. You'll all be fast friends in no time.'

He met her fervent gaze with a look of genuine doubt. 'Really think so, do you?'

'Can't hurt, can it?'

'I'm sure we'll find out on that one.' He sighed and sat back. 'Fine. You win.'

'Good.'

They watched the last of the light fade, the plains beneath dropping through violet and mauve into twilit gloom. He didn't look at her when he said, 'You doing all right then, pest?'

'I . . . I'm not sure.'

'Want to have a chat about it?'

She considered. 'No.'

'Fair enough.' The last of the shadows were subsumed by nightfall. 'We're friends, then, are we?'

'Yeah, I reckon so.'

'Do you think that's weird, us hanging around together?'

'Honestly?' She rubbed one hand over her one eye, then the other. It had been a long day. 'Yes,' she said.

'Fair enough.'

'Doesn't mean I want to stop, though.'

'Right.' He chuckled, just once. 'Fair enough.'

Years pass in seconds, in days, in centuries. A scene, an instant, an event reconstructed anew. Rai knows the place, the reeking crossroads alehouse, the drum of rain upon its bowing roof, and she knows the feeling that holds her, the listlessness, the inattention. The rest is shards, fragments reassembled.

She is tired of waiting around in these places, she is tired of these petty manoeuvres by petty men playing their games of narrowed power. She wants more than this. She is better than this. She can do something, something huge. She can move kingdoms. Her mug is empty again, and still she must wait, belittled or ignored by those indifferent to her, pestered by every third brute who is snagged by her looks. She pulls the hood forward, but it does nothing to drown out the laughter of the corner table. The fucking corner table. Drinking, laughing, revelling. Rai's hand is tight on the hilt beneath her cloak. She only just finished cleaning the blade.

'Four more, please, chief.' She is shunted aside, the dregs of her cup splashed over the bar. 'Aye, fuck, sorry there, pal. One for yourself and all.'

The creature at her elbow is foreign and freckled, pale and maned in a halo of orange. Rai is transfixed. This is not how it happened, of course, but this is how it is happening now.

'Can you believe this fucken ballad, eh?' The newcomer jerks her thumb towards the sweaty minstrel on the dais. 'Some bint pining over her lost love, turned her hair all griefy white? That's some proper bollocks there. Here, give me a hand with these.'

She is too stunned to protest, too outraged at what the throne of Arowan has done with her legacy, catches herself raising fingers to her cowled mop, dyed a murky black, then she is at the corner table, slopping mugs in hand. They barely look up from their mirth. There are tears in their eyes.

'Aye, right, cheers.' A pause. 'Fancy joining us for a swift one? If you're waiting around, that is.'

Rai hovers, uncertain. 'Who are you?'

'Aye, well, you could say we're in the business of freelance diplomacy. We're a novel endeavour, upstarting if you will, but with great things ahead, I guarantee it. This company's going to change the world.'

'And you're . . . celebrating something?'

'Ha, ancestors, no, but one day, eh? You got a name, pal? Not an actual name, that's for gimlets. A good nickname or moniker, a nom de guerre.'

'Aren't all noms "de guerre" around here?'

The orange person grins like the sun. 'See, man, that's what I'm always saying! So what do people call you?'

Rai considers, just for a moment, thinks of the name Varolo gave her, the one Zaven and the others have used with such glee, then translates it.

'Loveless.'

TWENTY-NINE

'Aye, right, so in the absence of what we might call . . . a trusted elder acting in a . . . supervisory capacity, duties fall to yours truly . . . in the Slayer oversight stakes . . . for this climb.' The Commodore paused her stream of verbiage for a moment while she hauled herself, grunting, up another layer of rock. 'You may save your professions of . . . gratitude-slash-flattery-slash-wonder for later, if you prefer, perhaps to take the time necessary . . . to craft particular verses of indelicate thanks, as the fancy takes you.' She flicked her mountain of hair back over her head. 'I'm not here to . . . tell you your business, after all.'

It was not yet dawn and the air was crisp and sharp against Javani's skin. Over the murky peaks to her right, little more than looming black teeth against the paling sky, the wispy clouds that scattered like wool tufts were edging pink. Despite the chill and the gloom, Javani climbed easily, her muscles warm even as her fingers and toes pulsed with cold. She had to keep waiting for the Commodore to catch up.

'Maybe,' she said quietly, conscious that they were getting close to one of the trade roads that fed the outpost, 'maybe we'd go faster if we devoted less energy to, uh, talking?'

'Aye, well, that's a . . . common misconception, you see.' The Commodore's words were breathy, and she certainly didn't seem as fighting fit as she'd claimed when they set out. 'Good bit of chat keeps the . . . lungs moving, works the breath, see? It's basically a catalyst for exertion.'

'A what?'

'It's science, girlie, and I doubt you've had the . . .' she took a heaving breath, '. . . education sufficient for full comprehension of the . . . pertinent factors.'

Javani suspected her raised eyebrows were visible in the gloaming. 'I think,' she said carefully, 'I might have a little breather here, if that's all right? Then we can cross over this last ridge and down to the road.'

'Aye, right, well,' panted the Commodore, 'as long as we're in position for the first shift . . . suppose you can have a wee rest here.' She wiped a hand across her brow, then flicked away thick beads of sweat. Javani edged back to give her space.

'Commodore?'

'Aye, Slayer?'

'Why are you here?'

The light was good enough to see the frown of bafflement work its way across the Commodore's face. 'Did you hit your head on the way up, girl? Did I drop a rock on you in my vertical alacrity?'

Javani had been hoping the Commodore would at least look beyond the literal. 'No, I'm fine. I mean why are you with us, against the diggers? Why did you, I don't know, come out of retirement or whatever it was, in Arowan? Like I said to Anashe, we were riding and raiding for two years while you kept out of it, so . . . I guess, what changed?'

'Ah.' The Commodore sat back against the striated rock, already splendid shades of magenta and vermilion in the budding dawnlight. 'Well, that's easy enough.'

'Yeah?'

The Commodore looked her dead in the eye, and Javani was unnerved to see not a hint of mirth in her gaze. 'That would be your mam.'

'You came out of retirement for Ree?'

'Aye, no, not exactly. We'd been, well, indirectly corresponding, for some time, and it's fair to say that both Anashe and I – and our agency pals – played our part in your wee undertaking, no matter that you saw us riding in no raid. But bringing about the meeting was my piece of resistance, as they say in Tokemia.'

'With the Swan.'

'Aye, the very same.'

'But then Ree was . . .'

'Indeedly-do. Made her a rash wee promise on the spot to go retrieve you from your mischief, and, well, you were present when we returned. So, once again, duties fall.' She gestured to herself with both thumbs. 'While she's out of commission, someone needs to keep the rest of you honest.'

'I thought I was doing that.'

'Aye, I bet you did.'

Javani frowned at that. 'I'm ready to move on.'

The Commodore pushed herself to her feet, dusting her palms then wiping them down her trousers. 'Aye, right, off we bugger then, eh?'

They resumed the last section of their climb, but the Commodore was quiet for mere moments before striking up again. 'Course, taking more direct involvement in the grand scheme is not without its side benefits.'

Javani concentrated on her handholds. They were easier to see as the light grew, and the pitted rock was, in truth, an easy climb, but the last thing she wanted to do was fumble her grip and make a tit of herself in front of the Commodore. 'Really.'

'Oh, aye. The diggers and I go back a spell, it's true – bad blood under the bad bridge, you might say . . .'

'Doubt I would.'

'. . . So the opportunity to stick the Bellend Brothers a wee shiv in their overstuffed undercrackers is not without appeal.'

'The who?'

'The Bellend— Are you telling me you don't know who runs the Guild?'

'Oh, yeah. Course I do.' Javani gave a coiled root a firm tug to see if it would take her weight. It would not. 'Just never heard them called that.'

'Clearly you've kept rarefied company,' the Commodore replied, and the mocking edge was impossible to miss. 'Beralas and Gurbun Verdanisi, then. Shitheads the pair.' She paused, took a breath. 'Aye, well, I say that – I had hopes for Beralas, when he took over from his old man. The old fella was a proper bastard, came up from the mines himself – well, from mining-adjacent activities, you might say – but friend Beralas always gave the impression of being a man who understood what mattered in life. Sadly, ascending to the height of authority over the Chartered Miners' Guild has left him just as much of a toad as the old man, just with better tailoring.'

'What about the other one? Gurbun?'

'Oh, he was always a tosspot. Thickest, angriest wee bastard I ever saw, and you know, coming from me, that means something.'

They crested the ridge and the outpost of Gonaraz spread beneath them, already bustling within and without the walls despite the early hour. The Commodore fished for the spyglass. 'Righty-ho, let's see if my lads got the early shift . . . Ah, crusty fuck-nugs.'

Javani squinted. It was still too dim to see much; lanterns still flickered at the gates, illuminating burnished breastplates and heavy coats. 'Bad news?'

'My lads are not on duty. Not going to chance the gate until I see some friendly faces. We'll need to bide here a time.'

'You really think they'll remember you?'

The Commodore affected disbelief, and wafted a hand over her face. 'No bugger forgets a day on the sauce with a true connoisseur.'

'What's that?'

'A drinking expert. A booze-master. A grog-guru.'

'You mean you?'

'Course I mean me, fucken hells. Those boys will light up like an alchemical enema when they see me coming.'

'Don't you owe them for drinks from last time?'

'Least said, soonest mended.'

'And this will get us the information we need?'

'In time, naturally. Can't rush these things.'

Javani tapped one finger against her chin. 'Is this entire reconnaissance outing just an excuse for you to go drinking again with your new friends?'

'No!' The Commodore almost looked hurt. 'Not entirely.' Her face lit with a cheeky grin, making her at once twenty years younger. 'It's important to play to one's strengths on the battlefield, you see, Slayer.'

'Could you . . . could you not call me that any more?'

'Eh? Slayer?'

'Yeah. That.'

'You'd prefer "girlie", would you?'

'I mean, I have a name that's reasonably serviceable, although not without its faults . . .'

'Ah, no, using actual names is for gimlets. A good nickname, a nom de guerre, that's what lends an air of mystery on the whispering battlefield. I thought Slayer was pretty good, wouldn't have minded that one myself in my younger days, but have it your way.'

'No, it's just . . .' Javani shut her eyes, then opened them again. 'I saw a man die, in front of me, in the animal pens . . . one of the slavers.'

'And you did him in?'

'No, it was . . . the other one.'

'Ah.'

'She . . . she cut him open. And then . . . You know what, I don't want to say. I don't want it in my head any more.'

'Ah.'

'It's just, every time you call me Slayer, I kind of . . . I remember it. I remember the noise it made. The look on his face. I remember how it made me feel. And . . .' She swallowed, her throat suddenly thick. 'I don't want to. I killed someone, once, for sure, and it was the right thing, but it was a horrible thing, and I didn't . . . I didn't see it happen – the moment he hit. I've watched people die, saw my best friend bleed out in the dirt, saw an old man murdered with an axe five feet in front of me. I've shot arrows at people; hit some, too. But nothing has ever made me feel like I did in that moment in the animal pens, and I never want to feel it again. I definitely don't want to . . . celebrate killing, with a nickname.' She pressed her hands together, rubbing cold fingers, holding tight. 'So . . . could you not?'

The Commodore didn't say anything for a moment, just gazing back with her pale, round eyes, ever more contrasted in the growing light against the freckled umber of her face, the grey-flecked rust of her mass of hair. 'No problemo,' she said at last, then, after a purse-mouthed pause, she added, 'although, in truth, girlie, you'll not be shaking those memories so easily. Such recollections have a tendency to loiter unwanted, to linger in the fringes, and travel with you in the onwards. Shaking them off is no small thing, take it from me.'

Javani matched the purse of her lips, nose twitching in frustration. 'It can be done, though? Right?'

'Aye, well, it happens, sure.' The Commodore brushed her fingers down her front. 'Course, the trouble with forgetting things is you can never be sure what you've forgotten, eh?'

'I don't think that's true.'

'Maybe you're right. Maybe not. Who's to say?'

'Then how do I forget? Short of suffering gods know what other manner of indignities to crowd out the first, which is not a course of action I'm exactly thrilled by.'

The Commodore squinted, appraising her. 'How old are you?'

'Fifteen. And a half.'

'And how are you on the consumption of brain-chemistry-altering volumes of rustic spirits?'

'What?'

'How much booze can you drink?'

'What? None. Gods. Ree would freak.'

'Aye, well, that's route one out the window.'

'Oh yeah? What's route two?'

'Same as route one, but with more blows to the head.'

'Fuck's sake.'

'Told you it was no small thing, didn't I?' The Commodore chuckled to herself, but there was an edge to it, something inward-facing, a note of melancholy that morphed into a sigh.

'Commodore?'

'Girlie.'

'I do have a name, we covered this.'

'Sorry, I don't make the rules. Had something to offer, did you?'

'Don't take this the wrong way – or do, what do I care – but, well, you drink quite a lot, don't you?'

The Commodore sniffed, chin lifted. 'Everything in moderation, including moderation, I always say.'

'Are you trying route one?'

The Commodore went to reply, then hesitated, her mouth half-forming a word, then her shoulders dropped, and she let out another sigh. 'Route two, maybe.'

'You're trying to forget something?'

'Girlie, there's a whole world of hogshite I'd be cock-a-whoop to flush from my cranium. By the time you've lived as long as I have – assuming you curb some of your less prudent instincts, naturally – you'll have no shortage of sluiceable bilge yourself.'

'But something in particular? Beyond . . .' Javani waved a hand, '. . . a general quest for amnesia.'

The Commodore sniffed again, harder this time, her nostrils momentarily flattened. 'Aye, perhaps.'

'What is it?'

'What kind of question's that? Hardly going to get the bugger forgot if you force me to dredge it up, am I?'

Javani put up her palms. 'No, no, it's fine. I mean, I told you mine—'

'Not in great detail.'

'—and if you've successfully forgotten whatever it is, good luck to you, and pass the, uh, whatever it is in that skin at your belt.'

'Arak.'

'Ugh, really? That stuff reeks.'

'Aye, but it keeps your teeth proper clean.' The Commodore flashed her an impressively dazzling smile, which held for a moment before drooping at the corners. 'Ah, well, fuck it.' She reached a hand down and hauled up her shirt, revealing a sudden, shocking expanse of pale belly. Javani was almost blinded, in testament to the burgeoning daylight, but after a few blinks she was able to focus on what she was being shown.

'This here is why I'm not likely to forget,' the Commodore said softly, not sad, but reflective.

'What in hells did that?'

'Crossbow. If you can call it that – one of them nasty mechanical buggers, in the days they were new. Two bolts here, side by side. Another one up here.' She gestured to her shoulder. 'I could have sworn it was seven in total, but somehow they only had three to show for it when they pulled them all out.'

'Nine hells. And you survived.'

The grin returned, if only briefly. 'Aye, well, course. But doesn't mean I enjoyed myself, and nor am I keen to repeat the experience.'

'What happened? Was this when you rode with Ree?'

The Commodore snorted, mouth pulled to one side. 'Funnily enough, it happened not long after she'd left us for good.'

Javani had a hand to her mouth, unconscious. 'You were one of the . . . at the siege, the people she . . .'

The Commodore pulled her shirt back down and shifted her shoulders. 'Aye, sounds about right. Course, she made the right call, getting out before they flattened the fucken place around our ears, but, well, I like to think we made a difference in the end.'

'Can you tell me the full story some time?'

'Which part of trying to forget were you unclear about, there?'

'I mean, not that bit, you can skip that bit, but the rest of it? And maybe . . . maybe some stories of what Ree was like, when you rode together. If you had time.' She had a sudden, jolting thought of Aki and Anashe, two years before, begging Ree for stories of their own mother from their days riding together, and she felt her cheeks burn.

The Commodore had made the same connection. 'Ancestors, you're as bad as Anashe and her brother were, when first we crossed paths. Fair wore me down with their pestering, and I'll not stand for any such emulation on your part.' She sniffed again and rubbed a hand beneath her nose. 'But maybe. If you're good. Although mostly she was a pain in the hole, always swanning about the place, batting her lashes, flaunting her, uh, lashes. Reckoned she could get any man to do whatever she wanted.'

'And could she?'

'I mean, mostly, aye, but that doesn't make it any less reprehensible as a fundamental strategy.' The Commodore took a long breath, her gaze drifting. 'Truth is, I've not thought about those days for a good long time, but they've never left me. Sixteen years since we rode together, since the siege, and everything after has travelled in its echo.'

Javani shifted, moving closer as the Commodore's voice faded. 'What do you mean?'

'You wanted to know why I'm here, girlie? Because I'm afraid. That's the truth of it.'

'What are you afraid of? Being shot by a crossbow again?'

The Commodore barked a laugh, sending nearby corvids into the lightening sky. 'Aye, right, fucken yes to that. But no, in more of a sense general, I am afeared of my own capabilities, should matters escalate and bums become squeaky.'

'You mean . . . What do you mean? If you're worried about your personal safety, then first, you seemed perfectly happy waltzing into Gonaraz and the teeth of the Guild's greatest concentration of tin this side of the expanse – and now seem happy to repeat the experiment, by the way – and second, why would you stay with us and not bugger off back to Arowan?' Javani shook her head. Sometimes adults baffled her, or those in whose company she found herself, at least; she wondered if somewhere there might be a community of rational, comprehensible adults, who said what they meant and meant what they said. She discounted the thought immediately.

'I mean,' began the Commodore, one finger raised, then paused. 'That is, it's . . .' She let out an exasperated breath. 'I spent much of my youth in direct combat, much of it deadly. Until the crossbow incident, I barely suffered more than a few scratches and a bruised ego.' She knocked on the top of her head, through the waving fronds of hair. 'Skull like a millstone, me. Thought nothing of facing down a gaggle of bastards if they needed downwardly facing, and more often than not, the crew and I came out smiling, if a little bloody. With the odd exception, it must be said.' She paused again, gaze somewhere around her knees.

'So . . . ?'

'I've not hefted a weapon in anger in sixteen years.'

'Oh.'

'I've dodged risk, girlie. I've skulked and I've wheedled and I've ducked and I've dipped. I've sent others in my place, I've delegated. Taken to life behind a desk – a nice desk, mark you, real blackwood, got it at an estate sale – and been happy to count the coin from others' misadventures.'

'And now you're here, putting yourself in harm's way again . . . to prove to yourself you can still do it?'

The Commodore released a long breath through her teeth. 'Aye, seems so.'

'Well, uh, so far, so good?'

'Ask me again when the bums get squeaky.'

'When you say that, do you mean—'

'Ah, at fucken last. My boys have shown. Right, clear yourself off, Unslayer. The Commodore can handle matters from here, and you've got a yard to watch.'

'You know, "Unslayer" isn't really any better than—'

'Go on! Off you sod, sharpish. I'll get what we need and return, or die trying.'

'Really?'

'Course not, you wee pillock. Now get up on that promontory and watch the yards, there's serious drinking to be done down here.'

'Good luck, Commodore.'

'Ah, luck's for fannies. I've got arak.'

Javani watched her go, her walk as incongruous as before, and shook her head. It was no good hoping that one day she'd understand adults; they were just people, after all, and – it seemed to her – people made no sense to anyone but themselves.

Javani watched the yards for hours, taking careful notes and the occasional sip from her waterskin, the spyglass pressed to her eye until it ached, until the sun passed its peak and Anashe came creeping alongside her to take over. Relieved in every sense, Javani made the careful climb down and slow ride alone back in the direction of the camp, the high sun casting the red rock with sharp shadows of purest black.

Without the focus of watch duty, her thoughts became unsettled on the ride. The Commodore's words had stuck with her, those she'd followed at least, and as she rode the hidden trail through a narrow defile, her mind became snagged on the impossibility of forgetting something you were all too aware of. Again, she was in the animal pens, again that moment of excitement, of anticipation, as Maral broke them free. Again, the shock, the disbelief, the unfolding revulsion at what the Mawn had done to the slaver. Reminding herself that the man was hardly undeserving did nothing to dull her shudders. Maral's acts dogged her. She could not escape the woman.

She reined in her pony with a sharp jerk. Perhaps it was the pattern of her thoughts, but she once again had the unmistakable sense of being watched, just as she'd had on the mesa after her exit from the *Illustrious Den*. She wheeled her mount around in a complete circle, scanning the steep slopes either side, the stripe of cloud-scattered blue overhead.

'Maral!' she bellowed, her voice coming back at her in waves. 'Is that you?'

One hand crept to the bow at her saddle, but if someone had a bead on her, there would be a shaft through her gut before she'd even drawn an arrow.

The echoes of her shout faded, but the feeling did not.

'You're working for bastards, Maral!' she called again, letting her words ricochet. 'You're helping them make everyone suffer. Including you.'

Dying echoes, distant birdsong, the lone cry of a hawk.

'He killed your family, Maral. He took you as a pet. You know it.'

Still nothing. She felt stupid – of course Maral wasn't there. No one knew where they were or what they were doing. To that end, perhaps she should be going easy on the shouting—

Something shrieked from a spiny bush along the trail and she whirled, but it was only a sad-looking, grey-plumed bird, finally making a break from the crazed baying human. It fluttered erratically up and out of the defile, then stillness reigned once more.

Javani shifted in the saddle. Something was different. The feeling was gone.

It did not return for the rest of the ride.

THIRTY

The dung diorama was back, but at least it had dried out. A bit.

'Aye, right, listen up,' the Commodore declared, stubby fingers hovering over painstakingly modelled manure. 'Courtesy of the hard work, skill and boundless natural charm of certain members of this here assemblage who remain too modest to be named, we have amassed the necessary to hammer this here shambles into something that might be called a plan.'

'Talking about the shit-heap, are you?' Anri might even have been serious.

'Shit-heap metaphorical. The shit-heap literal—' she gestured expansively, '—now offers a degree of fidelity apposite to our needs.'

'Are those little poo people?' Javani asked, peering.

'Aye, and significant is each.' The Commodore interlocked her fingers and pushed them outwards with a magnificent crunch. 'Going to let me do the talking this time, girlie?'

'I'll see how you get on.'

'Most kind, cheers.' Sarcasm dripped from her words like oil, but Javani didn't care. She was, she realised to her modest embarrassment, really, really excited.

With a theatrical in-breath, the Commodore began. 'Right. We now know the structure of the . . . what was it, wagon-train?'

'You can just say train.'

'Aye, right, train. They're putting one together here, one down in Kilale, uprating the chains and cables and whatnot between here and there as they connect the final stage. These trains will be bigger and heavier than what we saw out on the plains, armoured wee castles at each end like we thought. A bunch of Norts have been on site, but they've all fucked off back down to the port cross-country, ready to hitch a boat home come opening time.' The Commodore paused, rubbed a hand under her nose. The dung edifice had expanded in scope markedly since its first outing, with a trail of . . . something . . . now leading off the rocky table and across the arroyo's dusty floor.

Anashe was a little closer to the model than last time, her sharp features inclined in only modest distaste. 'What does it say that the architects of this monstrosity do not deign to travel on it themselves?'

'Aye, who knows, eh? Could be they've half-arsed it, could be they're comfy the fun part is done and all that's left is tedious drudge, best left to the diggers. One thing that's fairly clear is that this is not the first of these fuckers they've built, so prudence would suggest we give them the doubty benefit on this one. But, uh, let's look to minimise our own time aboard, eh?'

Anashe's mouth was as tight as a cat's backside. 'Agreed.'

'Getting aboard, now then.' Anri was keeping his distance, from the model as well as everyone else, but his head was inclined towards it as if drawn by its gravity. 'Plan for that, is there?'

The Commodore's eyes sparkled. 'Glad you asked, son of the Hindmarch. So: morning of, our passengers of note will be clambering aboard this brand-new construction, right *here*.' She pointed to a wedge of packed dung, laid out in a line with chunks and accumulations of varying sizes. 'The passenger wagon, freshly assembled in the Gonaraz yards. No more lumping it in with the ore for our Guild types!'

Anashe pointed with a slim finger. 'The direction of travel is . . . this way, yes? So it is the second wagon, after the front fortress.'

'Aye, we think so.'

Anri leaned halfway forward and pointed too, perhaps in a bid not to be outdone. 'That the only bit with people on it, then?'

'The greatest concentration thereof, aye.'

'But,' Javani pressed, keen to reward Anri for his engagement, 'there will be guards in both the front and rear wagons, the ones Anashe called fortresses.'

'Because they have high walls and fortifications,' Anashe replied reasonably, 'and many heavily armed people who will look upon our presence with displeasure.'

'Aye, which is why you'll be *havoiding* those bits,' the Commodore said, with such heavy emphasis that Javani worried her drinking had overpowered her.

Manatas cleared his throat, and Javani tried not to let it bother her. Although if he did it again, she might snap at him. If the man had something to say, he should just say it; this veneer of manners helped nobody and just slowed everything down.

'Yes, captain?' she said, a polite smile hammered across her face.

'We truly expect no other guards along this entire chain?' he said, eyes tracing the ribbon of lumped dung.

'Aye, well, according to my sources, which are both unimpeachable and possessed of questionable moral fibre, all the most valuable stuff is kept fore and aft in the,' she flicked Anashe a reluctant glance, 'fortresses. Monies, records, items of particular interest. Hence the concentration of guardage.'

Manatas sucked at his lip, rolled it against his teeth. 'Then must I be the one to say it? Surely that is the location for our quarry? An item of such value would be kept under guard and armour.'

Javani grinned. 'You're forgetting one thing, captain.'

'Please, enlighten me.' His eyes were earnest; here was a man who genuinely craved good news.

'They don't know it's all that valuable, because they don't know we intend to steal it. They've been ferrying it around in the personal effects of their ink-dippers for months, maybe even years. Two guards, tops, and an iron-bound chest.' She pictured the man on the *Illustrious Den*, his little chest behind him against the wall. 'And we know how to get into those.'

'Sure do,' Anri added, wearing a faint and bristly echo of her smile.

'Compared with, you know, actual treasure, and coin, and promissory notes and whatever else they're shipping down to Kilale, they're not going to waste space in their strongrooms on some transient auditor's paraphernalia, right, Commodore?'

'Aye, bang on, girlie. We can state with a *high* degree of confidence that the passengers' odds and sods – including said Great Seal of Arowan – will be in the baggage enclosure, just about . . . here.'

Anashe counted. 'That is the fourth wagon along. Why is it so far back from the passenger wagon? What if a passenger wishes to retrieve something once aboard?'

The Commodore looked a little pained. 'Can't say for certain at this point, although from what I could glean, it's possible the intervening wagon will be reserved for comestibles.' She paused. 'That said, crossing from wagon to wagon while this thing's at full speed would be the act of a maniac, so I think you'll be fairly safe from any shiny lad wandering back in search of his hanky.'

One of Anashe's eyebrows had risen in a delicate arch. 'We will not be crossing between wagons?'

'Oh, aye, well, ideally not, no. Girlie, do you want to fill them in?'

'As a reminder, I do have a perfectly functional name.'

'Was that a yes? I can't understand the impenetrable argot of today's youth.'

'Ugh, yes.' Javani took a breath and let some of the excitement bubble up again. 'The baggage is loaded through side doors, big sliding ones, pulled shut. Here, in the yard. It'll have to be done by eight bells – that's the scheduled departure time.'

Anri gave a sceptical snort. 'There's a schedule, is there? Like they'll stick to that.'

'They have to. Remember, they have to get underway at both ends simultaneously – if anyone's not ready, they'll get left behind.'

'Aye,' the Commodore added gleefully, 'or squished.'

Javani shuddered, nose wrinkled. 'Less of that talk, please.'

'Suit yourself.'

'So everything loaded here, in wagon four, and all passengers aboard here, in wagon two, then bells ring, signals flash across the plain, cables jangle—'

Anashe's eyebrow had yet to drop. 'You do not know how they signal from one end to the other, do you?'

'How they do it doesn't matter. They do it, and things get moving . . . slowly. Commodore?'

'Aye, here we go.' The Commodore reached out and grabbed the frontmost dung-block, representing the leading fortress wagon, and began sliding it across the rock towards the lip. Javani's eyes watered at the sight, but the smell wasn't as bad as she'd expected. 'All aboard, and such.'

'As soon as the wagons pass this point,' Javani gestured, although not too close, 'they're outside the walls. And just here is a narrow cutting along a curve, before things start to get steep. By the time the baggage wagon reaches it, the front fortress will be out the other side, and the rear will be around the curve, out of sight. This is our entry point.'

Anashe's narrow mouth twitched in thought. 'How fast will the wagons be travelling at this stage?'

Javani looked to the Commodore, who seemed to manifest confidence that Javani was unsure was warranted. 'Aye, barely walking pace. If my calculations are correct,' – this struck Javani as decidedly unlikely – 'the last wagon won't yet have left the walls by the time the gang's ready to hop aboard.'

'Hm,' said Anashe.

'That's the plan, then, is it?' Anri was short of his caustic inclinations, but sounded far from convinced. 'Lie waiting in this ditch by here, wait for the poo train to pass—'

Javani winced. 'Please don't call it that.'

'Call it what I like, won't I. We pop up, slide open a big door, jump ourselves inside and get rummaging, then hop back out quick-quick?'

'Exactly. It should be easy to spot, won't be guarded and we can be on and off in only a few breaths, back down into the cutting before they know we were ever there. Train rolls on, we stay hidden until it's safe to make our getaway.'

'Sounds too easy, it does. What if something goes wrong, like you can't find it?'

Javani tensed, Ree's words echoing unbidden around her skull. *You never think of what you'll do if something goes wrong.* Her nails pressed hard into her palms.

The Commodore answered when Javani didn't. 'Aye, well, it does bear consideration, should the item's location not be immediate, or the de-casing be an issue . . . Take too long in there, and old trainy will be out of the cutting, and moving briskly off downslope.'

Anashe's eyebrow had arched like a bow. 'And we will no longer be travelling at walking pace.'

'Aye, no.'

'Could be at full canter by then,' Javani confirmed. 'And travelling through some pretty rocky parts.'

'Is that a metaphor, or . . . ?'

'Both, I suspect.'

'Then what is the plan for extraction?'

Javani and the Commodore exchanged glances. 'We wait,' Javani said.

'Ride this device to the port? I imagine we will encounter an unfriendly reception.'

'Just until things flatten out a bit. Captain?'

Manatas stood straighter, and this time at least did not clear his throat. 'There is a stretch, beginning a little way before what I take to be the halfway marker, where the engineers have cut the tracks along the path of an old riverbed.'

'About here-sies,' called the Commodore, from some way along the arroyo. She'd tried to draw out the path of the tracks to scale, Javani realised, and was in danger of disappearing around the bend.

'While I am not yet certain of the precise dimensions,' Manatas went on, 'the terrain around offers sufficient undulation to allow for a measure of concealment. A party could await the train's approach, then ride up to speed in short order and get alongside it on a reasonably flat stretch.'

Both of Anashe's eyebrows were now up, and in danger of marching up over her scalp. 'The plan is to *ride* alongside a mechanised monstrosity that moves at the speed of a galloping horse—'

'Cantering,' Javani supplied.

'And . . . what, leap from this wagon onto horseback?'

Javani held her incredulous stare, but it was a challenge. 'We can use a cart,' she averred. 'With ropes. We've done it before.'

A faint smile tweaked the corner of Anashe's mouth. 'Of course, that boat you sank.'

'It wouldn't have sunk if they'd put the fires out faster!'

'One cart, approaching over open plain, will be hard to disguise.

Archers in the fortresses, or anyone elsewhere along the structure with a bow and a keen eye, will make such activities perilous.'

'Yeah, well, actually I thought of that.' In the back of Javani's mind, she directed her words at the spectre of her mother. 'As we said, best-case scenario, we jump aboard, find the seal immediately and get straight out, right?'

Anri snorted without mirth. 'Not going to happen, is it?'

'It should! But if it doesn't, we hunker down and ride out of the mountains, then at the old riverbed, out pops not one, but two carts. And some riders.'

'How is this better?'

'A cart from each angle, right?' Javani weaved her hands in and out. 'They won't know where to look. We'll have riders moving ahead, riders going behind, hanging at the edge of range, then when we're ready, the carts dive in, we rope out and away. They'll be expecting an attack, not an extraction – they won't know what hit them. Classic misdirection.' She folded her arms and nodded to herself.

Anashe rubbed at one eyebrow with her thumb. Perhaps it was tired from its exertions. 'It feels like there are many, many moving parts to this plan.'

'The core is simple,' Javani pressed. 'We get aboard, we get the seal, we get away.'

Manatas stirred, his face rumpled with discomfort. 'There is a lot of "we" floating around here . . .'

'Lot of poo, too,' Anri contributed, which earned him a smile from Manatas that was at least two-thirds wince.

'. . . exactly who will be clambering aboard this contraption and placing their life in our enemy's hands?'

He was looking at Javani when he said it, and she was already inflating in pre-emptive outrage. Anashe answered first, her flat hand raised like a blade. 'Once we are clear on the roles, each should be performed by those most able. By my count, we have a small team to lie in wait, then board the train as it passes.' She began to count on her fingers. 'We have drivers of at least two vehicles, and roping crew. We have riders, as escort or distraction. And then there is the matter of . . .' Her gaze flicked towards the shelter, where Ree lay sweating in darkness.

Manatas rubbed a hand over his jaw. 'Who stays behind.'

'Indeed. We may also require scouts and lookouts. Once we have confirmed the scope of each role, we must devote ourselves to training and preparation. Time is getting short, and we must make these decisions soon.'

Manatas sighed and dusted his thighs with one hand. 'I do not disagree.'

'Well bagsy me not getting on the train, then,' Anri volunteered bravely. 'Or riding in. Or being on a cart with ropes.'

Javani's nose twitched. 'And where exactly do you see yourself contributing on the day, Anri?' Over her shoulder, she heard Manatas murmur to the Commodore, 'Exactly what does "bagsy" mean?'

Anri's mouth pulled down in consideration. 'Something about lookouts, was it? Sounds ideal, that does.'

Anashe's eyebrow had moved to mid-level, hovering sharp like a hefted spear. 'Given the spare forces available, I am unconvinced we can afford the luxury of lookouts.' She gave Anri a pointed look. 'Or cowards.'

Anri puffed outwards, whiskers bristling. 'Now then just who do you think you—'

Anashe was already walking away. 'Is there not a less . . . feculent version of this layout we can study? The dimensions of the baggage wagon are vital for proper preparation.'

The Commodore gave an exaggerated sigh. 'Ah, fucken hells, I'd forgotten what you were like when it came to prepping.'

Anashe merely stared at her, and the Commodore seemed to wilt before the force of her gaze. 'Aye, right, fine, if you're so antsy there are indeed some rough sketches we've compiled. But they lack the full majesty and splendour of this here diorama!' She kicked something away that might have been a pebble. It was quite dark in colour. 'Didn't even get to the people part.'

Anashe gave a short, satisfied nod. 'Now all we need is something appropriate in size . . .'

A rumble and squeak from along the mouth of the arroyo drew their attention from the Commodore's tableau. Around the corner of the rock came the White Spear and Tauras, dragging after them a large, sun-bleached wagon, one of its wheel rims cracked and an axle wonky.

'Keep lifting, boy,' growled the White Spear as they approached. 'We are not stopping yet.'

'Right you are, Mistress Whitespear,' came Tauras's breathless reply. His face was rigid with concentration.

Anri shot Javani a hurt look. 'Oh, told them the plan already, did you? Sent them off cart fishing.'

'That's a wagon, not a cart. It has four wheels. And yes. We needed to get moving.'

'Fine. Don't care, anyway.'

'Decided where you want to be on the day, yet?'

'Anywhere but by here.'

Anashe was watching the wagon, one long finger tapping her chin. The wagon-bed was piled with cuts of wood, and at least one spare wheel. 'Yes,' she said abruptly. 'That will do nicely.'

THIRTY-ONE

Anashe, for want of a better word and much to Javani's consternation, *summoned* them as the last of the daylight was ebbing. She was standing in front of the newly arrived wagon, its broken wheel replaced and one side of it adorned with hammered wooden boards and marked with chalk, cast into ruby and amber by the sun's dying rays.

Manatas peered at the markings with undisguised suspicion. 'Exactly what stands before us, my lady Anashe?'

Anashe looked sharply around the group, ensuring sufficient attention was being paid before answering. 'This is our quarry.'

'Oh, saved a bit of time, that has,' came Anri's rejoinder. 'Turns out the real train was the wagon we found along the way.'

Anashe did not dignify that with a response. 'From the dimensions the Commodore supplied, I have drawn up the relative height from the earth of the doors we must traverse.'

'Don't see the need myself,' grumbled the Commodore, 'was all there on the model.'

Manatas lifted his chin, his neck long, seeing the adorned wagon with new eyes. He indicated the lowest chalk line. 'This is the base of the door in question?'

Anashe shook her head, once and firmly. 'That denotes the floor of the wagon.'

The captain licked his lips. 'This next line?'

Another shake. 'The likely travel of its wheels.'

By now the captain's brow was furrowed, eyebrows tight. 'You mean to say . . .'

Anashe jabbed a finger like a dagger at a line around the height of her ears. 'Here.'

'And that is the . . . *base* . . . of these cargo doors?'

'Unless the Commodore erred in her information gathering.'

'Hoy, get to fuck with that kind of chat, my gathering informational is *sine qua non* I'll have you know, dick-ears.'

Anashe's eyebrow rose and sank like a wave. 'Quite.'

Javani heard Manatas mutter, '. . . do not believe that means what she intends . . .' but it was tactfully soft.

Anri took half a step and whacked one end of his unstrung bow against the line, a hand's span from the unflinching Anashe's head. 'So it's anyone getting on the train is climbing up that, is it?'

This, Anashe deigned to answer. 'It is. While it moves at a speed somewhere between walking pace . . .' she gave the Commodore another look, '. . . and that of a cantering horse.'

'Aye, right, 's'why it's important to catch the bugger early, before it gets too carried away.'

Anashe pressed her palms together. 'Let us now settle the matter of assignments. Once our roles are set, we must devote the time that remains to preparation, and intensely.'

The Commodore took a swig from a heretofore unseen wineskin, which perhaps explained some of her crepuscular belligerence. 'Seems a good way to spoil a lovely evening.'

Anri chuckled, once. 'I'm with the orange one. Does this have to be now? Got toenails to pick, haven't I.'

Anashe wore the expression of someone who juiced citrus fruit between her molars on a regular basis, a sort of suck-mouthed impatience at the stupidity of the others. But there was something, Javani was sure, something in her eyes that was not all furious.

'We have one wagon, and one cart, which need a driver each, in addition to any further crew we require,' Anashe declared as if no objection had been raised. 'That is two. We will require outriders, each with spare horses in a string. That is another two, at minimum. That leaves at most four of us to board the baggage wagon and search for the seal, while maintaining a presence at camp.'

Manatas's nose twitched. 'Four seems on the side of generosity, given the challenges inherent to ingress and egress.'

'It does. But it also minimises the time required to search the wagon and locate the seal – as well as dealing with any nasty surprises found aboard. Four searchers could well be finished before the train leaves the cut and gets out into the open.'

The captain ran a hand down a gaunter cheek than Javani remembered. 'That does sound mighty appealing.'

'Then the question returns to who will go. I have already spoken to Tauras and Whitespear – they are best suited to the vehicles, and understand their roles. Sarian will act as a rider—'

Javani looked around. 'Hey, where is Sarian?' Despite their time at the camp, she still barely knew the soft-spoken scout, but thought he had kind eyes nonetheless.

'Preparing to go for supplies. I'm told there is a cache within a day's ride.'

'Oh. Right. I'll need to give him a letter to pass on.'

Manatas gave her a weary smile. 'Perhaps this is not the most apposite time for correspondence.'

'On this occasion,' Javani sniffed in a mock drawl, 'I'm inclined to disagree.'

'Was that an impression of me?'

'I'm disinclined to—'

'Your point is made, thank you.'

Anashe was not yet tapping her foot, but everything was in place for it. 'Roles and responsibilities, you remember? We have our drivers and one rider. We need one more rider and at least three infiltrators. I will be one. Who will be joining me?'

'Each of these infiltrators,' Anri rasped, looking uneasily at the chalked wagon, 'going to need to clamber up that nonsense, are they?'

'Yes.'

'I can do it,' Javani said quietly.

'It's bigger than your head,' Anri shot back.

'I'm a better climber than any of you. And if need be, I'll stand on someone's shoulders to get in. Once one person's aboard, we can rope up from there.' She gazed at the wagon, glazed now in pinks and golds. 'All we need is one.'

'Fuck's sake,' Anri moaned. 'Does this mean I've got to go with you then?'

'Only if you want to.'

'Not much of a choice, is it? It's that or lead a string of ponies across the plain in full view, or, what, ride in the back of a wagon? At least this way I might not get all my teeth shaken out like.'

'What's left of them.'

'Cheeky bugger.'

'Aye, well, there's one other role we've not discussed.' The Commodore shifted uneasily; her earlier (possibly booze-fuelled) joviality had left her. 'Who's lingering hereabouts.'

Javani felt suddenly cold, as if in an instant they'd snapped from sunset to dead of night. 'You can't mean . . .' She turned her desperate gaze on Manatas. 'You wouldn't make me— After everything, haven't I proved—'

Manatas raised his palms, his brows lifted, his eyes so tired. 'When Anashe said we needed the best people for each role, she was right. I cannot ask you to stay here, when you are . . . indeed, the best climber, and perhaps the best we have at getting into places they should not be. I trust you to get this right.' He nodded at Anri. 'If you can hog-tie this lump, you might even get him up alongside you.'

'None taken, is there.'

Javani's tide of cold ebbed just as fast as it had arrived, and she felt a curious heat below her ribs, something light and tingly. It was just so nice not to hear 'no' for a change. 'Th – Thanks. I guess. Does that mean you'll be . . . ?'

When the captain shook his head, it was as if it had the weight of a boulder. 'We are short one rider. And riding is something I am good at.'

Javani turned to the Commodore, who looked no more cheerful than before. 'Commodore? Do you . . . Do you want to stay behind?' She tried to add 'and look after Ree', but she found she couldn't force the words.

The Commodore chewed her mouth around, looked off to one side, wrinkled her nose and said, 'No need to decide right now, eh? I'll have a chat with those two useless bastards I dragged here from Arowan and see who's up for what.'

'Oh yeah,' Javani murmured. 'I forget Teg and Stefanna are here sometimes.' Officially, the two riders were on watch, but she was fairly sure she'd seen Teg dozing under a briar not that long ago.

'I'd like to say it's because they're excellent sentries who blend seamlessly into their surroundings,' the Commodore replied, 'but the fact remains that you just can't get the staff these days.'

Anashe's brows lowered. 'Why do you look at me when you say this?'

'Aye, no reason, no reason, just a couple of years ago I had a thriving agency, and then certain operatives went charging off half-cocked, and now I'm stuck with whatever I can get.' She sighed, then swivelled around. 'They're not up here, are they?'

'Then it is decided,' Anashe intoned, apparently approaching some kind of limit. 'Javani, Anri, I and one other will board the train. Captain Manatas and Sarian will ride the strings. Tauras and Whitespear will drive the vehicles. Those who remain will be left in charge of the camp, and . . . its occupant. Agreed?'

The general assent was mumbled and muttered with impressive ill-grace.

Javani flexed her fingers, which felt strange and tingly, and took a deep breath. It was happening. She was going to rob the train. She was going to save the day. She was going to prove she could do it, she could make the difference.

Now all she had to do was give Sarian her letter.

'Are you an investor, too?'

The man to Siavash's right was large, in all directions, his size amplified by the richness of his multilayered robes, which shimmered in the dancing light that crept beneath the sparkling canopy. The bulbous lanterns at the railing reflected in his eyes, and from the fine-worked filigree of his nose- and earrings, the stones set in the rings and bangles on his ample hands as they rested on the wood, Siavash felt horribly under-dressed.

'One does what one can,' he offered cordially, eyeing the man's girth with barely concealed envy. 'You're here for the . . .' He fluttered his fingers, which featured considerably fewer rings than his neighbour.

'Investiture, yes.' The man was older than Siavash, which made him feel a little better; perhaps in another twenty years he'd be filling his robes just as well, and be dripping in ornamentation. 'Wouldn't normally travel up from the city for such nonsense, but, well . . . there are some unusual opportunities in the offing.'

He turned his head towards the harbour, where through the cooling evening mist and over the bobbing forest of masts of merchant vessels large and small, a great black bulk lay anchored offshore. It was too dark to make out more than a vast darkness, but Siavash was well aware that even in daylight a Iokaran hulk looked much the same. Two smaller vessels lurked in its orbit, those Siavash had heard called blackblades, and at any other time he would have considered them the first wave of an invasion force.

This, however, was not any other time.

'I'd hoped we might see a delegation at dinner,' the man went on, 'maybe make some entreaties there, but of course, the rumour is the diggers have sewn up the overseas trade just as much as cross-country. So it could be a total waste of time, but you've got to take some risks, eh?'

Here Siavash was on safer ground. 'What is life, after all,' he rejoined, 'without a zest for adventure?'

'Well, I wouldn't go that far,' the man muttered with a dismissive wave of his hand, and Siavash deflated. 'At our age, life's comforts have a greater attraction than blazing trails, eh?'

Siavash nodded weakly. *Our* age? There were decades between them!

'If I've dragged my carcass and my retainers up to this armpit, I'd better be getting more out of it than a few undercooked meals in the shadow of . . . whatever the fuck they're calling that.'

As one, both men looked back over the rail to the expansive yard below. Great straight bands of iron gleamed up at them in the lantern-light, and beyond them rose and spread the covered bulk of the segmented vehicle that would ride the Iron Road, draped in a great swathe of roped canvas. Saving the grand reveal for the big day, Siavash presumed. Even at this hour, the yard beyond the canvas remained a hive of activity, teeming with the final, urgent efforts of construction and connection. Mere days remained until the ceremony.

'I believe it's called a rolling stack,' he said, doubting the words even as they left his mouth.

'Absurd name,' the man replied, 'for an absurd creation. Still,' he went on, pushing himself up from the rail, 'if it makes even a fraction of the promised returns, we'll still be coining it in, eh?' He nudged Siavash, jingling and rippling as he did so.

'Quite so.' Siavash was relying on rather more than a fraction.

'Can't believe the bastards have the temerity to demand more funds to finish it.' For a moment, his generous knuckles paled on the rail. 'That's the opposite of investing, the damned-by-gods parasites. The sooner those fuckers are swept from this earth, the sooner we can get back to some notion of traditional commerce in these parts.'

This notion alarmed Siavash. 'Is— Is that likely?'

The man gave a grim laugh, the nest of metal at his chest tinkling. 'Gods, no. It would take an act of the divine to burn these leeches from our collective veins, and if they've really sewn up a deal with our black-shipped neighbours, even that might not do it. Come plague and fire and famine, but the Guild will endure, and when the dust clears their hands will be out for their cut.'

'Oh, good. I mean, not good for, well, everything, but, you know . . .' Siavash swallowed. 'For the investment.'

The man nodded, a calculating gleam in his eye. 'That's right, my friend. It's the investment that gives us all a bit of common purpose, eh?' He went for another nudge, which Siavash endured with forced good humour.

The gleam faded. 'Still, we've all got limits, and the diggers are testing mine. Their thirst for this last round of coin has pushed them into bed with the unspeakable.' He glanced to the far end of the platform, then turned his head and actually spat over the rail. Goggle-eyed, Siavash almost dropped his drink over the railing.

Partially recovered, and still trying to act like he knew what the man was talking about, Siavash squinted in the direction the man had indicated and affected a knowing look. 'You mean . . . ?' He let the question dangle, as if he was unwilling to speak of the aforementioned unspeakable. All he could see at the far end of the platform, past the milling, drink-heavy worthies and their attendants, was a tallish man, lacking Siavash's heft, with a drooping moustache and a similar number of earrings to his neighbour, if of evidently lesser quality. His clothes were bright in the torchlight, garishly so, and when he spoke his teeth appeared to gleam.

Siavash's neighbour gave a confirming nod, which did not help, but went on, which did. 'The fucking Mercantile Brotherhood, welcomed as peers. It's enough to make a man vomit up his gizzard.'

Siavash nodded wholeheartedly, while wondering which of the dishes he'd picked at earlier had been the gizzard. 'Yes, yes, dreadful.'

'I mean,' his neighbour went on, 'I've done business with some types, I'll grant you. I've trafficked, I've dabbled, I've dipped in shades. But I have never exchanged coin for the life of a human being, and I never will.'

Siavash gasped. *Slavery?* He looked back to the man in the corner with fresh eyes. All those close to him wore the same bright and garish colours, and an invisible wall seemed to separate them from the rest of the gathering. The project's overseers might have welcomed them for their silver, but the other investors were retaining a wide berth.

The man beside him took the gasp as a measure of commensurate disgust, to Siavash's relief, then barked a laugh. 'Ah well, another few days, and all will be forgotten when the coin starts rolling in, eh?'

'Indeed,' Siavash replied with a nervous smile. 'So much to look forward to!'

Rai dreams splintered memories, faster now, jumping and merging and clashing against one another. She is feverish, she remembers. She is fighting something bigger than herself, stronger than herself, and she is tired. The leaping strands of memory unnerve her – is her mind unravelling? Is this how it will feel?

The shards of memory congeal, coalesce, and she dreams confected history, a moment of years. She is on a ship, a narrow vessel that cuts through iced waters, the night around her ferocious indigo, stars like crystals. She stands at the prow, gazing forward over freezing black waves, seeing nothing.

A companion joins her, a tall, angular woman many years her senior, her shaved head glowing almost blue in the starlight. When she speaks, it is with Anashe's voice, with her daughter's voice. It could not have happened like this. The dreams delight in distortion.

The princely young man they have found themselves escorting is asleep at last, she says, her hands still moving. He requires a little more care at sea, it seems.

Rai does not turn. Whatever she's searching for on the brooding horizon, she cannot see it. She expresses casual contempt for those who cannot care for themselves, mewling infants of all sizes. She says too much, and her companion stills.

The woman is quiet long enough for Rai to feel discomfort, and then, slowly at first, she speaks of her own children, of her pain at being forced to leave them behind. They would be older, now, she says. A little older than the prince in their care.

Rai is shamed enough to turn, to mumble apology, to confess a secret of her own, reassured enough that her mute companion will take it no further. Rai tells of her sale, of the man she was sold to, paraded through the hall of dance. How she poisoned them both, because she would not bring a child into that world, and despite her unexpected survival, she will never have children of her own. How she avoids even the subject's contemplation.

It is better this way, she says. What kind of parent would she be, with her own as templates? Her companion disagrees, but Rai is adamant. Why even consider the notion, after all.

The other woman is quiet again, as pale bergs glide by in silence. You keep one foot on the threshold, her companion says. Is it being comfortable you fear? Or is it family? Our little company may not be blood, but it is something. It is easy to undervalue what we have, to take it for granted, but life can change faster than we can ever imagine. Consider, perhaps, that home is something you carry with you, and it can be people.

I will always choose for myself, Rai avers.

That is your right, her companion replies, if you feel like that is what matters. If that is what you want.

What do you want?

Rai cannot reply, her eyes back on the sombre horizon. Perhaps there is a hint of land, a hint of light. The future approaches.

Her companion reaches over and flicks the object that hangs at her neck. And are you planning to keep that ridiculous jewel you took from the Reaver Queen?

Rai glances down at the blue stone, glittering in late starlight. Nah, she says. I'll probably pawn it the moment we make land.

THIRTY-TWO

The days leading up to the Big One were some of the hardest and most miserable of Javani's life, and yet somehow the most exhilarating. Anashe drilled them relentlessly, herself included, setting the wagon rolling gently on a slope, making them run alongside and throw themselves up and onto it. Then again. And again, sometimes with ropes, sometimes without. Javani's only consolation came from seeing Anri, the Commodore, Teg and Stefanna put through the same treatment, with which they coped hilariously. The Commodore and her people had hoped to dodge the training, but as one slot for boarding the train remained open and who filled it was yet to be settled, Anashe forced them all to suffer her preparations. The Commodore claimed to be joining in 'for morale', which fooled nobody.

Then, of course, came the exit training – leaping from an elevated platform on the moving wagon to the ground, onto a cart rolling alongside, onto a pony being led by one of the riders. That was far, far worse than getting aboard, made that much less bearable by the uncertainty that hovered over everything. If they were both quick and lucky, they'd be hopping off at walking pace within the cut outside the walls of Gonaraz and making for the scrub where their mounts were left.

If they were neither, they'd be attempting to exit the wagon train at what the Commodore repeatedly assured them was the speed of a cantering horse, which while at least not full gallop did not make any part of the endeavour particularly risk-free or straightforward. Then there was the uncertainty of which method would be available in the circumstances. They expected guards, and they expected the guards to be armed – the forts at either end of the train were designed to house elevated archers, of that there was no doubt, so any approach risked covering fire from the extremities. The horses could run anywhere the tracks went, but all it would take was a bolt or arrow to hit flesh and everyone's day took a nosedive.

The cart and wagon, meanwhile, could be plated, their occupants shielded, but would be sluggish on approach, and could only really get close to the tracks along the old riverbank around the midpoint. Timing would be crucial, and somehow the very thought of travelling at speed in an armour-plated wagon brought Javani out in a cold sweat. Javani did not want to end up taking that route, not again. They needed to find the seal fast, and get out before things got out of hand. Every night she collapsed to her bedroll, battered and shattered and convinced that oblivion was instants away, then found herself awake into the night, exhausted and worrying.

'Getting out quietly the goal, is it?' Anri gasped in a rare break in their drills, his hands on his knees and sweat making dark pools on the red earth between his boots.

'That's . . . the idea,' Javani responded, somewhat put out that she was as breathless as him despite being (probably) thirty years younger and in far better shape.

He wiped a grimy hand across his brow, which just left streaks. They both shone in the sunlight. 'Right, right, course.' He took another shaggy breath. 'Thought the idea was to be robbing them publicly, like, though?'

Javani paused. 'Um.'

'Just seems like a quiet getaway doesn't chime with the whole . . .' he lifted a hand from his knee, gestured feebly, then flopped it back, '. . . thievery circus, does it.'

'Well. Yeah.' Javani's lips pinched in thought. There was an answer to this. 'Thing is—'

'A public escape risks great peril,' came Anashe's voice in a tone that implied that a) no argument would be tolerated and b) if they had enough breath to be talking, they had enough breath for another run, which would start with grabbing hold of the cart's ropes and dragging it back up the slope to the starting point. 'Safe extraction must take precedence over any . . . circus.' She stepped into view around the cart, momentarily blocking out the sun where they crouched. 'Once retrieval of the seal is complete, and everyone involved is well away, we can make whatever declarations we choose.'

'Fine, fine,' Anri muttered, pushing himself vaguely upwards. 'Seems a missed opportunity, that's all.'

Even silhouetted as she was, Javani could tell Anashe's eyebrow was up. 'A missed opportunity for *what*?'

He shrugged. 'Don't ask me. Not much of a statement-maker, me. But, you know, nipping into their nethers and out again, feels like we should be . . . leaving a mark.'

Javani had her hands on her hips. 'You want to set something on fire, don't you?'

He didn't meet her eye. 'Didn't say that. Didn't not say that. Just thinking all that baggage might burn a pretty colour . . .'

Anashe sniffed. 'We have spent enough time on this. Come, take your places and—'

'What if it's not in there, then?'

'What?'

Anri was evidently in no hurry to lug the cart back up the slope, even if it would get them back in the shade. 'What if the seal isn't in the baggage wagon.'

Javani took the suggestion as a personal affront. 'It'll be there.'

'Might not be.'

'It will. It's travelling from Gonaraz to Kilale on the day, and that means it's on the Iron Road. And there's nowhere else on the wagon-train for it to be.'

'How big is it, then?'

'What?'

'How big? Like, yay big, or yaaay big?'

Anashe was now holding herself so still she was very faintly trembling. 'Time is precious. We have a countable number of hours—'

'I don't know,' Javani snapped, ignoring her. 'Big enough to be used to stamp laws and things. Bigger than a Guild seal, I guess – it's called the Great Seal, right? But it can't be *that* big.'

'Someone could be carrying it, couldn't they?'

'But why would they? It's a bit of metal that lives in a box. The box goes with the baggage, and that's where we'll find it.'

'But you've never seen it, have you?'

'Well, no.'

'Then how are you going to recognise it if you do find it, eh?'

Javani stared at Anri. Anri stared at Javani.

'Not like it's going to have "Great Seal of Arowan" engraved on it, is it?'

'It might.'

'For the love of the Goddess!' Anashe cried. 'I know what the seal looks like. I know its dimensions, I know the nature of its packing, I know the colour of the velvet that envelops it. As would you both if you had paid attention to the briefings I prepared!'

Javani and Anri shared a look that could only be described as Mutual Reproachment.

'I was going to—'

'She wouldn't let me—'

Anashe's hand chopped the air. 'Enough. Perhaps we are hungry. Find food, and we will continue after.'

Anri looked ready to moan, but by the grace of the gods held it in at the last moment. 'Fine,' he muttered, 'got some trail meat in my saddlebags.' He slouched away, still dripping with sweat.

Javani found herself alone with Anashe by the side of the cart, and burdened with an overpowering urge to apologise to her. She tried to fight it down, hot and tired and confused as she was, but a moment's reflection told her it would cost her nothing, no matter how irrational, and might soothe Anashe's evident irritation.

'Sorry.'

Anashe's head tilted, her long neck smoothly arched. 'For what?'

'Just now.'

'But not for ignoring the briefings?'

'That too.'

Some of the ire seemed to leave Anashe, her posture a fraction less taut, which was a step in the right direction. 'Anything else?'

Javani tapped a finger to her chin. 'What else is on the list?'

That got a flash of a smile, transforming Anashe's face for an instant. 'Too much for one day. Come, let us eat.'

They wandered back towards where the horses were tied, in grassy shade beside a sheltered creek that still had water at its foot despite the season. Javani watched the other woman sidelong as they walked, seeing the tension in her shoulders, the stiffness of her gait, but the purpose that powered it all.

'Anashe, why did you come here? After Ree was— Why didn't you stay at the club?'

'I believe I told you this. I wished to see your mother's work completed, and felt I must take a more direct hand in proceedings.'

'Yeah, but . . . you know, really. You sent your girlfriend away—'

'Sefi is not my girlfriend.'

'Suuuure, if you say so. But you know, you didn't have to, like, *throw* yourself into this, you know?'

'You said "you know" twice in one sentence.'

'Well, you do know, don't you.'

Anashe came to a halt still a few paces shy of the ponies and turned to her, and Javani was proud of herself for not taking an immediate step back. 'Perhaps I do.'

'Go on.'

'Do you remember, at Aki's Rest, when you asked me if I was happy? It is possible that the answer I gave, while true, was not . . . the truth beneath.'

'You're not happy?'

'Perhaps not all the way.'

Javani took a slow breath, trying to match Anashe's manner. 'You miss Aki a lot?'

This almost provoked a laugh. 'Of course, little one. How could I not? He was a part of my life, a part of me, for as long as I had lived, everything I ever knew, and to lose him so suddenly was to lose a piece of my heart.'

'I noticed . . . how you leave a space beside you, at meals.'

'He would only complain he was being forgotten.'

Javani gave a sad grin. 'Oh, no chance there. He's impossible to forget.'

The sadness of Anashe's smile matched Javani's. 'In all the worst ways.' She took a long breath, her gaze moving out past the ponies, past the rucks of striped red rock that marked their corner of the foothills, past where Anri was crouched and chewing something very, very deliberately. 'And perhaps that is why I am not as happy as I would wish.'

'I travelled once with a merchant,' she went on, 'who claimed what mattered most in life was adventure. He was wrong, and mad, but there was a grain of truth to his words. In all my travels with my brother, I craved nothing more than comfort, and in the last two years, in his absence, I found a measure of . . . let us call it . . . easy living.'

'And?'

She let her shoulders drop, her face fall. 'It is . . . hollow. Something is missing.'

Javani folded her arms, head to one side. 'You spent decades wanting to be comfortable, and then got what you wanted, and it wasn't satisfying? You're a damned-by-gods parable, Anashe, Ree would—'

She clammed up.

Anashe didn't seem to have noticed. 'My clothes are too soft, my boots do not chafe . . . Where is the burr beneath my shirt?'

'Anashe, are you saying you were too happy to be happy?'

Anashe lifted her head. 'I am saying a life without challenges gives me less pleasure than I expected. My happiness . . . it came too soon after Aki's loss, and too easily. How can I truly mourn my brother, the man who gave his life to preserve my own, if—'

'Come on, piss-drips, we doing this or not?' Anri was striding over, his chewing complete. 'Some of us have places to be.'

Javani rolled her eyes. 'Well, there's no shortage of challenges around here.'

Anashe nodded, something that could almost have been a faint smile at the corner of her mouth.

'Indeed.'

Sarian returned, and with him came the supplies. Not just victuals and consumables, but several ponies behind him in a string, loaded down with the product of the rebellion's hidden stores.

Manatas was all over the new gear, lifting each breastplate and sabre up to the light, checking for dents and nicks. Anashe began unpacking the weapons of range, the revelation of which caused Anri a near-terminal huff.

'Fuck's this?'

Javani stood beside him, affecting a look of practised expertise. 'Hand-bows, Anri.'

'Like that grubby little shitter you had in the village, is it?'

The affected expression vanished. 'Hey! That grubby little shitter saved everyone in the end, didn't it? And no I am not referring to myself!'

'Didn't say anything, did I?' he chortled, then looked back at the hand-bows. 'Not using one of them, though, I'm not. It's beneath me.'

'Nothing's beneath you, you grotty oaf,' came Javani's half-muttered reply.

Manatas swaggered over to inspect the bows over Anashe's shoulder. 'However much these items displease you, Anri, it cannot be denied that they possess many advantages for our current venture. They are designed to be aimed and operated with a single hand in tight corners, and will suit both our riders and infiltrators in their given circumstances.' He picked one up, unfolded and refolded it, twirled it around his finger and slotted it neatly into a sling at his belt.

'You can't make me use one.'

'Nor would I dream of such. However, you may find, should matters turn from us, that you are without room to operate your full-length bow.'

'Be the judge of that myself, I will.'

'I expect you shall.'

The Commodore moseyed over to cast an eye over the breastplates, gleaming in the sun. 'All this tin with their stamp on it,' she muttered, 'the wasted materials alone fair make me weep.' She tapped a finger to her chin. 'Still, this amount of Guild-stamped gear does pose the question, should we be trying to dress up in all this blether and sneaking into the yard the night before?'

They looked at each other.

'Nah, would never work, would it,' the Commodore sighed. 'Girlie would look like a toddler in a ten-coat.'

'I'm taller than you!'

'Oh yes,' grumbled Anri, 'let's stick to our original plan, shall we, that's much better. Nothing mad about it.'

Javani caught Sarian as he was leading the ponies to the corral. 'Sarian, wait.'

He turned, looking tired but patient. Javani found she'd missed having the young scout around, despite their relative paucity of acquaintance (and despite him being probably six years her senior, although she couldn't help thinking of him as 'young'). She liked his eyes. When the job was over and done with, she resolved to try to get to know him a little better, no matter what Ree might—

'Javani? Are you all right? You look like you're in pain.'

'I'm— yeah. Anyway, my letter. Were you able to pass it on?'

He nodded. 'Passed on as instructed, but no time to hang around for a reply.'

'No, no, that's fine.'

He offered a tight, controlled smile. 'Can I ask what was in it?'

'Just catching up with an old friend.'

THIRTY-THREE

Inaï Manatas sat quietly in the darkness, listening to the sound of his beloved's breath, watching the slow, sometimes pained, rise and fall of her chest, flinching at every grimace or spasm that wracked her taut features. Her hand was limp in his, and clammy, unresponsive to the gentle rasp of his calloused fingertips over her skin.

'It will be tomorrow, my dear.' He kept his voice soft, as if afraid to wake her. He took a long breath, matching one of her own. 'We are as ready as we can be. As ready as your absence would permit, perhaps. But if you could see how she has driven us on, how she has brought us this close . . .'

He swallowed. The dread was never far, his constant companion, but he could, at least, when he had the strength, keep it at bay through force of will. 'I wish you could wake, could return to us, if not for me, then for her. I wish you could see her.'

Manatas swallowed again. 'That which you asked me, back in camp, the thoughts unvoiced. It was my fear, then – richly – my greatest . . . that I wanted more than anything for this rebellion to be over, but I was not certain that without it, you would see a purpose to keeping me in your life.' He stood, head bowed against the shelter's low ceiling, the clammy hand still in his. 'It was selfish of me, I know. I would see you wake, even if it should cost me everything, if only that the two of you might reunite.' His throat was tight, his breath hot. 'I miss you, Ree. I do not know what tomorrow will bring, but we will see each other again, one way or another.'

He squeezed her hand and laid it gently across her abdomen. As he did so, she shifted, her eyelids fluttering, a moan escaping her lips that sounded almost like his name. For one sharp, glorious moment, she seemed about to wake.

'Ree? Ree, are you there?'

She slumped back, her face pained, and the wheeze of her breathing resumed.

'Any shirts today, Javani?' Tauras was doing the laundry again, the White Spear looming over his shoulder with a practised eye. Like his cooking, there was still plenty of room for improvement, but the trajectory of quality, as the Commodore liked to say, was upwardly inclined.

Javani pushed herself up from her bedroll, where she'd been lying in a still-dressed heap. It was not yet sunset, but her weariness was bone-deep, along with the bruises and abrasions she'd incurred in the days of training. Removing her outerwear for washing was a slow and painful process. She was on the verge of feeling bad for Tauras, now effectively the housekeeper of their little camp, rushing around after them, cooking their meals and washing their clothes (in addition to the wagon and cart drills the White Spear put him through when he looked like he had too much time on his hands), but she lacked the energy, and more than anything feared that someone would announce it was her turn to take care of dinner or her filthy shirts, which on top of her compounded exertions might have been enough to tip her into madness.

'Mngthankyou, Tauras.'

'That's all right, Javani. I'll dry them by the fire tonight and you'll have them ready for the big day tomorrow. Should be lovely weather for it.' Arms full, Tauras moved on.

Tomorrow. Javani swallowed. Was it really tomorrow? She felt wrung out, used up, strung flat and beaten with sticks. There was no way she was in any fit state to rob anything from anyone tomorrow, let alone do so at any kind of speed. She was exhausted, yet the thought that before dawn they'd be up and off on what was potentially a suicidal endeavour set her fizzing with nervous energy, her jaw trembling spontaneously, her fingers clenching and unclenching. She knew she needed sleep more than anything, but her heart fluttered in her chest, a sick feeling like acid churning below it, and over and over the thought that she needed to see her mother before she went. Just, you know, in case.

She groaned and squeezed her eyes shut, fists balled against them.

A foot nudged her. 'Eat. Then rest.'

'Don't wanna.'

A large hand seized her by the collar and hauled her upwards. She found herself looking into the implacable gaze of the White Spear. 'Many years ago, a warrior of my clan, a young berserker, refused to eat and rest before a raid. He claimed the blood gods would lend him strength for the slaughter to come, and he would cleave the path through which the rest would follow.' She sniffed. 'On the trail, he faded, then fell, long before we even reached our quarry, and it was the crows that cleaved a path into his innards. You need strength, child. You need food. Then you will sleep. Then you will rise, and we will complete this operation. Do you understand?'

'Nngh.'

'Do you understand?'

Javani dangled, resentfully. 'Yes, Mistress Whitespear.'

'Good. You will be useless if you are half starved. Someone must make sure you eat.'

There was just a hint of words unsaid at the sentence's tail, a gap where the phrase 'as your mother is not around' or something like it would have followed. Javani's stomach clenched again, and it was not hunger. Released to unsteady earth, she glared for a moment at the vast Horvaun woman, daring her to voice the unsaid words, challenging her to say anything in the direction of Javani's inability to mind herself. At the back of her mind nagged the thought that Manatas was right, that Whitespear was right, that the Commodore was right. Javani locked her jaw tight to stop it trembling again.

The White Spear said nothing. She only stared back, until the fire of Javani's pique guttered and fell away, and then she felt only self-conscious.

'Eat,' the Horvaun said, and turned away, calling after Tauras with chiding and correction. After a moment, Javani threw her blanket over her shoulder and followed her down towards the cook-fire.

'Aye, right, you bunch of bastards, did you save me any scran?' The Commodore came sliding into the camp. They'd been taking turns to watch the yard where the wagon-train slumbered and grew, and now one of the agency crew would have taken over for the penultimate shift. Whatever was left of Javani's hunger evaporated with the Commodore's arrival. This was the last time they'd all be together before the operation. The hairs were standing on her arms, and without realising it she'd turned to face the shelter, her weight already shifted, one foot leading.

Manatas emerged blinking into the firelight, and Javani started and looked away. The captain did not meet her gaze; he looked taut and hollow, eyes red, stubbled cheeks sucked against his jaw, but moved with fluid determination. 'What news in the camp?' he called to the Commodore as she hunkered down with a platter on her knees.

'Eh? I only just got here.'

He paused, lips pulled tight, took a breath. 'What transpires in the outpost?'

'Oh, right, aye.' The Commodore took a big mouthful, then went on, chewing. 'Everything's going to plan. They've loaded the cargo wagons with ore and whatnot, and hooked it all up to the cables. Seen a bit of baggage go aboard, presumably the rest arrives tomorrow with the passengers.' She burped. ''Scuse me. Whole place is guarded to fuck, no way we'd have got in there. But outside the walls, well—' She burped again. 'Who made this, it's got some bollocks, eh?'

Tauras raised his hand from behind the laundry. 'I did, Commodore. I'm sorry about the bollocks.'

'No, you're all right, young fella. We need some bollocks this evening, eh?' Her voice dropped. 'Some of us more than others.'

Manatas was leaning across, trying to regain her attention. 'Never mind the, uh . . . Is all in place for tomorrow?'

The Commodore swallowed her latest mouthful and nodded. 'Aye, in place, all right. It's on.'

Javani felt a shudder run through her, a tingle of pure adrenaline, pure dread. Her gut churned anew, and with fresh vitriol, and her mouth tasted of storms. Every negative thought of the previous week resurfaced at once, a screaming chorus of doubt and confusion. Without even realising, she pressed one hand to her chest, gripping the blue stone tight beneath her shirt until her knuckles paled, and did not look towards the shelter.

What if I'm wrong?

She batted the thought away. Whitespear was right about one thing: she needed to rest; but despite her exhaustion, she knew she'd never sleep.

She was wrong.

Anashe sat cross-legged at the clifftop, the warm wind ruffling the trailing straps of her clothing, facing the fading glow of sunset on the jagged western horizon. She held herself upright without effort, her breathing relaxed and chin lifted, eyes half closed. Before her, perched between sharp-edged stones, the last of her incense burned itself gently to ash.

'Well, brother,' she said quietly to the wind, 'perhaps tomorrow will be the day. Perhaps tomorrow I will join you and our mother in the heavens.'

She took a slow, hot breath. 'I miss you, Aki. No matter the time, the wound is raw. I have been adrift without you. I have tried to persevere, but I cannot be certain . . .'

She swallowed. 'I cannot be certain that I am worthy. That I am worthy of your faith in me. That I am worthy of living, when you did not. That I am worthy of living happily.' She took a tight breath of scented air, and let her head drop. 'Better, in truth, to be worthy of a cause. To give yourself for something greater . . . as is the way of our family.'

The windborne cries of roosting birds carried over her with the smoke, and she lifted her eyes to the horizon once more. 'The little one believes you menace us still from the air.' A melancholy smile pulled at her features, fleeting and involuntary. 'When it is time, brother . . .' Slow tears rolled over the stark planes of her cheeks, and her voice cracked. '. . . will you come to fetch me?'

Anashe remained motionless on the cooling clifftop, her silent tears darkening the earth, as the light faded to nothing.

At the crest of the trail, Maral was as still as a corpse, which she found came naturally. She'd always had the knack, from the earliest she could remember, and by now skulking from sight and blending into shadows was second nature. While her body stayed immobile, frozen but for the slow, steady rhythm of her breath, her mind whirled, and she almost missed the new arrival.

'Ah, Ziba, at last.' Beralas was looking resplendent in a new set of evening robes, the plumes of the carriage behind him a matching shade of rich crimson. The coach lights sparkled in the cascade of rubies of his earrings, the thick stone at the centre of his collar. Gurbun lounged beside him, leaning against a carriage wheel, its rim leaving slashes of murk on the brilliant white of his outfit. Maral's lip curled.

Beralas strode forward to meet the rider, hands clasped behind his back in an unconvincing bid to hide his impatience. 'What was the delay? We have places to be.'

Rahdat slid from the saddle before the horse had stopped, and dropped her head and one shoulder in deference. 'We have been deliberate in preparations, Chairman. Tomorrow's events carry great weight for the Guild and all who believe in her. Nonetheless, I apologise for the delay.'

'Fuck's sake,' came Gurbun's honk, 'we know tomorrow's important. We're the ones telling *you* that, you fog-eyed merkin. Is everything ready or not?'

'It is.' Rahdat dropped her voice, her gaze intent. 'For what comes.'

Gurbun's scowl slid smoothly into a smirk of anticipation, and he smacked his fist into his opposite palm. 'Now *that's* more like it. We'll finally get to see if our gift from those smug little pinheads is as impressive as they claim.'

'Hardly a gift,' Beralas snapped. 'The chiselling dogs bilked us enough for it all.' He ran a nervous hand through his freshly oiled beard, bracelets clattering. 'And my capacity for trust in their claims is greatly diminished.'

'Will you stop *whining* about everything?' Gurbun was away from the carriage now, indifferent to the soiling of his robe. 'Tomorrow's going to be a triumph, stop raining piss, will you.'

Beralas's glare would have melted anyone but his brother, who seemed impervious. '*Not in front of the help*,' Beralas hissed, and did not look towards Maral.

'A triumph,' Gurbun repeated, enunciating to excess. Beralas's fist clenched, and for an astonishing, intoxicating moment Maral thought he might punch his brother. But he only pressed his hands together, hissed out a hot breath then put one palm on Gurbun's shoulder.

'I'm trusting you with this,' he growled. 'I'll be late.'

Rahdat's eyebrow twitched, the closest the woman got to registering shock.

'Just go without them.' Gurbun sounded exasperated. 'You'll miss the good bit.'

Again, Beralas's glare was fearsome, but it washed over his brother like so much water over river rock. 'I will *not* ring in the next glorious era of our father's legacy without a wife at my side, or any of his grand-daughters in attendance. We will make a show of familial unity, or gods help them.'

Gurbun shrugged, sliding his brother's hand from his shoulder. 'Don't care.'

Beralas ignored him, chewing once more at the corner of a fingernail. 'Ziba, your man Guvuli has control of things at the port?'

She nodded once, curt and emphatic. 'Preparations were completed on time and on budget.'

'Hm. Most impressive. It's a pity we'll be retiring this fellow once the celebrations are done, eh?'

Rahdat's scarred lips flickered in what might have been called a smile by someone who'd never seen one before. 'Yes, Chairman. A double pity he lacks the wit to see it coming, but that, perhaps, tells its own story. I will depart directly, and ride overnight to ensure I am in place for arrival.'

'No, no,' Beralas said half-heartedly, flicking the corner of an incisor with his thumbnail, 'don't feel you must ride the plain overnight on our account.'

Maral was practised enough to recognise that Rahdat would most certainly be expected to ride the plain overnight. The woman nodded once again, and turned for her horse. 'See you there, Chairmen.'

'Ride safely, Ziba.' Beralas turned back to the carriage. 'Kuzari! It's time.'

Maral's confederate came rolling out of the carriage, tumbling towards the ground yet somehow landing elegantly on his feet before rising to stand at Beralas's side. He was eating a quince, and wiped the juice down the front of his coat.

'Ready, boss.'

'I'll be heading down then, shall I?' The sarcasm in Gurbun's question would have been unmissable to the liveried Goldhelms lined either side of the carriage, and again the whites of Beralas's eyes flashed in the coach lights. He reached out and caught his brother's exquisitely tailored arm.

'Do *not* fuck this up.'

'Speak for yourself.'

Beralas did not release his grip. 'Remember General Mangud's famous quote.'

'He the one who drowned in sugar?'

'It was honey. "Only the best plans survive contact with the enemy."'

Maral's cheek twitched. General Devad 'Sweetstiff' Mangud had not said that, and nor, most likely, had anyone else.

'I'm not going to fuck anything up.' Gurbun shook off his brother. 'I'm going to have some fun.' He began walking away. 'See you there.'

'Wait!' Beralas cast around. 'Take Maral with you. This is what she's for.'

Gurbun's expression told its own story. 'For the love of the gods! I do not need one of your ratcatchers stinking up the place.'

Maral was motionless, inert, barely even breathing, barely even there. An image, in her mind, a moment, an emotion – someone she cared about, in mortal danger, moments from death, someone she *loved*—

'You'll take her and you'll be grateful. Maral.' Beralas snapped his fingers. 'Maral, are you here?'

She stepped out of the shadows. 'Chairman.'

'Gods, there you are.' His tone softened, but he did not look directly at her. 'Maral, you know you can call me Beralas.' The formal edge returned. 'Go with Gurbun. Do what you're best at. Do what needs doing.'

She said nothing, but her expression betrayed her uncertainty, and he put up a hand. 'Yes, I know, but Kuzari knows where to go. Kuzari, take three of my Invincible Goldhelms with you. See, Maral, all will be well. You've done the hard part, and now you can reap the rewards.'

'Yes, Chairman.'

He went to pat her on the back, his hand sweeping a finger's width over her shoulder, then turned back to his brother, who was glaring at Maral. The contempt in Gurbun's eyes was thick as syrup as he locked gazes with her. Was there something behind it, though? Was that a glittering core of . . . fear? The questions swirled in her mind. Again, she pushed them to one side. She had a duty to perform.

'Gurbun, you know what's important. Don't—'

'I get it, by the gods. Go off after your women, then.'

'We will be there as soon as—'

Gurbun was already striding away. 'Fuck off,' he called.

Beralas stared after him, eyes hard, then clenched one fist so tight the rings squeaked. 'Go with him, Maral. Do what needs doing.' She noted that he did not say anything about keeping his brother safe, which seemed a curious omission. Beralas had already turned back to the carriage. 'Kuzari, get into position and stand by. I will see you all very soon.'

Maral trudged down the rocky path after Gurbun and his bodyguards, her mind less certain than ever, and a long way from joy.

THIRTY-FOUR

Anashe was shaking Javani awake, which seemed impossible because she definitely hadn't been asleep. Yet dreams fell away from her, dissolving like cloud, leaving only wisps and echoes. She'd dreamed of Moosh again, the first time for a while; he'd featured regularly in her dreams in the months after his death, sometimes as a major player, sometimes only as a background element, and his awareness of his own fate varied with his appearances. The dreams had intensified a year or so after the events in Kazeraz, then tailed away, and her cold shock of waking was coupled with an intense and twisting guilt, a feeling that she was forgetting him, that once she no longer dreamed of him he would be lost to the world. The fact that she rarely dreamed of Aki only made this worse, his sister being the first thing she saw upon opening her eyes.

All of this passed in an instant, but left her with a lingering sense of unease, of shameful trepidation. It was not the ideal start to the day.

'Little one, it is time.'

Javani sat up, yawning and shivering, her blanket wrapped around her shoulders as was her habit. Dawn was yet a long way off, the night above them blue and starlit. The air was cool, with a gentle breeze blowing from the south, and she wondered if her shaking was more adrenaline and dislocation than a reaction to the temperature.

'You should stop calling me "little one", I'm big now,' she went to say, then hesitated. Whenever Anashe used the name for her, she heard the affection in her voice, heard the echo of Aki's words in each saying. Rumpled and guilty as she was, she realised she didn't want to lose that. Not yet. There was already too little affection in her life.

'I'm up.'

A sound like someone in pain came from along the arroyo, a bitten-off yelp. For a moment Javani thought only of Ree, but the pitch was wrong, the voice someone else's.

'What in hells is that?'

Anashe pursed her lips in the moonlight. 'Teg has turned an ankle. He cannot walk.'

'The Commodore's Teg?'

'Indeed.'

Javani swallowed. 'The one who was coming with us?'

'Indeed.'

'Shit.'

'Indeed.'

There was little breakfast to be had, with Tauras engaged in last-minute preparations, but Javani would have struggled to eat anyway. The White Spear pressed some pocket hardtack on her anyway, 'as she'd only be hungry later'. Somehow the big woman made this seem like a tactical failing.

Amid the ordered chaos of the camp, Javani approached the Commodore, who was supervising the loading of the cart and the wagon.

'How's Teg?'

'Hm? Oh, aye, fucked. Daft bastard slipped getting out of bed. Life in your forties for you, I suppose.'

'What do we do? He was our backup man for getting aboard.'

'I am aware.'

'And?'

'Aye, well, lad's only fit to sit, as we used to say.'

'I gathered as much.' Javani fought down a yawn. Her initial disorientation was gone, but now she was swept by alternating waves of cold and fatigue, and the aches and bruises had not magically disappeared in the night. She almost had sympathy for Ree and her bad leg—

'So he'll be minding things here, along with Stefanna on watch.'

Javani hesitated. 'Does that mean . . . ?'

The Commodore gave a heavy sigh. 'Aye, it does. Gird yourself, girlie, I'll be along for the ride today, so you and the other jesters had best be on top form, eh?'

Javani searched the woman's pale eyes, gleaming in starlight. 'Are you sure? After what you said . . .'

'Aye, I am. Can't keep putting off confrontation, all the pamphlets say so, even if in this case my antagonist is a supra-national para-military organisation.'

'What?'

'Just get yourself ready, will you, girlie? Some of us need to tip out before an operation.'

Javani stood at the threshold to the darkened shelter, the blue stone gripped so tight she half expected to find cuts in her palm. She ought to say something, she knew, before she left. This might be the last chance. But what was there to say? How could she put it all into words?

She turned to find Manatas in front of her.

'Uh, hello, captain.'

'Good morning, Javani.' He licked his lips, face pallid in the camp's gloom. 'I wanted to speak, that is, before you left, this likely being the last chance we will have to converse in advance of today's events, and their outcome being clouded in uncertainty— Say, what is that?'

The stone glimmered treacherously from between her paling fingers in the lantern-light.

'Uh. It's . . . It belonged to Ree, she got it years ago, although she never told me where or how. It was her one true treasure, and I borrowed it in Kazeraz, and then may have been complicit in it being . . . mislaid.'

His head tilted. 'Yet you have retrieved it?'

'Yeah. It was why I was on the *Illustrious Den*.'

'And you . . . you were planning to return it to her, as a gift? An offering of peace?'

Javani sniffed, rubbed at her nose, her throat scratchy. 'Would you give me a moment?'

He was already withdrawing. 'On my honour.'

Her steps into the darkness of the shelter were unsteady, shuffling things. The figure on the pallet was little more than an indigo smear in the pre-dawn gloom. Somewhere in the murk, her mother lay, sweating and wasting. And there was a good chance that if something went wrong on either side of things today, this would be their last encounter.

Javani's hand was out, the blue stone barely a glimmer in the darkness, hovering above the invisible figure. The air inside the shelter was too warm and smelled of suffering.

'Ree?' Her voice was small and hoarse. 'I, uh . . . I got you . . .'

She swallowed. The stone dangled from her grip, inching ever closer to her unseen mother's chest as her arm lowered.

'I wanted to . . . After I . . . This is . . .'

She took a breath.

'I got this back because I wanted to prove to you that I could fix my screw-ups,' she said quietly. 'I lost it, I got it back. But I can do more than that, more than just . . . not screw up. I can make a difference. I could have done all along, if you'd let me, but you always held me back. Well,' she went on, softly, sadly, 'you can't hold me back any more.'

The stone clicked against something, and Ree gasped in the darkness. Javani's shoulders shook.

'You know what?' she said. 'We can do this when I get back.'

She snatched back the stone and stumbled for the doorway, missing, as she went, the fluttering of her mother's eyelids.

Manatas was not far, his attention so overtly fixed on the ongoing preparations across the camp he could not have been any less expectant.

'Javani? Are you—?'

'Fine. You had something you wanted to say?'

'Ah, indeed.' He took a slow breath, his eyes not on her, but lost somewhere in the darkness past her shoulder. 'The obvious things, of course – good luck, be careful, stay mindful of risk and reward. But such entreaties and provisos notwithstanding, there was an ounce of fresh material I wished to impart.'

Javani waited, part of her pre-emptively clenched. Her eyes stung for some reason.

'I know you have struggled with your mother's . . . condition. It is my belief that she will yet surprise us, and we will see her, and speak to her again.' He looked up at the stars, eyes shining. 'But she cannot be here now, to say the things to you that perhaps she should have already, perhaps she would have already, had matters not interceded so often and with such intensity.' His gaze dropped back to her, and the wet gleam remained at the corners of his eyes. 'I cannot speak for her, nor claim to know what she would have said had she known of this day, but I can speak for myself, awkward and ill-defined as our relationship remains.'

Javani squirmed, but discreetly.

'Javani, you are an extraordinary young woman. And while I am greatly afraid for you in the hours to come, had I any doubt in my mind that you were incapable of the feats today will require, I would have hog-tied you and buried you up to your neck in red clay before letting you stray a stride from this camp. I know you are up to the task, I trust you to make the right choices, and to come back here whole, and with that seal in your hand. And I can say this with confidence, because I have seen it with my own eyes in the years I have known you. I have seen you grow, in stature and capability, and I have seen you become everything your mother hoped for you.' His voice was shaking now, his words rough and cracked. 'And your mother has seen it, too. Although she never got to tell you herself, she was so proud of you, of all you are, of all you will be, and all that you'll achieve. And while I know that she'd have pitched a fit to think of what you're about to do out there, it would not have been because she did not believe in you. She'd only have worried about letting you down.'

He took her hands in his, his fingers warm, his gaze shining and intent. 'I will not let you down, Javani. You will find that seal, we will get you off that train, and we will all come home safe.'

All she could do was nod; if she'd tried to speak, she knew she'd have burst into tears. Not just from the faith in his words, but from the way he'd unwittingly said 'was' about Ree, and hadn't even noticed.

'I will see you soon,' he said, squeezing her hands and holding her gaze. She was abruptly aware that she didn't want him to let go. His grip was warm, his eyes earnest. Javani had never had a dad growing up, barely even a rotating stable of father-type-figures in the early days, and now suddenly she felt a hole in her heart for what might have been.

'Good luck.' He released his grip and her fingers were suddenly cold, alone in the universe. She stood motionless until Anashe steered her away and towards where the infiltrators were gathering. For a moment, Javani was almost overcome by an urge to tell everyone in the camp that she loved them, even Anri.

'Morning, dickhead.'

The urge passed.

Javani trailed Anashe through near-darkness, following a route that only the lanky scout could see. Not that that stopped Anri muttering criticism of her pathfinding from two paces behind. The first wash of mellow amber had appeared at the eastern horizon, the sky beyond it lifted from indigo to lilac, and their window to get into position was closing.

'Are you sure you want to be here, Anri?' Javani hissed over her shoulder.

'No,' came the reply, followed a moment later by, 'But . . . boring before, wasn't it?'

The Commodore laboured behind Anri, her progress marked by a steady emission of invective from every root-stubbed toe or hawthorn-scored arm. Javani dropped back to match pace with her.

'Are you all right, Commodore?'

'Fuck no, girlie, thanks for asking.'

'You're doing the right thing. I'm sure of it.'

'Aye, well, that's great reassurance, that is, thanks for that. That's put all manner of existential crises and soul-searching right to bed.' The Commodore shuffled the pack on her back, the spools of rope at her shoulder. 'Fancy carrying some of this shite while you're in the helping business?'

Javani hefted her own spool. 'Sorry, I've, uh, got to stay nimble.'

Ahead, Anashe had stopped at a ridge, one hand up, fingers splayed. It was time to descend into the cut. Javani swallowed. 'This is it. Once we clamber down there, we're not coming back up.'

The Commodore gave her a sidelong grin. 'Still certain we're doing the right thing?'

'Fuck no,' said Javani with a matching grin. 'But we're going to do it anyway.'

THIRTY-FIVE

The first hour was the hardest. Once they were in position, tucked beneath scrub (some hacked down by Anashe and hauled over for extra coverage) at the base of the giant gouge through the rock, there was nothing left to do but watch and wait. As the sky overhead washed into pinks and yellows and the light grew, the rocks around them came alive with the cries of birds and the hum and chirp of insects, and Javani got her first good look at the tracks.

They were so much bigger than she'd expected. Despite knowing the rough height of the wagon they'd be boarding from Anashe's ruthless practice, her head had still been at 'mine cart rails' for the width of the thing. This was not an accurate assumption. The rails were arm-thick wood, plated with iron, and set Anri's height apart. Ropes as thick as her neck were strung along the tracks, run through regularly spaced towers with a mechanism she couldn't follow and was happy not to. And, of course, there were two sets of tracks, one in each direction, with enough packed loose stone between them for what presumably counted as safety. The narrow cut she had imagined was wide enough to ride a brigade down.

Javani lay beside Anashe, rough rock digging into her belly, scratchy brush tickling and itching her back and arms, and tried to make herself comfortable. It was hard to escape the conclusion that she should have urinated before they descended.

'You are fidgeting.'

Anashe had a fabulous way of turning an observation into an

accusation. She was watching the upward curve of the tracks out of sight, laid out against the rock as if draped. She did not fidget.

'It's hard to, you know. Get comfy.'

'I'm sure. Do you need to void your bladder?'

'No.' Maybe.

'Remember, should things become fraught later on, there is no shame to soiling your underclothes in the name of expediency.'

Javani shot her a look. 'Are you making fun of me?'

Anashe did not meet her eye, but the corner of her mouth lifted, just a little. 'My brother used to say the same thing to me before a job.'

'Oh. Did he regularly, um, soil his underclothes?'

'He would never admit it. But the fact it was never far from his mind carries its own suggestion, does it not?'

They were quiet for a while, but for the increasingly deafening chorus of insects.

'I'm sorry about Aki, Anashe.'

'So am I, pain in my posterior that he was.' She released a breath that was on its way to being a sigh. 'And I am sorry about your friend, and about your mother, too.'

'She's not dead.' Yet.

'We will do this thing today, and will do it for her.'

Javani bristled, shuffling on her elbows. 'This one, I'm doing for me.' She froze. 'What in hells is that sound?'

A humming, then a squeaking, tremulous at first but growing in intensity, was coming from the tracks. The ropes were moving, one in each direction. Javani felt the hair rising on her arms, on the back of her neck, a ghastly liquid feeling in her gut.

'The trains are in motion,' Anashe breathed. 'There is not long now.'

Javani swallowed. 'Let's spring this trap,' she whispered.

Captain Inaï Manatas sat uneasy on his mount in the shadow of the great red rock pillars that marked the mountains' end. Behind him were a string of ponies cropping at the tall-grass, tails swishing and stamping the occasional foot, presumably from boredom. He had never wondered whether horses felt boredom before, and now it was impossible to escape the thought. Away to his left, a little higher up the slope, was the second rider, Sarian, and his string.

Miles downslope, hidden behind a bulging crag that stood proud from what was fast becoming slanting, sweeping grassland, were the two vehicles. Tauras was driver in the first, the White Spear in the second, roped behind enough horses to match the speed of whatever came around the corner through the bluffs and out into the open.

He hoped so, at least.

Manatas checked the mechanism of his hand-bow one more time, listening to the cries of birds echoing from the ridge. So many buzzards around, this early in the day. He frowned. What did they know? Who tipped them off?

With a grinding creak, the thick ropes that ran over the tracks began to move, seeming to ripple across the plain on their supports.

'Sarian,' Manatas called, and needed say no more to the other man's nod.

Inaï Manatas sat uneasy on his mount, and waited.

'Ulfat, must we really be here so early? It's barely dawn and the ceremonies won't start for hours.'

Siavash's aged clerk bowed his head. 'Thousand apologies, master, but the invitation was specific. I thought you might, uh,' he sniffed, rubbed a finger under his nose, 'wish to secure a good seat for the occasion.'

Siavash nearly stumbled out of his (hastily applied) best formal robes. 'The seating isn't allocated?'

'No, master. Only for, uh, premium investors.' Ulfat inclined his still-bowed head towards where the banks of galleries had been erected, either side of the vast, roughly square area that was currently obscured by dangling sheets of canvas from suspended wooden frames. People were milling in great numbers, despite the early hour and sharp breeze from the sea, and as Siavash watched, he saw a number of equally fancy-looking types and their trailing retainers ushered through a gap in the billowing canvas. 'The luncheon will take place behind the curtains, on an elevated platform over the tracks.'

'How extraordinary.' He paused. 'Will the train be leaving or—'

'The first is leaving now, master. The return train will arrive sometime in the afternoon, we're told, towards the end of the luncheon. Rumour has it the Chairmen will be joining you for sweetmeats and the renewal of the Guild's charter.'

'Extraordinary,' Siavash repeated. 'Well, let's make haste, Ulfat. We don't want to be stuck on the outside, sitting next to someone dreadful, eh?'

'No, master.'

'Gods, the sound!'

Javani clamped her hands over her ears, squeezed her eyes shut, for all the difference it made. From all around them came whistles, horns, and the terrible squeak and creak of cranking machinery and ropes under terrible strain. The noise seemed to echo in the cut, barrelling back from the rock, doubling and degrading into a wall of near-physical force.

Anashe nudged her, hard. 'It comes,' she mouthed, but Javani had already known. The rails had started to quiver, the already cacophonous air in the slice of mountain now joined with an eerie metallic song from the trembling iron.

'It comes!' Anashe repeated, this time as a shout, and from around the wall of rock at the top of the cut came the train.

Ever since that first day with the spyglass, when they'd seen the half-train climbing into the red cliffs at Gonaraz, Javani had known the head of the train would be big. She had watched it assembled in the yard from their vantage in the mountainside, witnessed the great crenellations of its fortress walls, the arrow-slits and spool-wheels, the mesh of metal at its nose like teeth, a vast shield of the Guild its prow.

Still, she screamed.

Anashe clamped a hand over her mouth, dug them both into the earth as the ground beneath them shivered and jumped, all the time whispering, 'Remember the plan, the rest will be smaller. Remember the plan.'

Javani focused on the plan. The plan had momentarily left her mind, but she was confident that with a few deep breaths once the appalling, bone-shaking noise had passed, it would come sauntering right back. Then the realisation hit. The noise would not pass. They were supposed to climb aboard the noise.

She screamed again, into Anashe's paling palm.

'You can do this.' Anashe's words were hot in her ear, loud and urgent. 'We can do this. We will do this.'

Her shudders passed. Already the constant noise seemed familiar, its novelty lost. 'We can do this,' she repeated into Anashe's hand.

The hand released, and their eyes met.

'The head is passed. Two more to go.'

They waited, clamped together beneath their verdant cloak, coiled like snakes as the earth rumbled beneath them.

'One more.'

She watched great wheels turning against the rails, rolling past at a heavy, inexorable crawl, loose stone around it jumping like drops on a stove. From ground level, they were absurdly tall.

'Now.'

They moved.

'It was never this big before!'

'Keep up, Anri!' Javani shouted over her shoulder.

'Call this walking pace, do you?'

'Come *on*!'

Anashe moved with loping strides beside her, but Javani refused to let anyone else reach the train first. Anri wasn't completely wrong; it was already moving faster than the comfortable walk they'd been promised, and picking up speed as the slope ahead steepened. She was level with the baggage wagon now, somehow far more towering and oppressive than the mock-up they'd constructed for their practice, great sheets of silvered wood overpainted in Guild colours with haphazard levels of diligence. It stretched high overhead, the panels capped with strung canvas at the edge of their view. The two doors themselves resembled nothing more than sliding barn efforts; taller than Javani, their disparity exacerbated by the additional height of the grinding wheels either side.

Walking faster than was strictly comfortable, she planted both hands on the corner of the leftmost door and began heaving, letting the train's forward movement drag it back in her grip.

The door did nothing more than rattle, and she lurched forward, nearly losing her footing. Anashe was alongside her in an instant, steadying her gait, placing a hand of her own on the door's edge.

'It won't budge!'

They tried again anyway. It made no difference.

'Hoy, what's the fucken hold-up? Some of us are proximal to top speed here.'

'The doors are locked shut,' Javani called back.

'This not on your list, then, was it, robber?' Anri retorted, his ire directed at Anashe. 'This bastard is only getting faster, and our time in this here little gulch is limited.'

'I am aware of these things!' Anashe's breathing was still, even, her pace assured, but her elbows were beginning to pump in a way that suggested jogging was imminent. 'I assumed the locks would be external,' she continued in a mutter. 'We must force our way in, and quickly.'

Javani fell into her own jog, scanning the great sides of the wagon in desperation. 'It's going to take too long to batter our way in . . . Hold one end of this.' She slipped her spool of rope over her head and pressed one end into Anashe's palm, then began to twirl the other, weighted end. Jogging as she was, she told herself it was just like rope tricks from the saddle, except the saddle was in her mind and she had to keep her legs moving.

She flung, and the rope sailed up and over the top of the wagon, looped over one of the struts that held the taut canvas roof, and clunked back down the side into her waiting grip.

'Keep hold of that!'

As Anashe wrapped the other end around her body and braced her arms, Javani seized the rope with both hands and leapt for the wagon-side.

THIRTY-SIX

Javani climbed, the rope raw in her hands, her boots thudding against the wood of the wagon-side. Hand over hand, propelled by adrenaline, she near ran up the wagon as Anashe anchored her below. As soon as the top was in sight, she threw herself forward, ignoring the shrieks of her existing bruises as she thumped against the wooden lip, scrabbling with her feet until she was fully over, suspended by the sagging canvas. She swivelled, looked back over the side, down what seemed an impossible distance to the valley floor where the others jogged alongside.

'Now you climb!'

Anashe flicked a look back at Anri and the Commodore, who were keeping up but at visible cost. 'There is not the time for us all to make it.'

'Fuck it.' Javani slid her trail-knife from her belt, jammed it into the canvas roof, and sliced. Her cut was halfway done when something beside her pinged and the section of roof supporting her gave way. She plunged.

Javani bounced and thumped her way into the darkness of the wagon, hitting a suspended rack of something before teetering and crashing down onto a stack of crates. She lay immobile for a moment, her body a screaming bruise, as around her boxes and cases shivered and dropped.

'Fuck it,' she groaned.

The wagon was dark and shaking, but for the slash of light from the rent she'd left in the roof, which gave her just enough to make out the shape of the doors, and the metal pin driven through the locking bars. She pushed herself to her feet, wobbled, nearly fell, then scrabbled towards the doors, held up by unseen stacks. She stumbled to her knees before the pin, reached for it, and just for a moment two thoughts sprang to the forefront of her mind.

The first was, *Why was this locked from the inside?*

The second was, *Am I alone in here?*

There was no time. She hauled the pin free, threw up the locking bar and dragged the door sideways. Light flooded in, red and amber and flashed with green, and an instant later Anashe cleared the wagon floor, nimbly hopping up as if simply leaping a low fence. The rope was still wrapped around her, and in short order they had dragged the loose coils from the wagon-side and were throwing the end at the chasing Anri and Commodore, both of whom were now undeniably running.

'Stop throwing it past me, will you?'

'Aye, fuck, you're getting in the way!'

The light in the wagon seemed to be getting brighter. Javani risked a look out of the doorway up the train, towards the front. 'Nine hells, we're almost out in the open. Get on board!'

'Fucking trying, I am!'

'Try harder!'

Anashe, the loose rope hauled in once more, flung it out in a loop and bagged the Commodore. 'Help me pull,' she said, and she and Javani between them hauled the Commodore up off the ground and swung her in through the door, just as Anri dragged his wheezing carcass over the threshold and rolled to a stop inside.

Javani leaned all her weight on the door, driving it closed, as just for a moment the rushing red rock vanished and a flash of clear blue nothing appeared, then was gone, and the wagon was once more in near-darkness.

'I feel like we made that harder than it needed to be,' she said, hands on her knees. Her entire body throbbed.

'Told you I could do it, I did,' came Anri's breathless voice from the wagon floor.

'You certainly took your time,' Anashe replied. Even she was breathing hard, and had one hand pressed to her ribs in the gloom. 'We are too late to find the seal and depart in the cutting.'

'Aye, right,' came a voice from the floor. 'But hard part's done, now, eh? All downhill from here.'

Javani could barely stand. Somewhere in this shaking, shuddering darkness was the target of their search. All they had to do was find it. Then came the getting out.

She'd worry about that later.

'Yeah. All downhill from here.'

Tauras sat on the bench of the big wagon and waited for his friends. Not all of his friends were on the train, of course, or waiting up the slope. One of his friends was sitting on the bench of the cart just across from him, half-turned to look back past the big rock that blocked their view of the plains and the Iron Road that ran over it like a big dark line. He was also pretty sure he was friends with the ponies that were harnessed in the traces in front of the wagon. He'd given them names, because they hadn't had any before, and nobody had said he couldn't. His favourite was Svon, the barrel-bodied little chap on the left, who seemed to eat double what the others did. Tauras could respect that.

'Boy.'

Mistress Whitespear did not normally smile, and she was not smiling now.

'Yes, Mistress Whitespear?'

'You must concentrate today. No, do not remove your sunhat. You must keep it tied under your chin, or your brain will cook, and it will not take long.'

'Yes, Mistress Whitespear.'

'You remember where you must drive the wagon, when it is time?'

'Yes, Mistress Whitespear.'

'You remember why it is important?'

Tauras remembered. He didn't even have to think hard.

'Because our friends could be in trouble. They could get hurt. We need to rescue them.'

'That's right.'

'Mistress Whitespear?'

'Yes?'

'After today, when all our friends are safe, do you think we can have the feast? Down at the lake? I think I can cook one now.'

Mistress Whitespear didn't say anything for a moment, and her face didn't move. After almost long enough for Tauras to worry that she hadn't heard, she said, 'Maybe.'

'What if—'

'Boy, concentrate on today.'

He had displeased her again. He knew it, even if it didn't show on her face, because nothing showed on her face. Tauras felt sorry, and ashamed. He thought of Captain Manatas's words on what to do when he had disappointed someone. He had to make her proud. And he knew how to do that.

'Yes, Mistress Whitespear. I won't let anyone get left behind.'

Javani was upright, although the punishing swing of the baggage wagon was doing its best to undo it, throwing her one way then the other. 'We need to . . . gods above . . . get searching!'

Anashe was doing a better job of keeping her balance, one hand against a rocking wall, her eyes lost in the gloom that stretched away on either side of their splash of daylight. 'The scale of this thing,' she whispered, 'is beyond reason, beyond nature. It defies the will of the Goddess . . .'

'Yes, it probably does, which is why we should get off it as soon as we— Whoooooah!'

The front of the wagon tipped downwards, and everything in it that wasn't strapped or roped in place began to slide, Javani and the other infiltrators included. Anri crashed against a stack of chests and bounced off with a howl. The Commodore had grabbed hold of the net over a tidy display of barrels and seemed to be grinning, although in the murky chaos it was hard to tell.

'Aye, right, that would be the start of the descent, eh?'

'Gentle slope, you said!' came Anri's growl.

'It looked gentle from a distance!'

Javani kept herself standing, feet braced, teeth gritted. She was beginning to get used to their new angle. 'Guess this means we're not hopping off at a walk.'

'Nope.' The blade of the Commodore's hatchet gleamed in the darkness. 'Now let's get hacking about, shall we?'

There. A distant flicker, a blur through haze. Manatas snapped the spyglass to his eye, peering through its distended smear at the mountains' flank.

'They are in the open.'

A jingle and snort announced Sarian nudging his mount closer. 'That's good? Or is it bad?'

'It simply is.' Manatas could not unwind the knot of worry in the pit of his stomach. To have left Ree in the care of Teg and Stefanna felt bad enough, but what might she have said to hear he'd allowed Javani to embark on so rash a course while ostensibly under his protection . . . ? There was no right path, he knew, and he was no one to tell the girl what she could and couldn't do. But it did not make the worry go away.

'There is . . . That wagon, at the centre . . . Its shape is . . . unexpected.'

'Which one? Can I have— Thank you.'

'First is the head fortress, then—' Manatas recounted the order of the wagon-chain from memory, the spyglass now pressed to Sarian's eye, '—the enclosure for passengers, then what may be food stores, then the baggage, then general storage, then it is ore and cargo all the way to the tail fortress.'

'Which is the middle wagon?'

'The first of the ore and cargo, two beyond baggage. Its shape is different, see how it humps?'

'Not really. Maybe just a tall ore pile?'

'Hm. Maybe.'

The knot tightened.

'You know, Ulfat, it's really most irregular.' Siavash peered along the queue of similarly overdressed and shining worthies, some fanned or shaded by huffing attendants, all waiting to be admitted to the enclosure that surrounded the terminus of the rails. 'Made to wait like this, in full sun. You'd think they didn't value our investment!'

'Worry not, frater,' came a voice from beside him. 'For our value is precisely that which can be taken from us, and no more.'

Siavash turned, wondering if his interlocuter from the previous dinner had reappeared. Instead, he found himself meeting a wide smile of many golden teeth. The gold-toothed man bowed, just a little. His robes were fresh and no less garish than the last time Siavash had seen him, in the distance at the evening reception, and his moustache had been brushed out and waxed into points. 'Ishir Kusan,' he said, holding Siavash's eye with a dead-eyed stare. 'Delighted to place oneself at the service of those present.' Behind the man, his retainers lurked, their bright colours in stark contrast to their menacing aspects.

'I've . . . I've heard of you,' Siavash replied, matching the man's bow from habit alone, all the while feeling he should be backing away.

Again, the slick row of gleaming teeth, wet and fulsome. 'One trusts such tidings were all to the benefice?'

'Um . . . probably.'

The smile widened, which was not what Siavash wanted at all. Between the man's glass-eyed gaze and the slick lustre of his teeth, Siavash felt there was nowhere safe to look. 'But frater, you have one in that most perilous position of disadvantage, for your moniker is not yet disclosed.'

Siavash at least managed to exchange a glance with Ulfat at this point, who answered for him. 'We present Siavash Sarosh, merchant of merchants.'

'Oh, no, really . . .' Siavash waved a nervous hand. 'Just a low-level investor, no one of particular importance in this venture . . .'

'And here we stand the pair,' Kusan said, one thumb tweaking the end of his moustache, 'as compeers nonetheless.' He leaned forward and placed a hand on Siavash's shoulder, a startling breach of etiquette. Siavash was so shocked he could think of nothing to say.

'One feels we will have *much* to discuss at the luncheon,' Kusan continued, and gave Siavash's shoulder the sort of squeeze that he might use for testing the ripeness of a fruit. 'And one, for one, cannot wait.'

THIRTY-SEVEN

Javani hurled the broken chest across the wagon in frustration, where, to her great disappointment, it did not burst into fragments. 'Not here, either.'

They were used to the slope now, and the rocking, and the constant juddering shake of themselves and everything around them, the dancing shaft of light from the rent in the canvas roof. They'd started almost at random, tearing into anything that looked large enough to hold a Great Seal of Arowan, or hold something that held one, but at Anashe's insistence they had become more systematic, working their way through one section of the wagon at a time, cracking each case, chest, crate and barrel, ripping open sacks and bags, throwing open bundles. The wagon was a scene of rolling devastation.

And they were running out of things to check.

'Not here,' came Anri's voice from the rear of the wagon.

'One item remaining,' came Anashe's echo, with a mild hint of reproach.

'Nearly not here,' Anri corrected.

'Fucking hells,' Javani hissed. 'I'm going up the other end. Give me the hatchet, will you?'

The Commodore was having another breather on a clasp-smashed sea chest, the tool across her lap. 'Aye, right, fine. Don't break it. I'll be hacking away again in a mo.'

Javani snatched the hatchet without a word and stalked, bow-legged as a feast-day rider, towards the front end of the wagon, her free hand bouncing her from the wall with the vehicle's sway as she stepped over the piles of wreckage. Some of the loose items had slid or bounced towards the front when the train had tipped, and she hoped the seal's case might have been among them.

The front wall of the wagon had a sort of door, another sliding panel much smaller than those on the side, and a set of empty racks and shelves for what she assumed were smaller objects, straps and ropes hanging loose. As she caromed her way towards where the loose odds and sods had gathered, one little box in particular the object of her attention, something, absolutely and without question, moved in the corner of her eyeline.

She froze, or did the best she could in the circumstances, feet slipping on loose debris. She fixed her gaze on the banked shelves. Something there had moved. Something had definitely moved.

The wagon rocked, the straps swayed, small things moved in small ways, but nothing else. It was pointless trying to listen; the thunderous rumble of the train obscured all but shouts. Still, she gripped the hatchet tightly, and moved forward with slow, careful steps, then grabbed the shelves with one hand and swung herself around them, hatchet raised.

Nothing.

She edged backwards, daring the empty boards to spring into life, then a hand grabbed her and she spun, swinging.

Anashe caught the wrist with the hatchet with a look of only mild irritation.

'Little one, we have a problem.'

Sarian had not surrendered the spyglass, and Manatas was getting twitchy. 'Well, what do you see? Anything . . . untoward?'

'It proceeds at a constant speed. Hard to tell at this distance, everything is still so small, but it seems slow, for travelling down a mountain like that. You'd think it would pick up speed.'

Manatas flicked the reins in his hands, flexed his jaw. 'The mechanism prevents reckless acceleration, or so I am informed. Every stride that wagon-snake travels downwards, its force lugs the counterpart in the upward direction. Equilibrium is maintained through wheel-boxes and counterweights.'

Sarian looked up from the spyglass. 'Really?'

Manatas lifted his shoulders. The day was getting hot, even in the shade. 'So I am informed.' He pointed back in the direction of the distant train, shimmering over the waving plains, drawing ever closer. 'Remember the signal. If a door is wide open, we are to approach. If it is open only in part, they have already left. And if the doors are closed—'

'We bide our time. I remember.'

Manatas could not relax. Waiting was anathema. 'What of that middle wagon, the humped creature? Two back from where our friends should be. Do you notice anything about it now?'

The scout returned his attention to the streaked brass. 'Nothing. Are you sure this hump is a cause for concern?'

'At this juncture,' Manatas replied, chewing at his lip, 'I am sure of nothing.'

They were seated opposite each other beneath the canopies, which was bad enough, but then the retainers were shooed away by Guild flunkies, and Siavash was deprived of the company of Ulfat, at that moment what passed for his only friend in the world – a thought which gave him pause. He missed Ulfat more than he'd expected to, a feeling worsened by the identity of his dining companion.

The grand table between Siavash and Kusan, the gold-toothed slaver, was decked and draped in Guild colours, groaning with confections and delicacies that were far from appropriate for the early hour. The leering presence of the man on the cushion facing him had taken the edge off Siavash's appetite, and then there were the stacked benches of spectators in ranks beyond: presumably, said galleries had been constructed to allow the great unwashed a view of the grand arrival and subsequent ceremonies, but for now they afforded only an unobstructed view of some of the plateau's most notable merchants and political representatives stuffing their faces. For Siavash, it was enough to stamp away any residual thoughts of breakfast.

He fell back on small talk.

'Dining above the tracks of this, uh, great endeavour . . . strikes one as a bold choice, no?'

Kusan smiled again, and Siavash managed not to shudder. 'The inbound conveyance should not be expected until the unblinking eye has reached the mountains, and our terrain resides within its penumbra.'

Siavash tried not to stare. 'Come again?'

The smile broadened. Saliva glistened from golden teeth. 'The train from the mountains will not be reaching us until nearly sundown, frater. Time is ample for full repast in advance of its entrance.'

Siavash did his best to match the smile, closed-mouthed and discomfited as he was. 'Splendid,' he said, 'I suppose.'

'What do you mean, not here?' Javani's voice was a shriek over the thunder of the wagon. 'It has to be here!'

Anashe's voice carried just enough above the clamour. 'Every case or container that could have contained it, in its setting or otherwise—'

'But we saw it brought aboard! Right, Commodore? We saw them load it in its fancy little case.'

'Aye, well, right, you see,' came the reply from a dumped mound of clothes, 'we saw it carried into the yard, aye, for sure, and up to the loading dock, and into this very wagon, but as to where in precise terms it ended up on this here endeavour . . .' She spread her hands, one of which was holding a wineskin.

'Are you— Are you fucking drinking? Now?'

'Ah, well, as to that, found this here wee skin amongst the effects of those not present, and thought I'd best check, you know, in case the seal was within.'

'You have got to be—'

'Hey, don't dismiss a wee loosener in times of peril. I've done a lot of my best work while half-cut. 'S a long and honourable tradition.'

Javani wanted to scream. Instead she turned back to Anashe, one hand gripping the other woman's arm with a ferocity that would have driven a yelp from anyone else. Her words came out as a plea. 'You said something about an idea?'

Anashe's gaze was intent and unblinking. 'We have overspent our time in this wagon – the longer we wait, the greater the risk of discovery, or missing our exit.'

Javani cast a look back towards the sort-of door by the wagon's end with the shelves, half to remind herself what it looked like, and half just in case whatever it was that had moved had reappeared. There was too much chaos to feel watched, not like the eerie stillness of the plains and valley, and the thought that there could be anyone in the wagon along with them seemed ludicrous, and yet . . .

'We shouldn't panic.' She returned her focus to Anashe. 'We probably just missed it in the first rush. And we should be safe from discovery for a while yet, nobody's going to be moving between the wagons on this thing . . .'

Anashe's expression brought her up short. 'There are wagons either side of this one that may yet contain it,' the scout said, holding Javani's gaze. 'They should be less densely packed, but there may be people aboard them.'

'Are you saying we're going to—'

'Anri and I will move to the one behind. Carefully.'

Anri's head popped up like a prairie dog. 'Hoy, I'm doing what now, then?'

Javani had a sense of what was coming, but tested the water anyway. 'And, what, the Commodore and I go forward to the other?'

'Absolutely not. You are to stay here and hold this position.'

'Well how is that fair? If time's so much against us, why do you and Anri get to go exploring while—'

Anashe was implacable. 'Little one, Anri and I between us have fought, and killed, enough to make it,' she paused, 'ordinary.'

'Speak for yourself,' Anri muttered. 'More into maiming these days, anyway.'

'That is not what any of us wish for you,' Anashe continued.

'Hey, I can—'

'You should also remain close to the doors, in case matters do not go as we had hoped.'

Javani stood her ground, chin jutting, fists balled, swaying in time to the wagon's rock. 'And I'm supposed to, what, just sit here babysitting this booze-guzzling reprobate?'

'Hoy, don't leave me out of the murder stakes, I've cut up some fuckers in my days, I'll have you know.' The Commodore hiccuped. ''Scuse me. You know, on one occasion I split some fella in half with a two-hander, but in my defence he was an irredeemable tosspot.'

Javani glared at Anashe, but she might as well have been glaring at a cliffside for all the effect it had. 'Don't leave me here, Anashe. This is my gambit.'

'Sometimes we must play to our strengths,' came the cheerless reply. Anashe extricated her arm from Javani's grip, then, despite the aggressive motion of the train, put both hands on Javani's shoulders without losing her balance. 'If we do not return, and you do not find the seal in this wreckage, please leave when it is time. There will be other chances, other battles, but not if you are lost.'

Javani seized her wrist in one hand. 'I could say the same to you. No heroic sacrifices, you understand?' Javani remembered Anashe's brother, and the stories of her mother. This was a family who travelled beneath a fated cloud.

'I hope we will see each other again. I am . . . proud of you.' And with that, Anashe slipped from her grip and stalked towards the rear end of the wagon, travelling easily over the sliding carnage of their search. Anri watched her go, started, went to follow, then turned back to Javani.

'I'm not intending to die, pest, so see that you don't either, eh?' With that, he hefted his bow, and made considerably less graceful progress after Anashe. A flashing glare and a shriek of chains a moment later announced they had opened the door at the upper end, and then Javani and the Commodore were alone.

'D'you, uh, d'you want some of this while we wait?' The Commodore wafted the skin in her direction. 'Found a wee stash down here. Ghastly stuff, of course, but buggery choosers and all that.'

'I can't *believe* you've turned to booze at the first opportunity. I *asked* you if you were sure you wanted to come.'

All mirth left the Commodore's voice. 'If you'd had half the life I've had, girlie, you'd not begrudge a daughter of Clyden a wee drink.'

'Consider yourself begrudged. I've no idea what kind of life you've had because nobody tells me anything. Were you always called Commodore? That can't have helped.'

'Commodore is more of a title, an alias, a nom de guerre.'

'Huh.' A thought occurred. 'Did Ree have a nom de guerre? Before she was Ree.'

The Commodore was quiet a moment. 'She did. A few in fact.

But they're not who she is now, just who she was then. Now are you going to sit down or what?'

'What.' Javani snatched up the hatchet she'd jammed into a post. 'I'm not done here yet.'

She spun on her heel, or tried to, and marched back down towards the shelves.

And as she did so, she saw exactly what she'd expected.

The tide drags at her, carries her, throws her forwards across the years. Rai stands before a table, a rickety, cratered thing of gnarled driftwood. On the table is a basket, and in the basket is a baby.

'It's sick.'

The voice is a man she rode with, a pragmatist. A killer. A man she stayed close to, for longer than she intended.

The infant in the basket writhes and whimpers, restless in sleep. Pained. A hot little thing, skin flushed and sweaty.

'You can't care for it. Look at you. Look where you are.'

Rai swore she'd never return to Serica, to Arowan, she'd never see the gorge again, let alone cross it. Yet here she is, north of the Grey Hills, the expanse stretching out before her. Behind her is war and chaos and collapse. Behind her is what had passed for a family. Ahead, there is nothing. Nothing but possibility.

And the basket.

'Look at it! Tiny, frail, wretched. You can't keep it alive. You'll only doom the pair of you.' The voice tells her what she knows. It couldn't be otherwise. 'All this will do is hold you back. You need to choose yourself.'

He's not there, of course. No one is; the room is empty. She's alone, completely alone.

They both are.

Rai leans forward. The baby has a thick head of hair, familiar eyes that blink open at her proximity. 'Ratty little weed, aren't you?'

Then the child is in her arms, hot and tight against her, little lungs fighting, heart like a hummingbird's.

'You need to choose,' the voice says again.

'Not yet,' Rai replies, fingers gentle in the infant's curls. 'Not today.'

'You can't be a mother.'

'I don't have to be. But we all need someone to look out for us, don't we, kid?'

The little eyes open again, meeting hers, then close again with a sigh, and some part of her is changed forever.

'I promise you, I will never treat you the way my parents treated me,' she whispers.

'You need to choose. It will only hold you back.'

'I'm choosing. It's you and me against the world now, Javani.'

The room dissolves, the voice with it, then her arms are empty.

Javani?

Kid?

THIRTY-EIGHT

Anashe stepped carefully over the grinding, thundering chain that lashed the wagons together, doing her best to ignore the whipping blur of track and ground passing in the gap beneath, then had to snatch at the wagon-side as Anri stumbled into her, teetered at the edge, arms windmilling, then righted himself with one desperate hand on her arm.

'By the Goddess, what are you doing?'

'Not my fault, was it. Bastard thing keeps moving when you're trying to walk, it does.'

'This is not new information. Can you not move with care?'

'That was with care. Normally I'm a lot more jaunty, like.'

'I find that difficult to believe.'

She went to haul the narrow panel that passed for a door aside, but he didn't release her arm. 'Do you wish to spend the rest of the day out here?' she snapped.

'How do we know what's in this one, eh?'

'"Light goods", according to our intelligence.'

'Yeah, but half the stuff that should have been in the other one wasn't there, there could be anything in here and all.'

She pried his fingers from her humerus. 'That is what we shall endeavour to discover.' With her hand freed, she slid the long knife from the sheath at her thigh. 'There should be no one present, but we should be prepared.'

Now pressed against the wagon-end beside her, he shrugged the bow off his shoulder and checked the string. Anashe watched with her lip curling.

'Why you would even think to bring such a weapon along is beyond comprehension. The space to draw, let alone shoot—'

'Hoy, I don't question your choices, you don't question mine, eh?'

Anashe's eyes narrowed. 'What choices of mine do you consider worthy of question?'

'Not getting into that, am I. Pits and snares all the way down, that is.'

'But you would criticise something?'

'Not saying.' The string to his satisfaction, he slipped an arrow from his quiver and gripped it in his bow hand, an approximation of ready. 'Besides, you're the one who wanted me along with you. Recognised my qualities, you did.'

Anashe's grip on the door-panel was beginning to throb. 'The reason I brought you along, you malodorous incompetent, was that I did not trust you to be left alone with the young lady.'

'Eh?'

'The moment my back was turned, she would have proposed some outlandish scheme divorced from the very concept of risk, and you would have nodded her on her way, no doubt with some aphorism about true independence being the separation of thought from action, or something equally bovine.'

'Done something to upset you, have I?'

'Better she is left in the care of the Commodore, who will at least keep her in one place while we achieve our goals.'

'Just feels like "malodorous incompetent" was coming from somewhere specific, that's all.'

'Let us proceed!'

'Granted a man's smell can become somewhat pungent on the trail, but I don't feel my competence has—'

Knife in hand, Anashe hauled the panel aside.

'Huh,' said Anri. 'Weren't expecting that, were you.'

Javani beheld the source of the movement, and the source of the movement beheld her in return.

'I knew it was you,' she growled. 'I fucking knew it.'

Maral said nothing. She seemed to fill the space between the shelves, dark-garbed and stocky as she was. Javani was certain she'd let herself be caught, but the only question was why.

'What are you doing here, Maral? What are you doing in this wagon?'

The Mawn watched her with deep, dark eyes beneath the hanging strands of her knotted hair. 'You should go,' she said, the rasp of her voice barely audible over the clatter and roar.

'*You* should go,' Javani retorted, but the hairs on her arm were standing up, goose-pimples travelling up her legs. If Maral was here, had been in the wagon all along, she'd heard everything. If Maral was here, she'd known to get aboard. If she'd known to get aboard, it was because she had known they were coming. And if Maral knew, that probably meant . . .

'You should go,' Maral repeated. She had no obvious weapon, but Javani was under no illusion that made her harmless.

One hand hefted the hatchet, the other gripped the spool of rope over her shoulder. 'Going to make me? I don't need to cut you. I can down you and fetter you with just a rope if I want, remember?'

The corners of the Mawn's mouth twitched, just a fraction, as if a smile had momentarily broken containment and been hastily recaptured. 'You really should go.'

'You know what, Maral? You *are* the one who should go. When I asked you why you were here, I didn't just mean standing in this ridiculous vehicle. I meant, what in hells are you doing still working for these people? You've done more than enough to walk away now, unless you're happy with the way things are, the way they're going?' She moved her hand from the rope to her chest in a gesture of sweeping magnanimity. 'I'm even willing to overlook the fact that you *almost* successfully poisoned my mother, if you clear out, right now, and let us do what we came to do.'

This time, it was Maral's brows that tweaked, a flash of surprise. 'She still lives?'

'Well who can fucking say, but she was alive when I left camp.' Javani's cheeks were burning. There was no way she should have surrendered that information, she could almost hear Ree's rebuke in her ear. But in her defence, she was feeling very, very angry, and beneath that lurked a roiling tide of dread at exactly how discovered they were.

'You . . . you want her alive?'

'Are we still on this? Of course I do, she's my ma, and even if she wasn't, she's the person who's done the most for me in the whole bastard world.' The horrible truth of the words hammered home as she said them, and suddenly her throat was tight and tears formed in her eyes. 'Of course I want her to live, gods damn it all, I nee— Never mind.'

Maral said nothing, her eyes like onyx pebbles in the dark.

Javani wiped her sleeve across her eyes. 'So why don't you do us all the favour of buggering off before you cause even more damage, eh, instead of doing whatever it is they sent you here to do.' Kill us all, presumably. Gods, how much do they know? 'Did you even go back and check the archives?' She kicked a pile of discarded books and ledgers across the floor. 'If there's one thing these bastards pack a hundredweight of – apart from shoes, for some reason – it's records. They take note of everything in the Guild. I bet there's a little entry in the archives somewhere, from all those years ago – "fabulous day slaughtering, wiped out a whole camp of Mawn, kept one for a treat, might make it into a murder-slave for shits and giggles." Except it won't be worded so delicately.'

Javani was breathing hard, her face hot, her back sweaty and legs trembling. Her mouth tasted of adrenaline, which was not a flavour she would previously have thought she'd recognise. From somewhere behind came a slurred call from the Commodore, which she righteously ignored.

Maral hadn't moved, hadn't said anything, gave nothing away, but the tilt of her eyes was . . . just . . . a little different. Javani's heart leapt in her chest. Had she got through to the Mawn? Was she about to turn tail and leave them to complete their mission? Would she – gods have mercy – would she even lead them directly to the seal?

The narrow panel behind the Mawn burst open in a dazzle of glare, and Javani recoiled, one hand before her eyes. It took seconds of blinking to adjust, just in time to witness a new figure stepping carefully into the wagon from outside, one hand on the frame, glorious white robes smudged and grubbed. Maral slid to one side as the man advanced with swaying steps, and behind him brass-fronted guards filled the doorway.

The man cast a disgusted look at Maral. 'Where in fuck have you been? Know what, don't care.' He took his hand off the wall to crack his knuckles, and gazed at Javani with what she could only feel as hunger.

'Hello, little rat. Do you know who I am?'

She nodded. Gurbun Verdanisi, Second Chairman of the Chartered Miners' Guild of Serica, just as the Commodore had described him.

'Good. Do you know what I'm going to do to you?'

She shook her head, trying to back away but not trusting her feet on the crowded, tilting, swaying floor.

'Good.' He squinted. 'How old are you? Know what, don't care either. Let's get your friends together, shall we? We have such japes in store.'

'Shit,' whispered Javani.

Anashe moved cautiously into the wagon, one hand kept on the rough wood boarding of its perimeter. Behind her, Anri ducked inside and pulled the panel back across. It did little to dim the racket of the train.

'Why is it empty?' Anashe murmured. 'There should be more than enough in tradeable goods—'

'Not completely, is it?' Anri replied, kicking at a low stack of small crates. 'Probably didn't want to risk putting anything valuable in this one, what with it not having a roof.'

Anashe cast her eyes up at the crystal blue of the sky above. Distant wisps of cloud strolled softly overhead, distance dulling any sense of the train's alarming speed. 'We are hardly at risk of a storm.'

Anri had found a rack of wound chains, much like the ones that held the wagons together, and some giant reels of arm-thick rope, spooled around stout wooden spindles. He kicked at them as well. 'Not much to go on, is it, hiding-wise. Looks like spares for the couplings, or whatever they were called.' He lifted a fat link and let it drop with a clatter. 'Fucking daft, it is.'

Anashe was prying the lid off a crate, more in hope than expectation. 'To what are we referring now?'

'The whole thing, isn't it. The chains, the cables, the ropes, strung across miles. How does it work? How can it work? The stress, the distortion, the tension should just—'

'Anri!' Anashe barked. 'That it *does* work is all we need to know. We are on it, and it moves, and we should concentrate our energies on completing our task and removing ourselves from it with the greatest possible alacrity. All being well, there will be time to postulate on the alchemy of this infernal contraption when we are well away from it.'

'Would say that, wouldn't you,' came the muttered response. 'Got no respect for physics.' He squinted into the morning sky. 'What do you make of that?'

Anashe did not look up. The crate was useless, of course, as she'd known it would be, but she felt honour-bound to try the rest.

'Next wagon along. Kind of . . . bulgy, isn't it. Like there's something poking up from the canvas.'

'What do you mean, something poking up?'

'Mean what I say, don't I. That one's got a roof, this one hasn't, that one's got some big old something under it, tenting it like a morning bedsheet.'

'Why would a bedsheet . . . oh, by the Goddess.'

'What? It's an indelible image.'

'*You* are an indelible image.'

'Thank you.' He squinted again. 'You know,' he said, 'I reckon there's something moving under there . . .'

'Let's get some light in here, lads,' Gurbun called, free hand swiping in the direction of the cargo doors. He carried a sword at his hip, a fine one, but the number of armoured guards who suddenly seemed to fill the carriage immediately doused any thoughts Javani had kindled of snatching it, stabbing him and making a run for it.

'Stay on your pimply arse, paleface,' Gurbun bellowed at the Commodore as he advanced, Javani backing cautiously away in his path. The incline of the wagon was decreasing, suggesting they were through the worst of the mountain descent and making for the gentler slope of the great plains crossing. Which meant they were coming up on the first of their departure opportunities . . .

Then they were bathed in daylight as the guards dragged the loading doors wide, and the wagon filled with the rush of air and the swirl of dust. A blur of open ground beyond, flashes of green and grey, barren stretches of red earth, until her eyes adjusted again. The Commodore had been right; they were moving at the speed of a cantering horse, travelling a declining slope, and the plains were beginning to stretch out beside them.

'That's better, eh?' Gurbun roared. 'A fellow can see his own fists in here. Now!' He slapped a fist into his palm. 'Where are the rest of you hiding? Is this it? A child and . . . and . . . whatever the fuck you are.'

'None taken,' came the Commodore's voice from her pile. She had yet to surrender her skin, to Javani's mounting fury, and seemed to be working her way through several others piled between her knees.

'Get up,' she hissed. 'Get up and fight and we could take these bastards.'

The Commodore burped. 'Aye, right, no. Not as the odds are currently, y'know, stacked.'

'What happened to your place on the kill stakes? To splitting some tosspot with a two-hander? To putting the last fifteen years behind you and facing your fears?'

'Right, aye, but, counterpoint . . .' She burped again. 'No. Ooh, this one's got a kick, eh. I think this is the fella.'

'Gods above, I thought Anri was a coward—'

'Stop talking!' Gurbun bellowed. 'You're not in charge of this, understand? I am, Gurbun Verdanisi. You're going to do what Gurbun says. And right now, Gurbun says, "time to have a look out the side" because our grasping little friends from over the sea have gifted us a few little extras, and you don't want to miss what happens next.'

THIRTY-NINE

'You see it?' Sarian thrust the spyglass back towards him, but Manatas had no need of it. The train was already in plain view across the sweep of the landscape.

'The doors lie open, wide as can be.'

'The signal! Ride, ride, ride!'

Sarian was away before Manatas could reply, spurring his mount off down the hillside with his string of ponies taking up the gallop in pursuit. Manatas took only a moment to stuff the spyglass back into his jacket, then with hue and cry he followed.

Gurbun was right up against the loading door, hands gripping the post, leaning out as far as he dared as the wind whipped at his glorious, tarnished robes. He was grinning, hair blasted against his scalp. 'Here they come now. Wondered how you'd do it, and here's the answer come charging over the hill.'

He turned back to Javani and the Commodore, who were corralled at the wagon's centre, disarmed and surrounded by smashed baggage and its innards, and as many as nine guards. 'You see, we're not as thick as you vermin think. We always figured someone might try to come after the Iron Road, might try and intercept or sneak aboard. We've been on to you from the start.'

A tiny noise caught Javani's ear, from down the wagon, where Maral still lurked half-hidden in shelving. Had that been a . . . snort? Of derision?

Gurbun affected to ignore it, although the stubble of his jaw flexed with tension. 'It's a shame the view from here isn't ideal, but you'll get a better one presently. For now, you can just enjoy the overture from in here.' He barked over his shoulder. 'Signal it!'

In the distance, Javani saw the telltale feathers of dust, the rising kick of horses on the move. The riders were coming. And Gurbun was grinning.

Anashe clapped her hands over her ears, barely keeping her balance as the wagon rocked. 'What in the name of the Goddess is that noise?'

'What?' Anri roared back.

'What is the noise?'

'What?'

Whistles, whistles and horns – they seemed to come from all around, piercing sharp and blaring over the thunderous clatter of the train. Then at once they fell away, the din of wheels on rails suddenly almost sedate by comparison.

Anri removed his hands from his ears, stuck a finger in his ear and waggled it. 'Kypeth's puckered ring, what was all that about?'

The moment passed; Anashe's mind kicked in with possible explanations. None of them were good. She scanned around them, her sense of unease growing, grip tight on her blade. Movement caught her eye.

The canvas roof of the next wagon was peeling away, hauled down by unseen ropes, revealing a towering structure, a steeple of spars, drawn up from somewhere within the wagon body. Someone was climbing it, a pair of someones, rushing up a ladder at its back towards the boarded platform at its summit.

'What in the name of . . . ?'

Anri was beside her, hand pressed to his brow, shielding his eyes. 'Know what that looks like?'

'What?'

'Hunting hide.'

'Hm.'

'Don't usually smoke, mind. That's new.'

Gurbun paced before the open doorway, stance wide, steps heavy. Javani itched to leap forward and kick him clean from the train, but she knew the guards would likely stop her, and the pointed end of any number of spears and sabres would go through her like knitting needles. The knowledge did nothing to make the urge go away, though.

'Get off your arse,' she hissed at the Commodore, who still sat pretty on her mound, surrounded by her bottles and skins, pilfered from wrecked baggage. 'We don't stand a chance with you down there.'

The Commodore fixed her with a beady glare. 'Girlie, there is a time for fighting, and this is not it.' She rummaged in a broken chest at her side and produced a long clay pipe and a flintbox, which she set about loading.

'You're sparking up now, are you?' Javani couldn't keep her voice in check. 'Now?'

'Hoy!' Gurbun slammed his palm against the wagon-side. 'No conferring! Eyes front, you pestilent little maggots. You're not missing this.' He stuck his head out the side again, then turned with a vicious grin.

'Fifteen years ago,' he went on, 'or was it more? Probably before you were born, squirt. Anyway! Years back, the dung-eyed fucks down south crossed paths with our esteemed friends from across the sea, and got a little taste of their temper. BANG!' He clapped his hands together with a mighty slap, almost lost his balance, jammed a hand against the doorpost.

'Anyway,' he repeated. 'Turns out some mad king had kidnapped an alchemist, and made him spill his guts. Before you know it, within the year, said king has run riot, charged north to wage war on Sainted Arowan with heathen witchfire. Remember the siege? Not you, titch, you were gloop back then, but the rest of us, eh? Blasted the fat city to dust.'

In the corner of Javani's eye, she saw the Commodore becoming increasingly fidgety, unlit pipe in hand, and increasingly red in the face. She probably needed to relieve herself after all the grog she'd guzzled. Javani was infuriated by the woman's cowardice, after all the big talk of facing down her years of fears.

'But the secret was out,' Gurbun droned on, 'and Arowan got its own alchemy. Fought off the stunted inbreds, and then . . . well, we got our blasting powder. Revolutionised the expanse. Revolutionised the Guild. Made us who we are today.' Gurbun stuck a thumb in his lapel and preened for a moment.

'But the funny thing about the march of science,' he went on with a devious grin, 'is that it just . . . doesn't . . . stand . . . still.'

The wind whipped at Manatas as he rode, full gallop, across the waving grass of the plateau, dust mask up against the choking kick of Sarian's string ahead. Exhilaration flooded him; he felt like whooping, yelling his glee to the sky as they broke across the open ground. It had been an age since he'd ridden so hard, so fast, with such purpose and determination in service of a truly vital goal. And it was in sight, as they cut their diagonal, curving path towards the tracks. Across the narrowing strip of plain came the wagon-train, its head fortress lumbering black steel, the chained wagons rattling along in its wake like the wooden segments of a child's toy, the door-panels of the baggage wagon hanging wide and dark against the glare of the morning sun. The horses in his string ran clear, his own mount alive with sympathetic energy, while far ahead, narrow smudges marked the distant passage of the cart and the wagon, making for the dry riverbank to come.

Sarian was closing, mask loose around his neck, a visible smile on his young face, as the string of ponies raced out behind. They were riding too hard to even consider the spyglass, but Manatas shot what looks he could at the train as they narrowed the gap, peering beneath the wide brim of his (tightly tied) helmet at the maw of the baggage wagon, the odd flash of figures within like a break in moonlit clouds.

Then the wagon two behind it drew his eye, its canvas roof pulled back, the curious hump he'd spied from so far away, so long ago, revealed as an equally curious tower of crossed beams, topped with a walled platform that threw a trail of black smoke into the morning air, a line like a slash of charcoal staining the sky in the colossal vehicle's wake.

Without conscious thought, and to the consternation of his enthusiastic mount, Manatas slowed to a canter, his attention now fixed upon the mysterious middle wagon and its smoking tower. Was that movement at its summit? His eyes were not good enough, not without ground glass and twenty years knocked off.

'Sarian!' he called, 'Sarian, hold!'

Sarian would not hold. Whether he heard or not, the younger rider ploughed on, leading his string of ponies on a course to intercept the baggage wagon at a gallop.

Manatas unstrung his hat and waved it in desperation. Glimpses at the baggage doors suggested too many figures lurking in the darkness within, shaded against the bleaching sun-wash. The smoking tower concerned him greatly, its sudden appearance, the strange noise that had preceded it, horns and whistles over the growing thunder of the train.

'Sarian!' he tried again, kicking his mount back into pursuit, still waving his hat. 'Sarian, hold!'

This time Sarian turned, confusion on his young face, mercifully slowing the pace of his mount and its chasing companions.

'We can reach them now,' he called back over his shoulder, 'before the carts need close.'

Manatas gestured furiously with his hat, trying to keep his horse at speed and his balance in the stirrups. 'The middle wagon! The tower!'

The boy merely shrugged. 'Could be anything. They gave the signal, captain – they need us!'

'We don't know it's— Sarian! The smoke!'

But the young man had put his heels to his mount and was off again, barrelling towards the train, looking to curl his path alongside and bring the horses in line with the doors.

'We needed a better signal,' Manatas muttered as Sarian's dust trail washed over him, wafting his hat and stuck with the terrible indecision of holding back or charging after.

Then something sparked and fizzed on the strange tower, a flash like ball lightning in the clear of day, and a black arrow ripped through the air. Manatas saw only a blur before the ground between him and Sarian erupted, the earth bursting upwards in gouts of sod and torn grass, showering Manatas with a plume of pulverised rock. His horse screamed and shied, almost rearing, and behind him the string was in chaos. Manatas fought to stay in the saddle, his hat lost, reins gripped white-knuckled, whatever soothing sounds he could muster drowned by the pulsing whine in his ears and the shrieks of the panicked and milling horses.

'What in the name of the gods . . .' he would have whispered, had words been possible to form. From the corner of his eye, through the falling patter of debris, he saw Sarian, still mounted, still riding, dragging his wide-eyed string ever towards the train. The train where the foreboding tower still smoked, and whence another black arrow was only a matter of time.

Manatas squeezed the reins, pressed his knees against his jittery mount and fought down his own wave of panic. He had no idea what to do.

Javani stared, open-mouthed, so stunned that her pulse had yet to rise, just a cold and tingling feeling all over her body, numb even to the rocking sway of the wagon beneath her.

'Like that, parasites?' Gurbun's grin was so wide there seemed a vague danger the top of his head would fall off. Some of his guards had cheered when the object had smacked into the flat of the plain and detonated like a wagon full of blasting powder.

She couldn't speak, her throat thick and closed, couldn't even turn her head to check the Commodore had seen it all. She was light-headed, a taste like metal on her tongue, and the dim sense of relief she'd felt at seeing the riders scattered but whole after the terrible explosion was fast being gnawed away by the certainty of the next projectile.

'Fifteen years ago, or whenever it was,' Gurbun chuckled as he swung over from the doorframe, one-handed and ape-like, to leer into her face, 'our pals the Iokara could scare their enemies plain shitless with a volley of these bad boys. But truth be told, back then they rarely went where they were pointed, half the time they didn't go off, and even a hit meant little more than scorch marks. Well, maggots: Things. Have. Changed.' He chortled, attention switched to his guards. 'Who wants to guess what happens next? Anyone? Come on, lads, let's make it interesting.'

'Horse goes up,' called one.

'Two!' cried another.

'Two and a rider,' went a third. 'We'll see some legs fly!'

Now Javani could move again, she turned her furious, impotent gaze on the Commodore, who was unmoved on her mound but now striking the tinder box against the pipe with a fixed and glazed determination, her gaze somewhere out over the distant horizon. In desperation, Javani scanned the debris-strewn wagon around her, searching for something, anything that could turn the tide. Instead she found only Maral, the Mawn looking back at her with an expression as taut and blank as the Commodore's.

Javani felt hatred, rage and disgust, and a desperate, miserable pleading. 'Help,' she mouthed.

Maral did not react.

'Kypeth's rotten todger, what fuckery was that?'

Anashe had barely the mind to shush her companion, her attention locked on the rising black blast of smoke from the towertop, trying to gauge where its missile had travelled from the sound of its impact.

'Alchemy. They have bought or borrowed witchfire from the Iokara who engineered this abomination. And they know we are here.' Anashe's mouth was dry.

'What do you reckon they're shooting at?'

Anashe cocked an ear. It was hard to make much out over the constant cacophony of the train, but the shrieks of panicked horses carried over the wind.

Riders. Closing. The signal.

'There are two possibilities.' Anashe spoke slowly, trying to form the thoughts into coherence by force of will. 'Javani and the Commodore have found the seal, opened the doors, and we have been discovered at the riders' approach.'

'Think they might have stuck a head through and mentioned it, eh?'

'Then the other is that we are in a great deal of trouble.'

Anri took a moment to digest this.

'Balls,' he said at length.

'Indeed.'

A hissing noise was coming from the tower ahead, loud enough to hear over everything else.

Anashe hefted her blade. 'We must return to them, they are likely—'

Anri's jaw jutted. 'Piss off back there if you want to, but from the noises and emissions coming off that tower of power up by there, another one of them screamers is on the way.' He fixed her with a boss-eyed glare. 'Then another, and another, until we're all blown to bits across the plain. Or someone does something about it.'

'What are you saying?'

'I'm saying we don't know what's going on behind us, but we can see what's ahead, and it's a pain in everyone's arse.' He flicked up his bow and slid an arrow to the string. 'Also, got a little glimpse of one of the bastards up there, I did. He's going to pop his little head up in a moment, and when he does, I'm going to have him.'

Anashe hovered. 'They may come through the door behind us at any moment. Or in front of us.'

Anri appeared to be smiling through his dreadful beard. 'Don't worry. I've got a plan.'

FORTY

Manatas made his choice, cursing the lost seconds of indecision. He released the string of ponies, letting them run free behind his own. 'Sarian! We must draw them from the carts! Cut the string and spread the horses!'

Sarian didn't hear; the young scout was still trying to close on the open baggage wagon, hunched tight in the saddle as if presenting a smaller target would make some measure of difference to the fury of the black arrows from the train. Manatas slapped at his side for the signal horn, realising too late it was lost, its strap cut by a jagged shard of flying rock.

Then the tower belched, and another black bolt screamed through the air, blasting great lumps of earth higher than the train and scouring Manatas and the ponies with a wave of vicious scree. Horses cried and stumbled, his own included, and he fought to keep the saddle once more. So much for drawing their shots; he was stuck in a no-man's land, too far from the train to aid those within it, not far enough to escape its alchemical lashing. Now he understood Sarian's intention – if he drew up along the body of the train, the tower would have no line to him and his ponies, and could not risk detonating one of its missiles so close to itself. He just had to buy Sarian time, and not be burst in the process.

'Come on, girl,' he murmured into his anxious horse's ear, 'one last wild ride.'

Javani flinched with her entire body at the sound of the second explosion, feeling its thump even through the rattle and shudder of the train. The scene from the open door of the baggage wagon was chaos and dust, the landscape rolling past at uncommon speed as a great eruption remodelled it at the edge of her vision. Still she saw riders, or horses at least, through her streaming eyes as the gritty wind whipped at her. Gurbun lurked at the doorway's edge, peering round it with a grin like a gutter-boy plotting his next purse cut.

'You,' he called to the nearest of the overdressed guards who ringed Javani, and the now pipe-smoking Commodore, with spears and sabres. 'Give me your stick.'

Puzzled, the guard complied, passing his spear over and drawing his sabre the moment his hands were empty, furnishing Javani and the Commodore with a fierce look of determination lest either of them for a moment get the idea that he would be somehow harmless. Javani did not give a toss. Her attention was fixed on Gurbun, and whatever he was up to that required a spear. She realised she was counting in her head, counting heartbeats as she sometimes did, tracking how long until the next black arrow came screaming from the tower and immolated someone she cared about.

Gurbun was looking at her, his eyes wide and expectant. 'You're going to like this bit,' he said, his mouth a smirk of tall, ivory teeth against the thick stubble of his jaw, his white robes gleaming and smeared. She lacked the energy or inclination to respond, her mind divided on tracking the time between alchemical missiles and counting the guards around them, their armour and armaments, their likely reaction if she were to try something more adventurous than sneezing. She wiped at her streaming eyes again, furious most of all that Gurbun would think she was crying, not wind-chapped, because she was not crying, not even a little bit.

A bobbing shape appeared in the doorway, dark against the glare of the rushing landscape beyond, and it took a moment for her blurring eyes to resolve it: a horse's head, followed by more of the horse, followed by Sarian, riding at a canter, his head turned to peer into the gloom of the baggage wagon.

'Anashe? Javani?' he called, 'Move quickly! I have—'

Gurbun stepped around the door-panel, swinging the spear in a wide arc, and slammed it against Sarian's head. He dropped from the horse without a sound, lost from sight in less than a heartbeat, and the horse kept on running.

Javani didn't even scream. She was numb to Sarian's loss, his appearance and departure so sudden, the incongruity of his mount running on beside the train. Even Gurbun's laughter seemed distant, muted by her own confusion, and the little counter in her head that was telling her the next missile was now overdue. Her gaze drifted, unfocused, skimming past Gurbun and the open doorway with its rushing vista of bleached plains and cerulean sky, past the immobile Commodore and her growing wreath of smoke, a clay jar of something acrid in her drinking hand, past the brass-fronted, leering guards, and came to rest on Maral, half-hidden in darkness, eyes as black as sin, her expression as blank as a training dummy. Javani said nothing, felt nothing, but fixed her eyes on that black gaze and held it with all her strength that remained.

'A couple more rats left to swat,' chuckled Gurbun in the background, his voice as if he were in another room, 'and we should . . . huh. Where's our next screamer, eh?' His eyes narrowed, thick brows lowering like a portcullis. 'You two, find out what's going on back there. Maybe there were more vermin aboard than these two after all.' He turned back to the open door-panel as two of the guards stumbled off through the end door that Anashe and Anri had taken what seemed like an age before. 'Look at this fucker run, eh?' he chuckled at Sarian's still-cantering mount. 'Run, horsey, run!'

Seven guards remained in the wagon with them, as well as Gurbun, who seemed to be moving towards the notion of stabbing the cantering horse with the spear in his hand, if only to see what would happen. The very idea of it sent a flash of furious hate through Javani, who kept her gaze locked on the half-shadowed Mawn. She'd seen what Maral could do. The Mawn could cut down the guards and Gurbun with them, probably using nothing more than hairpins. All she needed was the right motivation.

'Maral!' she hissed. 'You owe me. Remember? You owe me.'

The Mawn stirred, blinked twice. Awareness seemed to come back to her. She no longer bobbed and swayed in time with the rock of the train, but moved apart from it. Hope flared within Javani's chest, hope and gleeful anticipation. This was it. Gurbun was going to be laughing on the other side of his—

Maral surged forwards, towards Gurbun, towards the open panel. Javani's heart rose with her, her breath caught, the hairs on the back of her neck standing and waving in furious salute.

Maral leapt from the train and onto the horse's back, seized the reins, and vanished from view.

'Shit,' said Javani.

'There, see that? Got the bugger, I did.'

'Very good, Anri. It was a challenging shot.'

'You taking the piss?'

'No. It was commendable. The movement of both tower and train added a great deal of complexity.'

'Oh. Felt like you were taking the piss.'

'Why would you say that?'

Anri sniffed, scrubbed a hand under his nose. 'Just, you know, people tend to—'

'Behind us!'

'Could be the pest . . .'

It wasn't. Anashe waited, crouched behind a roped crate, until the two men were through the doorway and into the body of the wagon, then rose and threw in a single motion. Her blade caught the first man in the cheek as Anri's arrow bristled from his companion's eye. Without a word, they rushed to the stricken guards and finished them where they lay, before their shrieks and gurgles could carry above the thunder of the train.

'See that, got him right in the—'

'Yes, Anri, very good.'

'And you said my bow wasn't worth bringing.'

'Your perspicacity and ability stagger the very soul.'

'Now you *are* taking the piss, you are.'

'And I was before, you witless oaf! This situation is very bad, Anri, do you understand? Two guards came from where we left Javani and the Commodore. We do not know how many more—'

'Cheeky bastard! There's another bugger on the tower. Have that, you crusty gimlet.'

Anashe hovered, pulled in two directions at once – towards the front of the train, to find the others, or backwards to the tower, to save those riding to rescue them.

'Come on, misery guts. There might be other buggers up there, or ready to scamper up it if we give them the chance. We're going up that tower – can't come at us both ways then, can they?'

Anashe's breath felt too hot in her chest. 'And then what? This is the plan you mentioned?'

Anri flashed what for him probably counted as a grin. 'That would be telling!'

Siavash was just resigning himself to perhaps a candied cherry or two and some pistachios, when he was startled by singing. Away to his left, along the grand platform that sat over the extraordinary iron-clad tracks of his greatest investment (a modest principal wagered, but with great expectation of returns), a curious cart had been wheeled by unseen flunkies, a tumbrel of sorts, draped in colours much like those worn by Kusan and his ilk, and barred at the sides as if caging the occupants – which surely could not have been the intention, as the occupants themselves were children. Said children had now, spontaneously or at a discreet signal, broken into song, giving a spirited rendition of what had, in Siavash's youth, been a hymn to hard work at the feet of the gods, yet had mysteriously transformed in the recent decade to a paean on the virtues of the Miners' Guild, and all who engaged in the glory of commerce.

'Such indulgence, is it not, to be serenaded as one dines?'

The man opposite was smiling again, a dribble of fruit juice running down his chin. Siavash tried not to look at his mouth.

'You know of this, Master Kusan?'

'Why yes, Master Sarosh.' He placed a hand at his colourful chest, silk rippling and shimmering in the early light. 'A token, no less, from my fraternity. A gesture of our beneficence and magnanimity, in the spirit of mutual commercial endeavour.'

Siavash looked back at the singing children. They were close enough to make out the looks of desperate hunger they shot at the groaning tables, their faces thin and drawn as they warbled. He'd heard worse, certainly, but there were one or two in the barred chorus who looked like a stiff breeze might carry them away.

'The children are yours?'

'Why, yes, frater, in a sense. I lay no claim to their parentage, but my fraternity is the current holder of their bonds.'

Siavash started, a quince tight in his hand. 'They are . . . Those children are slaves?'

Kusan's gilty grin widened, sending a fresh dribble of juice down his chin. 'Of course not, good master merchant.'

Siavash harrumphed his pointed satisfaction, but it was hard to shake the feeling he was being mocked. He glanced either side in search of anyone else to converse with, but the other diners appeared to have left a suspiciously wide berth around them, shuffling their cushions away unconsciously or otherwise. He recognised the man he'd conversed with at the evening reception, the man who'd cursed both Guild and Fraternity. He was three cart-lengths away, his back emphatically turned. There was nobody within conversation range, none but Kusan. It was either tolerate the man or sit in awkward silence until the dinner ended, hours hence.

'The master merchant searches for our illustrious cousins.'

'Hm?'

'One must admit, one has been struck by the same curiosity. Might we be graced with the presence of the delegation at our feast? Do the Iokara lurk among us, as we delect, amongst these senators and townships' chosen?' He stuffed a date into his mouth as punctuation. 'Rest assured, master merchant, they are watching, even if they cannot be seen.'

Siavash attempted a polite smile. 'Tremendous.'

Only a few more hours to go.

FORTY-ONE

'Well, that's a turn-up, eh?' Gurbun leaned out of the door into Maral's dust cloud, staring after the departed Mawn. 'Know what? Don't care. Didn't need her anyway.' He swung back in, then tossed the spear back to the guard who'd provided it, making the man drop his sabre to catch it.

'You three, find out what the fuck's going on with the tower, and why the other two didn't come back. And go carefully! These little weasels can nip. And you – go forward and set the signal, just on the off-chance. Yes, the second signal.'

'Four of us gone, Chairman? Is that wise?'

Gurbun pulled himself up to his full height, which wasn't *that* much greater than Javani's, his chin jutting. 'Are you saying that . . . one, two, three of your colleagues can't keep me safe against these two, guardsman? This girl-child and that pile of sacks on the pile of sacks? What are they going to do, nag me to death?' He swung a hand, half a punch, half a dismissal. 'Get out of here. Question me again and I'll burst you beneath the wheels.'

The guards exited promptly, three following after the previous two towards the rear, one going forward. Javani and the Commodore were left alone with Gurbun and the three remaining guardsmen, who now seemed somehow diminished without their comrades. Javani was sweated through, without even realising it. What had happened to Anashe and Anri? Why hadn't they come back? Were they hiding? What about Sarian? What about everyone else?

Gurbun was pacing, his gait adjusted to the rock of the train, one hand never far from the wall. 'Looking for something, were you?' He jerked his head towards the devastation that littered the wagon, the smashed cases, the torn sacks. 'Having some trouble finding it?'

He laughed, a sort of galloping bray, nasal and irksome, then thrust a hand into his brilliant white robe and jerked out a familiar shape on a fine silver chain. 'Did it look anything like this?'

'The seal!' Javani lurched towards him, hands grasping. 'You bastard, you had it!'

'*Sit* down,' he barked, driving his foot into her midriff and sending her stumbling back, gasping, crashed to the floor beside the Commodore in her shroud of pipe smoke. The Commodore yanked her clay flask of musty spirits out of Javani's path as she fell. 'Careful, now.'

'You're staying quiet until the rest of this shit is cleared up, then we're having a party at the dock,' Gurbun spat after her. 'A flaying party.'

Still wheezing, Javani shot the Commodore a look of dark-faced fury. 'He's got . . . the seal! Are you going to . . . do . . . anything?'

'Three brass-bellies, one pillock,' the Commodore muttered. 'Remember when I said before, about it not being the time to fight?'

Javani snarled through the pain that glowed up from her gut. 'How could I forget?'

'Aye, right,' said the Commodore, huffing on the end of her pipe. 'Well, times change.'

The Commodore took a giant swig from her bottle, then hopped to her feet in a manner that belied the volume of booze she'd ingested.

'Hoy!' cried the nearest guard, brandishing his sabre. 'The Chairman said to sit down.'

The other two crowded closer, their own weapons leading by the pointy end. 'Yeah,' one added, in case the message hadn't been clear.

The Commodore offered them a brilliant closed-mouthed smile, put the bowl of the pipe up to her lips, and blew.

A great billow of flame lit the wagon, a ruby burst that scorched the eyes and set the nearest man's sleeve on fire. The guards fell back, screeching and howling, as the Commodore flung her bottle into them, then kicked up two more from her feet for good measure. The bottles burst and sprayed, and the flame spread, liquid and dripping, leaping from the first guard onto the others. They yowled and beat at their clothes, fumbled with the buckles of their toasting breastplates, their weapons dropped and movements frantic.

'Move fast, girlie,' the Commodore called as she snatched up a fallen spear, then with minimal ceremony set about belting the guards with its flat, herding them as they blazed towards the open door-panel.

Javani was still staring open-mouthed, her gasps stilled despite the bruise to her solar plexus, smoke stinging her eyes. 'Do what?'

'Get him! Get the seal!' the Commodore shouted back as the first guard fell screaming and burning from the train, leaving a puddle of glowing flame on the boards by the door in his wake. 'There you go, fella, have a nice wee tumble in the dirt there, that'll sort you out.'

Javani cast around. 'With what? They took everything!'

'I don't fucken know, you were the one who was so bleeding keen to fight!'

There was . . . One of the guards had dropped his sabre, when Gurbun had thrown him back the spear, it had to be—

Steel was at her throat, blissfully cold, horribly sharp.

'Still looking for something?' came Gurbun's condescending sneer from the sabre's far end. 'Orange thing! Drop it and back away, or we'll see what colours this little creature is on the inside. You two, stop being on fire. Fucking *stop* it, you're embarrassing yourselves.'

'Girlie?'

Javani swallowed, feeling the sword-tip move up and down with the bob of her throat. 'The seal is all that matt— aargh!'

'You keep your mouth shut,' Gurbun hissed as he pushed the blade hard enough to sting and itch. 'Last chance, outlander! I don't want to kill you here – not when we've got all the gear for something *spectacular* rigged up at Kilale – but test me again and you are ruptured, yes?'

The two guards were beginning to beat themselves, and each other, out having finally twigged that mutual assistance was better than smouldering onanism in this case, and the rebels' advantage was dying out with the flames. Javani wanted to shout, 'He's bluffing!' or 'Don't worry about me, do what you must!' but in truth she was rigid with fear. The vague knowledge that Gurbun intended to kill them had been there for a while now, but distant, out of sight, a future concern; when the blade of his sword was drawing a thin line of blood from her twitching throat, it was a harder concept to ignore. All she wanted was for the Commodore to see off the guards, and disarm Gurbun before he exsanguinated her, and for them to make off with the seal, flee the train and ride away in safety. Was that so much to ask? I mean, really?

'Ah, fucken hells,' sighed the Commodore, and her spear hit the boards with an unmissable thunk.

'Marvellous choice,' Gurbun growled, 'although you scrofulous little pissants have tried my patience. Maybe we *should* start the party now, after all.'

He began to move the sabre in a gentle sawing motion, a rictus grin on his blocky, formerly handsome face, something unhealthy in his leer. Javani couldn't even scream, for fear the movement of her throat would make it worse. She shrank backwards, pressed against the wall of the wagon, as the Commodore moved helplessly back from the open panel and the two singed guards turned to retrieve their weapons. She couldn't scream, couldn't shout, couldn't even react when in the corner of her eye a darkening shape appeared at the hatchway behind the guards. She stayed rigid, even when the shape resolved itself into the galloping form of Captain Inaï Manatas, taking careful aim.

Anashe moved fast, her decision made for her by the thump and jingle of an unknown number of guards coming through the doorway from the baggage train. She dragged Anri behind her through the end door, then paused, feet braced over the rocking, juddering chain that linked the wagons together. Rails and rock rushed by beneath them, the thought of slipping through or falling clear somehow more terrible than an equivalent tumble from a horse travelling at the same speed – itself not an experience to be sought. There was something so unnatural, so manufactured and obscene about the great wagon-snake, slithering too fast across the plain, befouling the landscape and all who came near it.

'We must be careful,' she growled to Anri, keeping her voice at a level just audible over the thunderous clatter, and gestured towards the doorway to the next wagon, its tower now lost to them behind the tall silvered panels. 'There could be—'

'Charge!' Anri barked and kicked the door in, which was far from ideal as it was supposed to slide. The wood splintered inwards from its narrow fixings and clattered to the wagon floor, revealing the wide base piles of the tower, its braces and spars like rigging, some stoutly packed crates, a mountain of discarded canvas and a number of surprised men in Guild colours and patchwork armour, one of whom was halfway up the first of two ladders that worked their way up to the towertop. The tower itself seemed suddenly much, much taller than it had from a distance, but Anashe had less time than she'd have liked to dwell on the perils of perspective as those at ground level were registering exactly who had kicked the door in and their likely relationship to the two bleeding men at the tower's summit, and consequent lack of flaming missiles.

'What is wrong with you?' she hissed at Anri, snatching the long blade from its sheath. 'We could have done this quietly!'

His bow was already in his hand, arrow nocked, steadying himself against the train's sway with wide feet and a fixed expression. 'Just can't stand the fucking hanging about,' he said, letting fly and precipitating a shriek from halfway up the tower.

Anashe counted the men before her – all men, once more; she was beginning to suspect a policy lay somewhere behind it – and counted them again. Shock had given way to confusion had given way to increasingly murderous intent, but each was blessed with the caution to see which of his comrades would charge first. This gave her an opportunity, a window in which to plot her approach, to narrow the angles, force them to—

Anri flighted an arrow into the nearest man's leg from barely eight feet away, and as he collapsed the others realised they all needed to move. They charged, brandishing axes, hammers and at least one long pole with a curious hook at the end.

'Goddess curse your impetuosity,' Anashe snapped as she held the blade before her, coiled for the first strike.

'Oh boo hoo,' came Anri's reply. 'You telling me this lot will cause you any fuss? Look at them.' Another arrow whistled over her shoulder, hitting a man barely a stride from her in the chest and most certainly ruining his already questionable day. 'Bunch of pie-eyed piss-gobblers.'

The piss-gobblers were on them now, long poles jabbing, axes swinging, and Anashe had no room to manoeuvre. 'We need to fall back! There is no space here.'

'Arse-apples.' Another arrow struck a man who was lunging at her with a whistle-sharp axe, hitting him in the teeth with barely a hand's span between the fletchings and the quivering bow. The noise he made was distasteful, and put the comrades around him off their own attacks. Anashe whipped the long pole from the grip of the first with a flicker of her blade, then, kicking loose fingers, put two deep cuts into his fellow's forearm, sending the man's prying bar clattering to his feet. The tide was turned.

Wounded and traumatised, the men fell back, stumbling through the ropes and beams that anchored the tower towards the wagon's far door, crying for mercy and salvation. Anri put a final arrow into the last man's back, then turned to Anashe with a look of near-heroic smugness. 'See? Pointless bringing a bow, she said. No room to use it, she said.'

'You are . . . an extraordinary human being,' Anashe replied, hands on her knees.

'In a good way, you mean?'

'No.' She stood, feeling a fighting ache for the first time in years. She thought she had missed it, but in the moment, she wanted to be anywhere else. She wanted to be with Sefi, back at the club, nursing a small cup of wine and preparing to sing. She did not want to be on some infernal machine, haring across the landscape, trapped inside with what had to be the worst people on the continent, some of whom were on her side.

'Come on, chin up.'

'You are enjoying yourself.'

He met her questioning stare, jaw loose and chin jutting. 'Honestly, no, my breeches are fuller than the privy chute on Saints Morning. But we're doing something, eh? We're fucking doing something.'

'That much is inarguable.' She cleaned her blade, resheathed it and stretched out her back. 'You mentioned a plan, I believe? Those who fled from us did not do so without direction – they went seeking help.'

He scoffed. 'Nothing back there but ores and whathaveyou, isn't it?'

Anashe sucked her lips against her teeth. 'So we were told. Yet there is much aboard this contraption that is not as it should have been.' Her gaze travelled to the tower that loomed over them, casting them in its rolling, chequered shadow. 'Your plan.'

'Right, so.' He pointed at the lower ladder. 'Get climbing.'

'Me first?' She did not like how the tower swayed as the wagon rocked. It seemed to bend.

'Might still be someone breathing up there.' He winked. 'You can bore them to death.'

'You are a contemptible wretch,' Anashe replied, grasping the first rung, and found she was smiling.

FORTY-TWO

Javani stared along the length of the curved blade that was wedded to her throat, gleaming and flashing as the train thundered on, to the hand and outstretched arm that held it, white robes brilliant in the narrow slice of sun from the wide-open side panels, to the gurning, slavering face beyond the arm, and held her breath. Give nothing away, give nothing away, don't let the hope show in your—

A slim bolt punched through Gurbun's hand and came to rest, point jutting from his palm, as the sabre dropped to the wagon floor. Gurbun and Javani stared at the bolt, each marvelling at its sudden appearance, before his face curdled in pain and rage and he shrieked, clutched the hand to himself, and forever doomed his robes.

'Chairman? By the gods, fuck—' The guards were still coming to terms with their recent near-immolation, and were desperately unprepared for the arrival of a former mercenary captain at the doorway, standing proud in the saddle, fingers smoothly cranking the hand-bow and slotting the next bolt home. Javani felt a flash of admiration, a sudden, lurching and disorientating flare of respect for Captain Manatas, for all he had done, for all he could do. She wished Ree treated him better. She wished Ree treated everyone better.

'Get him!' Gurbun roared between agonised bellows, injured hand cradled at his gut, the other wrapping it in a bloody embrace. 'Kill that bastard!'

The guards moved to snatch up their weapons, but the Commodore was faster. 'Cheerio, fuck-stick.' The spear collided with the first guard, driving him out of the doorway and past Manatas and his horse, as the captain levelled the hand-bow at the second. The man froze, caught in two minds, his knife unsheathed and ready, but the loser in a numbers game. He made a half-hearted swipe towards the Commodore, then dropped the weapon and ran for the head-bound doorway. The bolt caught him in the back of the leg as he ran, and the Commodore was on him as he bounced off the broken shelving and collapsed.

'Don't move,' Javani snapped, grabbing the fallen sabre and pointing it at the hunched form of Gurbun. It was heavier than she'd hoped.

'Javani, time is short,' Manatas called from the loading door, cranking the hand-bow once more, 'and my horse cannot run forever. Where is the seal?'

'Dickhead here has it.' She jabbed the sword towards Gurbun, who snarled. His own sword, long and straight, still hung from his belt, and for a moment she thought he might go for it left-handed.

'Do you know what I'm going to do to you, you cretin, you worm? You and the rest of your worm kind? Think you can hide? Think you can—'

'Shut your mouth or the captain is going to drive a bolt through your eye and into the walnut that passes for your brain.'

Gurbun went silent, although his look towards Manatas and his bobbing hand-bow was a little short of convinced.

'Now hand over the seal, and nobody else gets hurt.'

His uninjured hand flashed to his chest. 'Never going to happen.'

'Aye, right, you know we could all save a whole lot of bother if you just dropped this shite-hawk now. We could fish old sealy from his cooling corpse. I know it's not very sporting, but expediency is its own reward, eh? No? Aw, come on, where's your sense of urgency?'

Manatas had one hand on the doorframe, easing the burden on his mount, if only a little. 'The Commodore is not without reason. Our horse strings are lost, but we are coming up on the old riverbank. The wheeled conveyances will shortly be able to close, and you must depart in them. Where are Anri and Anashe?'

Javani nodded towards the tail of the train. 'They went that way. I think they stopped the alchemy.'

Gurbun was wheezing, his shoulders shaking, and Javani realised to her disquiet and disgust that he was laughing. He tweaked the seal from his bloodied robes, showing her a flash of its edge on its gleaming chain. 'You think you've won? You think even if you take this, victory is yours?' The grin slipped easily into a snarl. 'I want to see it. I want to see it in your eyes, when you realise—'

'Captain,' called the Commodore, 'will you kill this tosspot so I don't have to?'

A terrible noise filled the wagon, whistles and horns, discordant and wrong. 'Not again, what in hells is it?' Javani slapped her hands over her ears, sabre and all.

Gurbun didn't hesitate. He barged past her, knocking her to the ground, and was past the Commodore before she could raise her spear. He dived through the end door towards the train's front, the bolt from Manatas's hand-bow left quivering in the wall beside it.

'Shit,' said Javani.

Manatas folded in the arms of the hand-bow, twirled it over his finger and stowed it at his belt. 'I will come aboard. Injured as he is, he cannot travel far, and we may yet catch him before we run out of riverbank and are forced to depart.'

The Commodore was shaking her head. 'Aye, right. Didn't care for that noise the first time we heard it, and, like Anashe's poetry, it's not improved by a second outing.'

'Wait . . .' Javani said, tossing the sabre to the Commodore. 'We heard it before, right before . . .'

They looked at each other.

'Shit,' said Javani, and the outside world exploded.

'What now, Anri?'

'Eh?'

'This was your great plan. What do we do now we are at the top of this . . . unnerving . . . edifice?'

'Oh. Well, wasn't a proper plan, was it. More of a, uh, notion.'

'A notion.'

'An inkling, then. Here, give me a hand kicking these tosspots over the side.'

The tower's sway was almost too much for Anashe, who prided herself on delicate poise, excellent balance and tremendous leg strength, but was finding the way the whole thing ducked and bobbed with the movement of the train beneath far too close to a voyage across choppy waters, something she would not have relished at the best of times.

'Anyway, now we're up here, you cut up any bugger that tries to come up the ladder, and I'll put some shafts in anyone who tries to get past down there.'

'I see. And then what?'

'Hm?'

'When you run out of arrows, and we must flee this horror. How do we get down?'

'Uh. Like I said, more of an inkling, really.' He cocked an ear. 'Hear that? It's that fucking racket again.'

Anashe froze, or did her best being bodily lurched from side to side. Her eyes travelled along the length of the train, forwards and backwards, and noticed at last the telltale ribbons of black smoke rising from the little forts at each end.

'Anri.'

'Aye?'

'What do you make of the alchemical construction before us?'

'Oh. Not going to lie, I've got no idea.'

'I think it would be best to learn what we can about it. Very fast.'

The first black arrow streaked from the rear fortress, five wagons back, churning the air with alchemical filth. Anashe whipped her head around to see it detonate not far from the baggage wagon ahead of them, sending a great plume of pulverised rock and earth into the brilliant sky. The wagon yawed from the impact. Anashe tasted acid and dirt.

'Very fast indeed.'

Tauras geed the ponies back up to speed. Behind him, his cargo lolled in the back of the cart, battered and dusty, but safer to be moving again. Tauras urged Svon and Woolley (he named the other pony Woolley because he had a thick coat and could barely see out from under the fringe of his glossy mane) back over the lumpy ground. They were behind where they were supposed to be, he knew that. It was going to take hard running, fast running, to catch up again. But the ponies wouldn't let him down. Just as Tauras would not let his friends down.

The ponies ran.

Manatas whirled, dazed and lurching, then the ground came up to meet him and flattened itself against his jaw. Noise and movement were everywhere, impossible to fathom, impossible to catch, and his body flopped and spasmed as he tried to right himself. Somehow he was prone, his horse gone, hands and head stinging from a mess of impacts. His ears rang and hummed, and the ground seemed to tremble and jump beneath him. His thoughts were fled like spooked cattle, and just as hard to corral. At last mind and senses aligned, and the world rushed back into sharp relief.

'Ow,' said Captain Inaï Manatas, and pushed himself gingerly to his knees. The rumbling of the earth had not abated, and at last his memories rejoined the party. 'Gods, the train. The horses.' He staggered upright as the train thundered on not three strides away, the last few of its wagons passing, its monstrous rear fortress growing ever larger in his vision.

He searched left and right. His horse had fled, and the rest of the strings they'd brought ran wild across the plain, some in line with the train, others veering off to explore the new opportunities afforded by infinite grassland. Ahead, in the distance, he saw the White Spear rolling on in the cart, cutting now towards the old riverbank where the vehicle would be level with the train wagon-beds. If he ran, he might just—

He tried to run. His ankle screamed, and one hip lodged a pretty sharp complaint. An elbow added something, but it was lost in the noise. Captain Manatas was running nowhere.

The wagons rumbled on in front of him, throwing dust and shaking the earth. Just a couple left now.

Manatas took a breath, braced himself, and leapt.

'What happened?' Javani knew she was screaming, and pointlessly so. 'Where did he go?'

'Aye, fuck, guess he fell somewhat by the wayside.'

Javani stuck her head out of the door. 'He's alive, at least. I saw him get up, but he's miles back. What do we do?'

The Commodore had brushed herself down, scooped up the sabre and given it a swish. 'Get after Chairman Ballbrains and cut his fucken legs off?'

'What about Anashe and Anri? We can't leave them behind.'

The Commodore gave her a look which brought her up short. It was not a cold look, nor was it dismissive or exasperated. It was instead a look of great solemnity, a look that set its foundations in a bedrock of compassion and built itself from great stones of understanding, the result a monument that reflected Javani's great unspoken fear back on her with quiet sympathy.

They may already be dead. If they are not, they knew the risks, and made their choices. They would want us to push on, they would want us to succeed, even if it costs them their lives. We both know this, and we both wish it was otherwise, but the facts are as stark as they are immutable.

She knew Ree would agree to the letter.

'No, fuck it, I'm at least going to check.'

From outside came the crack and boom of another explosion.

FORTY-THREE

'Come on, come on, how hard can it be?'

'This is a delicate piece of alchemical engineering, Anri, it cannot and should not be rushed.'

'Righto, lovely, no bother there, is it, except down there is our way off this horror show, rattling along and weaving between these fuck-off holes that keep opening up in the fucking ground!'

'Do you think shouting and cursing will make me work any faster?'

'Not like you could go any slower, is it? Kypeth's dangling arse-grapes, you're fussing over it like an old pettifogger.'

'These tubes are packed with blasting powder! One slip and we could immolate ourselves, this tower, the wagon beneath and Goddess knows how much of the train. Is that what you want?'

Anri folded his arms. 'Would at least make things interesting. Oh.' He straightened.

'What? What is it?'

'Pest. Javani. She's at the doorway. She's alive!' He waved down, arm a blur, a huge, gappy grin plastered across his bristly face.

'Goddess be praised. Does she have the seal?'

'Doesn't look like it. She's waving us to come down, come with them.'

'I see.'

Another black arrow screamed out from the rear tower, tearing another gouge in the plain barely a spear-length from where the White Spear swerved in their rescue wagon.

Anri met her eye. 'Nobody's getting off safely with that tower belching out those bastards, are they?'

'I suspect not.'

'How many people does it need to operate this alchemical nonsense?'

Anashe swivelled the tubing on its mounting. She was pretty sure she had the measure of it now. 'One to aim, one to set the fire.'

'Thought so.' He sighed. 'Ah well.' He leaned over the towertop. 'We'll catch you up!' he bellowed. 'Oop, ram-nuts, the guards are coming back. Crack on, pest!'

He swivelled, shrugged his bow into his grip, and put an arrow through the shoulder of the first guard to near the tower base. The others scattered and fell back, bellowing for shields and plating. Anri hissed as his next shot thumped into the mottled wood beside a retreating guardsman.

'Ah, donkey's dung-hole.'

'A miss?'

'Had to happen sooner or later, I suppose. And not many of my little shafted friends left now.'

'I will take that to mean your arrows.' Anashe stood back. 'But I have the measure of this device now – the greatest challenge is matching the tower's sway. I will aim, you can set the fire.'

'Righto, looks like we've got a moment or two before those buggers come back. At least they're not likely to try to burn us out, eh? Not without sending half the train skywards.'

'Indeed,' Anashe replied, sighting along the tubing. 'And we are perfectly capable of doing that ourselves.'

'They're not coming. Let's go.'

'Aye, right.' The Commodore took a breath, tried to twirl the sabre, gave up halfway. 'Could be all sorts in the wagons to come. You ready for this, girlie?'

'Yeah. I reckon.' Javani had retrieved her trail-knife, along with another that someone had dropped by the door. She wondered if it had been Maral, but it seemed unlike the Mawn to have been so careless with a blade. She looked back to the trail-knife. It had been a present from Ree. A good, solid, reliable knife. She swallowed. 'You?'

'Oh, aye, no bother. No worries on that score. Tip top over here.'

'That thing you did, with the fire. And the spear. That was amazing. I'm sorry about what I said before, about saying you were a coward. I didn't know it was a gambit.'

'Ah, no harm done. Can't say I wasn't all the way committed to not necking the stuff anyway.' Both hesitated, eyes flicking from each other to the distant door. 'Still, thing is . . .'

'Yeah?'

'There's a difference between doing something in the heat of the moment, and having a bit more of a run-up, if you follow.'

'Yeah.'

'It's the contemplating that gets you. I swear to the ancestors, if I see another fucken crossbow—'

'Nobody's had a crossbow so far. And we took him before, we can take him again. Him and his army.'

'Aye. Right. Brave bastards we be.'

'You know, Ree said once that bravery was a myth.'

'Sounds like her.'

'No, I mean, fearlessness. How not being afraid wasn't something to be proud of, especially if what you weren't afraid of was, you know, well, dangerous. If anything, fearlessness was a mental defect.'

'And you're saying what, exactly? Am I or am I not defective?'

Javani couldn't help her smile. 'Just that knowing something is dangerous, and facing it, doing it anyway, and doing it right – *because you know where the risk is* – that's worth celebrating.'

'It's a weird fucken time to be grinning, girlie, but aye, fine. Let's get to it.' The Commodore twirled the sabre again, properly this time. 'Your mam wasn't always wrong, you know.'

'Yeah, maybe. *Maaaybe*.' As an afterthought, Javani swept up her spool of discarded climbing rope and slung it over her shoulder. 'You never know. Now let's cut that bastard's legs off.'

The White Spear weaved. The White Spear swerved. Long ago had she abandoned any notion of reaching the train. Now she was concerned with occupying the operators of the tower, who blasted witchfire across the landscape in their pursuit of her, until either their ammunition ran out or her luck did. One or the other, it was coming. It was only a matter of time.

She had lived a long time, she knew, far longer than she'd had any expectation of surviving. She'd witnessed more deaths than she could count across the years, some noble, most otherwise, but a handful she might have considered 'good'. Her end was inevitable, but when it came, she, at least, would make it count.

Manatas held onto the wagon's side with every fibre, straining every sinew, teeth gritted, bursts of hot pain exploding from every wound, ancient and fresh, and still his grip was slipping. Wind tore at him, whipping him with his clothes, and waves of choking dust rolled unstoppably over him. A fall would not be fatal, but it would likely add to his compendium of injuries, and once he dropped he knew he would never catch the train again. He would be left, somewhere in the centre of the plains, without horse or supplies, to stagger, starve or die of thirst before he could make it back to safety.

And still his grip was slipping.

'I am not, by nature, a praying man,' Manatas mumbled to himself through gritted teeth, 'and considered as a pantheon, our contact has been infrequent and, to my shame, somewhat driven by expediency, but were any of the gods to somehow be listening, it would be incumbent upon me to—'

'Captain Manatas? What are you doing up there?'

A voice, a voice he knew, and so close behind him.

He turned his head slowly, unwilling to let the hope escape all at once.

Tauras extended a hand from the driver's bench. 'Can I give you a lift, cap?'

'Say when to set the fire.'
'One moment . . . now.'
'Now?'
'Now! The fire, now!'
'Righto.'

A seething hiss, a horrible stink, and a great fizzing from inside the tube, then Anashe choked on a blast of fumes, recoiling in a retching heap on the tower's boards. Movement in the corner of her streaming gaze, that terrible screaming, and then . . . nothing.

'Missed,' came Anri's bitter voice from above her. 'Still, reckon I know where you went wrong.'

Anashe wiped at her eyes and tried to cough the stink from her lungs. 'You did not set the fire when I said. When I say "fire", you set the fire. The concept is far from elaborate!'

'Budge out the way then, I'll aim this one.'

'You dare—'

'Come on, bet you can load it faster than those lads on the other tower.'

'Perhaps, indeed, but—'

'I mean, you'd better, 'cos they know we're not on their side now and they're aiming at us like.'

'What? What happened to not immolating the centre of the train?'

'Tell them that, not me! Looks like they're rather happier being immolators than immolatees.'

Anashe gritted her teeth and set about loading. Swiftly.

Javani and the Commodore hesitated before the narrow door to the next wagon, standing in the awkward, swaying nether-ground between, heavy chains and cables twisting and grinding beneath their feet. Javani didn't look down, just braced her feet and kept one arm on what passed for the doorframe. A bloodied handprint marked it, just above her own.

'Chairman Gobshite came this way, then.'

The Commodore was adjusting the tilt of the sabre in her hand, searching for the perfect angle for their great entrance. 'Aye, not like there was anywhere else for him to go, was there?'

'I guess not.' Javani swallowed. She was used to the noise now, and the constant, bone-rattling movement, but her mouth was dry and her stomach churned with a thousand worries, and her strategy of Trying Not To Think About Them was beginning to fall short. 'What do we think is through there?'

'This one? We thought maybe food, then passengers beyond, then it's the wee fortress.'

'Right. Ready?'

'Don't rush me.'

'It's just, the longer we're out here—'

'I said don't rush me!' The Commodore licked her lips. 'Should have brought some of that arak with us.'

'To use to clear a path?'

'Aye, and that.' She hovered the tip of the sabre a finger-span from the door. 'Here – we – go!'

She hauled the door aside.

'You're praying there, cap?'

'Hm? Indeed, Tauras, I find myself in some degree of debt to our fair pantheon, and given I am unable to name precisely which of our deities, large or small, I am indebted to for my salvation, relative as is, I feel it is incumbent to offer some measure of my gratitude in the more general sense, lest I be considered churlish or lacking in appreciation for their actions, an outcome which would render far greater peril in the round than my original predicament. You understand?'

'Yes, cap. Definitely, cap.'

Manatas smiled and shook the ache from his arms as they barrelled forward in Tauras's wagon, its two shaggy and tireless ponies outpacing the train, gaining along its length as they raced along the old riverbank. They were close against it, close enough to ease some of his concern that a black arrow would hit them before they could reach the baggage wagon at the midpoint of the train. Assuming that's where the others still were, which he suspected they were not.

A groan from behind him drew his attention to the wagon-bed. 'Sarian!' The young scout was bloodied and battered but breathing.

'Yes, cap. Picked him up after he took a fall, cap. Thought he should probably come too.'

'That's why you were so far out of position. Good job, Tauras.'

The big man glowed. 'Thank you, cap.'

'Now where is Mistress Whitespear? We are travelling the riverbank now, meaning the midpoint of this journey is upon us. We will not have the bank forever—'

A black arrow screamed from the front of the train ahead of them, and any hope of seeing the White Spear and her cart was lost in a wall of fire.

'What is your delay? I see them, I see them in their turret. They are aiming for us!'

'Don't rush me, woman. Can't balls this up like you did.'

'That was your doing! If you had set the fire when I said—'

'Fire!'

Swallowing her fury, Anashe snapped her arm to the rear of the tubing, setting the slow-match to the exposed clip of propellant. The slim disc sparked and flared immediately, then she fell back as a blast of stinking smoke engulfed her. She collapsed to the tower floor, which still lurched alarmingly, hacking and wiping at her streaming eyes, and then, just for a moment, over all the other commotion she thought she heard a distant echo of a scream.

'Anri, did it—'

It was a thunderclap, but in mute, a soft and brilliant flare of light in the corner of her streaming vision. The great steel plates of the fortress at the train's rear were blanketed in a wash of flame, buckled and twisted, then the fire rolled up and over the turret's edge and the entire thing blew outwards in a catastrophic eruption of bilious gouts. It was too bright to watch, the top of the fortress split wide and ripped into the air in shards. Its lower section rattled on, chained to the rails beneath, trailing poisonous black smoke from its dismembered ruin.

'I'd say that was a hit, I would.'

'Beginner's luck.'

Something on the plain exploded in echo, and they snapped their heads around. What looked like the White Spear's cart had become a blackened crater, ringed by scorched and flaming wiregrass.

'Kypeth's hairy arsecrack, there's one at the front and all!'

'I will load.'

'Happy for me to aim again, are you? What happened to beginner's luck, then?'

'Perhaps it would be best for all of us if your luck held, just a little longer.'

'You know, you're not all bad.'

Anashe slid the next of the alchemical monstrosities home into the smoking tubing and locked it in place. 'Loaded. Really?'

'Yeah, only most of you. Fire!'

'What is that, ahead? Beyond the front turret?'

'I said fire!'

Anashe fired.

In the abandoned stillness of the shelter, a cracked voice whispered in the darkness.

'Kid?'

FORTY-FOUR

The Commodore hurled aside the door, and the entire train shuddered. A great shock travelled along it, lifting the wagon on its tracks, sending the Commodore sprawling and leaving Javani clinging to the doorframe for dear life as, a heartbeat later, everything came crashing down once more.

'What in hells did you do?' Javani bawled at the Commodore, who had pitched into a nest of sacks just inside the doorway.

'Fucked if I know,' came the muffled response.

After another moment of clinging to the structure of the wagon and not looking down, that seemed to be it for train-quakes, and Javani peeped inside. 'Oh look, windows.'

'It's a big old fucken chuck wagon in here, eh?'

The wagon was lined with crates and shelves down one side, now in some disarray, and its canvas roof was punctuated with ventilation holes. The wagon's other side featured widely spaced hatches, open to the vista beyond, where people dressed as kitchen servants were clustered around a number of work surfaces and what looked like a broad cast-iron stove. Despite an abundance of kitchen paraphernalia, very little cooking seemed to be happening, and all eyes in the wagon were turned on the Commodore, who was pulling herself upright from her sack stack and grumbling. Javani watched the staff; looks were exchanged, mutters shared. They might not have been dressed as guards, but they looked far from pleased to see the rebels.

'Listen,' Javani called from the doorway, one hand still clasped tight around the splintery wood, 'we mean you no harm.'

A kitchen knife whipped across the wagon towards her, vicious and twirling. Rising from the ground, the Commodore snatched it from the air and sent it winging right back, where it thumped into the chest of the man who'd thrown it. He collapsed with a screech.

'All right,' Javani sighed, 'we mean you *some* harm.'

'Cheeky bastard,' the Commodore muttered, lifting the sabre and flicking it forwards. 'Right, yon fuckers, girlie here and I are coming through, and you can get out of the way or you can get cut to fucken pieces. Makes no odds to me either way, but anyone who thinks they're going to land a blow as we pass is going to find themselves with a punctured spleen faster than you can say "Oh no, my organs". Savvy?'

The murmurs and mutters of the cooking staff intensified, underpinned by their colleague's plaintive moaning from the floor before them.

'Let me take a wild stab at this, eh? Some golden fuckwit came buggering through, pissing blood out his hand, offering you fame and riches to take us out. Well, Chairman Dickfingers neglected to mention that we're savage killers, and, bluntly, you're not. This wee one to my left is called Slayer, and not a week back she strangled a member of the Mercantile Fraternity to death with his own guts.'

'I did not,' Javani muttered.

'And you may not have heard of me, but that's because I tend not to leave survivors, or at least any fucker with their tongue still gabbing in their head if they cross my path in the dark. So that's the summary, folks. Hate to rush you, but it's decision time. Get out, or get cut, 'cos we're coming through!'

She charged, and, almost apologetically, Javani charged with her.

'Bollocks! That was your fault, that was.'

'You see, it's not so easy as . . . Oh, by the Goddess!'

The black arrow had burst from its launcher in a filthy cascade, blasting across the sky towards the front of the train, trailing a vicious plume. It had sailed right past the crest of the fortress at the train's head, missing it by a few agonising feet, and flown on, towards . . .

'Oh fuck me,' Anri breathed.

How could she have forgotten? The old riverbed augured the

halfway stage of the Iron Road, the midpoint, and there, just as predicted, as expected, as mandated, came rolling—

'The other train,' she said aloud.

The black arrow slammed into its nose and exploded, blasting it open like a sneeze, sending up a wall of flame over the oncoming train's front.

Anri hissed through his teeth. 'That's not ideal. Do you think they've got the same alchemical—'

The fortress of the oncoming train erupted in a firestorm, a jet of incandescent hues surging into the clear blue sky and scattering wildlife for miles around. The explosion dwarfed those which had come before, its shockwave thundering outwards in a wave of flattened grass and baking air. Their own train rocked and shuddered as the impact worked through it, and then they were passing, the oncoming train already a boiling cauldron of flame, fire spreading from it in a smoking, choking mass as the two trains began to overlap. Flames leapt from the incoming conflagration onto the turret at the head of their own train, climbing the plating of the fortress, towards where their alchemical foes lurked. Said foes were, it seemed, alert to the danger. As the trains passed and fire crept over the fortress towards them, the operators took to throwing barrels and packages over the far side.

'Kypeth's chapped bumhole, they're ditching their screamers,' Anri said, peering alongside her. He frowned, one hand to his whiskers. 'Reckon they'll manage it?'

'Some of them evidently think not,' Anashe replied, watching dark little figures leaping from the towertop, down to the rushing plain below. A moment later, something flashed on the turret, and things began to pop and hiss.

Then the train was passing them, in heat and fury and boiling flame, a skin-blistering wash of roaring savagery, then a blanket of blackness, a tail of smoke so dark and thick it felt like the night was strangling her. Anashe pressed herself to the tower floor, which lurched and swayed undaunted, feeling her hair sizzle, hands stuffed over her nose and mouth. Anri was beside her, hunched over her, inadvertently shielding her from the worst of the heat.

At last it lifted, the air clearing with callow indifference as the train rattled on and left its companion heading up the climb to the mountains, burning itself steadily to death and leaving a pall like a blazing city in its wake.

Anri wiped at his eyes and looked back after it. His hair and beard were singed in patches, and he was smeared with soot. Anashe imagined she looked the same.

He took a breath, hacked a cough, and tried again, then jerked a thumb towards the retreating conflagration. 'Think we'll get the blame for that?'

'I am more concerned about how much of our own vehicle remains . . . a little fiery.'

Anri peered after the departing train, the light of its flames still stark as the distance increased. 'What was it someone said they were using these things to send up into the mountains?'

'Mm? I believe it was principally matters of supply. Food, wages, equipment, items of that ilk.'

'And what kind of equipment are we thinking they use then, when they go blasting out the sides of mountains?'

Despite the fierce heat on her skin, Anashe felt suddenly cold.

'. . . Just wondering, so I am, if that thing keeps burning like that, whether there's going to be an almighty bang in the not-too-distant.'

'It is not . . . inconceivable.'

'And given, you know, how this train and that one are all tied together like, in the same little loop, what happens to us then?'

Anashe rubbed at her eyes, tried clearing her throat. 'Well, I am not an expert, but if the link were severed, we should continue moving under momentum, less the drag of friction of course, and we remain on the downward slope, so . . . Mm.'

'We might start getting faster?'

'It is not inconceivable.'

'Speed of a cantering horse, she said,' he sighed. 'Neglected to mention flaming chariots to the afterlife.'

'I suspect that your afterlife will be somewhat different from mine.'

'No argument there, you'll probably come back as a heron.'

'What?'

'No, not a heron, those gawky fuckers that stand on one leg.'

'What do you—'
The other train exploded.

Charging in the Commodore's wake was exhilarating, and left Javani with an overwhelming sense of guilt. She knew it was wrong to enjoy it, utterly wrong. The speed, the power, the way those in the chuck wagon scattered before them, their looks of unambiguous terror. She didn't want to hurt anyone, not really, not unless they'd done something to deserve it, but she was gliding on a thermal of implicit violent threat that made her skin tingle and her hair stand on end. Her pulse thumped in her ears, and the knife in her sweat-glossed hand had become totemic, capable of sending their adversaries diving from her path with the merest movement in one direction or another.

They reached the wagon's end in a handful of strides, finding the doorway half-barricaded with a crate and small barrels, some evidently marked with bloody handprints. Gurbun had passed through, and was running out of places to hide.

'One mo.' The Commodore grabbed up the loose lid of a crate and began lashing its rope handles around her arm.

Javani nodded at the half-blocked doorway. 'What was through here?'

'Next one is passengers. Load of gilded nibbers, cowering under their benches.' Satisfied with her improvised shield, the Commodore hefted her sabre and shouldered a barrel aside.

Javani kept her voice low. 'Are they going to come after us, the kitchen people? Like, stab us in the back?'

The Commodore turned back to the anxious faces peering from behind benches, and in one case, the stove, and the stricken man with the knife still embedded in his chest. 'There will be a few more of us coming through in the nearish future,' she called out, 'so were I in your dapper wee shoes, I might think about how to get myself off this whole show, before something *really* nasty happens. Cheerio.'

She flung the second barrel down and heaved herself over the crate. 'Coming?'

Javani slid over the crate with considerably more ease, and if she were being less modest than usual, substantially more grace to boot.

They leapt across the wagon-gap, and, as one, they kicked the next door off its runners.

'We mean you no harm!' Javani bawled.

From behind them came a phenomenal boom, and the whole train lurched and rocked. Things fell from other things, one wall slanted, and Javani and the Commodore were thrown into a heap, Javani's legs swinging dangerously off the door lip and between the two wagons, her toes lost in rising dust. The Commodore had one hand on her shirt, the other gripping the doorframe, and gradually, with savage grunts, Javani got herself back aboard.

'Fucken hells,' the Commodore panted, 'do you think perhaps you should stop saying that?'

'What in hells was that? Did one of the wagons explode down the end?'

Around them, the train groaned and convulsed, shuddering as if on the verge of an emetic episode. Javani stared down at the tracks beneath them, conscious of the clattering cadence of wheels over rail.

'Wait . . . do you hear that?'

The Commodore cocked an ear. 'What?'

'It's getting faster. The rhythm.'

'Eh?'

'The train is accelerating.'

'It's not supposed to do that. Speed of a cantering horse, all constant like across the plain. There's machinery and whatnot, and the counterweight of the other train.'

Javani swallowed. 'Might that have been the boom we heard?'

'Oh. Right.' The Commodore pushed herself to her feet. 'We'd better get a fucken wiggle on, then, eh?'

Something caught Siavash's eye, away to the horizon, past the exhausted, breathy children in their wheeled container sitting so neatly over the tracks, past the spars and scaffolds that lined the arrow-straight iron path from the distant plain to where they sat.

'Did you see that?'

Kusan looked up from his platter, where he was midway through tearing the wings off what had possibly once been a partridge. The stuffing contained diced apricots, a fragment of which currently decorated the slaver's golden smile. 'See what, frater?'

'There was . . . a sort of flash, over in that direction. Like lightning.'

'The celestial sphere is limpid. Was the master merchant distracted by a momentary reflection of our glorious sun?'

Siavash frowned, his lips pursed. It had been no reflection. This whole affair had robbed him of his appetite, and dishes lay piled before him like missed opportunities. He wondered if he could divert some of the wilting food in the direction of the children in their mobile enclosure, but the liveried servants who buzzed around the tables appeared to be matching the other diners in giving his end of proceedings a wide berth. His discomfort was reaching measurable levels.

'Perhaps it is time we began relocating matters, don't you think? We're dining over the tracks that the great wagon-train will be—'

'Come, master merchant.' Kusan interrupted with masterful condescension. 'The arriving contrivance is hours away, and we have such delights yet to come. Repose yourself. Nobody is going anywhere.'

Ree was awake, and her mind churned. Memories seethed and faded, the cobwebs of dream. She couldn't think straight, couldn't move. She was very thirsty.

'Kid?' she tried to say again, but the word was only a croak.

She lay in darkness, stillness, in a damp sickbed, her eyes half-closed, her senses dulled. She ached. Her body itched, throbbed and hungered. Where was she? Where was everyone else? Where was the kid?

Anger flared, residual and fresh. Had they abandoned her? Had Manatas left her to die? Had Javani?

And why?

And had she deserved it?

Something inside her hurt beyond the physical, something sharp and stinging in her gut. A phrase rang around her head, a memory, or something still echoing.

You can't hold me back any more.

She knew the words. They resonated.

Sounds came from beyond, somewhere at the fringes of her darkness. She wanted to call out, afraid of who might be there, of who might not, but she was so weak. Already fatigue was reclaiming her, her thoughts muddied and sluggish.

You can't hold me back any more.

FORTY-FIVE

Shapes swirled in smoke and blowing dust as the wagon rattled over rough, unyielding ground, jolting Manatas up from the bench and down again with pelvis-shuddering indifference. He did his best to ignore the thud of the semi-conscious Sarian's skull against the wagon-bed behind him.

'Tauras! You are diverting! Why are you diverting?'

'Can't leave anyone behind, cap.'

Ponies milled from the miasma, then he saw it: the wreckage of the White Spear's cart, one wheel snapped and shattered, the other simply absent. The ruined wood was blackened and smouldering, delicate fingers of flame licking along its edges. More shapes lay strewn around it, lumpen and disarrayed, their origin and nature unclear.

'We do not have time to stop, Tauras. The velocity of our quarry has increased somewhat, and—'

'Can't leave anyone behind, cap.'

Manatas chewed back his reply. Attempting to talk Tauras out of a fixed idea was a road to nowhere. His eyes fell on one of the ponies, milling not far from the wreckage and cropping at the flattened grass.

'Tauras, is there any rope in this wagon?'

'Certainly is, cap. I packed extra.'

Manatas prayed pardon from Sarian as he dug beneath the man's docile form, and an instant later he was knotting.

'A little to the left on approach, if it please you, Tauras.'

'Righto, cap!'

'The train is untethered.' Anashe could not keep the edge of anxiety from her voice. 'We are gaining velocity.'

'Knackers to that, we've got company down there.'

Wild-eyed and raw-throated, Anashe leaned over the tower's rail. The guards were back, moving up from the cargo wagons at the rear of the train, and in much greater numbers than before.

'There's hundreds of the fuckers.'

'There are not. But it is . . . more than I expected.' She glanced at the smoking ruin of the fortress at the tail of the train. Its billowing devastation seemed so small and demure compared with the horror show that had just come roaring past then torn itself apart. Barely a shred of the other train remained, only the crater where it had detonated. 'It is possible there were more stationed in the train's rear, and they are moving away from the flames.'

'Or something tipped them off there was mischief afoot, like, say, a series of fuck-off explosions. Strikes me they knew we were coming, isn't it? All these extra guards, this alchemy bollocks. That was for us.' He chuckled, then laughed, breaking into a wheezing cough. 'Look how well that's gone for them, eh?'

Anashe did not share his mirth. 'How many arrows do you have left?'

'Six. If I'm careful.'

'Mm.' The guards were hovering at the wagon's end, staying behind the crates and boxes, keeping from Anri's line of fire, but more kept arriving, and some had shields. 'There are more than six men down there. They may swarm the ladder, or just cut the mooring ropes and let us fall. At least they will not risk burning us out – there is as much powder down there as there is up here.'

Anri flighted an arrow straight down, through the boot of a guardsman who had made a tentative sortie in the direction of the tower base. 'Or they just charge on past us after the others, I suppose.' He sniffed and rubbed soot around his face. 'Thought maybe we could detach this one from the rest, if we got down there fast enough, but . . . well, you saw those chains, eh? We're not shifting them by hand, we're not.'

The thought of the dozens of guards below charging up the train after Javani and the Commodore brought Anashe up short. She met Anri's watery eye, then as one they turned to the alchemical monstrosity on its sweeping pivot.

'Yeah,' said Anri, 'can't say I'm wild about the idea, myself.'

'My feelings are similar, but I am running short of alternatives.'

Anri swallowed, then leaned over the rail and loosed another arrow at the press of guards at the tower's base. He leaned back in as someone threw an optimistic spear well wide of them.

'I could—'

'Why don't you—'

They spoke over each other, then stopped, then hesitated to start again.

'It requires two to operate,' Anashe said in a soft voice, after a suitable pause.

'Yep.' He sighed. 'Bugger.'

Manatas rode hard. The train's speed was picking up now, rolling down the gentle slope of the plains towards the distant coast, trailing plumes of filthy black smoke as it went. He'd kicked the pony into a gallop and was gaining on it, but at nowhere the rate that he'd hoped, despite his mount's relative freshness. The rear fortress was a wreck, flattened and flaming, but the tower at the train's centre still seemed whole. He gave it a wide berth, just in case, geeing his pony hard as they raced through drifting dust clouds, one arm across his mouth. There was the baggage wagon, its doors still hanging wide and black like a toothless maw. Gurbun would be somewhere beyond, towards the head of the train, and Javani and the Commodore would be in hot pursuit.

'Come on, girl, don't fail me now,' he murmured to his flagging mount, and with his free hand, reached for his hand-bow.

Tauras hauled Woolley and Svon to a stop just beside the cart's wreckage, and leapt to the ground, some of which was black and broken up. The White Spear looked up at him, her head a hand's width from the wagon's front wheel. She looked unhappy.

'Boy.' Her voice sounded strained, like she had bad gas.

'Mistress Whitespear. I'm here to get you.'

'You should not have come. You should stay with the train.'

'Can't leave anyone behind, Mistress Whitespear.'

'That is not what I told you.'

'It's what I decided, mistress.' Tauras knelt and fed one arm beneath her, then the other, and lifted with his legs.

She watched the wagon wheel bob past her head as he made her upright. 'I am,' she said, in a tired voice, 'a little weary of close encounters with wagons.'

'We'll get you on board, Mistress Whitespear. You'll be just fine.'

'Boy. You should not have come for me. You have made a poor choice.'

Tauras hung his head and said nothing.

'But,' she said as he lowered her gently alongside Sarian, in that tight, gassy voice, 'I am glad you did.'

Tauras was beaming as he leapt back aboard.

The passenger wagon was in a sorry state by the time Javani and the Commodore tumbled inside, the former crouched behind the latter and her shield. Benches were upended, plush seats and tables in disarray, and some of the thick curtains fallen from the half-shuttered windows. The ceiling was proper wood, nicely vaulted, and compared with its canvas-roofed predecessors, the wagon felt gloomy and claustrophobic, narrow shafts of sunlight from the shutters casting glowing lines of dust at sharp angles, one candelabra still burning on the only table that hadn't been tipped.

'Going to say it again?' the Commodore hissed. There were faces in the gloom, and movement: the passengers, the notaries and functionaries, the cowering scribblers the Commodore had predicted. A trail of splatter marks on the rugs – silk rugs, in a place like this! – announced that Gurbun had already passed through.

'I don't know,' Javani growled back. 'Are you going to give them the gut-strangling speech again?'

'Aye, well, a little goes a long way, I always say, and diminishing returns is one of life's great perils for those who reach my ripe old age.'

'Is that a yes?'

'Get out of here, bandits!' came a voice from the back. It didn't sound wholly convinced, let along convincing. 'We're armed! Leave here or we'll cut you down!'

Javani put a hand on the Commodore's shoulder. 'Maybe I should—'

A crossbow bolt whistled out of the darkness and thunked into the shield, spraying them both with splinters.

'Fucken hells!' The Commodore roared. 'Now you're all getting the beats!'

'Are you aiming the device correctly? Some of them have started on the ropes; we may not have long if we are to detach this wagon before they either down us or cross over.'

'I'm aiming it just fine.'

'Then why do you not say "fire"?'

'Priming pan is too hot! We go now, it'll take our faces clean off.'

'Why did you not mention this? We should be cooling it, somehow!'

'Because I'm having serious second thoughts about this whole enterprise, all right! I signed up for a bit of light rebellion and a sprinkle of maiming, not to blow myself up in the service of . . . whatever it is we're doing this for.'

'You are doubting yourself?'

'Course I bloody am! We could be . . . I don't know, firing these black arrows into those buggers down below and, uh, working out how not to take ourselves up with them.'

'That is unlikely.'

'We could be leaping to safety then.'

'Perhaps onto the train you just destroyed?'

'You helped with that!'

Anashe put her hand on his arm. She half expected him to recoil. 'There is nowhere else to go, and our time is running short.'

'I know, I fucking know, don't I. Ah, sod it, I've had a good life, I'm ready to go.' He snorted. 'No, bollocks, I've had a shit life, it's been miserable, and so have I.'

'Anri, this is also a difficult moment for me too, and you are not making it any easier.'

'Oh, I'm sorry! The impending end of my existence and the *utter* lack of delight I have at the notion is making *your* life difficult, is it? Whole thing is hardly fair.'

'Anri! Do not pretend to subscribe to some concept of a fair existence. You are a wiser man than that, and you are fooling nobody.'

'Don't need to tell me that life isn't fair, do you – I spent half my life nursing a wife who couldn't love me even when she was conscious! Been an exile and outsider everywhere I've ever been.'

'You preach to me of unfairness? My mother was banished when I was but a babe, my traitor father murdered soon after, and I spent my adult existence following my brother on a doomed quest across continents, only for him to die and leave me completely alone!'

'Oh. Does sound a bit rough, that, fair play.'

Anashe sniffed, then cleared her throat. 'It seems neither one of us has perhaps enjoyed the life we might have wished for.'

'Yeah, quite a pair, eh?' He offered her his whiskery, gap-toothed grin. 'And now we're ending them in a big old bang.'

'At least this will leave some mark— Whoa!' The tower lurched beneath them as one of its mooring ropes flashed loose. 'They mean to bring us down. The priming pan?'

'Close enough.'

'Then let us do what we must.'

'Yeah, fine. Give me a hand, will you.'

Between them, they hefted the tubing and pointed it towards where the wagons joined.

'Ready?' said Anri, as the tower lurched again. Another spear came sailing past, lazy on the wind, lost somewhere in the rolling sweep of the passing landscape. Anashe's gaze drifted out over the impossible blue sky, unbounded and limitless and limpid, but for the soaring specks of distant birds. Her breath came easier, now.

'Fire,' she said.

The mood in the chuck wagon was fractious and volatile. The men – the six who still stood – had yet to reach agreement on their course.

'We should go after them,' said one, to a chorus of variable agreement. 'There's more of us than them, and if we go fast they'll have their backs to us.'

Another had his hand in the air. 'Lads, lads, I really think we should consider trying to get off. We're going way faster than we're supposed to, look. And things keep going boom, yeah?'

'Horseshit,' declared the first man. 'Any minute now, our boys are going to come storming through here, and it'll be heads galore for those rebels. And then there'll be no more bangs and booms, because they'll all be fucking dead. You mark my words.'

It was at this moment that Captain Manatas chose to stride into view, a hand-bow in one fist and his sabre in the other, streaked in blood, soot and dust and resembling nothing more than a fearsome spirit of plains vengeance.

'Good day, friends,' he said in a voice that was both affable and spring-loaded with unspent violence. 'Might I enquire as to whether you have seen a young lady come through here, in the company of a curious, orange-haired woman with an uncommon accent?'

The faces before him were hardened but brittle; angry, confused eyes and tight jaws. The nearest man's hands were shaking.

'I have no wish to press you,' Manatas said, aware his eyes were a little wider than normal, 'but a prompt answer would go a long way to avoiding any further unpleasantness.'

At that, a mighty blast detonated behind them, throwing the wagons up and forward, rocking them on their wheels, bending and creaking as at least one axle snapped. The contents of the chuck wagon took momentarily to the air, then crashed down in a sharp and heavy rain. Through it all, Manatas kept his balance, years in the saddle and campaigning through mud and desert steering him with preternatural poise. As things began to settle once again, and the train picked up ever more speed, its chuntering rhythm now an urgent tattoo, he looked around the scene of devastation and the disarrayed staff with the air of a disappointed governor.

'Well?'

Almost as one, the inhabitants of the chuck wagon made for the windows, and hurled themselves out.

FORTY-SIX

'No crossbows, you said. "Don't worry Commodore, there'll be no crossbows on this train, I swear it on my pretty wee girlie head."'

'I said nothing of the sort!' A bolt punched into the overturned dining table that formed Javani's cover. 'All I remember is someone using the words "cowering nibbers."'

'And they are! Just with a crossbow. Or two.' Another bolt winged the bench behind which the Commodore lay prone, tearing a chunk from it on its way to judder from the wall. 'You're wronger than I was.'

'Maybe if you'd let me reassure them, they'd have let us by, like the chuck wagon crew?' Someone threw a candelabra over the table at her. She threw it back.

'Oh aye, right, like it was your reassurances that cowed them, not the gut stuff.'

'I could just—'

'At this rate, you tell anyone else we mean them no harm and the planet splits in two and drops us into the sun.'

'How is it my fault things keep exploding?'

'How is it not?'

Javani poked her head up. The wagon remained in darkness, but for the brilliant shafts of angled light from the half-shuttered windows. Things moved in the gloom, people and objects, as they rattled along on the straining rails. Someone was going to throw something again in a moment, then a bolt would follow.

'Listen!' she called out to the darkness. 'We're not here for you.

We're just here to take back something that your dickhead Chairman stole. We only want him, and what he's holding. Let us pass and be at peace. We—'

'Don't you fucken say it.'

'—mean you no harm!'

She felt the blast before she heard it, that tremor, that pop in the air, and deep down she'd half expected it. At least this time, as the shockwave travelled along the train, she was already crouched on the floor, hunkered against the table. From the crashes and cries that came from further along, others had not been so lucky.

Her ears were still ringing when the Commodore grabbed her arm and dragged her up. 'Go, go, go! Before they rally!'

They pelted through the ever more jumbled wagon, hurdling upended furniture and the odd occupant, the Commodore charging shield-first.

'Had to say it, didn't you?'

'It was coincidence! Gods know what that one was . . .'

'That's as may be, girlie, but now I'll make you a liar when I do *this* . . .'

The Commodore diverted to kick the crossbow from the hands of a rising man, then brain him with the hilt of her sabre. 'Prick,' she spat, then they were off again, through the door and onto a narrow gantry that led up to the suddenly towering form of the train-head fortress. Its iron was scorched black and smoking, flames growling at its battered rampart, a great chunk missing on one side as if bitten away by a monster beyond comprehension. Up close, the scale of the thing brought Javani up short, so much taller, so much longer than the other wagons. She'd seen it from across the plains, inspected it through the spyglass, cowered as it shuddered past, but standing at its foot as they rocketed over the earth, its battlements torn and belching smoke, a great rent in its side, she was suddenly uncertain. It was too massive, too intimidating. A thousand Guild Goldhelms would lurk inside, with Gurbun at their head, laughing.

'Fucken crossbows, man, I am so sick of— Why've you stopped? Hoy, girlie! Fuck's up?'

'It's . . .' She swallowed. 'It's too big. We can't . . . I can't . . .'

'Bollocks. Come this far, haven't you? What's left that could possibly put the wind up you?'

'I need . . . I can't . . .'

'You can and you will. Remember why you're doing this? For your mam, was it? For Ree?'

The world dropped into focus again, the industrial lines of the fortress suddenly in stark relief.

'No. *Fuck*, no. This is for me.'

'Aye, right. To prove you can. And you can, girlie, so pick up your knickers and let's get a move on. At the speed we're going, we're out of that old river way sooner than expected.'

'What? What do you mean?'

'We're going faster now, right? For whatever reason. Faster we go, more ground we cover, harder it is for our exit team to keep up. So let's catch our wee dingleberry pronto, before we end up riding this flaming cock-proxy all the way to the coast and a fair way out to sea.'

Javani squared her shoulders, shifted the coils of rope on her shoulder and lifted her knife, as the Commodore reached for the door-panel with eyebrows raised.

'Do it.'

It was hard to say who the black arrow's impact surprised most. For Anashe, who at least knew it was coming, the impact rippled up the tower towards her as the far wall of the wagon disappeared in a sheet of flame and a flowering eruption of smog. The separation with the front half of the train was immediate, exacerbated by the shock of the explosion in the wagon's leading edge, which incinerated the first of its axles and sent the remaining structure tipping and grinding along the railed path in a rolling bloom of sparks, flames and smoke.

This came as a considerable shock to the Guild men, who were thrown forwards, backwards and downwards, towards a boiling inferno at the wagon's front. Those who survived the initial impacts became steadily aware of the hungry spread of the flames across the slowing ruin of the wagon, the blaze crackling its way towards the reinforced crates of alchemical ammunition that lay neatly stacked at the beleaguered tower's foot.

The tower itself lolled, first across, then around as the last of its ropes creaked back, giving its occupants one last sweeping vista to go with their breakfast-launching swerve. The heavy alchemical launcher pitched and tumbled away to the rough plain below, splintering and shattering on impact. Behind and beneath them, wood crisped and burned, and overworked ropes began to fray and split in their tormented moorings.

'This is it, then, is it,' Anri muttered from the opposite corner. One of his arms was bent across his body in a way that suggested it wasn't working very well, and his breathing had a hitch that implied at least one broken rib. The creak and crack of rope and spar were unmissable now. The tower was not going to spring back, and they dangled out over the whispering plain, a conflagration building at the drooping tower's foot. 'Either we fall to our deaths, or the rest of that powder goes up and takes us all with it.'

Anashe was jammed into her own corner, her left leg bent useless beneath her, a deep cut at her temple, and her gaze fixed out into the soothing azure, away from carnage and flame. She watched the birds, soaring and turning. Not buzzards this time. Not yet.

'Didn't think we'd have time to think about it, if I'm honest,' Anri went on. 'Thought, you know, boom, that would be it. Didn't think we'd be sitting here afterwards, waiting for the rest like.' He hissed out a breath. 'Kypeth's fetid fistula.'

Anashe's eye remained on the distant avians. 'Why do you profane your deity so readily?' she asked in a sluggish voice. 'Surely now of all times you would wish to plead his favour.'

Anri's laugh was so sharp it made him wince. 'You what? Kypeth's not a god! Just some git I grew up with, from the other end of the village.'

'Then why do you invoke him so?'

Anri tried to shrug, failed, and winced again. 'Dunno,' he offered. 'He was an odd sod, I just enjoy carrying him with me, I suppose. Pox took him before I moved on, and, well, you know . . .'

'So long as the story is told, the life remains.'

One bird was closer than the others, a small thing, and dark, with a flash of white at its collar. Anashe felt her chin lift, her eyes narrow, peering at it as it turned.

'Anyway, I suppose we'll be reliant on others invoking and profaning us from here, given the imminent and all.' He tried to take a deep breath, caught himself, then hissed slowly through his teeth.

Anashe was staring at the bird. A falcon, perhaps, each of its turns bringing it closer to the wreckage of their half-train. She could not shake the impression that the bird was inspecting her every bit as much as the other way around. The unsinged hairs on her arm lifted.

'Thing is . . . call me mad if you like,' Anri went on, 'or stupid, or sun-touched and brainless, but I like to think in other circumstances, in another time . . . perhaps we'd have been something like . . . friendly.'

This tore Anashe's gaze from the sky, swinging her head around. 'What? Your company has been nothing but vexation and provocation. You have driven me to levels of ire I have not felt since . . .' She tailed off, her breath caught.

He was grinning, gap-toothed and bloody. 'Yeah, me too. It's been a laugh, eh?'

Something snapped and the tower lurched, dropping them another foot. The contents of the ruined train wagon were hissing and fizzing as the flames ate away at the reinforced crates, charring and curling their cargo. It all smelled terrible.

'Ah well,' Anri said. 'Another life, eh?'

Anashe snapped her gaze back to the bird, the hawk. It was gliding on a thermal, seeming to hang motionless, and it met her glare with a single black and yellow eye, then with the slightest duck of its head, it dipped its wing and wheeled down and away, dwindling with astonishing speed.

'Not today,' Anashe said aloud. Something burned in her chest, something more than loss. Her eyes stung.

'Eh?'

'It is not today,' she repeated, her certainty growing. 'Anri, come, we are leaving.'

'I mean, doubt it, like.'

She hauled herself forward, dragging her useless leg, peering over the buckled floor of the sagging structure. 'We have dropped a little closer to the earth, and perhaps with a— By the Goddess! Whitespear! Tauras! Up here!'

'Hello, friends!' came the voice of Tauras from the swirling murk beneath. 'If we *promise* to catch you, how do you feel about jumping?'

Ree drifted in and out of sleep. She couldn't stay awake, couldn't shake the phrase, the words that haunted her. She was so weak, in one part amazed she still lived, yet increasingly conscious that her end might yet be close. Her thoughts were whirling and incoherent – dreams lingered, or memories, or memories of dreams. Something needled her beneath it, a gnawing anxiety.

I must be dying, she thought, my life is flashing before my eyes.

But not all of it.

Not the Before.

The feeling lurked still, beneath the claws of sleep, beneath the torpor. Nagging like a hangnail, a loose tooth; what was it?

I made the girl a promise. I promised to keep her safe. I promised to treat her better than my parents treated me. And I kept that promise.

I kept that promise.

Still, the phrase haunted her, unshakeable: *you can't hold me back.* Where was everyone? Where was the kid? How could she leave her, after everything she'd done? After she'd kept the promise. Given so much in its name . . .

As she slipped beneath sleep again, from outside came the sound of hoof-beats.

FORTY-SEVEN

'So that's where the rest of the fucken guards were!'

The men inside the shell of the fortress were wide-eyed and sweating, almost certainly in no small part from the volume of fire that surrounded them. The fort's original construction had been blasted apart from its roof, then steadily eaten away by lingering flames, leaving a hollowed-out carcass with two sets of stairs, one smouldering, running up to the mauled remains of the upper floor and the rampart. The wind-whipped flickering of the burning walls lit the interior in a kaleidoscope of demonic shades, and the space swirled with squalls of roasting air and scorching embers. The noise was constant, like being trapped inside a whistling, howling, heaving bellows, belching snarls of fire through the widening cracks in its walls.

'What are you waiting for?' came a familiar voice from behind the manic guards, two lines of three, spears levelled, their burnished breastplates slick and steaming. 'Stab them to chunks, you dullards!'

Gurbun was halfway up the stairway that wasn't yet blackened and smoking, edging backwards up it with his good hand on the still-sheathed hilt of his long, thin and expensive-looking sword. In his other dangled the seal, held up to the shifting light, blood-slick and lurching on its chain. He was taunting them, goading them, to charge the spears of his last line.

The Commodore seemed only too happy to oblige, the sabre already hoisted above her head and a wild look in her eye. Her improvised shield was nearing the end of its useful life, and Javani was struck by a sudden and immediate feeling that their luck had run out.

She shot out a hand. 'Wait!'

The Commodore faked a swing and growled at the guards, all six of them, then whispered, 'What?'

'He wants us to charge.' From the corner of her eye, she caught Gurbun tucking the seal back into his robe.

'Aye. So?'

'Well, you remember what you said before about not wanting a repeat of what happened to you before?'

'Fucken crossbows, man.' The Commodore squinted. 'None of these bastards packing one, though.'

'I just think . . . there's six of them, they've got spears and armour, they're not backing down . . . and it's just you and me on this side, and if I'm completely honest I never really learned how to fight with a blade.' Now at the top of the stairs, Gurbun had ducked down, the seal stowed, and was rummaging around for something, she couldn't see what.

'You what?'

'Look, I'm a fantastic rider, I'm superb with a bow, I can run, I can climb, I can, uh . . .'

'Chat shit?'

'Well, yeah.'

The Commodore glanced at her sidelong. 'Well, girlie, momentum and first impressions are what's got us this far, and if I'm being frank the longer we give these lads to think about how best to come at us, the worse we'll be doing out of it, so I suggest you spend the next few seconds putting that big old brain of yours towards coming up with something you can do within our current confines, given that's about as long as we've got before they start taking steps.'

'Wait, what?'

'Time's up. Come taste some Clydish hospitality, you brass-fronted bastards!'

From the very top of the stairs, Gurbun loosed his crossbow.

'Thank you for the lift, Tauras,' Anashe called over the fearsome wind of their travel. They thundered along the bank of the old creek, the two stout ponies galloping tirelessly despite the populous nature of the wagon they hauled. Every bump and jolt sent them rocking, jarring her throbbing leg, but she fared better than Anri who lay in the wagon-bed beside Sarian, tossed from side to side and cursing as they raced.

'Can't leave anyone behind, mistress.'

'Where is Whitespear?'

'She's rounding up the horses, mistress.'

They were closing now, albeit slowly, on the flaming ruin of the train. Trailing bilious smoke laced with tongues of flame, half of its length missing, the five front wagons barrelled on along the Iron Road, scorching and warping the tracks as they came. Severed ropes and chains, seared and bitten, rattled along in the wreck's wake like guts. And still it seemed to be picking up speed, coasting down the gentle slope of the plains before the final swoop from the plateau down to the coast. Anashe wondered if there was any way to stop it, disconnected as it was from its mechanical workings, the restraining mass of its sibling. The train was on fire, out of control, and heading for the port.

And her people were on it.

'Can these ponies run any faster?'

'Not really, mistress. They're happy at this speed, but faster will tire them and we may not catch up.'

Anashe sucked at her teeth. 'We may not catch up anyway.'

They hared over a rut or divot, the entire wagon see-sawing for a moment, then settling back into its urgent clatter.

'Tauras, why did the axle not shatter just then? Surely we are not that lucky. How is the wagon able to maintain this speed over such broken ground?'

'Oh. I made some changes to it, mistress. I was worried about the weight, so I used some straps and belts to give it a bit of spring. It's, uh, suspended, in a way. I hope that's all right.'

'It is . . . good, Tauras.'

He glowed.

'Thank you, mistress.'

Siavash almost reached across the table. 'Did you see that? Another flash. Sounds like thunder.'

The slaver raised one grease-slick palm. 'What can I say, master merchant. Perhaps a tempest gathers itself out over the plains. But regard the firmament! Our skies remain crystal, and we shall feel not a particle of precipitation.'

Siavash tugged at the neck of his robe. Beneath his cushion and their temporary platform, the chains and cables that ran along the tracks seemed to be moving a great deal faster than before, their noise now hard to ignore. 'Perhaps we might consider moving the children along now? Their singing has been lovely, but it feels—'

'Frater.' Kusan's voice was hard, all synthetic mirth shorn. 'Do not concern yourself with the urchins.' The chunk of apricot was still in his teeth, and Siavash realised he probably couldn't tell it was there. The slaver spread his fingers across the silken tabletop. 'Master Sarosh, we are both men of commerce. We understand—'

'We are not the same.'

'We are men of commerce, master merchant, and all that differs is the nature of our merchandise. We buy low and sell high, we move product from where it is plentiful to where it is sought, and we collect the margin as profit. It is the law of markets, master merchant, and it is the will of gods.'

'Slavery is forbidden by law!'

Kusan's eyebrow climbed. 'Law? How amusing. The law of markets cares nothing for the laws of men. And the laws of men are . . . changeable.'

Siavash looked around, at anywhere but the man opposite, and tried to ignore the trembling in his legs. Surely there was someone else he could engage? Where was Ulfat?

Kusan would not let his attention escape. 'You may not like me, master merchant,' the slaver said, leaning forward, his robes straining, 'but the market demands our cooperation, just as it demands our so-called "betters" admit us to their feast. We are engines of wealth, and wealth means power. We are but human, master merchant, paradox made flesh. All of us aspires to success, to greatness and, yes, wealth, while vilifying precisely those who have achieved it. Not from some worthy notion of redistributive equality, but from our own greed. Our avarice. That is what drives the market, master merchant. That is what drives us all.'

The golden teeth gleamed. Siavash became dimly aware that the trembling in his legs was in fact coming from beneath him. The cushion he was on was quivering, because the iron-clad rails they were perched on had begun to jitter.

'Take our friends the Guild as apotheosis, frater. They are despised, yet they flourish. They flourish, therefore they are despised. And every man here wishes he could tap a fraction of their success.' Kusan sat back on his cushion, his teeth slick and gleaming. In the distance, Siavash heard odd noises, over the general hubbub of merriment and conviviality, the murmuring press of their adoring audience in the gallery above, the constant background clamour of the port, the rattle and clank of machinery. The rails were now singing in a most disquieting way.

'I think, perhaps—'

'The advent of the Iron Road brings with it a great overture, an expansion of our collective horizons. New lands, new customers, new . . . markets, with new hungers to be fed. We are here, master merchant, because they know they need us, and they wish they could be more like us. And they shall be.'

Siavash's chin jutted. 'I am not like you.'

'Not yet, perhaps, but the day is young.'

Just over the horizon, something definitely went bang.

FORTY-EIGHT

The bolt whistled under the Commodore's shield and buried itself in her thigh.

'Oh you have got to be fucken . . . come *on*!'

A line of spears closed in.

'Commodore, are you all right?'

'I've got a fucken bolt in my fucken leg, do I look all right?'

'You know, it's really hard to tell.'

'Do something, Slayer!'

And Javani realised exactly what she could do. She stashed her knife in its sheath, then shrugged the bundle of rope from her shoulder. As the first rank of spearmen closed, she began to swing the rope around her head, the weighted end humming like a vengeful insect. Javani stood over the crouching Commodore, whirling the rope around her, its sharpened tip flashing in the demonic firelight, daring the guards to advance. When they did, she snapped the rope at their hands, at their knees, at their faces. Small wounds, but upsetting nonetheless, and debilitating, and their cohesion began to creak.

Gurbun bellowed from the top of the stairs, encouragement or beration or just a sort of furious animal lowing; it was hard to tell with everything else that was going on. He seemed to be having trouble reloading the crossbow with his injured hand, but Javani knew time was against them.

'Commodore,' she growled through gritted teeth, 'what is the plan here? I can't keep them back forever.'

'Aye, right,' came the strained response. The Commodore was trying to get up, and it was not going well. 'Joke's on them, they're exactly where we want them.'

Javani lashed the rope at the nearest guard, who gave a little yelp and took a step back, to the caustic consternation of the men behind him. 'And where's that?'

'Off . . .' the Commodore huffed, stumbling forwards with a wild swing of her sabre then collapsing sideways, '. . . balance.'

A noise of triumph issued from the stairtop, and there was Gurbun, standing proud, the blood-smeared crossbow drawn and levelled in his grip. Javani threw herself over the Commodore as the bolt flashed through the air and thumped into the wall behind her.

Gurbun snarled his frustration, then bellowed, 'Will you just fucking kill them, you useless bastards? I am so bored of this.'

Javani and the Commodore were a heap on the floor, the rope in a tangle, six men with spears bearing down on them. 'Fuck,' muttered the Commodore from beneath Javani's chest. Javani tensed every muscle. She'd never been stabbed before, certainly not with a spear, and wasn't relishing the prospect.

'Fuck,' echoed Javani.

The speartips did not arrive; instead a great clang echoed in Javani's ear, followed by two more and a shout. She looked up in time to see Captain Manatas hurdle over her, clearing her huddled form by a finger's span, then loose a hand-bow into the face of the central guard as he landed. The man staggered back, screaming, and Manatas hacked smartly at the lunging spears of his confederates, then inclined his head a fraction towards where they lay.

'Kindly withdraw the Commodore, if it please you.'

Gods damn the captain, he was still polite, even when giving orders. Javani didn't argue, perhaps for the first time in recent memory, and scampered around behind the Commodore, hauling her half up and half backwards and towards the narrow door and the gantry beyond, leaving a slick ruby trail as they went.

'Hoy, what are you playing at?' The Commodore's thick mane waved as she struggled to right herself on her good leg as Javani dragged her backwards. 'We've got them on the run, the dusty pricks.'

Javani had one eye on the five remaining guards and one on the

Second Chairman at the top of the stairs, who had the crossbow jammed between his knees and his tongue poking from the corner of his mouth in concentration.

'Call it a tactical retreat,' she replied, then marvelled as Manatas beat away an attack from two men – trained, professional soldiers, with six-foot spears – with his sabre, somehow making enough space to re-crank his hand-bow, then loosing it into the foot of one and carving a nasty chunk from the working arm of the second. Then he was away, dashing backwards after Javani and the Commodore as they stumbled their way onto the wind-whipped gantry, feeling the creak and groan of the tortured wood as they thumped down onto it. Manatas dragged shut the fortress door behind him, barring it with a pilfered spear, and an instant later the door bulged beside his head with a resounding clang.

'I see that fellow got his bow loaded again,' the captain said, his back against the door and breathing hard, sweat gleaming from his skin, the sabre back in one hand and the small bow in the other. Javani had never seen Manatas fight before, not properly. She'd seen him on rides, on raids, commanding and scheming, and occasionally menacing and threatening, and of course, doing his little tricks with a hand-bow around their training grounds, but she'd never actually seen him in combat. She realised that on some level, she'd always seen him as Ree's shadow, her totem, her second and attendant. Maybe he had a decent tactical brain on him, and he'd seen a few engagements long ago, but she'd taken his position to be principally one of sentimental attachment on Ree's part, or perhaps his willingness to do what she said, when she said it, because for whatever ghastly reason he seemed to love her and be willing to put up with her intolerable shit. But at no point had Javani considered that maybe, just maybe, Manatas himself was worthy of some level of admiration.

'Gods' golden shit, captain,' she breathed, 'you're amazing.'

He looked up, brows lowered, his eyes little more than creases against the glare. 'I, uh, appreciate the compliment.' He cleared his throat. Around them, the train roared and rattled, belching flame and smoke and feeling ever closer to shaking itself apart. They were going far faster than before, almost at a full gallop, and the plains tore by on either side in a pure blur of emptiness. The gantry felt entirely unsafe. 'I apologise for my tardy arrival,' he went on. 'I was delayed by the need to convince a number of people that leaving the train before matters became very much worse might be in their collective interest.' Javani noted the splatter marks on his jacket, the fine mist on his boots, darkening the dust.

'You're not going to get knocked off again, are you? Once is misfortune, twice is—'

Manatas put up the hand with the bow. 'I will endeavour so not to do.' He nodded overhead at the smouldering fortress, its armoured panels blackened and warped. 'Was it not a touch afire within for a pitched battle?'

'Gurbun has the seal. We had to get to him.'

'He also had, from the look of it, a fine mechanical crossbow, a Shukla if I'm not mistaken.'

'Fucken crossbows, man.' The Commodore sounded a little delirious, but Javani recognised it was never going to be entirely conclusive either way.

'Bastard's clearly got too much disposable income,' Javani muttered. 'What are we going to do?'

Manatas inspected the bolt in the Commodore's leg. 'Missed the artery, but we need to get her off this train, and ourselves with it.'

Javani's chin jutted. 'Gurbun has the seal. He's the other side of that door, and he's got nowhere left to run.'

Manatas stowed his sabre on one side of his belt and tucked the hand-bow at the other. 'He also has at least three trained and armoured guardsmen, the high ground, and the advantage of cover. This vehicle is only getting faster, and if we do not leave it soon it may become too perilous to even make the attempt.'

'Yeah? What then?'

'Then we are doomed to remain aboard as it accelerates down the final stretch to the port. A long, steep downhill, you may remember. The chains are cut, we are unmoored. This flaming contrivance has no means to slow itself, let alone reach a controlled halt. The remains of this train are going to hit the end of the Iron Road like a runaway . . . uh . . . horse. A heavy one. That is also on fire.'

'The *seal* is *in there*!'

'Aye, right, come on,' came the Commodore's voice from the gantry, 'just let me strap this bugger up and I'll be in there with you. Let's lop off some limbs!'

'See, the Commodore agrees.'

'I am far from convinced that the lady in question retains full control of her f— By the gods!'

Javani turned, and gaped. Pulling slowly up alongside the gantry were two stout, shaggy ponies, galloping to the very limit of their determination, and pulling a narrow, bouncing wagon containing a bloodied and bandaged set of people.

'Tauras! Anri, Anashe!' Javani cried. Tears were in her eyes, from nowhere. She'd had no idea of the level of worry that she'd kept suppressed. 'You're alive.'

'No thanks to this one,' Anri bellowed. One of his arms was strapped and he had a face like thunder.

'Nonsense,' Anashe retorted, 'you were the one making peace with Kypeth's divine nethers.'

'I told you, woman, Kypeth had nothing divine about him.'

'Yet your fixation with his underparts remains.'

Javani stared, dumbstruck. It was one of the strangest sights of her life: both of them were trying not to smile.

'It's rude to rush people,' Tauras called from the bench, 'but Svon and Woolley can't run this fast for very long.'

Manatas snapped into action. 'Then let us make haste. We must depart, and promptly – the Commodore is injured.'

Anashe took the reins as Tauras moved to the wagon-bed, then ropes were thrown and a rough bridge formed between speeding wagon and gantry. Despite her furious protestations, the injured Commodore was trussed and rolled, transferred to the wagon-bed with minimal fuss, where Anri set about inspecting her injury, one-handed.

Manatas turned to Javani. 'Javani, it's time for us to leave.'

She shook her head, jaw clenched to hide its tremble.

'Javani, please.'

'It's rude to rush people,' came Tauras's voice again, 'but I can see the end of the riverbank and it's getting closer.'

'Javani.'

'I'm not going.'

'If you do not leave now, you will not be able to jump. You will ride this train into the sea if you are not killed in there.'

'I can take him.'

'Not alone.'

Javani clenched her fists, swaying on the gantry as it groaned. 'We can't leave now! We don't have the seal, and it's so close!'

'Then let them keep it, for today at least. Better we leave this place with our lives and take it another time. There is always tomorrow.'

She shook her head, the wind stinging tears from her eyes. 'If we don't get it today, they renew their charter, they go on forever. We have to take it today. We have to break them today. We cannot let them roll into the port with it safe in their hands.'

'They may be going a little faster than that . . .'

'Hoy, you bastards!' The Commodore was bellowing at them from the wagon-bed. 'What's the fucken hold up? If I'm not allowed to do any dismembering, don't you even think about doing any without me!'

'It's rude to rush people—'

'Yes, Tauras, I am aware!' Manatas called over his shoulder. 'Javani, for the love of the gods, if you do not leave now you will throw your life away, and it will be for nothing. It is too much for you alone. You'd have to be a damned-by-gods fool to even attempt it. The last thing your mother would want is for you to die for the cause.'

'Isn't that what she's been doing?' Javani snapped. Sand was whipping in the wind, and there was maybe just a hint of salt on the air. 'Killing herself in the name of the cause?'

'Perhaps,' Manatas acknowledged, 'but not by intent – and you have far more to live for than any of us.'

Javani took a deep breath. Her hands were shaking, her teeth on the verge of chattering, and her whole chest felt very light. 'Captain Manatas, I'm not going. I can't let them win.'

'Will yous two hurry the fuck up! We're running out of river-road!'

'Javani—'

'You know what Ree would say?' Javani wiped at her nose with the back of her hand, her eyes crusty with grit and tears. 'You know what she'd say, if it was anyone else up here?'

He sighed. 'I do.'

'Finish the mission.'

'Finish the mission,' he echoed. Manatas released a long breath, letting his head sag, be bobbed and swayed by the judder of the train. 'I will never convince you, will I?'

'No.'

'And we are out of time.' He turned to face the wagon. 'So be it.' Manatas whipped the sabre from his belt and sliced through the ropes in a single sweep, sending them pinging apart with a collection of twangs. Immediately the wagon slowed, the exhausted ponies easing their pace as the riverbank turned away from the course of the train, and the vehicle and its confused occupants dropped swiftly back into the rising cloud of dust, lost but for the echoes of their cries.

'Manatas you fucken . . .'

'Could have untied them, eh, cost me a few . . .'

Javani and Manatas were alone on the blood-stained gantry, barrelling over the last of the plains and towards the port. Around them swirled noxious black smoke, lit with incessant bursts of flame from all along the structure, the surrounding landscape lost to swirling murk.

'Captain Manatas. You're still here.'

'That I am. If I cannot rescue you, I will not leave you.'

'I'm touched.'

He cracked half a smile. 'Do you imagine I have any wish to return to your mother to inform her of your demise under my watch?'

Javani flinched at the thought of Ree, pushed the images away. 'What happened to "only a damned-by-gods fool would even attempt this"?'

'I have, in truth, been referred to as such.' He wiped a hand across his brow, leaving filthy streaks. 'On multiple occasions.' He reached to his belt. 'I believe you know how to use one of these?'

Javani took the hand-bow, inspected it, unfolded the arms and got cranking.

'I've been known to use one.'

'Then all is where we would wish it.'

He moved to the barricaded door, sabre in hand, and reached towards the spear that barred it.

'Ready?'

The hand-bow ready, Javani scooped up her loose rope and re-spooled it over her shoulder. 'Ready. And captain?'

'For the last time, I invite you to call me—'

'Thanks.'

'Well. Yeah.' He gripped the bar. 'Just please do not embarrass me by dying.'

'Likewise, old man.'

He slid the spear aside.

Ree lay in silent darkness, awake but drifting. Her weakness left her sluggish and delirious, unable to follow her surroundings. Had there been someone there, a moment ago? An age ago? She could not be certain. Why did the words haunt her?

You can't hold me back any more.

Why did she feel so . . . *guilty?*

The dreams lingered at the edge of memory, drifting but jagged.

I made the girl a promise. I'd never treat her the way my parents treated me.

And I kept it. I kept it.

Didn't I?

Then like the lifting of a fogbank, an image surfaced, as bright and sharp as yesterday.

She was arguing with her parents, the clarity of the memory almost heartbreaking. The angle of the sunlight through the high windows, the way the motes of dust danced in the latticed shafts. Her mother was crying, her father's face dark. Her siblings were elsewhere, out of sight, their ears no doubt pressed to the mottled doors.

The last time she was home, the final argument. She was telling them she had made her choice.

Her mother pleaded. Her father growled. Had they not done enough for her? Their chosen child, their golden path? They'd sacrificed everything so that one of their children might yet make something of herself. How could she do this to them?

She was resolute. They would not keep her cloistered, locked in studies and learning. She knew the shortcut, the quick step to the life she desired, the life she deserved. The whispers of the dancers had proved true, as she'd hoped. Arowan's heir took an interest in the daughters of the upper city, and he had yet to choose a bride. She was choosing her own path, and she was betting on herself.

Her father paced, he wheedled and bluffed. But she knew it all, their secrets, their shames. They had held her back too long, kept her from living, from tasting the life she was entitled to. They had stifled her, their constricting attentions, their rank desperation, all their hopes balanced on her slim shoulders. They had implored devotion, prudence and patience, that one of their children might yet attain a better life in the upper city for them all. They caved on the dancing, her mother heartbroken that she had spurned music, but relieved that she had some artistic pursuits beside her studies. She was so bright, and so beautiful. They had shielded her from everything, but she was fifteen and a half years old and she knew what she wanted.

And what she wanted was to rule Arowan beside the husband she had chosen.

She'd seen him in the gallery, in the wings. She'd felt his eyes on her. She knew the rumours. And she was hungry for what would follow.

Her parents had smothered her with their overprotection, and she was breaking free. She was choosing for herself. A life of glorious luxury awaited, and if they tried to deny her, she would expose them. She would burn them down, and the rest of her family with them. Every oversight, every peccadillo revealed unless they buckled. And they would buckle. Because they were weak, and she was strong. She was determined. She was doing what she was always meant to do.

I am fifteen and a half years old. She stared them down, imperious, intransigent. *And you can't hold me back any more.*

Ree gasped, a pain like stabbing in her chest, then a scream pierced the darkness.

FORTY-NINE

They caught the occupants of the fort by surprise. Two of the guards were on the lower floor, knelt over the casualties the rebels had inflicted in their first visit, although Javani couldn't tell if they were tending to the men or emptying their pockets. Her expectations of the kind of people who would take the Guild's specie were already pretty low, so she wouldn't really have been shocked either way. The other guards, presumed at two, were up the working stairway to the flaming gantry above, where Gurbun's choleric bellowing suggested that they were in the process of removing the slim bolt from his hand.

Manatas didn't hesitate, so Javani didn't either. Ignoring the men on the rampart above, the captain made for the two guards at the fortress floor, lit strange as they were by the manic flutter of flame through the gaps in the outer plating. The groan of rushing air accompanied the train's chuntering shudder, the fort's interior a rattling kiln, the wash from the cracked and burning nose like a blast of midsummer desert air. Manatas braved the gale without a word, his boots thudding from the blistered wood of the floor, leaping an overturned storage rack to deliver a savage cut to the neck of the man who was closer to standing.

Javani followed, the little bow slick in her palms, stifling the tremble in her arms through sheer force of will. Her chest still felt light, oddly hollow, and she moved after Manatas with a curious ease, a distance from the world around her, everything muted and dim. Still no one spoke, the stricken man falling with barely a gurgle, fingers wrapped at the captain's blade while his colleague scrabbled for the spear at his feet. Javani watched them moving impossibly slowly, Manatas yanking back on his sword as the dying man grasped it bloody, the second guard fumbling to bring his weapon from the floor, levering it up towards the captain with incomprehensible lethargy. Then it was in his hands, brought to bear on Manatas as the captain wrestled to free his sword, their panic-wide eyes locking as each turned to end the other.

Her tongue electric in her mouth, pulse rushing in her ears, the world a strange, underwater place around her, Javani squeezed the hand-bow's trigger.

The bolt caught the guard square in one eye, and the sound it made brought the world rushing back. Force, sound and movement came crashing over her, and Javani dropped her hands to her knees, suddenly overcome and feeling the urge to retch. Something splattered, hot and wet, across her hair, and she looked up to see Manatas's earnest eyes looking back. Two eyes, whole eyes, nothing jutting from either. She fought the urge to gag again.

'Are you well, Javani?'

'Popped,' she gasped.

'What's that?'

'His eye . . .' She stood, swallowing bile, wiping a hand across her mouth. 'The sound it made.' She shuddered again, unsteady against the ever-more manic rocking of the train. 'It popped.'

He looked her over for signs of injury, then pressed the small bow back into her palms. 'Are you all right to continue?'

'Shouldn't have been able to hear it. Sound like that. Over the noise.'

'Javani . . .'

She slapped herself in the face. She'd seen Ree do it once, although the exact circumstances were long forgotten. It seemed like the right thing to do.

'Ow.'

'Javani?'

'I'm fine. I'm all right.' She shook herself again. Droplets flew from her head, which didn't help. 'Just . . . ugh.'

His eyes were urgent but understanding. 'You have the right of it. This is an ugly business, but we must—'

'Alarm! Alarm! They're back!'

Manatas flashed his teeth in a grimace of disappointment. 'Ah well.' He grabbed her by the sleeve and dragged her towards the functioning stairs. 'Quickly now.'

Javani's fingers were numb and unresponsive. She knew she needed to crank the hand-bow and reload it, she knew time was short and the guards would descend on them in an instant, that somewhere above them Gurbun would be preparing his own crossbow, which shot bolts a great deal larger than hers. But her bloody fingers wouldn't work.

Manatas charged up the stairs as the guard charged down. Two other figures at the summit, Gurbun and the final guard, a large man whose polished breastplate glimmered like a bonfire in the light of the flames around them. As the guard started downwards, Gurbun thrust the crossbow at him with his non-bandaged hand. 'Load this.'

'Chairman, they are—'

'Load it, you chump. Think you're here to make decisions? You're here to do what you're told. Now load it. Fast!'

Manatas ducked and swayed on the stair, his sabre leading, as the first guard worked to keep him at bay with his spear. The captain was disadvantaged in both reach and height, and once more Javani was struck by the man's combination of poise and skill; Manatas was pushing the guard steadily backwards up the stairs, feinting and flashing and cutting as he went. Javani followed, as close as she dared, clumsy fingers still struggling to reload the hand-bow.

'About time!' Gurbun snatched the crossbow from the large guard and levelled it at his shoulder, wincing as he tried to fit his bandaged hand around the weapon. The wince became a snarl as he sighted along the weapon's length, down the stairs and towards Manatas and Javani. The snarl became a grin.

'Down!' Javani shrieked, and flung herself forwards, dragging Manatas downwards by his shoulders. She heard the snap and thrum of the crossbow, the meaty thud of impact, and a gasp from above. She looked up to see the guard who'd been duelling with Manatas totter forwards, then drop from the stairway, a thick bolt jutting from the back of his head.

'Sight's off,' Gurbun growled. 'You fucked the fucking sight, you imbecile.'

Manatas was moving again. 'Come on!'

They were up the stairs in a heartbeat, Javani's breath burning in her chest, then doubly so from the billow of filthy smoke that met them on the rampart. Gurbun and his guard had backed away along the wreck of the upper floor, which once must have covered the body of the turret, and now ended in ruined planks and splintered and blackened wood over a drop to the floor below, or over the side to oblivion. The wind whipped at them, and all around were flames, the air hot, thick and smothering, greater than a desert gale, blasts from an oven. Views of their surroundings flashed past through roiling belches of smoke, the land steepened, a hint of oyster blue at the horizon. Kilale Port lay at the end of the tracks, and the end of the tracks roared ever closer.

The guard was at the crossbow again, cranking it with looks of frustration and no small hostility towards the Second Chairman, who had withdrawn to the rampart's far end. He stood, bandaged hand extended, his once white robes soot-blackened and blood-stained, the elegant sword still at his hip and madness in his eyes.

'Hurry up, you septic dunce. I'm waiting.'

Manatas slowly closed the distance on the guard, who was finding loading the crossbow while backing away along a ruined, burning battlement far from simple.

'Our quarrel is not with you,' the captain said in a low voice, the sabre easy in his hand. 'We just want the seal. Go on your way and we'll do nothing to stop you.'

Perhaps it was the fresh air, or the lack of it, but Javani's fingers had come back within her control. She shuffled the coiled rope on her shoulder (heavy, sweaty, chafing, why had she brought it?) and slotted the last of the little bolts into place.

'Come on, you mouldering fathead. Why in the name of the gods must my brother employ simpletons at every turn? Come the renewal, I'm taking command of recruitment. I am sick and tired of being surrounded by bloody idiots!'

Manatas addressed the guard. 'Your Chairman's charm is . . . undeniable. Help us take the seal and he'll be nothing but a bad memory.'

'Stop talking to my staff! I am warning you. You've made me

pretty angry already, but you won't like what comes next, you goat-fucking maggots.'

'How would a maggot fuck a goat, then?' Javani called, half in an effort to distract the Second Chairman, and half because she really wanted to say the words out loud.

'What? Don't talk back to me.'

Manatas was still murmuring to the guard, now within a few paces of the man and the crossbow, stepping carefully over the broken timbers. The wind whipped tongues of flame from the rumpled iron sheets at their periphery. 'Think how he treats you. He killed your confederate and laid the blame at your feet.'

The guard looked at the weapon in his hands, then glanced towards Gurbun, who paced behind him with quivering impatience. 'You know what . . .' he said, turning back.

A sword blade erupted from the man's mouth, spraying Manatas in gore, and the big man convulsed and spasmed, his eyes rolling back into his head. The crossbow clattered to the ground as Manatas fell back, one bespattered arm raised, and Javani shrieked.

'Bored!' barked Gurbun, placing one foot on the collapsing guard's back and dragging his beautiful, befouled blade clear. 'I told you you wouldn't like what came next.'

Manatas wiped matter from his face. 'What in the name of—'

Gurbun lunged across the smoking gap and stabbed him.

'Weren't expecting that, were you, dullard?' Gurbun tossed the blade in his uninjured left hand, his bandaged right tucked into his robe, as Manatas staggered back, palm clapped to the fresh wound in his arm. 'Didn't think I'd be able to use both hands, did you?'

Gurbun lunged again, scoring Manatas across the thigh. The captain tried to raise his sabre, but his swing was weak and directionless. Around them, the train thundered on, fuming and aflame, rattling its way down the plain towards the port, juddering and jolting with such force it could only be a matter of time before important things started falling off it. The fire and smoke surrounded them, wind-smeared, creating a blistering bubble of their own little hell on the ruined fortress-top. Gurbun laughed, blood-smeared and blackened, tossing his head and swishing his glistening rapier as

Manatas struggled back and away from him, and Javani was overcome by a sudden, crushing, hair-tingling sense of déjà vu.

I am in a place of darkness, a place of danger, and I am watching a duel. I am watching someone I care about facing off against someone greater than them, someone with more, someone who has cut them and pierced them and is moments from killing them, and there's nothing I can do, I am paralysed, I am useless ...

She looked down at the hand-bow, rigid in her grip. Cranked and loaded.

I am not *useless.*

'Hoy!' she called, the bow level in her hands, her grip steady, sighting along the bolt at Gurbun. 'Drop the sword.'

He turned to her, incredulous. 'There is no fucking way—'

'Bored,' Javani snarled, and shot him.

The bolt hit him in the upper arm, driving into the meat of his shoulder until it hit bone. Gurbun howled, a bellow of pain and outrage, but he did not drop the rapier. He turned to face her, bolt jutting, shoulders warped, then grabbed for the bolt with his injured hand. 'How dare—'

Manatas cut him across the calf, and he dropped to one knee with a snarl. He flashed the rapier around, sending Manatas sprawling on his own injured leg, then Javani lashed him with the rope. Once, twice she whipped him, until at last the sword clattered from his hand.

'Quick, get the—'

Gurbun staggered to his feet and hurled himself towards the blasted battlement at the head of the train, slumping over the buckled iron, his bandaged hand thrust out into space. Dangling from it was the Great Seal of Arowan, swinging and jumping on its chain, blood-streaked and glowing amber and ruby in the demonic firelight.

Javani charged towards him, the rope snapping in her hand, and Manatas limped after, sabre loose at his side.

'Stop!' he bawled. 'No closer, vermin.'

'Captain, are you all right?' Javani whispered sidelong. 'Can you take him?'

'No talking!'

'I fear I cannot reach him before he does something undesirable.'

'I said no fucking talking!' Gurbun stretched further over the front of the train, his hand and the seal momentarily obscured by wafting clods of filthy air. 'One more word, one more *step*, and it goes over the side.'

'Wait—' Javani cried, hand reaching.

'What did I just fucking say?' Gurbun screeched, letting the seal drop on its chain by a hand's span. 'You stay there, you stay silent, or the one thing you came all this way, and shed so much blood for—' Javani cast a glance around the devastated battlement, the sticky, smoking pools, the carmine sheen of the captain's fingers, pressed to his arm, '—goes under the wheels, never to be seen again.

'You're probably thinking, "Oh but Chairman, you need it for the renewal, you wouldn't take the chance."' Gurbun was smiling again, his teeth impossibly bright against his coating of filth. 'You fucking dolts, you imbeciles! Nobody knows what this looks like, and nobody cares but you! We can have a man in Kilale knock out a replica in an hour, and no one will give a *shit*. The Guild is eternal, and it does what it wants.' He laughed, too long and too hard, the whites of his eyes gleaming yellow in the light of the flames.

Javani stood rooted, exchanging an angry glance with Manatas. The captain was upright, but paling, and now blood trickled from his boots to the charred timbers beneath. They could not rush him before he dropped it. Perhaps, if she looped the rope, she could—

'Didn't you wonder, you maggots, you vermin? Didn't you wonder how we knew you were after the seal? Why we packed this show with alchemy and blasted your rat friends into chunks?'

Javani suppressed a smile. He didn't know they were alive. Hells, he probably had no idea that the back half of the train was—

'Any moment now, a battalion of guards is coming up those stairs. They're not going to kill you, though. It's a peeling party when we reach Kilale, and you're going to be front and centre.'

'How, then?' Javani risked it. She didn't want him setting what passed for his mind to assessing the state of the train and the unlikelihood of his reinforcements showing. Not while there was still a chance they could get the seal off him, and then . . . um. 'How did you know?'

'A traitor, obviously. Turncoat in your camp. Sold you out.'

Javani and Manatas exchanged a look, then both laughed, the captain with a matching wince.

'Hoy! No laughing! I said no fucking laughing. Fine, nobody sold you out, it was a spy. Followed you, watched you, came crawling back at every turn.'

Javani's laugh died away. Maral, the cow. Another crime to add to her tally. If Javani ever saw that Mawn again, she'd give her exactly what she deserved . . .

'But the important thing here, you dopes, you clots, is that we were ahead of you and your rotten bunch every step of the way. You have done nothing to surprise us, nothing we weren't expecting. It's a shame you won't see it, the big finish. You see the key to ratting is purging the nest, and when we get to Kilale—'

Javani let fly with the rope. It sailed from her hand, arcing across the ruined rampart, over Gurbun, and wrapped around his extended arm with a whispering snap.

'Gotcha!' Javani hauled on the rope, and Gurbun dropped the seal.

It fell in slow motion, twisting in the air, its chain streaming out behind it, lit on every side by pulses of flame, cast dark by thunderous smoke. It turned, lazy in rotation, then was gone from sight, gone forever.

Javani stared, open-mouthed, the rope at her feet and her hands at her head. 'No! Why did you—'

'I warned you, you—'

Manatas, who had used the opportunity to limp closer, punched Gurbun with the sabre's hilt in the side of the head. The Second Chairman dropped to the tortured wood without a word, the rope still wrapped around his arm.

Javani dashed to the captain's side. 'Do you see it? Where did it fall?'

They both peered over the twisted battlement, wafting and wheezing at the caustic smoke that billowed over them.

'I see it! It's there! It's caught on the . . . the . . . thing.'

The seal dangled, snagged on the projecting prow of the giant Guild shield sculpted onto the train's nose. It was too far to reach, but maybe, just maybe . . .

'Quick, help me with the rope.'

'I apologise for my lack of assistance in this regard,' the captain murmured as they unwound her grappling rope from the groggy Chairman, 'but I fear I must devote some energies towards the prevention of further blood loss.'

'Yep, sure, whatever you need.' Javani's eye was on the seal and only the seal, fixed on its bobbing, jumping form through the scuds and clumps of black smoke. 'I can . . . I need the angle, if I can just . . .'

Manatas put his good hand on her shoulder. 'Uh, Javani.' He nodded ahead, through the streaming pillars of filth, to what lay before them. 'We are about out of time.'

'Oh, shit,' said Javani.

'Language,' said Inaï Manatas.

Siavash drew himself up, the rails beneath him now juddering quite considerably. Unease was manifesting around them now, several diners already likewise on their feet and looking to move away, and a growing susurrus from the galleries and watch-stations. Slowly, but with increasing certainty, people were beginning to move away from the train yard and its magnificent canopies.

'The laws of the protectorate are not so easily discounted,' Siavash said grandly, mentally appending a footnote concerning the trade of certain rare reagents and mechanical components that really wouldn't do anyone any harm in the right hands, where the discretion of the merchant in question was unimpeachable. 'We are all bound by society's compact.'

Kusan remained sitting, his bright robes spread around him like the petals of a glistening flower, his smile thick and oily. 'The laws of the protectorate are what the senate dictate, and come the imminent conclave, when *Exalted Matil*,' he spat the name, 'announces her withdrawal from stewardship of the senate, our generous benefactors the Chartered Miners' Guild of Serica,' he spread his hands around him, taking in the pavilions, the gantries, the outer port and plains, 'will propose a candidate to replace her. A moderniser, with one eye on the future and our relationship with our most prosperous trading partners.' His gesture swung towards the black vessels docked in the bay: the Iokara, who were very relaxed about the flesh trade. 'The Guild knows who funds it, and it will not forget.'

Again came the gleaming smile, wet and bright and still adorned with apricot flesh. 'The laws of men are nothing to the law of the markets, and the former will align to the latter. This is your chance, master merchant: for a modest buy-in, this very day, you may guarantee your share of the glorious future to come, and all the new experiences a young man could desire. What do you say?'

Siavash stared, dumbfounded, but before he could formulate a reply, the screaming began.

FIFTY

Kilale Port spread before them, vast and gleaming beneath the midday sun, the outlying farms and forts already flashing by, the emerald sea beyond the distant wharves and cranes rich and sparkling. The port was enormous, far bigger than she'd expected, stretching across the curled horizon in each direction, encircling a bay thick with masts and jostling vessels. The path of the rails ran straight into its heart, twinned black lines shimmering through haze towards boxy assemblies, scaffolds and gantries decked in bright flashes of colour, at its end a large domed construction of pale stone, perhaps once a grain store, that housed whatever remained of its screaming machinery. It was hard to be certain through the sweltering air, but there seemed to be objects and people at the track's end, square in its path. The train had begun to produce a dreadful rhythmic grinding noise.

'Quick, hold my legs, maybe I can—'

'Javani, I lack both the strength and the inclination – we must depart this situation, post-haste.'

Javani stretched, her eyes streaming, the seal bobbing through smoke and blistering heat. It was too far, the angle was too great, there was no way to reach it, not without roping herself and climbing down. The train's shake had become so violent that it wasn't hard to imagine being thrown sideways into flames or beneath wheels.

'How long do you think we have?'

'I cannot say.' Manatas grunted as he pulled himself upright beside her. He was favouring one leg and a torn-off sleeve served as a bandage around his arm. 'Enough time to descend, but beyond that I cannot say. Our velocity is substantial.'

Javani jumped as the groggy form of Gurbun staggered up on her other side. He was bleeding freely from the blow to his temple, the fresh red mixing with the thousand other shades of filth that marred his once glorious robes. Her bolt still stuck from his shoulder, and one of his legs was near black with a venous flood.

He ignored her, woozily placing both hands, only one of which was bandaged, on the sizzling iron of the battlement, and gazed dully out at the onrushing port.

'Huh. Early. Not supposed to be there until nearer sundown.' He shook his head, showering Javani with beads of cranial matter. 'Party won't be ready yet.'

Javani began to edge away from him, attempting to wipe at her face without attracting his attention.

'Going a . . . touch fast.' He leaned forward, over the crenellations, indifferent to the steam rising from his hands. 'Should be . . . slowing down.'

Javani cast another look towards the seal's resting place, then looked to Manatas. The captain seemed worn through, paled by blood loss and exertion, and a sudden memory of a burning gambling boat and his part in her escape came galloping to the forefront of her mind.

'When we get there . . .' Gurbun continued idly, '. . . when we get there, we're going to string you fuckers from a flagpole. There's stages, and performers, and they'll roar from the cheap seats, the dung-brained mass. Love a flaying, they do.' He turned his gore-slick face towards her. 'So do I.'

'Just try it.' The trail-knife was in Javani's hand already, its blade gleaming firelit and trained upon his filthy chest. 'Think I won't? You cut my neck, you bastard. I'll return the favour in a heartbeat.'

She realised as she said it that she really, really, didn't want to, although if she was perfectly honest, she'd have been completely at home with someone else doing it.

'You think you can kill me?' His eyes were wild and bloodshot, whites yellowed in the light, but at least he came no closer. 'I am the Guild. The Guild is me. And the Guild is eternal! You can't kill me, any more than you can kill a mountain, than you can kill the sea. You hear that, you diseased little oaf? Eternal!'

Beneath them, the train groaned and rocked, then one side dropped with a grinding clang, throwing them all sideways. Towers were rushing by now, arching structures of poles and planks, curving over the body of the train. Javani guessed they had something to do with its function, loading or unloading or some form of stabiliser, she didn't care. The most recent one whipped past them at great speed, barely a foot above their heads.

'Javani—' Manatas's hand was at her shoulder, sweat gleaming from his rictus-warped face. The man was suppressing a great deal of discomfort. In the dancing, flame-lit smoke behind him, for a moment she thought she saw Ree's face, shaped by cloud. It looked disapproving.

'Fuck it,' Javani muttered, and grabbed the captain's arm. 'We're leaving.' She gave one last, disconsolate look towards where the seal had landed. 'I'll see you again before long,' she whispered.

The train groaned again, and lurched further to the right. Gurbun staggered away from Javani as she clung to Manatas, who had dug his sword into the ruined wood of the rampart floor in an attempt to stay upright.

'Where do you think you're going?' Gurbun roared. The crossbow was sliding along the angled deck, and in two steps he could claim it. Javani searched around them in desperation. They'd have to pass Gurbun to reach the stairs, assuming they could cover the distance without being thrown through the blasted gap to the floor below. She turned back towards the front, and gasped an involuntary breath of acrid fug.

The port filled the horizon, buildings already at their sides. The train ploughed on, belching smoke and showering flame and hot iron, but even now she could see where the Iron Road reached its end. The way was packed with tables and benches, overlooked by galleries and wooden structures strung with festival hangings, and there were *people* everywhere and at last, very clearly, she could hear the screams.

'Well this isn't good . . .'

'I asked you a question, rodent.' Gurbun was upright, and he'd found the crossbow. His monstrous, bloodied grin was a sight to behold.

Another arching tower whipped by overhead to her left, then the train smashed through the body of the next. Its spars collapsed, and a huge, dropping beam flew across the sloping fortress-top, clipping Gurbun and spinning him around. The snap of his arm would stay with Javani a long time.

More towers and structures ahead. The impact had slowed them, but even if they hit every one of them they'd still be careering into the building at the tracks' end at a terrible pace. And between them and the building, there seemed to be an awful lot of people.

'Javani . . .' Manatas was fading, sliding from her grip.

'No you don't, captain.' She kept her eye fixed on the projecting gallery ahead, overlooking the tracks, its occupants sensibly fled. 'Get your arms around me and hold on tight.'

The knife was stowed, the rope back in hand, ringed thrice around them and cinched. She began to swing.

Here we go, this is it, Javani. Don't fuck it up. Don't fuck it up.

Gurbun was moving, crawling across the slanted floor. She tried to ignore him, even though he had the crossbow in his bloodied grip. 'I said . . . where . . . do you think . . .'

Feel the weight in your hands, feel the flex, the heft.

'. . . you're . . .' The weapon was pointing at them now, propped on the corpse of the big guard; she could sense it in her peripheral vision.

Lift and swing, swirl and sway. Get the rhythm, get the pace . . .

'. . . going!'

And release—

'By the gods!' Siavash had found his feet at last, the judder of the platform be damned. 'The conveyance, the conveyance arrives!'

At last his dining companion appeared to register the panic around them, the quiver of the ground beneath them, the urgent clinking of their tableware.

'The consignment is premature by hours.' Somehow he conspired to smirk. 'Such transit, such alacrity . . .'

'It is on fire!'

The gleaming smirk faded, if only a touch. 'Perhaps an effect of the speed of their passage . . . To travel faster than a galloping horse, across such terrain, perhaps the air itself would combust from the force of the traversal . . .'

The gallery around them had emptied itself, the other diners surging up from their generous cushions and waddling away as fast as their engorged bellies would allow. Siavash looked for dear Ulfat, last seen pushed to the perimeter by now bolting Guild personnel.

'Ulfat? Ulfat? Oh, gods have mercy, the children!'

There they sat, their feeble songs a memory, yet still trapped in the barred-over cart, parked square over the tracks. Beyond them, blurred by haze and distance but growing ever larger at a pace that terrified him, came the head of the arriving vehicle, a vast fist of twisted iron, blackened and flaming, throwing spark and flame like a demon of the earth. It charged down the slope towards the port, smashing towers and gantries in its inexorable, furious path. Siavash had never in his life seen something with such murderous and infernal intent, and he was the first to admit he'd seen more of life's ghastliness than he'd readily have preferred.

'It will slow.' Kusan was still eating, his mouth half full and eyes only on the shuddering dishes before him. 'There are devices to impede and retard, and obstacles at the track's extreme. Such fluster over trifles.'

Siavash watched the ravening beast smash a gantry clean from sight.

'It will not slow. Quickly, Kusan, you must help me. The children are trapped over there, and they are in its path.'

'And?' The man did not even look up.

'Kusan, they will be crushed! Have you no . . . no . . .'

The slaver cocked his gaze upwards to meet Siavash's imploring stare. 'None.' He popped another date in his already congested maw. 'Should they be lost, it is merely the advancement of a schedule already set.'

'Gods have mercy upon you, Kusan,' Siavash snapped, and set off towards the cart with the boldest strides he could muster on the shaking platform. Laughing now, Kusan went to rise, then flopped back upon his cushion.

'Frater, attend. One's robe, the most hapless occurrence. It lies snagged beneath.'

'Then remove it, and lend a hand!'

The other man smiled on, but the mirth was leaking from his eyes. 'One regrets that one cannot – without assistance of some form. These robes were—'

Siavash flashed his gaze to the pavilion's edge, still devoid of his attendant, then back to the cart, and the growing dark and burning mass of the onrushing train. It was moments away. 'Cut yourself free, then, I cannot delay!' He set off once more at some speed for a man who was not a natural athlete, and wearing a particularly fine outfit he was still hoping not to spoil. He'd never be able to shift the cart, but the bars had a gate, and the gate had hinges, perhaps if some of the children helped, then could all—

'Master Sarosh! Come back! Please! I'll reduce your buy-in, double your share. Sarosh!'

Anxious eyes met his as he reached the cart. 'Good day, urchins,' he said, suddenly aware he was not accustomed to greeting anyone who was not a potential customer. 'I'm going to push this up, and I would be most grateful for any assistance you cared to lend.'

'Sarosh! Sarosh! You snivelling wretch, you worthless shit bucket. The Brotherhood will cut out your tongue and sell your family to the savages across the water. Sarosh! Come back this instant or face the consequences!'

The entire cart was rattling at the train's murderous approach. He could see it now, from the corner of his eye, hear the feral, howling grind of its arrival, feel the rush of pulsing heat it pushed before it. Sweat flooding him, Siavash strained, some of the children mimicking his actions, then another pair of hands appeared next to his own.

'Ulfat, my dear, dear friend, what a joy to see you.'

'Sorry I'm late, master, I was detained at the perimeter.'

The hinges eased, then popped, and suddenly the way was open. 'Quickly now,' Siavash urged, bodily heaving the half-starved little bodies onto the platform one at a time. Ulfat steered them down and away, behind a building they hoped would provide safety.

The final child freed, Siavash turned to flee, gasping and sweated through. As he dragged himself to the juddering platform's edge, the heat and terrible cacophony at his back, his gaze landed one more time on the isolated form of Kusan, struggling and writhing at the abandoned luncheon table, dark-faced and weeping.

'Sarosh!' the man called once more. 'No buy-in, you can have my share. You can have everyone's. Take my estate, it's yours. Sarosh, please. I'll give you everything!'

'I want nothing from you,' Siavash replied, and leapt from the platform.

Ree lay in darkness, with incredible thirst and hammering heart. She burned with shame and loss and heartbreak.

Everything she knew was a lie, and the lie was her own. Her parents never sold her. She sold herself. She walked willingly into the lair of that monster, that indescribable *fuck*, and she did it against the wishes of those who cared most for her. And why? Because she was bored. Because she was impatient. Because she felt . . . smothered.

My parents wanted to protect me, and I reacted with insanity.

The kid. The pattern was repeating. Just like her own parents, she'd tried to keep her child from harm, from risk, from even the *potential* of suffering. She'd kept her from the harsh reality of her life, squirrelled away, safe from danger. Safe from connection. Safe from attention.

I have driven her away.

But Javani could not be contained. And now she was loose, and likely to do something irredeemably stupid. Just as Ree herself had done.

She had repeated all her parents' mistakes, and made entirely new ones of her own.

If I was wrong about this, what else have I been wrong about?

She had to talk to the kid. They had to reconcile, before it was too late. Before nothing could be repaired. Before the kid walked into the lair of her own monster.

Where was she? And where was the kid? Ree was fully awake now, jolted by her thoughts, wide-eyed and sweating.

And with her growing awareness came the knowledge that she was not alone.

FIFTY-ONE

Siavash felt the impacts as much as witnessed them. The train, or what remained of it, snarled through the last of the tracks on its terminal path towards the blocky building that housed whatever miracle machinery had kept the thing moving. One by one its axles failed, its mangled nose dipping, throwing sparks in a great scorching shower either side and a blizzard of oily black smoke. Siavash cowered between the thick posts of the pavilion, its bright canvas ripped away, his hands pressed to his ears to blot out the shriek of agonised metal, his eyes mere slits from the punishing glare. He was all too aware there was a chance his eyebrows were already gone.

At last, it tipped, flopping onto its side like a dying beast, the wagons that tailed it thrown out in a spasming wave. With a bowel-stripping groan that lasted longer than Siavash thought he could ever bear, the blasted, burning assembly finally came to a crumpling rest, crushed against the ruined walls of the machine house. Flames licked along its broken, smoking length, metal hissed and pinged, and one by one the pillars of the gallery dropped away and the entire wooden structure collapsed on top of it.

Siavash counted to ten, then added another ten to be safe, then an extra five for insurance, and removed his hands from his ears. He sat up slowly, eyes still pressed tight, one arm over his mouth as choking fumes roiled over him, along with drifting waves of pulverised wood and stone. Everything was oddly quiet, compared to the ghastly tumult of a few moments ago at least. He was dimly aware of bells and shouts and the general sounds he associated with catastrophe at the edge of his hearing, but at that very moment, he seemed to be the only living thing within a hundred strides of what remained of the Iron Road.

He walked slowly through wafting smoke and splintered wood, sleeve tight against his nose and mouth, feeling his way. Ulfat and the children were back and to the left somewhere, he thought. His foot squelched through an upturned pewter dish of mousse, until that moment miraculously undamaged, and he gave a rueful sigh. There, ahead, something glinting in the blackening mire. Something out of place.

Siavash approached cautiously, and bent to inspect his find, half buried as it was in rubble and ruin: a single golden tooth, the little square of apricot at its edge unfathomably preserved.

He shuddered, and then he saw what was beside it.

'Captain Manatas?'
'Hm?'
'You still with me?'
'Mm-hm.'
'You're bleeding on me, captain. That's not polite.'
'My most . . . sincere . . . apologies . . . I shall . . . endeavour . . . to cease . . . forthwith.'

Javani took the deepest breath her situation would allow. Her arms were burning, her ribs and pelvis crushed by the rope, and she was desperately worried about the captain, who was beginning to sag. They dangled on her rope from a projecting spar of one of the gantries that had lined the Iron Road on its way into the guts of the port. Beneath them lay devastation and smoking ruin, the tracks warped or torn clear, the earth churned and scarred. Curtains of black smoke rose from ahead, where somewhere, by the sound of things at least, the mutilated train had come to rest. Now the crashing was over, they were surrounded by the unsettling groans of heavy, damaged things under strain reaching the fringes of their tolerance.

'I'm going to start lowering us down now. We might go a bit fast, 'cos, well, to be honest, you're a lot heavier than I am, and you're not really pulling your weight.'

'Mm . . . sorry.'

They were at least tightly bound, the rope looped around waists and thighs, but there were limits. One of her legs was numb already. And she did not like the noises coming from the listing stilted gallery that peeped through the noxious fug.

'Here we go . . .'

A pillar gave, and the gallery shifted, then one corner dropped. One by one the pillars beneath it fell, crunching towards Javani and their gantry with ponderous inevitability.

'Going to go a bit faster . . .'

Pillar fell against pillar fell against pillar, each pitching into the next, the pace of the staggered collapse increasing. The grinding thumps grew in volume and frequency as Javani spooled with frantic urgency, hand over hand, one eye on the twisted hemp that rasped her palms, the other on the projecting spar from which they dangled. It had begun to quiver. A fall from their starting point would likely break her legs, and almost certainly kill the captain. Every hand-span of rope she played out brought them a fraction closer to the safety of the ground.

Assuming all the collapsing crap didn't land on them.

Crash, crash, crash-crash-crash-crashcrashcrashcrash—

'Captain, brace yourself, and get ready to roll.'

As the pillars hit their gantry, Javani let go.

'I cannot say . . . I cared for our landing.'

Javani looked back at the ruin of the timber edifice that had lined the tracks. Waves of dust rose from the rubble, mingling with the drifting mire, blotting the sun. 'Could have had it far worse, believe me. Now let's take a look at you.'

She tore the remaining sleeve from her shirt and bound the wound to the captain's leg, then stood, puzzled. Blood was still coming from somewhere, bright spots vivid on her clouded fingers.

'Captain, are you injured somewhere else?'

He was half propped up now, his colour a touch better with the immediate danger of exsanguination abated, and the constricting rope cut free from his nethers. 'I do not believe so. I am very sorry about your shirt.'

'You can buy me a new one.' She ran her hands through her filthy hair, and stopped. One of them had hit something sticky. Then it all rushed back to her: Gurbun, prone on the deck of the shifting turret, the crossbow propped on his murdered guard, the twang as they leapt clear, a rush by her ear, a lingering sting . . .

'That bastard! That absolute bastard! He shot my ear!'

She touched a tentative finger to the wound and recoiled, the very notion of damage to it appalling. 'How bad is it, captain?'

He cracked a grin, teeth white against the coating filth. 'Your survival is far from imperilled, but at last we are twins.' He touched a finger to his own ragged ear, missing a chunk from its upper half, and Javani shrieked.

His laugh was one step above a wheeze. 'I jest, I tease, my apologies once more. You are barely nicked. Keep your curls long and none will ever be the wiser.'

'Easy for you to say,' she harrumphed. 'I cannot believe that rotten bastard shot me.'

'I believe you shot him first.'

'That was with a hand-bow! And you shot him before that.'

Manatas coughed. 'I fear perhaps we are becoming bogged in matters academic. The gentleman in question is unlikely to trouble us again, irrespective of the precise order of our actions.'

'Yeah.' She sniffed, then snorted filthy air from her nose, wafted a hand. 'Yeah. He was riding that disaster all the way to the end.' Things had cleared, if only a little, and the light of small fires flagged a nervous path towards where the train-head had come to rest.

'Wait here,' she said, starting over the broken ground towards it.

'Wha— Javani!'

'I'll be right back. Don't go anywhere!'

It was an odd thing to find, there amongst the wreckage, Siavash thought, trying to put the lone tooth from his mind. A thick disc of metal, milled at the edges, still gleaming beneath the murk. It was attached to a chain, its links swallowed by charred beams and ash, and he poked it with a toe of his ruined shoes. Toasty, but not scalding. With a cautious hand, he bent to retrieve it.

The disc was fist-sized, heavy, warm to his touch, its edges pleasingly fashioned. A bas-relief occupied the upper side, smeared and gummed with grime, but it had the look of something official. Siavash pulled gently on the disc, easing its chain from the rubble link by link, wondering exactly what the item was, and what it was doing there. He was aware of shouts and calls at his periphery; the feeling that he was alone in this ruined world ebbed away. People were entering the train yard, dim shadows in the drifting murk.

The chain snagged, so he gave it a more forceful tug. The chain came a little more, so he pulled harder.

The chain lurched backwards into the debris, almost yanking the disc from his hand. Siavash gasped, took disc and chain in a firm two-handed grip, set his feet, and hauled.

The chain strung taut for an unbearable moment, then at last it gave, and Siavash thumped backwards onto the ruined ground with a cry, the disc and its chain free at last. He sat, panting, wondering at the object in his hands, its likely significance, and more likely owner, when the rubble in front of him began to shift.

Siavash froze.

The rubble erupted, and *something* emerged from within it. Siavash screamed.

Javani heard the shriek as she jogged, high-pitched, a woman or child in distress, and just the other side of the tumble of detritus to her right. She gripped her knife tight and ran towards it.

FIFTY-TWO

Siavash quailed before the apparition. It lurched like a creature of the seventh hell, bloodied and blackened, spikes and protrusions jutting from it, lit by infernal flame and wreathed in smoke, its claws grasping as it staggered towards him, yellowed eyes wild, bloody froth at its mouth. He shrieked again, scuttling backwards on his heels and elbows, bumping over wreckage, the disc grasped between sweaty fingers.

Then there were people around him, boots and legs and hands reaching beneath his arms and lifting him to his feet. Guild troopers, at last, combing over the wreckage, their mail and breastplates gradually losing their lustre as dust clagged. Two of them guided him backwards, their gauntlets at his armpits, while another one stepped in front and belted the apparition with the butt of a spear, sending it crashing sideways into the rubble.

He turned his head from side to side, burbling his thanks, but a moment's glance told him these were hard, true mining types, their features set, their faces scarred, not like the smooth-cheeked prancers he'd seen in gleaming Guild gear at so many functions in the past. The man and woman who had righted him each wore a scarlet sash on one arm, which also struck him as novel, but all he really cared about was the creature from the wreckage, and the fact it was now prone, hissing, snarling and writhing, but a safe distance from him.

A filthy young woman came haring over the ruin of the train, scrambling over twisted metal and blackened timber, then came up short at the scene before her. Her eyes fixed on the creature, at bay beneath the point of the Guild man's spear, then on Siavash, flanked as he was, then on the disc in his hands. The eyes widened, her mouth forming a little O, and Siavash swallowed as she slowly unsheathed a long-bladed knife.

A rumble of footsteps forestalled her, a sudden rush of breastplate-clad troopers into the crash site, ringing Siavash, the young woman, and the hell-creature. Each wore a scarlet sash at their arm, which Siavash now considered rather fetching. He wondered if he had any clothes of that particular shade, which he was sure would offset his eyes. He resolved to have Ulfat—

Ulfat. He'd seen nothing of his dear attendant since the crash, or the children left in his care. Not far from where he stood lay the shattered ruin of a familiar-looking cartwheel. Siavash swallowed again.

The line of guards to Siavash's right parted, and a new figure walked through, her strides coming easy over the spread of devastation. She was tall, her silver hair close-cropped to her scalp, her skin like old leather. She came to a stop on a fallen heap of timber, surveying the scene with a jaundiced eye, scarred lips twisted in distaste.

'Well,' she said after a moment, as flames sputtered in the background and swirls of dust ebbed around them, 'this is a fucking disaster.'

Her gaze settled on Siavash, who felt immediately exposed. One of her eyes had a milky cast to it, but it did nothing to lessen the force of her stare. Her attention shifted to the disc still tight in his soot-slick grip, and the scarred lips twitched minutely upwards.

'Not all bad news, though, it seems. Commander!'

The burly trooper who'd struck the creature down with the spear butt turned and advanced on Siavash. The man moved with a pronounced limp up the slope, his face heavily bearded beneath his helmet, thick with silver, and a faded smudge on his cheek that might once have been a mark of conviction. There was something ever so familiar about him.

'I'll be taking that,' he said to Siavash, who was staring at him with lowered brows, trying to place the man. He prided himself on never forgetting a client or customer, but this one was nagging at him. Someone from his trips north, up the mining road?

'The seal, if it please you,' the trooper said, extending a patient hand. The hand was missing its lower two fingers.

'Have we met, by any chance?'

The bearded man would not meet his eye. 'Couldn't say, master merchant. The seal, if it please you.'

'Yes, yes, by all means.' Siavash at last relaxed his death grip on the metal disc, feeling a little lighter for returning it to what were presumably its rightful keepers.

'Good.' The silver-haired woman sniffed. 'Now, the other matter.' She gestured towards the young woman who still stood, brace-legged and panting, on the twisted summit of the fallen train. Her narrowed eyes were fixed on the disc, brows tight, and Siavash did not like the way she held her knife or the fixed set of her jaw. There was something achingly familiar about her, too, now he thought about it.

'It seems we have a few leftover insurrectionists to sweep up, commander. I understand another is not far from here, the rest left scattered along the plain. Take these two into custody, and set up hunting parties for the others. When the Chairman returns, he will no doubt be delighted to combine the renewal ceremonies with a very *official* end to our little period of unrest.' She brushed settling flakes from her shoulder. 'Although perhaps we will shift the venue to somewhere a little less . . . untidy.'

Before the bearded man could reply, the hell-creature lurched to its feet with a roar, sending Siavash back onto his backside. It produced a horrendous sound, an animal howl, bitten and breathy, and after a moment Siavash realised it was laughing.

'You like that, vermin?' it bellowed, astonishing Siavash with its powers of speech. 'You maggots, you filth. The best you had, your guts and blood, and it's nothing. You're nothing. You'll be tasting your spleens come sunset, worms. You cannot kill the Guild, the Guild is eternal.' It raised one crimson arm in triumph. 'Eternal!'

'Trooper,' said the bearded man to the guard beside Siavash. 'Restrain the prisoner.'

The creature had begun to caper, shedding a black and gory crust. 'You tried to cut me, you tried to shoot me, but I'll be dancing on your graves—'

The Guild trooper marched over to the creature and struck it across the face with a mailed gauntlet. It dropped with a howl, and before it could scrabble away, the trooper hauled its broken arms around its back and lashed them together with a leather thong. It bucked and kicked, squealing and shrieking, and was swatted again for its trouble.

The bearded man ambled up to the creature as it snarled and spat, the trooper on its back, and advised it to hush.

'You cretinous goon!' it hissed. 'Do you know who I am?'

'No,' the bearded man replied with an affable smile. 'Nobody does.' He looked up. 'Stick him in the cells with the others.'

The gag went over the creature's mouth before it could speak again, then it was dragged, broken body thumping over every jut and lump, its anguished screeches muffled to mere dwindling whimpers.

The silver-haired woman was staring at the bearded man with a suddenly guarded look, lips pressed together. 'Commander . . .' she said in a voice that lacked its previous conviction.

'Mistress Rahdat.'

'Perhaps you had best pass me the seal, while you collect the . . . other prisoner.' She gestured towards where the young woman remained, perched on the ruin of the overturned train, except now she was sitting, her legs dangling over the side. She was sitting, and she was grinning.

The hairs stood up on Siavash's arms, and he had not the first idea why.

'I'm afraid I must politely decline, Mistress Rahdat,' the bearded man replied, folding thick arms across his beefy chest, his scarlet armband shimmering as the sun found a path through the miasma of the crash.

'Commander, you serve the Guild. What is this? Mutiny?'

'Nothing of the sort, Mistress Rahdat.' The bearded man squinted upwards, scrunching the mark on his cheek. 'See, as of, let's say for the sake of argument, an hour ago, the charter of said Guild expired, and with it its authority, and the monopoly on many things, among them labour organisations. We stand before you as the representatives of a new workers' collective: the Miners' Co-operative of the Northern Expanse, incorporating Eastern United Miners.'

Rahdat's mouth hung open. 'You cannot be serious. The Guild's charter doesn't expire until . . . It will be renewed within hours, just as soon as . . . as soon as . . .'

The former commander lifted the metal disc to his eye, dangling it on its chain, watching it turn in the drifting sunlight. 'Indeed, Mistress Rahdat.'

Rahdat's features twisted in a vicious snarl. 'You won't get away with this, there are a thousand men who wear the stamp of the Guild on their chest in this port alone, and—'

'Seem mighty convinced of their loyalty, there. Perhaps you'd like to see some familiar faces in the cells, too. Take her away, boys.'

Troopers flocked to the silver-haired woman, lifting her from her feet as she struggled and kicked. 'Go quietly, or go unconsciously, Mistress Rahdat,' the former commander called, and a moment later she took a hefty blow to the head. Troopers carried her away and out of sight in very short order.

'Nobody ever listens to me,' sighed the bearded man, and set off towards the wreck of the train with his rolling limp.

'Uh, what about me?' called Siavash, half sitting as he was, and completely unmoored. 'What should I do?'

The bearded man barely turned his head. 'Might want to think about leaving the immediate vicinity, master merchant. Things are apt to get a little . . . *hectic*. But the thanks of us all for your service today.'

Siavash stood, uncertain and increasingly alone, and dusted himself down. 'Well,' he said to himself, as he assessed the direction of the harbour, 'that was stimulating.'

He set off on unsteady legs, wincing at every step, and wondering if perhaps excitement and adventure were not, in fact, his heart's desire, after all.

FIFTY-THREE

Javani slid down, carefully, mindful of sharp edges and still smoking metal, her knife returned to its sheath and an enormous grin on her face.

Movos Guvuli stood with his arms folded across his chest, the Great Seal of Arowan dangling from his two-fingered fist, and a look of deep suspicion carved into his bushy features. Javani landed a stride in front of him, a little wobblier than she'd hoped, and pushed her aching body upright once more.

'Guvuli.' She nodded to him.

'Urchin. This nonsense your doing?'

'The, uh, train, and stuff? Yeah, maybe.'

'Maybe.'

They regarded each other for a few breaths, appraising.

'You got my letter then,' Javani said.

'And you got mine.'

She nodded again, fighting to keep the grin from taking over her face.

'You got taller, I see,' he said.

'Yeah, so I hear. You got older.'

He ran a hand through his beard, which was a good deal more silvery than on their last acquaintance. 'Only on the outside.'

'Well, Guvuli, you finally robbed the Guild.'

He cracked half a smile. 'Looks like we both did.'

'Better late than never, right?'

A hawk cried somewhere overhead, lost in the drifting murk.

'So . . .' She reached out a tentative hand. 'Can I have it?'

He didn't move. 'Why is it you want this thing?'

'So they don't have it.'

'They already do not have it.'

'Yeah, but . . .'

They stared at each other a moment longer, then Guvuli tossed the Great Seal of Arowan into the air, and she snatched it cleanly, to her inward delight.

'May it bring you luck.'

'I reckon it will.'

'And once again, urchin, you are making off with my haul.' He wasn't smiling when he said it, but his eyes twinkled.

A trooper was approaching over the devastation, one wearing a scarlet armband, and waving for the commander's attention. 'Duty calls,' he said, acknowledging the approach.

'What will you do? Are you going to . . . take over?'

He paused, half-turned. 'While we have a number of interested chapters who wish to join our collective, we'll be looking to keep things small and local, I believe. Empowered and self-organising groups anywhere there is mining, or mining trade. No more monopolies. No more rent-seeking and extraction.'

'Sounds good,' Javani said, following maybe half of the words and guessing at the rest. 'What about . . . What will you do with Gurbun, Rahdat and the others?'

'Well, Mistress Rahdat once made me a generous offer, so I'll extend the same courtesy. She's a pragmatic woman, I'm sure she'll come around. Aside from that, well, you can't have an insurrection on your doorstep. If those in our custody won't swear to the collective, they'll be seeking new opportunities . . . overseas.'

'And Gurbun?'

'Who?'

'The, uh, Second Chairman. The man you took away.'

Guvuli winked. 'Who?'

The trooper was hovering to one side now, looking impatient, and Guvuli waved an acknowledging hand. 'Yes, Nilam, I am coming. See you, urchin.'

'See you, Guvuli. And, you know . . . thanks.'

The harbour was in uproar, and Siavash wasn't the least surprised. The main thoroughfares were jammed with abandoned wagons and carts, their drivers fled in the excitement of the train's premature arrival, the draft animals turned or spooked, the result total seizure. Boats had attempted to flee the dock en masse, jumbling spars and stays and snagging on each other's rigging as puce-faced sailors screamed abuse at each other from abutting rails. The denizens of the port ran hither, then thither, the footways packed with alarmed but confused port dwellers and itinerant visitors who knew only that they needed to escape, but had no clear notion of to where or from what.

At least the fires of the impact hadn't spread, and the thick pall of filthy smoke that hung over the ruin of the train yard was steadily being whittled and dispersed by the stiff salt breeze from the dazzling sea. Siavash took a seat upon a whitewashed bollard at the harbour's edge, letting the world rush past him in every direction, and loosened what was left of his finest robe. The unfiltered sun beat down without mercy, the whistle of the breeze through the tears in his robe taking the edge from its fierce heat, if only just. Siavash was very sore, and very thirsty.

'No, no, fight them if you must – the messages must go without delay.'

Siavash blinked to realise he recognised the speaker – the obscenely wealthy man from the drinks reception, who'd cursed both Guild and the Mercantile Brotherhood while rubbing his hands at the profit to be made from the Iokara. He looked far less salubrious now, his robes almost as torn and dusty as Siavash's, and his face was flushed and dark from shouting. People clustered around him, a few with ponies or mules dragged behind, those Siavash took to be his staff.

'Clear a fucking path however you must,' the man bawled at his cringing personnel. 'We must get the news to every outpost, you hear me! Every moment wasted is money lost. The Guild is done, the markets are open, and it is every man for himself. Now go! Go, you bastards!'

The messengers struggled to disperse, elbowing their way through crowds, or in one case attempting to leap a mule over a stranded cart. Siavash applauded the attempt, if not the execution.

At last the man was alone with only his guards, and his eyes landed on Siavash. A smile broke out on his face, wild-eyed and wary-edged, sizing Siavash up as a rival predator in whatever this uncertain new world had to offer. 'Exciting times, eh?' the man called. 'The first movers are going to reap fortunes.' His trembling eyes dared Siavash to try moving ahead of him.

Siavash returned a polite, tired smile, and a nod of vague assent. The sea air was beginning to lift the stink of smoke and blood that seemed to coat him, although it was replacing it with the salty reek of fish guts, tar, and effluent, so it wasn't exactly a vast improvement. He pushed himself to his feet, mopped at his face and brow, and looked around. Things were thinning out, a little, some of the abandoned vehicles reclaimed by returning owners (or enterprising passers-by with an eye for opportunity), the footways no longer packed with the milling and the panicked.

Siavash began walking back towards the smoking wreckage of the train yard, offering the other merchant a polite nod as he passed him. The man had lost interest in Siavash, his attention now on the harbour's edge. 'The Iron Road is a ruin,' the man dictated to a scholarly-looking woman scribbling on a palimpsest at his elbow, 'but the Iokara may still—'

A flat, metallic noise – plangent notes like those from a discordant horn – played out over the harbour in an even, steady rhythm, silencing conversation and much of the activity. All eyes around Siavash leapt to the great black vessels that moored out in the bay, so Siavash stopped to join them. He saw movement on the decks of the ships, as great crimson sails unfurled and the equally crimson oar banks extended into the bay's clear water. The unsettling horns played out another signal, varied in pitch and rhythm, then as one the ships began to turn, slow at first, smoothly around until their anchors weighed and they were away into the vast north-east horizon.

'. . . and they've left,' finished the merchant with a heavy sigh.

'Scratch all that last section.' He took a breath, pulled himself straight. 'They'll be back,' he declared. 'But for now, we have more than enough opportunities to exploit. Fat times are ahead, my friends!'

Siavash walked on, feeling oddly dispirited, and still very thirsty. One of his fancy shoes was an utter ruin, hanging from his ankle, and he was having to be quite careful about where he walked, especially when so many nervous animals had been corralled for so long.

'There you are, master. We were about to come looking for you.'

Ulfat. Ulfat there, within a shaded nook, clear of traffic and excrement, and pressing a wrought silver cup of water into his hands. Blessed, divine Ulfat. Beyond him ranged a gaggle of smudged faces, eyes wide with wonder or anxiety or, for all he knew, hunger.

'Hello, Ulfat. Hello, children.'

Some of them waved back.

'Have a seat, master. You've had a tough day.'

Siavash obliged, resting on the stub of an old pillar. His legs still trembled. 'I have, haven't I?' He paused, gaze drifting to his clerk and the children beyond. 'Although I suspect that others may have had a harder time of it than me.'

He raised the cup to his lips, and found himself deeply relieved to see the children passing a pitcher around – a pitcher that he was fairly sure had been on the feasting table a little earlier – and drinking their fill. He sipped; the water tasted sweeter than nectar.

Siavash sat quietly for a moment, feeling the throb of his feet and the ache of his muscles, the pulsing heat of the strange little cut on his arm that he had no memory of acquiring, and looked out over the harbour. The merchant was still on the dockside, barking at anyone left within range, and he was not alone. Siavash spotted other figures, familiar faces from receptions and shindigs, engaged in urgent conference in huddles along the harbour, their brows furrowed, sweat gleaming upon them as if varnished. None of them looked happy, as such, and while many wore expressions of zealous excitement, the emotion he read in all of them was . . . fear.

Siavash looked back to his dear, loyal clerk, and the collection of increasingly giggly orphans crouched in the dust behind him.

'I think, Ulfat,' he said, 'it might be time for a change of scene.'

* * *

When Javani made her triumphant way back through the shattered ruin of the train yard, the seal tucked in her jacket and its chain wrapped around her wrist, composing a song in her head to her single-handed victory as she weaved through wafts of the smoking dust of pulverised constructions, she found Manatas was not where she'd left him.

Her panic was momentary. The captain came walking unsteadily out of the murk, one arm across his face wafting away particles, the other, blood-hued, hanging loose, thumb tucked into his belt like the very first time she saw him.

'Where did you go? You're not safe to move on your own.'

'I could say the same thing to you, young lady.'

'You rebandaged yourself?' She sniffed. 'Something wrong with the job I did?'

'It struck me that a clean dressing and some water might be prudent, once it became clear I could not catch you.' He leaned against a broken post with a barely suppressed wince. 'You have returned, though? You are whole?'

Javani nodded. 'I am.' She could barely keep the grin down, she could feel it fighting its way out, her mouth widening, her teeth desperate to put themselves on display.

The captain's eyes widened. 'Are you . . . did you . . . ?'

She whipped the seal from her jacket and let it dangle from its chain.

'I'll be fucked,' breathed Inaï Manatas, his mouth agape.

'Language,' said Javani.

'I had worried that our departure from the port might prove somewhat conspicuous,' the captain said as they reached the wreckage of the palisade that had once partitioned the Iron Road and its terminus from the fringes of Kilale, the plains a rolling sweep before them through the gap in the town wall, the fields and farms they'd flashed past at such velocity on their arrival now impossibly distant and sedate.

The roads around the port teemed with traffic, most of it travelling away, and much at high speed. Messengers, both liveried and impromptu, tore away down the trails, some in obvious competition with others. Whips and spurs were seeing liberal use, and not just on the mounts.

'I can see my fears were misplaced,' Manatas concluded.

'News travels fast.' Javani peered out through the haze, still smoke-washed, the land shimmering pale and golden beneath the summer sun. She was beginning to feel stiff, hot and tired, but she fairly thrummed with energy at the thought of what was now chained at her neck, never far from her straying fingers.

'Our rendezvous is lost to us, as is the reserve, and a mount of any kind will be hard to come by, but perhaps if there are . . .'

Javani raised a finger. 'Hang on for a moment.' She put the finger in her mouth, along with another, and blew.

'Was that supposed to be a—'

'Give me a *moment*!'

She blew again.

'Perhaps I might—?'

'Fine. Go on then.'

Manatas whistled, the piercing note echoing from the ravaged, deserted train yard, the broken chains and cables, the smashed towers and cranes. The sound came back in waves, bouncing from scorched and crumbling walls, from still smoking rubble, the collapsing tomb of the Iron Road.

They did not have to wait long.

'Would you perhaps care to explain to me,' Manatas said as he eased himself into the saddle of his newly received mount, 'how a groom-looking fellow wearing the colours of our mortal enemies, that which we swore to destroy, has presented us with not just the means of our escape, but supplies and fresh water besides?'

Javani mounted up alongside him, and placed a borrowed hat square upon her head. 'Some things you're best off not knowing.'

'Including how you came to be in possession of our quarry, in spite of everything?'

'Including that, captain.'

They set off at a gentle walk, the horses stepping carefully over debris, Javani mindful of the captain's injuries. The others should be waiting for them, somewhere along the route back to the camp, and there was no need to rush. They'd laid out a series of fallbacks and staging posts, spare mounts waiting, just in case, but now the danger had passed.

'For the last time,' Manatas sighed, 'you can call me Inaï.'

'You always say that.'

He chuckled, then winced. 'I will not give up.'

'Maybe I won't either.'

'You are your mother's daughter,' he said, then fell abruptly silent, their shared mirth dissipating at a stroke. Javani's thoughts turned inward, to Ree, her condition, her unknown future. It was so unfair. She finally had the one thing that proved she'd been right all along, that not only could she be trusted, that she could triumph where others failed, that she could be useful, that she could do great things . . .

And the thought that Ree might still be unconscious, or worse, brought a bitter twist to her gut. What's the point in doing great things if there's no one to impress?

What's the point of achieving greatness if there's no one to share your victory with?

Her gambit had succeeded. She'd planned for the worst. She'd won the day. And the one person, more than anyone else—

'Say, what do you suppose that fellow meant,' Manatas broke in, his own mouth downturned in thought, 'about ratting?'

'Hmm?'

'What was it he said? "The key to ratting is purging the nest"? Something of that ilk. The man was rambling.'

Images flashed through Javani's mind. Gurbun leering, his smug pronouncements, even as he was cornered and alone. *You think you've won?* Maral, leaping from the train.

Maral.

Ree.

Shit.

Her entire body went cold, her tongue tingling against her teeth. Sweat broke on her brow, at her back, her mouth dry and throat tight.

'Ma,' she gasped, and kicked her horse into a wild gallop.

'Who's there?' Ree wanted to cry, but she could not find her voice. Her throat was locked, parched and panicked. Her body was waking, properly now, her awareness of her surroundings growing as the fog lifted from her brain, as her limbs and digits began to respond once more to her commands. Her leg still hurt, which was fucking rich.

'I'm going to ask you some questions,' came a low, ragged voice from the dark, not one she'd ever heard before. 'And I'd better like the answers.'

Ree swallowed, hard, and levered herself slowly and painfully up against her bedding. The iron tang of blood was in the air.

'You and me both,' she whispered.

FIFTY-FOUR

Javani left Manatas in her wake somewhere along the way, and blazed past the first few possible rendezvous points without stopping, without even looking. The Guild horse was decent, but tall-shouldered and grain-fed, not a match on the plains ponies she was so accustomed to riding for hours at a stretch, and before long the poor thing was lathered and blowing, compelling her to slow her pace. She forced herself to make for a staging post to change mount, every moment of delay grinding her teeth to powder, and then change again when the next pony began to flag. The sun was low in the west, the shadows long and the wind cool at her back, by the time she reached the gully where they'd laid their camp, and she knew immediately that she was too late.

No guard at the gully's neck, no one on watch on the bluffs above, no challenge or signal at her approach. Just deathly silence, but for the roar and chirp of insects, the ringing screech of carrion birds, circling ever lower.

She slid from the exhausted horse, tied it beside the trough with trembling fingers, padding up the sandy earth with her knife back in her hand. Tracks ahead, many boot prints in the drifting dust, and more horses with them. Someone had come, more than one someone, but now there was no sign of anyone. She leaned against the warm rock, counting breaths, heart hammering in her chest, obliterating her attempt to listen for movement, for anything. At last she registered the slumped form of Stefanna, curled around a gory wound to her abdomen on the lookout shelf, runnels of blood striping the red rock black below her.

She risked another peek into the gully, and this time spotted Teg, face down and motionless, his bad ankle still bound and crutch beside him, halfway between the cold cookfire and the corral. Still nothing moved, not even the air. The gully was still as death.

Javani could wait no longer. She dashed into the camp, across it, making for the shelter at its end, ignoring the passage of footprints, the dark splotches and smears along the ground in her periphery, Teg's splayed corpse.

She screeched to a halt in the shelter's doorway, free hand gripping the bleached wood of the frame, pale-knuckled, her breath coming in shallow gasps. The interior was pitch, not a lamp or candle.

And all she could smell was blood.

'Ree?'

Javani tried to call, her throat locked, her voice stolen by fear. The knife dropped from her nerveless fingers, its dull thump muffled by the roar of her pulse in her ears. She took a step into the darkness, then another, until she was lost in it, the doorway a low, narrow rectangle of fading ruby light at her back. The smell of blood was overpowering, thick and rich with iron, and she reached out a trembling hand, then pulled it back, terrified of what she might find. Only then did she hear the flies.

'Ree?'

Her eyes were adjusting, the gloom gaining depth and shape as she stared into it. At last she could make out the shape of the pallet where Ree had lain. At last she could make out the outline of the figure on the pallet, beneath an undulating blanket of flies. And the hilt of the blade that jutted from its motionless form.

Javani took an involuntary step back, feeling as she did so the sticky pull of pooled blood at her feet, a shudder of involuntary horror rolling through her.

So. It was over, then.

She'd had a rehearsal of the moment already, when Ree had first been injured – the look on Anashe's face, the catch in her throat – and some part of her had been working in preparation for a repeat since: building a wall of emotional distance, stone by stone, idle thought by idle thought. It had been coming, one way or another; the only surprise here was the means.

Javani did not scream. She did not cry. She stood, feeling tremors ripple over her, feeling light and thirsty and very, very sick, but not sad. She wasn't sad.

'You fucking cow,' she growled at her mother's corpse. 'You fucking . . . awful . . . shit!'

She wailed and kicked at the pallet, stubbing her toe and redoubling her cry.

'How could you? How the fuck could you?'

Javani's fists were clenched, her face dark, sweat standing proud on her brow. 'For *years* I didn't know what I wanted, how I wanted my life to be. I thought I wanted excitement and adventure. I thought I wanted a quiet, normal existence, farming something easy somewhere beautiful. I thought I wanted to destroy the diggers and save the land. I thought I wanted to blaze my own trail into lands unknown. But you know what?' She jabbed a finger at the dripping body. 'You know what? I worked it out, at last. What I actually wanted was to have my mother in my life, and to be in hers in return. That's it! That was all!'

Her hands lifted, palms inward, fingers clawed in entreaty. 'You have been so *distant* in this mission, this quest to destroy the Guild. The *General*,' she spat. 'My only importance was my relation to you, but you wouldn't let me anywhere near anything. I thought if I showed you what I could do, how great I'd become, you'd finally let me be a part of things.' She wrestled the seal from the sweat bath of her jacket. 'I did it, Ma. I beat them. And I did it to impress you. I wanted . . . I wanted you to be proud of me . . .'

Now tears were in her eyes, furious unwanted tears. She was too enraged to cry, she knew it.

'I just wanted—' Her voice hitched. 'You had someone, lots of people, whether it's the captain or the rest of your crew, you weren't alone. And you're leaving me and I don't have anybody. I'm not ready. I'm not old enough to do all this on my own.' Her nose scrunched, her breath hot and urgent, fighting sobs. 'I'm *not* a kid any more. But . . . But I still . . .' Her lip was trembling uncontrollably, her tears brimming over. She forced her words out in a rush. 'I still need my ma, gods damn you. So you can't be dead, you hear me? You can't be dead because I haven't finished being angry with you, and I'm nowhere close to forgiving you, not yet. Hear me? You can't leave me!'

From behind her came a lung-wracking sob.

Javani turned, hot tears streaming down her cheeks, her nose stuffed and throat blocked.

Ree was propped in the doorway, and she was weeping.

'Ma?' Javani blinked, blinked again, rubbed at her eyes with gritty fists. 'Am I hallucinating?'

Ree fell against her, stick-thin and feather-light, tears rolling from her reddened eyes. 'Oh, kid. Oh, my baby, I am so sorry. I am so, so sorry.'

'You're alive? You're really alive?'

'I am. Not very, but I am.'

Javani took a deep, shuddering breath, wrapped her arms around her mother, buried her face in her hair, the tears coming hot and thick.

'You fucking cow!' she bawled.

Ree was too weak to make it to the top of the bluffs, so instead Javani half-carried her to the neck of the gully, shocked at how little she weighed, and settled her at the base of the cooling rock, looking out over the twisting briar and the great ruddy sweep of the plains beyond, watching the sun redden and bloat over the distant western peaks. She dashed back for hardtack and a waterskin, her own aches forgotten and in spite of Ree's feeble pleas not to leave her, then sat down beside the hollowed shell of her mother to watch the sunset.

'You're not dead, then.' Some part of her still wasn't sure. She kept reaching out to touch her mother, to reassure herself she was real. Ree seemed to be trying to do the same, one weak hand forever reaching for her, stroking or squeezing with what little strength she had.

'I'm not, kid.' Ree needed help to sip the water without soaking herself. 'I woke up.'

'Who was . . . the body on the bed? Where did all the blood come from?'

Ree took a long, wheezing breath. Her colour was improving, assisted by the ruby light of sunset, and although her clothes hung off her, the flint was returning to her eyes. Javani marvelled at her recovery, at her very life, clinging on after everything with impossible, bloody-minded stubbornness. The hot feeling lingered in Javani's chest, every breath like steam.

'I had some visitors. Invincible Goldhelms, by reputation.'

'Are you about to tell me you—'

'No. I had another visitor, who came late to the party. A friend of yours, I believe. It seems she knew the others.'

'. . . Maral?'

'Is that her name? We only met briefly before. You know, when she tried to murder me.'

'You spoke to her?'

'We had a little chat. She seems to think very highly of you.'

'What?'

'Anyway, upon her arrival, there were . . .' She tailed off, beckoned weakly for more water. '. . . Some disagreement ensued. The bodies were the eventual result.'

'Bodies, plural?'

Ree's eyebrow lifted, just a little. 'I know one was hidden beyond the bed, but are you telling me you didn't see the one on the floor? You kicked him at one point.'

'I thought that was the pallet.'

Ree made the effort to roll her eyes.

'Wait, how long were you standing there? Or leaning there?' Javani shot her mother an accusatory glare. 'Why didn't you say anything?'

The amusement faded from Ree's haggard face. 'I wanted to. It took me so much just to drag myself outside, then you came running in, I hadn't the strength to call out. By the time I made it back in, you were . . .' She swallowed. 'You were in full flow. It seemed . . . rude . . . to interrupt.'

She was gazing at Javani with wide and sunken eyes, suddenly full of unfamiliar doubt, of relief tempered with a lingering anxiety, her frail fingers clinging to the sleeve of Javani's jacket. She did not look herself.

'Well.' Javani folded her arms. Emotions still boiled within her, her own flood of relief and outrage and extraordinary surprise rolling back and forth in waves. Had Ree truly apologised to her back there? She couldn't trust her own memories in the moment, and it was hardly in character. 'I stand by everything I said.'

Ree nodded, slowly, her eyes shining in the sunset, her pale hair cast rose. 'You should.'

Javani sniffed. 'Oh yeah?'

'Yeah. I, uh . . . That is to say . . .'

'What?' Javani's breath was still too hot, her lungs feeling too big for her chest. 'What, Ma?'

'I . . . owe you an apology, kid. You were . . . right.'

Javani's jaw was trembling, just a shade, just enough to make her notice. 'About what?'

'About more than you weren't. About things where I should have known better.'

Javani stretched out her legs, mindful of keeping Ree supported, and leaned back against the rock. The hot feeling was moving down her chest, now a glow beneath her heart. 'Seems pretty . . . non-specific.'

Ree sipped more water. She didn't smell great, it was true, but she looked healthier with every hit from the skin.

'The last time we spoke . . . after the meeting with Exalted Matil . . .'

'I remember.'

'I was so angry . . .'

'I noticed.'

'. . . because I was embarrassed. Not of you, kid. Of myself. Of my . . . piss-poor parenting. To have shown myself up in front of that woman.' She tried to lift the skin, and Javani leaned across to help her. 'When I was your age . . .'

The hot feeling faded. 'Oh, here we go.'

'No. I mean. I . . .' Ree swallowed again. 'I may not have remembered things as clearly as I thought. When I was your age, I was already making choices, life-altering choices, and . . . they . . . weren't always good. But I should have respected you enough to help you, to support you, in making choices of your own, instead of shutting you out, shouting you down.' Ree gazed at her with her wide, sunken, tear-filled eyes. 'I'm so sorry.'

Javani wanted to quip, to deflect, but the words wouldn't come. The hot feeling rebloomed, the hairs standing up on her arms, tears pressing against her eyes, a feeling like she couldn't keep everything in, like she would burst. 'I just . . . I just wanted to make you proud of me,' she whispered.

Tears rolled down Ree's gaunt cheeks, racing down the hollows. 'That's backwards, kid. It shouldn't be on you to make me proud. It should be on a parent to make their child proud, and I've been failing you. I'm sorry. You deserved better.'

She lifted her arms, and Javani hugged her tight, as carefully as she could, feeling the press of her mother's bones against her as she cried.

'Go easy . . . Ma . . . you need that water.'

She released her grip and settled Ree back against the rock, the skin back in her hand. 'You called me "Ma",' she said quietly, looking in danger of bursting into tears again.

'And I'll stop doing it if you keep crying. You'll need another skin to make up for what you just lost.'

Ree's delicate fingers traced the side of her face. 'When did you get so damned-by-gods sensible, kid?'

Javani sniffed again and rubbed at her eye. 'Had a good teacher, that's all.'

They sat quietly while Ree chewed on softened hardtack (making Javani wonder if that just made it 'tack'), listening to the chirps and squawks of the plains, the whisper of the wind through the tall-grass, as the horizon began to swallow the sun. Javani watched the rise and fall of her mother's chest, the slow movement of her jaw, marvelling on both her miraculous survival and her more miraculous apology.

I'm sorry, kid. You deserved better.

'Speaking of making me proud,' Ree said without prompting, making Javani blush, 'do you want to tell me exactly what that is hanging around your neck?'

'Oh, Ma.' Javani felt the excitement building within her like steam, a desperate urge to gush forth with the full story. 'We beat them. I beat them. Just like the Exalted Swan wanted. We took the seal, and we wrecked the Iron Road in the process. When we left Kilale, people were falling over themselves to spread the news. Just like you said, it's open season on the Guild, they're being carved up from inside and out. And . . . and . . . I even planned for things to go wrong!'

Ree's gaunt cheeks crinkled in a smile of utter delight. 'Well, *now* I'm proud of you. I guess this explains why my visitors were in such disagreement over whether they should be killing me. The ones in fancy armour were very much in favour, it seems, and your little chum . . . vigorously opposed.'

'Maral really saved you?'

'She did. Although seeing as she was the one who laid me out in the first place, it seems the least she could have done.'

'What happened to her? Afterwards.'

'I couldn't say. She helped me out of bed, if only to dump corpses, but by the time I made it two strides outside, I was alone.' Ree took another drink, her stamina clearly reaching its end. 'Kid,' she said, 'how long was I . . . asleep?'

'A long fucking time, Ma. Did it feel . . . Was it like . . . ?'

'It felt like years.'

'Did you dream?'

'I . . . I'm not sure.'

The sun dipped further, spreading as if melting at the umber crest of the landscape. Ree looked like she was dozing, and Javani checked twice that her chest still moved. Her mother's words played over and over in her head, and the rocky hillside beneath her melted away like cloud.

'Kid?'

'Yeah, Ma?'

'You said "we" left Kilale. Where's everyone else?'

'Ah, yeah. I, uh . . . Wait, look! There, they're heading up now.'

Ree rubbed at her eyes with a tired hand, then peered forward at the narrow convoy of horse and wagon making its steady way up the trail towards them.

'Kid.'

'Yeah, Ma?'

'What in nine hells have you done to my rebels?'

FIFTY-FIVE

The palazzo echoed with clangs and distant shouts, so many it was impossible to be sure of their origin. The situation at the outer walls was already dire, and guards were leaving their posts as the whispers spread. Some simply walked off the job, others turned inwards, with gold in their eyes and greed in their hearts. The palazzo was a big place, but one could not hide in it forever.

Beralas hurried along the marble passageway towards the south wing, noting as he passed that tapestries had already been torn clear, and one of the gilded busts was missing, another lying smashed. The pouches and small chests he cradled in his arms jingled as he trotted, but the true wealth was still ahead of him. Safe and imminent departure was assured – the tunnels and chambers beneath the gardens had many advantages, and a hidden exit down to the little smugglers' dock in the valley below was chief among them in his current frame of mind.

As he reached the grand double doors of the residence, he turned to the Goldhelms who remained at his back, his pride, his honour.

'Wait here, my lionhearts. I shall return in but a moment. In the words of the Immortal Pislik: "hold fast, or fast hold."'

This got a set of salutes along with a couple of confused looks, but he was already pushing through the doors, his bundle balanced beneath his chin.

'Yzra? Darling? My daughters, we must . . .'

The rooms were empty. Not just empty, they were eviscerated. Every chest was open, every almirah thrown wide. Dresses and clothes strewn across floors, but, he noted, not the ones they truly loved. The jewellery was gone, of course, and their favoured art. He wondered how long ago they'd left.

Beralas stood in the empty hallway, the smooth stone cool beneath his fine slippers, and took a long breath, then pushed open the door to his wife's chambers. Empty, too; if anything more viciously voided than his daughters' rooms. He took another long, shaking breath, steeled himself, and marched to the hallway's end, to the private room, to which only he, Gurbun and their steward Magallu had a key.

The door was ajar.

Beralas rocked on his heels, his mouth working, throat dry. A cursory peek through the door's crack confirmed his worst fears, but no matter. He had working capital in his hands, he had his Goldhelms, he had his exit. The Guild and the Brothers Verdanisi might have suffered a setback, but a setback was all it was. The Guild was immortal, immaculate, indestructible. They would come back stronger, he averred as he walked briskly back down the hallway to the double doors. They would build their strength in secret, then they would strike, and sweep all before them in a righteous tide. There would be other wives. There could, in time, be other daughters.

'As you were, my lionhearts, we make for the—'

The floor was oddly warm and sticky beneath his feet. Beralas looked past his bundle, then down to the suddenly glossy marble of the hallway floor.

Dead.

All of them.

Eight men, their throats cut, their eyes wide in bloody horror. Their armoured corpses lay scattered and piled, their glorious golden breastplates sullied by gore, as if they had run in every direction and met their ends nonetheless.

The hallway was otherwise deserted.

'Who's— who's there?'

Beralas licked at dry lips, swallowed rancid air. He looked left, then right, and seeing no one, bolted for the western passage towards the garden terraces. He shed a pouch or two as he fled, slippers leaving bloody streaks on the marble, but he still had plenty. He had plenty, and his escape was in sight. He no longer needed to pay off the Goldhelms, for a start.

The western terraces were empty, but for a single white-smocked gardener, still toiling in the shimmering heat beneath a wide-brimmed hat. The dedication in the face of such upheaval pleased Beralas as he trotted along the manicured path beneath a florid trellis, shooting what looks over his shoulder he could manage without risking the loss of any more of the cargo piled in his arms. Over to the pergola, along the low hedge past the sunken fountains, then two turns around the maze and past the turquoise fountain would see him to his escape. The end was in sight.

He looked to his left, then again. The gardener had moved, and was now working two gardens over, parallel with him, head down against the fierce sun. That was irregular; most of the staff stayed within one section of the estate.

Beralas increased his pace, just a little, jingling with each step.

When he looked again, the gardener was gone, his view of the flowering oleander unobscured. He slowed, taking the corner towards the maze at almost a jaunty pace.

The gardener was directly ahead of him, one garden away.

Beralas came to a stop. The bags were beginning to feel very heavy in his arms. He shifted his grip, rolled his shoulders, irked at the sweat dampening his collar. It was hotter than it should have been, no breeze, only the ceaseless drone of insects drowning the sounds of chaos from elsewhere.

The gardener toiled on, head down. Beralas watched, sidelong, then slowly turned about. It might be prudent to take the long way there after all.

A right, then a left, and he was in the maze, but not from his normal entrance. No matter. It was a modest contrivance, even if he said so himself, and within a dozen paces he'd see something he recognised. There was another entrance already, probably the one he—

The gardener was beyond it, pristine smock near blinding in the sunlight. Back to him, head down . . . But perhaps another exit might make for a better choice. A right, then a left – by the gods, how could it be so hot, how was there no shade from these towering hedgerows? – then another left, and . . . No, that wasn't right. He'd erred the step before. Retracing, right this time, *then* left, then another left should . . . another dead end. The bags were so heavy, but if he put them down, he'd never manage to scoop them all up again. He took a hot, shaky breath. Focus, Beralas. You came in from the north. Or had it been the east? The sun was directly overhead, the shadows mere stubs. The way out was simple – there were only so many paths, after all. A left, then a left, then . . .

The maze's centre, a wide hexagon of spectacular tiles, two marble benches and a vacant wellspring in the form of a household god. A figure waiting on the shaded bench, sitting across its back, boots on the seat.

'Good afternoon, Chairman,' said Maral.

The Chairman was slick with sweat, staining through his robes, fat drops dripping from his brow, mottling the sacks and pouches crooked in his arms.

'M— Maral,' he stammered. 'What are you doing here?'

'Enjoying the gardens,' Maral said. She watched him, unblinking. 'Is that permitted?'

The Chairman swallowed. 'Of— of course. The gardens are yours to enjoy. As a valued member of my . . . family.'

The desperation was clear in his eyes. She saw it now. It leaked from them like sweat and tears, dribbling down him, his fear left bald beneath.

'Are you going somewhere, Chairman?'

'Maral, please, you know you can call me—'

'Answer the question.'

He took half a step back, easing towards the pale marble of the wall behind him, the empty fountain.

'Just going away on business, Maral. I won't be away long.'

'Alone?'

His eyes fell on the items beside her on the bench. The blade was not very long, but it was very bloody.

'Shall I come with you?' she said.

'That . . . That won't be necessary, this time. But— but I'll send for you. When I'm settled.'

She watched him, saying nothing, marvelling that she could have found him so compelling, so accomplished, so erudite. So assured and in command. She'd thought it was confidence born of great learning and drive. But it had been nothing of the sort.

She saw him now as he really was, shorn of minders, shorn of wealth, shorn of reputation – beneath it there lay nothing. His assured air had stemmed solely from the oblivious arrogance of wealth and privilege, and now he saw it, too.

'Maral, what happened? With Kilale, the Iron Road . . . with Gurbun. I thought you must have been lost along with him.'

She reached down to the bench, and he took another step back, the pouch pile swaying and clinking in his arms. Maral picked up a battered ledger, the leather of its cover paled and shiny, and laid it across her knees.

'She was right about one thing, after all,' she said.

'Who was? The . . . the insurrectionist? Maral, did you . . . did you kill Kuzari? He was like a brother to you.'

She leafed slowly through hoary pages, the parchment crackling from her touch. 'The Guild records everything. You . . . recorded everything.'

His neck stretched, peering over the bags, his throat bobbing. 'What . . . what is that book, Maral? Did you . . . have you been in—'

She turned another page. 'You drowned his mother. Kuzari. She was inconvenient, so you drowned her. And then you wrote about it.'

'Maral, listen, that . . . It's not . . . Sometimes I'd conject, make things up—'

'The hunting parties, though.'

'Maral, please . . .'

'I enjoyed the little markings you made, your trophies from your trips.'

'I had . . . we had no idea . . .'

'She was right about that, too. You *orphaned* me. You *stole* me. You *enslaved* me.'

'I gave you everything! Took you into my home, fed and clothed you, gave you an education—'

'You trained me, Chairman.'

'I made you part of my family!'

'Yet every time you looked at me, your eyes told me different.'

Maral snapped the book shut, dropped it to the bench seat, and stood. The Chairman took another hurried step back, his shoulders almost brushing the glowing white stone of the wall, a single small bag tumbling from his stack, hitting the bright paving with a sad tinkling thump.

'I always thought it was contempt. My whole life, within these marble walls, I thought I disgusted you.'

'How could you say such a—'

Maral took a slow step down from the bench. 'She told me I was wrong. She told me it was fear.'

'Please—'

'But that's the one time she wasn't right. It was not fear.' Maral took another step, the bloody blade still on the bench behind her, her hands empty.

'Maral—'

'It was guilt.' Another step. 'It was shame.'

'Maral, think about it, please—' his hands went up, the bags and sacks hitting the paving like meat. 'In the grand scheme of things, look at the life you've had, look at the luxury of your circumstances! I gave you that. And I can give you so much more. What kind of existence would you have had, out on the plains, a savage Mawn?'

She looked back to the ledger, gave a slow shake of her head. 'I'm not even Mawn. My family were Ireti nomads. But they were all the same to you.'

'Please, Maral, forgive me. Did not Feransis the White preach that forgiveness is the soul of humanity?'

'No. She did not.'

The wall behind the Chairman cracked open, then swung silently inwards, a great rectangle of darkness spreading behind him. Still he faced her, desperate, oblivious.

'Maral . . .' He licked dry lips. 'You've been like a daughter to me.'

'My name means "tool".'

'Have mercy, please! I gave you everything!'

She gazed at him for a moment, and felt nothing at all.

'I am what you made me.'

From the hungering dark swept Kuzari, still in his gardener's robes, long arms sweeping, wrapping the screaming, struggling Chairman, dragging him backwards, thrashing and kicking, muffled and crushed, swallowed by night—

And gone.

Maral stood alone at the centre of the maze, and yawned.

FIFTY-SIX

The lake sparkled, the descending sun draping a column of gleaming stars across its crystal surface. Wisps of cloud drifted high overhead, fringed golden and copper, the billowing puffs of cook-smoke from the clay stoves rising in optimistic pursuit. Boisterous chatter echoed from the creaking timber flanks of the lake house that perched on the wooded slope above them, the faded pillars of its projecting balcony pitted but sturdy, its well-worn steps to the shore glowing polished in the sunlight.

Javani milled uncertainly in the hubbub, shooed away from the flaming stoves by the White Spear, one of her arms still in a sling, with only a rueful smile from Tauras by way of apology, then glowered away from the drinks table by Anashe. Most of the adults were clustered around where Ree perched, although for once it seemed her mother was listening more than she was talking.

'Aye, well, word from my contacts across the expanse—'

'Contacts, eh?'

'Aye, contacts. Word from them is the diggers are falling apart, Guildhouse by Guildhouse, territory by territory. The loss of their charter went across the plains like a fucken firestorm, it's every vagrant and vagabond for him- or herself. Buggers are tearing themselves apart trying to keep the current holdings. The destruction of their biggest investment, no way to pay their creditors, and the disappearance of their two Chairmens won't have helped there, ha. Meanwhile the new players are organising, now the trade and craft monopolies are dust. We're looking at a time of upheaval, folks.'

The Commodore tapped the side of her nose, then slapped her non-bandaged thigh. 'And upheaval means opportunity, eh?'

'And Arowan?'

'Aye, general consensus is Matil will give them a few weeks to eat themselves, then sweep up the remains. New session of the senate is going to bring more than a new executive. No fucker wants to see another Guild in their lifetime, sure as boiled brass bollocks.'

Ree raised her bottle. 'Cheers to that.'

Movement from up the trail drew Javani's attention, followed by a squeal of unmitigated delight. Weaving down the hillside towards the shore came Vida and Mariam, the smiths and defenders of the village of Ar Ramas (and, in Mariam's case, Javani's recent tutor by correspondence), and – bounding ahead of them, great slobbery tongue trailing like a scarlet scarf – the vast and ancient form of Tarfellian, their best and most loyal hound. He made a beeline for Javani, checking his charge just before he knocked her clean from her feet and sent her windmilling into the lake.

'By the gods, boy, what happened to taking it easy in your old age?'

His wagging tail thumped her leg with enough force to leave a bruise as he circled her, pressing his flank against her and pushing his great anvil-block head into her midriff by way of affectionate greeting.

Mariam was only a few steps behind, radiating joy despite the pack on her back and the evidently heavy bags she carried. Vida followed at a steadier pace, watching every foot placement on the slope, and no less heavily laden.

'Gods be praised,' Mariam breathed, dropping her bags and grabbing Javani by the shoulders, 'Javani, look at you!'

'I'd rather not,' Javani said, feeling a blush come roaring up the back of her neck towards her face, and acutely mindful of Sarian at the foot of the steps, watching with obvious interest.

'You got so tall!'

'Didn't mean to.'

'Come here, you.'

Javani was hugged, the very air crushed from her, while Tarfellian wagged and thumped and circled and occasionally licked at her flailing hands when he felt he was being excluded. Vida offered a pat on the back and an approving nod, which left her with a warm feeling that was more than the blush.

'Right, where are we putting the food?' Mariam heaved up the bags again. 'Over there by the big lad, is it? Anri, you rogue, I hope you're making yourself useful.'

'Bugger off, Mariam.'

Javani eyed the groaning sacks, and the way the pack straps pulled at their shoulders. 'Can I carry something? Nine hells, did you bring the entire winter stores?'

'Well, you can't turn up to a party empty-handed, can you, and it was such a long trip we thought we'd best pack extra, just in case anything spoiled, but we made such good time in the end, didn't we, Vi? Anyway, the rest is up on the cart back at the ridgetop, didn't want to risk running it down the slope, did we. Maybe Tauras can give us a hand once he's finished his cooking.'

Javani shot a look to where the soot-blackened Tauras laboured over multiple stoves, bubbling pots and steaming irons, his face fixed in delirious concentration. He was growing his hair out, half-dyed swathes bunched in fistfuls at the back of his head. 'That may not be for a while.'

'Ah, it'll keep. Now, where's that terrible mam of yours?'

Ree's grin was like a sunrise. She really looked better.

'Vida, Mariam, what a treat. Forgive me if I don't get up?'

'*Two* walking sticks now, Ree? Can't trust you for a moment, can we?'

'I'm saving up for a third. Now tell me you brought the *kipir*!'

They ate, they drank, they told stories, as the sun made its slow descent, casting the lakeside in a ruddy glow to match their mellow hues. Javani was even allowed some *kipir*, which seemed only right, as she was very nearly sixteen now, which was basically an adult. She listened to the stories in a happy trance, letting them wash over her, while Tarfellian huffed happily at her feet beneath the table, gorged on table scraps; she'd heard most of them before by now, but she was soothed by the familiar, and occasionally piqued by a new addition. There was a man, there was a woman, there was a boy, there was a general . . . One day, someone would tell a story about her. The thought made her tingly inside.

'Right,' Anri barked as he pushed his platter away. 'Which of you bastards is doing the music?'

Anashe looked at Sefi, who had made the long trip with such alacrity that even Anashe herself had seemed taken aback, and was now snuggled against her on the long bench. 'I did bring a few instruments,' she replied, 'but can anyone else play?'

Anri made impatient grabbing motions. 'Come on, give something here.'

Javani started. 'You play, Anri?'

'If it's got strings, why not. No different from a bow, is it?' He met her disbelieving stare with a bristly wink.

And so the dancing began, much of it stilted and painful, given most of the dancers were recovering from a variety of injuries, some more serious than others, but certainly not lacking in enthusiasm. Javani watched open-mouthed as the White Spear executed a series of dazzling manoeuvres, still with one arm slung, before returning to Tauras to ensure the last of the cooking remained up to standard.

'I heard she was taking classes,' Manatas said from beside Javani, a fresh wine cup in his hand.

'I thought that was a joke,' Javani replied with an astonished shake of her head.

'Uh, Javani . . .'

'Captain?'

He went to say it, bit his lip, released a breath from his nose. 'I wanted to say . . . what you did, and the way you did it . . . was just . . .' He opened and closed his mouth, clicked his tongue. 'I cannot find the words,' he said at last.

Javani was swelling with pride. 'Thank you. That means a lot.'

'Tell me, though – your man in Kilale, if you had him on hand for the duration, why not simply let him take the seal when it arrived? Why did we—'

'Well, captain,' Javani interrupted, folding her arms and leaning back against the table, 'as I see it, we needed to do what we did to have had any chance of success. And as for Guvuli? Call him . . . "insurance against the unforeseen".'

'A safety net.' Manatas nodded, a mixture of satisfaction and what had to be admiration in his eyes. 'I am glad that it worked, whatever it was.'

'And, listen, thanks for your part, as well. I . . . I couldn't have done it without your help, without everything you did, and I want you to know that I'm really grateful, Thank you, Inaï.'

There were tears in his eyes as he hugged her.

Ree shifted on her bench, stretching out both legs beneath the table. 'And how's Camellia?'

Vida only chuckled.

'Oh, she abides,' Mariam sighed. 'She's coping, she is. It's been quite the couple of years.'

'For us all,' Vida added. 'We got the waterwheel up, though. You should see that bastard turn, a true thing of beauty.'

Ree smiled. 'Maybe one day I will.'

A lean shadow fell over her as the music started up once more. Captain Manatas cleared his throat. 'My lady Ree, may I have this dance?'

Ree looked down at her legs, the two sticks either side of the bench not a great deal thicker. 'In this state?'

'I am,' he said with a twinkle in his eye, 'willing to do most of the work.'

Ree extended her hands with the grace of a duchess.

Javani sat down beside where Anashe, Anri and Sefi played beneath the spread of an ancient olive tree. Anashe was singing again, her voice so clear and pure it astonished Javani that she didn't sing her every word from day to day. Anri performed quite brilliantly on a zither, the bastard, while Sefi drummed. They all seemed to be enjoying themselves to a degree Javani found unnerving.

'What was that you sang?'

Anashe looked up, her face flushed and eyes shining. 'One of our own composition.' She flashed a glance at Sefi, who beamed back. 'The words were Aki's, and to his credit, required only minor improvement.'

A bird fluttered down overhead, Javani couldn't tell what in the fading light, landing in the branches above them and settling there.

'You can really play, then?' she said to Anri. 'You never said anything.'

'Never asked, did you,' came the deadpan reply, and Anashe laughed.

Anashe laughed.

'What's . . . Look, what's going on here? Are you two . . . three . . . like, up to something? This isn't normal.'

'She's the judge of what's normal, is she?'

Anashe and Sefi giggled. Sefi, who Javani had known for all of a few hours, was laughing at her.

'Explain yourselves!'

Anashe's palms were up, even as she wiped a tear from one eye. 'My apologies, Javani. We are . . . We are perhaps friends.'

'Perhaps?'

'Look, you,' Anri said with a jabbing finger, 'there's nothing weird about adults of opposite sexes being friendly, right?'

'I didn't say—'

'And if we have a, uh . . .'

'Satisfactory partnership,' Anashe suggested.

'One of them, yes, then it's our own business, and nobody else's, right?'

Now Javani had her hands up. 'Right, right. Absolutely.'

'Good.'

'Good.'

Above Anri's head, the unseen bird voided its bowels directly onto his shoulder.

'Ah,' cried Anashe, 'the seal of approval! He wills it!'

They collapsed in mirth once more, to Javani's eternal bafflement. On the ridge above, framed by the dying sunlight, something caught her eye. 'Excuse me, won't you?' she said, leaving them to their giggles.

'Hoy!' came Ree's voice from what passed for the dancefloor. 'Less yap, more slap!'

'Righto, General!'

They struck up again.

'You are moving well, my lady Ree.'

'Considering?'

'Well, yes, considering.'

Ree clung tightly to the captain, who bore her without complaint, despite his injuries. For once, she did not mind being supported at all.

'I used to dance,' she sighed. 'How I used to dance.'

'You have fallen from the habit?'

'I'd say I've lacked opportunities in the recent past.'

'We could, perhaps, seek to remedy that?'

'Captain Manatas, what are you proposing?'

He took a long breath, and she felt the rise of his chest against her. 'Only that, when considering your future, I would be honoured to feature within it.'

'I fear my legs are weakening, Captain Mantilas. Would you mind holding me a little tighter?'

'It would be my honour to assist.'

'This concludes the opening day of the Siavash Sarosh School and Boarding House for Gifted Orphans and Deserving Infants of the Locality.'

'Very good, master.'

'Ulfat, please stop calling me master, we're married now, and it calls our dynamic into question.'

'Very good, m— my husband.'

Siavash brushed down his teaching robes (new, finely worked, educational embroidery throughout), straightened his teaching hat, and beamed.

'I hope you enjoyed your first day, children. Did I do well?'

'Yes, Master Siavash,' they chorused.

'In the coming weeks, we are going to learn the most important lesson of all, the one thing you *must* understand if you are to make your mark on the world: the greatest thing life can offer. What is it, you ask? Is it a zest for adventure, a life of unbridled excitement and exploration? Children, there is something greater, and more true.' He met Ulfat's eye, and his heart soared. 'But first, and only slightly less great: compound interest!'

FIFTY-SEVEN

'All's I'm saying is that chaos is a wossname, a . . . y'know, think of trying to get somewhere vertically, right, and then there's all this chaos, right . . .'

Ree arched an eyebrow. 'Tauras, I think the Commodore has had enough to drink for now.'

'Right you are, General!'

'Not General any more, Tauras.'

'Right you are, Mistress Ree!'

'Aye, right, listen, will yous? Honestly. And what happened to colouring your hair again, eh? Fair scorches the eyes, it does.'

'I decided I like it like this. This is me.'

'Aye, that it is.' The Commodore snuffled, then belched. 'You given any thought to what's next? Now we slayed the dragon? Slewed. Slathered.'

'Are you going to beg us to come south and set up with you?'

'Fffffffuck off, can't imagine anything worse than having you pissing in my professional porridge every day. No, no, word's reached me of a successful wee horse farm, not that far from here, and in need of new stewards. Big working staff, would need someone of *implacable* steadfastness to keep them in shape . . .'

'Is that a fact?' Ree tapped a finger against her lip.

'Give yourself a chance to get back on your feet and all, but one to ponder, maybe?'

'Maybe. Let me . . . Where's that kid got to now?'

* * *

Javani was breathing heavily by the time she reached the top of the ridge, on the verge of regretting the volume she'd eaten, but not quite. She came to rest with her hands on her knees.

'So,' she said, which was about all she was up to until her wind returned.

The figure at the tree-side was little more than a blocky silhouette, cloak-wrapped and square.

'So,' the figure replied in a low, raspy voice.

'You found us, then? I thought you would.'

Maral said nothing.

'Do you want to come down? We're having a party. Or are you here to murder someone? I'd offer to fight you for it, but I've just had a big meal and I'm really not in the mood.'

Maral said nothing, then shook her head.

'Was that no to the party, or the murder?'

'Both.'

'Shame. For half at least.' Javani pushed herself upright. 'I wanted to thank you, for saving my ma. Even though you left me completely outnumbered to die on that train.'

Maral produced a little snort from her nose that could conceivably have been a laugh.

'You were in no danger.'

'No danger?!'

'I knew you could take them.'

'Wha— With what? They'd disarmed us!'

'There was a coil of rope at your feet. I fought you myself already, remember?'

'Oh. Right.' Javani cleared her throat, then stuffed a hand into her jacket. 'Anyway, I wanted to give you something. Here. You can sell it, if you want, but I thought . . . well, I thought . . . you might like to wear it. It would go nicely with that bit of silk, if you've still got that.'

Maral said nothing, only stared at the object in her hand.

'If you don't like it, that's fine, I just thought, you know, you didn't have to—'

'I don't understand.'

'What? What don't you understand?'

'You want me to kill for you? Am I to be your red hand now?'

'What? Gods, no, shut up. It's a gift, Maral. To do with as you please. I got it to prove a point that doesn't need making any more, and I wanted to say thank you.'

'Th-thank you,' Maral echoed. The words ground out of her, like she'd never said them before and didn't know how.

'My, uh . . . Are you . . . all right?'

Maral nodded, her shining gaze still locked on the thing in her hand.

'You look like you might—'

'I do not cry.'

'Right, sorry, forgot. Sure you don't want to come down and say hello? There's still loads of food, Tauras can't seem to stop cooking. I know it might be a bit weird, with the whole assassination attempt thing, but they're a forgiving bunch, especially after three flagons of wine. Each.'

'I . . . must go.'

'Where? I mean, what are you going to do now? Assuming murder for hire is off the table.'

The other woman stared again at her palm, then tucked her gift inside her cloak. 'North. There is a library, and I have some . . . gaps . . . in my education. Then into the plains, to the high places. I may still have . . . family there.'

'After all this time?'

'Does such a thing expire?'

'No, I guess not. Well, if you're ever passing back this way, maybe pop in, eh? Just give us some warning first.' Javani shot a look down to the bottom of the slope, where lanterns were being lit and fires rebanked. 'Goodbye then, I guess. Safe travels, and all that.'

The trees were empty.

'Here you are, cap.'

'What's this, Tauras?'

'It's some of the breaded fish, cap. I kept it back, wanted to make sure I made it properly. Because it was Lieutenant Arkadas's favourite, cap. And he's not here.'

Manatas stood at the lake shore, watching the crimson water lap at the toes of his boots as the distant horizon swallowed the last of the sun. His mind travelled through years, rehashing visits past, and company passed.

'No, Tauras, he is not.'

'I thought it might be nice, cap. To have some fish, and think of him, and Captain Kediras, too. Wherever they are.'

'That was a very good idea, Tauras.'

'Is the food all right, cap? Did I do well?'

'Tauras, you were perfect.' Manatas took the offering, and lifted it to the sunset. 'To absent friends.'

He stood arm in arm with Tauras, watching the dying of the light, and cried for the lost.

'Was that your little friend popping in for a visit?'

'I really don't think she's my friend, Ma. Do Mawn even make friends?'

'Huh. Now I think about it, she looked more like an Ireti to me, but I never really got a good look at her.'

'Got space for me here?'

'I can make room.'

The sun was gone, just a thick russet band, diminishing over the distant water, mirrored in its undulating surface. They sat up on the bank above the shore, listening to the raucous conversation, the laughter and cries ringing through the landscape. Around them insects chirped, the night warm, the air clear. The first stars were out above them, twinkling pinpricks in a dusty spread across the gathering indigo of encroaching night.

'Ma?'

'Yes, kid?'

'This place . . . the lake. It's Arestan.'

'Come again?'

'Rice and wine and water as blue as sapphire,' Javani recited. 'It's what we were looking for, all along. Just . . . on the wrong side of the mountains.'

'Huh.' Ree was quiet a moment. 'What do you know.'

'I'm just saying, because, I know there's an election coming up in Arowan, with the Exalted Swan stepping back, and I know they're looking for candidates to take over . . .'

'Let me stop you there, kid. I am going nowhere near the senate.'

'You sure? I mean, you beat the Guild. You're the General.'

'Yeah, maybe, but the best thing a general can do after a war is step down. You know, thinking about the Ireti, they have this concept of war leaders, and peace leaders, and they're never the same people. Once the battle is done, it's time to take up the ploughshare again. Just like Camellia said.'

'Are you sure you can turn your back? I mean, you'd get to boss an entire continent around.'

'Don't push me, kid.'

'I guess we can't always get what we want. I didn't get to be a princess, you don't get to be Keeper of the Serican Protectorate, so fair's fair.' She sat back, looking up at the stars. 'So . . . what are we going to do next?'

'It's "we" again, is it?'

'Well . . . I guess if I learned anything from all of this crap—'

'That's a big "if".'

'—it's that I can stand to be around you a little more, if you can stand to be around me.' She turned to face her mother. 'But, I'm . . . I'm bigger now. Things have changed. We need to . . . work out . . . who we are to each other.'

Ree met her gaze, her gaunt face shining in the firelight from below. 'You're right, but who we are to each other is never going to be static, it's going to keep changing as we change ourselves. You are going to go out into the world and do *amazing* things, Javani. Even more amazing than what you've done already, which I have to say is pretty fucking amazing indeed.' She put a narrow hand on Javani's. 'All you need to do, my dear, is decide who and what you want to be, what you want to do, and where you want to go, and I will be here to support you all the way, for as long as I have breath and blood. I love you, kid, and you are the best part of me.'

'Uh, right. Wow.' Javani rubbed at one eye. 'I'll . . . can I come back to you on that?'

'Gods, kid, you don't have to have all the answers now. You've got the rest of your life, and the secret is you can keep changing your mind.'

'So, for now at least . . . partners?'

'Partners.'

They shook hands.

'Do I need to stop calling you "kid" again?'

'I think I could stand it a while longer.'

Ree turned and rummaged in the twilight, then turned back with barely a wince and something long and narrow across her spread palms.

'I think it's time you had this.'

Javani stared at the drab scabbard, the filigree of the fine-worked hilt, gleaming in the distant firelight. 'Gods, Ma, your sword . . . Are you sure?'

'My fighting days are done, kid. And while I hope you never have cause to draw it, better to have it along and not need it than the reverse.'

'Does this mean you'll finally teach me the forms? When you're better?'

Ree's eyes crinkled and shone. 'If you're up to learning, at your age. If it's really what you want.'

Javani was quiet for a moment. 'Thank you for not raising me to be a tool.'

'What?'

'Just . . . I get it now, what you were doing. And I'm sorry, for what I said, and what I did. I love you, Ma.' The words burst out of her, unprompted, unplanned, and Ree's dumbstruck expression made everything worth it. Their hug was twisted and awkward, but neither wanted to let go.

'Is it true you got that bandit Movos Guvuli to bail you out?' Ree said at last, half-muffled in Javani's hair.

Javani sniffed. 'You're not the only one who corresponds, you know.' She sniffed again. 'I can't believe all it took was a poison coma to get you to rest your leg.'

Ree released her. 'It's recovered enough to kick you up and down the shingle, you irascible tyke. Oh, and *on the subject* of water as blue as sapphire, did I hear there was something you were going to give me . . . ?'

'Ah, yeah, Ma. About that . . .'

Kuzari was waiting by the horses, somehow managing to lounge vertically.

'What are you eating?'

'Found a cart, over at the top of the trail. Loads of food in it. What? They won't miss one cheese.'

Maral swung up into the saddle, then reached into her pocket with gentle fingers.

'Anyway,' Kuzari went on, 'it's a long journey, might as well pack heavy. You know I get hungry on the road.'

Maral withdrew her hand, then very carefully, feeling her way, she tied back her hair with the folded rectangle of silk.

'Ready?' He was still chewing, even as he mounted. The dying dregs of sunlight filtered through the trees, lighting them in profile. 'Hey, is that new?' He gestured to her neck, where her gift dangled, shining in the light.

'Looks good,' he said, then turned his horse and set off along the trail.

'It does,' Maral said quietly to herself. 'It does.'

She put her heels to her mount and set off in his wake, cantering into jasmine-scented twilight, the wind teasing at her hair and the blue stone bouncing at her collar, her face stretched in an unfamiliar grin. Maral knew she didn't cry. Where the tears had come from was a mystery.

Maral rode north into the fragrant evening, and knew joy.

ACKNOWLEDGEMENTS

Deepest thanks and gratitude to the following, for all they have done for this book, and the trilogy as a whole:

To my exhausted agent, Harry "Baby Daddy" Illingworth, and all at DHH;

To my sublime editor, Laura McCallen, and the editorial team at HarperVoyager: Natasha Bardon, Elizabeth Vaziri, and literal superhero Chloe Gough; to copy-editor Edward Wall, and proofreader Rhian McKay; to the cover art dream team of Emily Langford and Gavin Reece for completing the series with another scorcher;

To fabulous subject matter expert and BBC correspondent Bethan Hindmarch, voice coach and corrective influence to Anri (and not forgetting Mariam);

To my fellow Illers' Killers, the collective padded cell; to my convention stalwarts, too numerous and splendid to name in toto, but with special mention to Anna Stephens, Ed Crocker, Richard Swan, Tom Lee, Sunyi Dean, David Goodman, Jen Williams, Pete Newman, Steve Aryan, Stew Hotston, Justin Lee Anderson, RJ Barker and Ryan Cahill; to Francesca Haig;

To the reviewers and broadcasters who have done so much to support me and the series, not limited to: Nils and Beth of the Fantasy Hive, Holly Hearts Books, the Brothers Gwynne, Stefan of Civilian Reader, David Walters and Adrian Gibson of FanFiAddict and SFF Addicts, Night at SoManyBooks6, Kayla of Kay's Hidden Shelf, and so many others;

To Matt, Emi and the team at The Broken Binding; to Phil,

Magnus, Adam, Caro & everyone at SRFC; to Adam Iley, James G Smith and Laz Roberts; to Katie Bruce, who also bakes with aplomb; to Raph, Paul and Mark, who buy the hardbacks; to Alexey, who would;

To the works of Bret Devereux, Phillips P. O'Brien, and Jackie Chan;

To my spectacular wife Sarah, and my increasingly massive daughters, to whom this book is dedicated, if only in the hope they'll stop asking such difficult questions;

To you, my readers, for coming on this journey with me. The path to *The Iron Road* began in 2019 with the first draft of *The Hunters*, but as you've probably spotted by now, its roots go all the way back to *The Black Hawks*, a book I was first tossing around notions for circa AD 2009. It's been a long old road, if you'll pardon the expression; thanks for joining me on it.

Love and thanks to you all.

Hitchin, March 2025

CREDITS

Agent
Harry Illingworth

Editor
Laura McCallen

Voyager Editorial Team
Natasha Bardon
Elizabeth Vaziri
Chloe Gough

Audio
Fionnuala Barrett
Sarah Allen-Sutter

Design
Emily Langford
Gavin Reece

Production
Emily Chan

Marketing
Sian Richefond

Publicity
Susanna Peden